CURSE OF THE
ATTACK-O-LANTERNS

Chris
Schweizer

PUBLISHER'S NOTE:
This is a work of fiction. Names, characters, places, and incidents are either the product of the author's imagination or used fictitiously, and any resemblance to actual persons, living or dead, business establishments, events, or locales is entirely coincidental.

Library of Congress Control Number: 2016936953

Hardcover ISBN: 978-1-4197-2190-8
Paperback ISBN: 978-1-4197-2191-5

Text and illustrations copyright © 2016 Chris Schweizer
Book design by Pamela Notarantonio

Printed and bound in China
10 9 8 7 6 5 4 3 2 1

Amulet Books are available at special discounts when purchased in quantity for premiums and promotions as well as fundraising or educational use. Special editions can also be created to specification. For details, contact specialsales@abramsbooks.com or the address below.

ABRAMS The Art of Books
115 West 18th Street, New York, NY 10011
abramsbooks.com

TO MY SISTER, LINDY

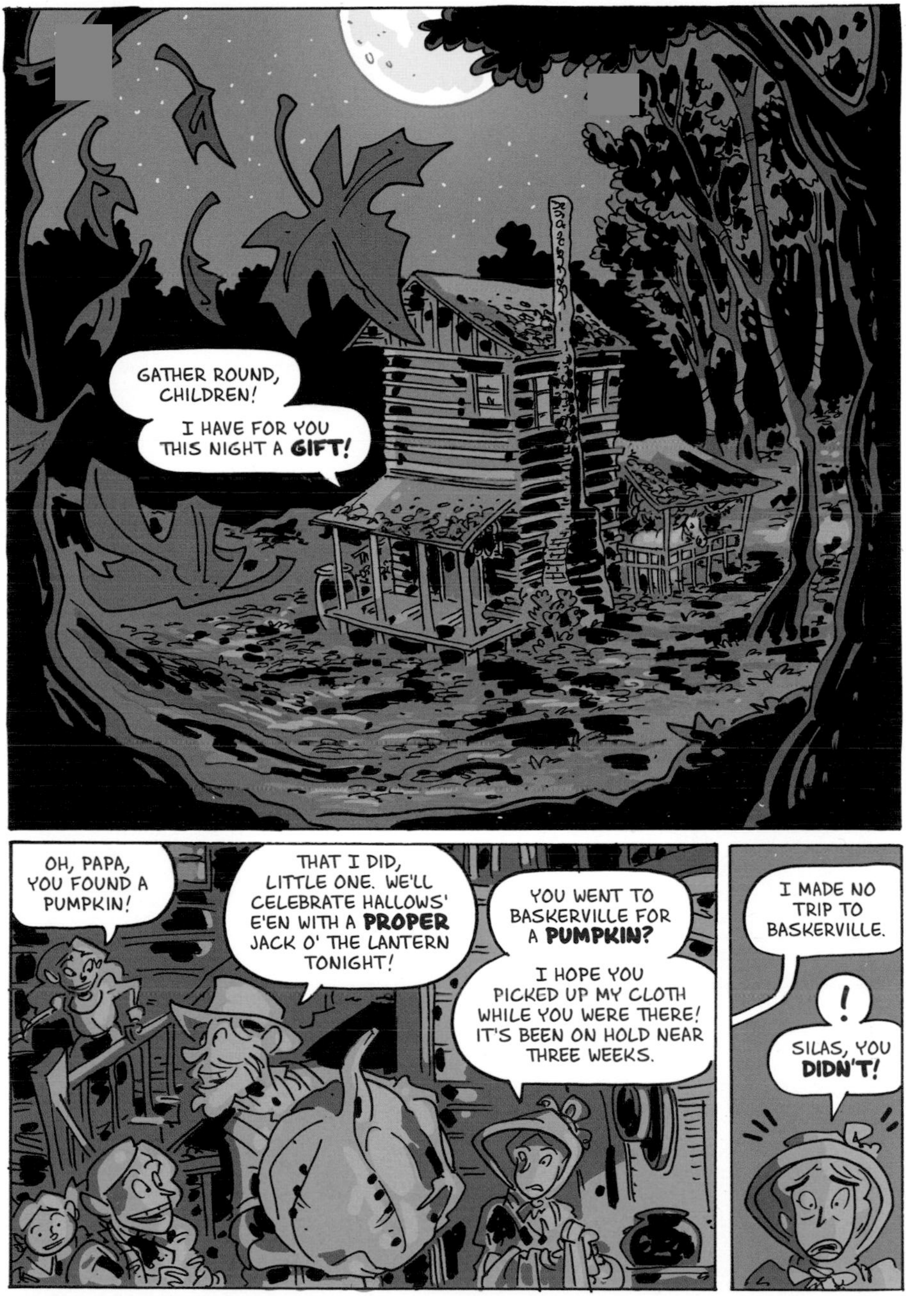
GATHER ROUND, CHILDREN!
I HAVE FOR YOU THIS NIGHT A **GIFT**!
OH, PAPA, YOU FOUND A PUMPKIN!
THAT I DID, LITTLE ONE. WE'LL CELEBRATE HALLOWS' E'EN WITH A **PROPER** JACK O' THE LANTERN TONIGHT!
YOU WENT TO BASKERVILLE FOR A **PUMPKIN?**
I HOPE YOU PICKED UP MY CLOTH WHILE YOU WERE THERE! IT'S BEEN ON HOLD NEAR THREE WEEKS.
I MADE NO TRIP TO BASKERVILLE.
!
SILAS, YOU **DIDN'T**!

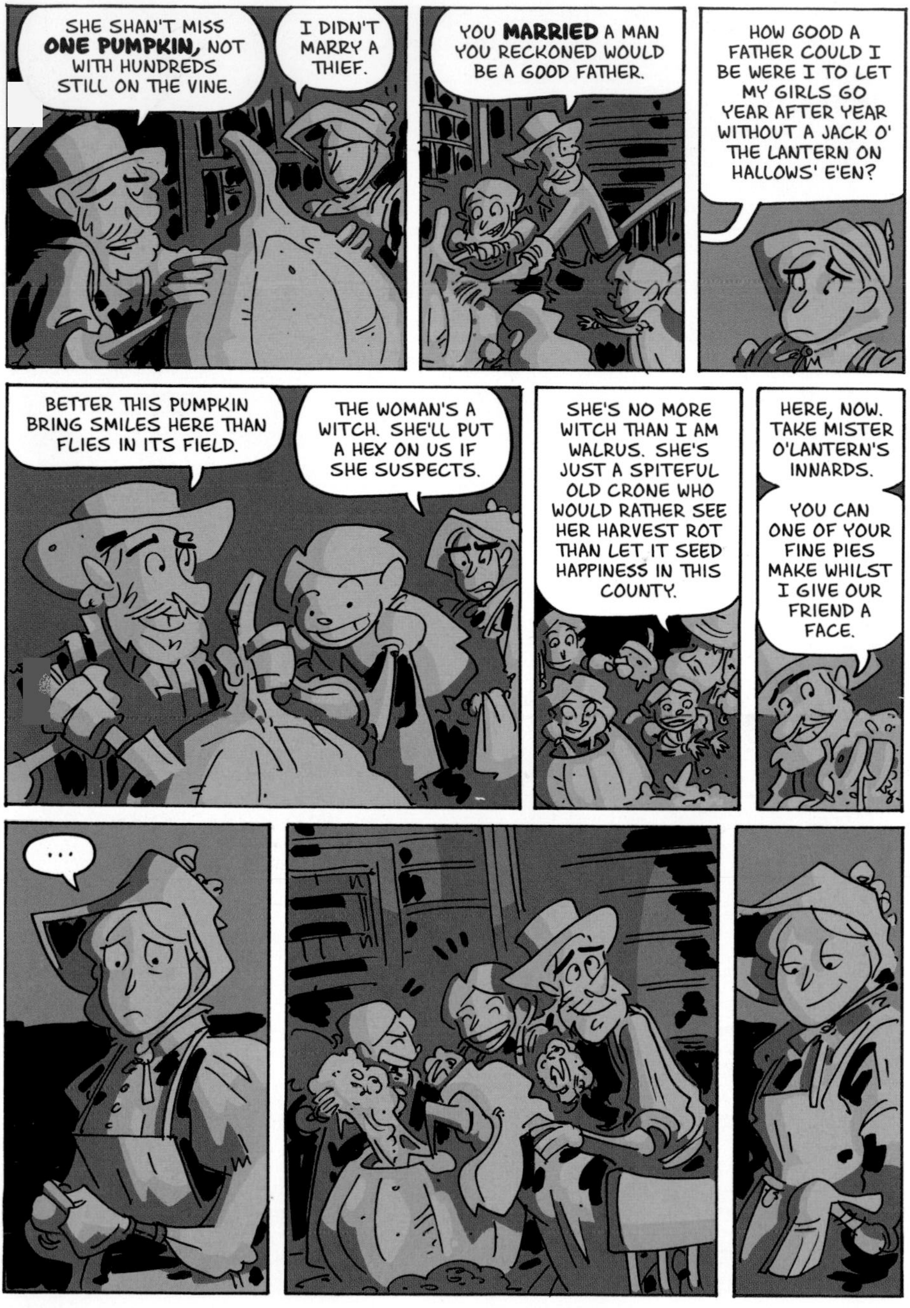

SHE SHAN'T MISS **ONE PUMPKIN,** NOT WITH HUNDREDS STILL ON THE VINE.
I DIDN'T MARRY A THIEF.
YOU **MARRIED** A MAN YOU RECKONED WOULD BE A GOOD FATHER.
HOW GOOD A FATHER COULD I BE WERE I TO LET MY GIRLS GO YEAR AFTER YEAR WITHOUT A JACK O' THE LANTERN ON HALLOWS' E'EN?
BETTER THIS PUMPKIN BRING SMILES HERE THAN FLIES IN ITS FIELD.
THE WOMAN'S A WITCH. SHE'LL PUT A HEX ON US IF SHE SUSPECTS.
SHE'S NO MORE WITCH THAN I AM WALRUS. SHE'S JUST A SPITEFUL OLD CRONE WHO WOULD RATHER SEE HER HARVEST ROT THAN LET IT SEED HAPPINESS IN THIS COUNTY.
HERE, NOW. TAKE MISTER O'LANTERN'S INNARDS.
YOU CAN ONE OF YOUR FINE PIES MAKE WHILST I GIVE OUR FRIEND A FACE.
...

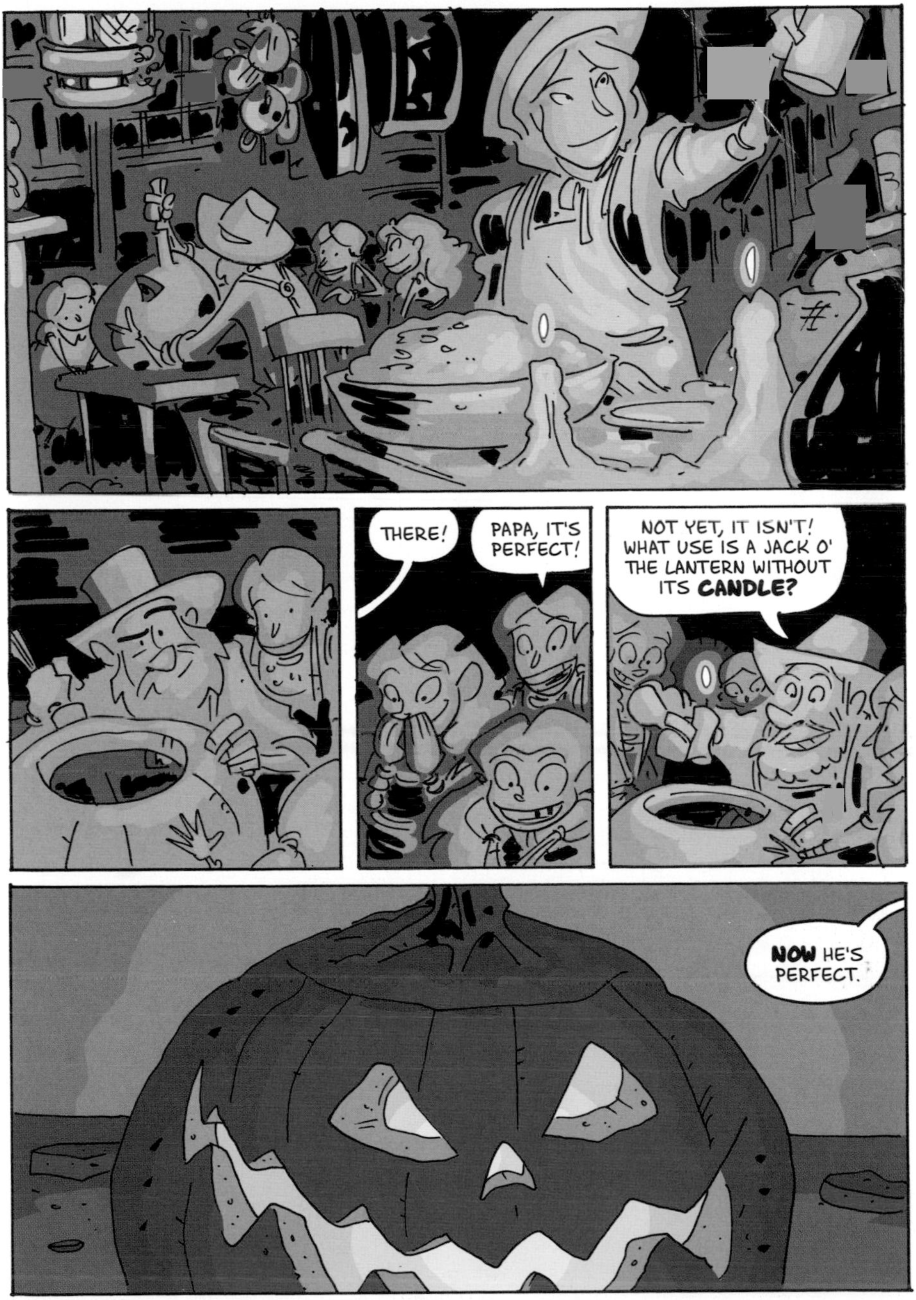
THERE!
PAPA, IT'S PERFECT!
NOT YET, IT ISN'T! WHAT USE IS A JACK O' THE LANTERN WITHOUT ITS **CANDLE?**
NOW HE'S PERFECT.

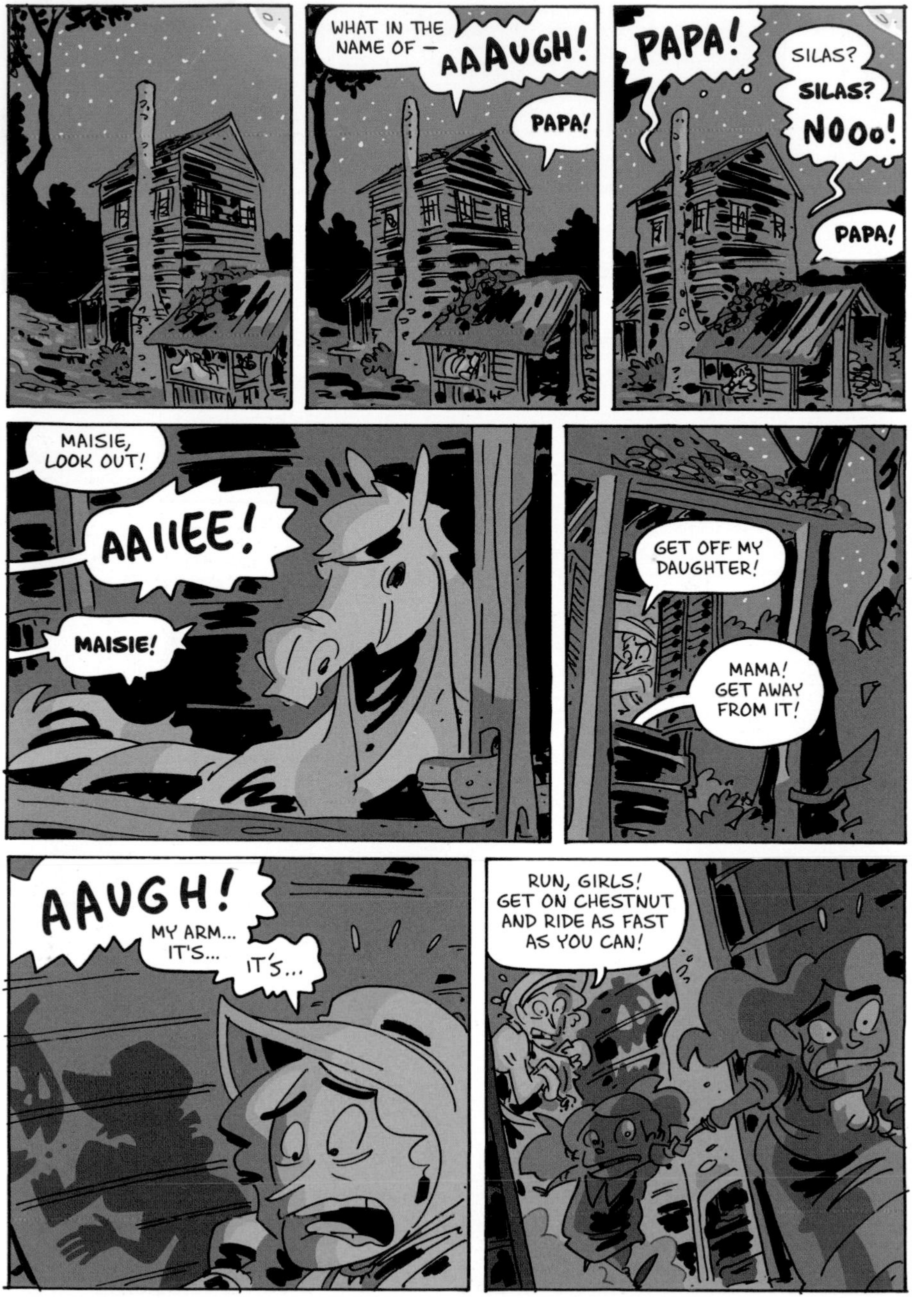

WHAT IN THE NAME OF —
AAAUGH!
PAPA!
PAPA!
SILAS?
SILAS?
NOOo!
PAPA!
MAISIE, LOOK OUT!
AAIIEE!
MAISIE!
GET OFF MY DAUGHTER!
MAMA! GET AWAY FROM IT!
AAUGH!
MY ARM... IT'S...
IT'S...
RUN, GIRLS! GET ON CHESTNUT AND RIDE AS FAST AS YOU CAN!

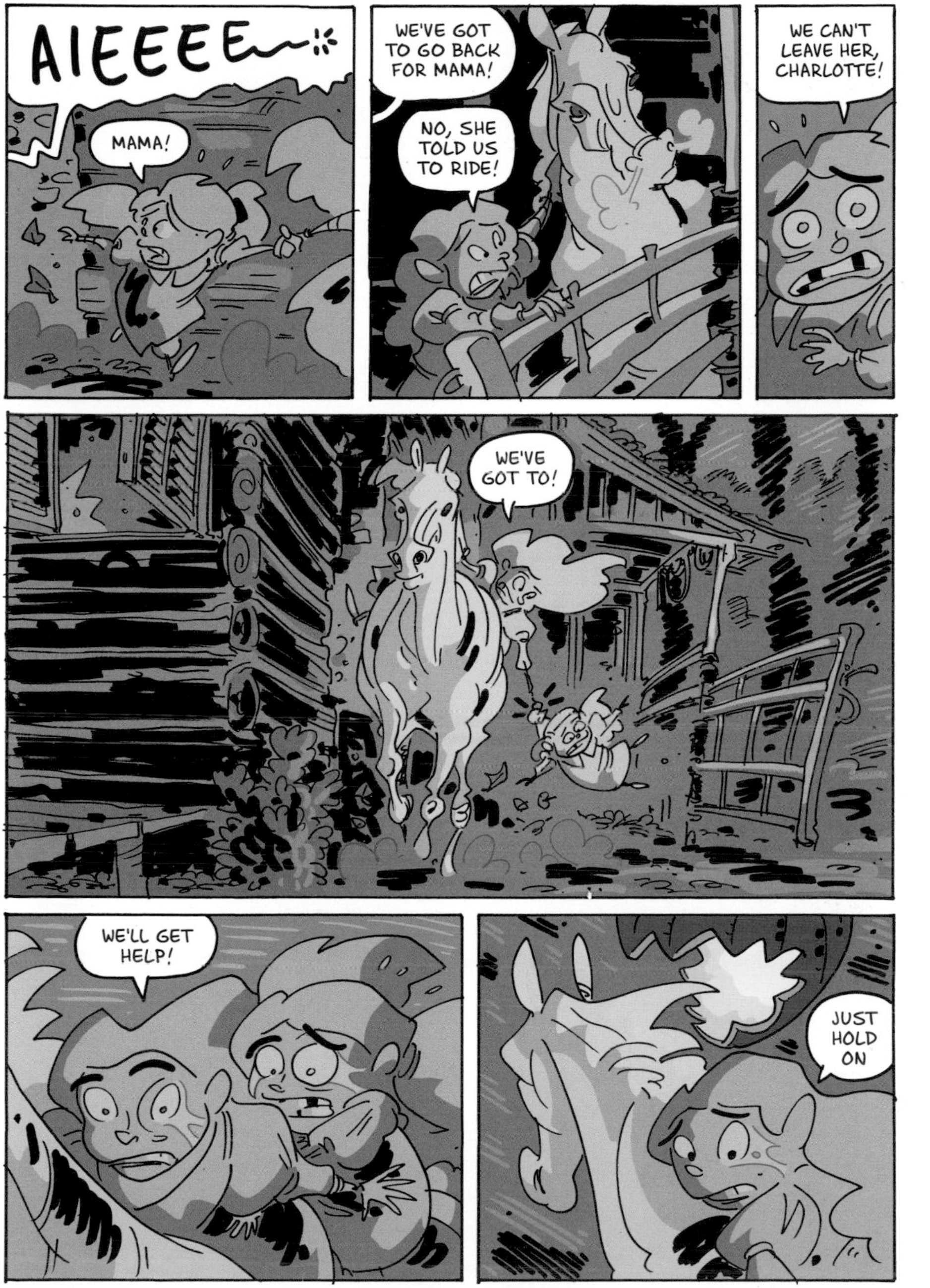
AIEEEE
MAMA!
WE'VE GOT TO GO BACK FOR MAMA!
NO, SHE TOLD US TO RIDE!
WE CAN'T LEAVE HER, CHARLOTTE!
WE'VE GOT TO!
WE'LL GET HELP!
JUST HOLD ON

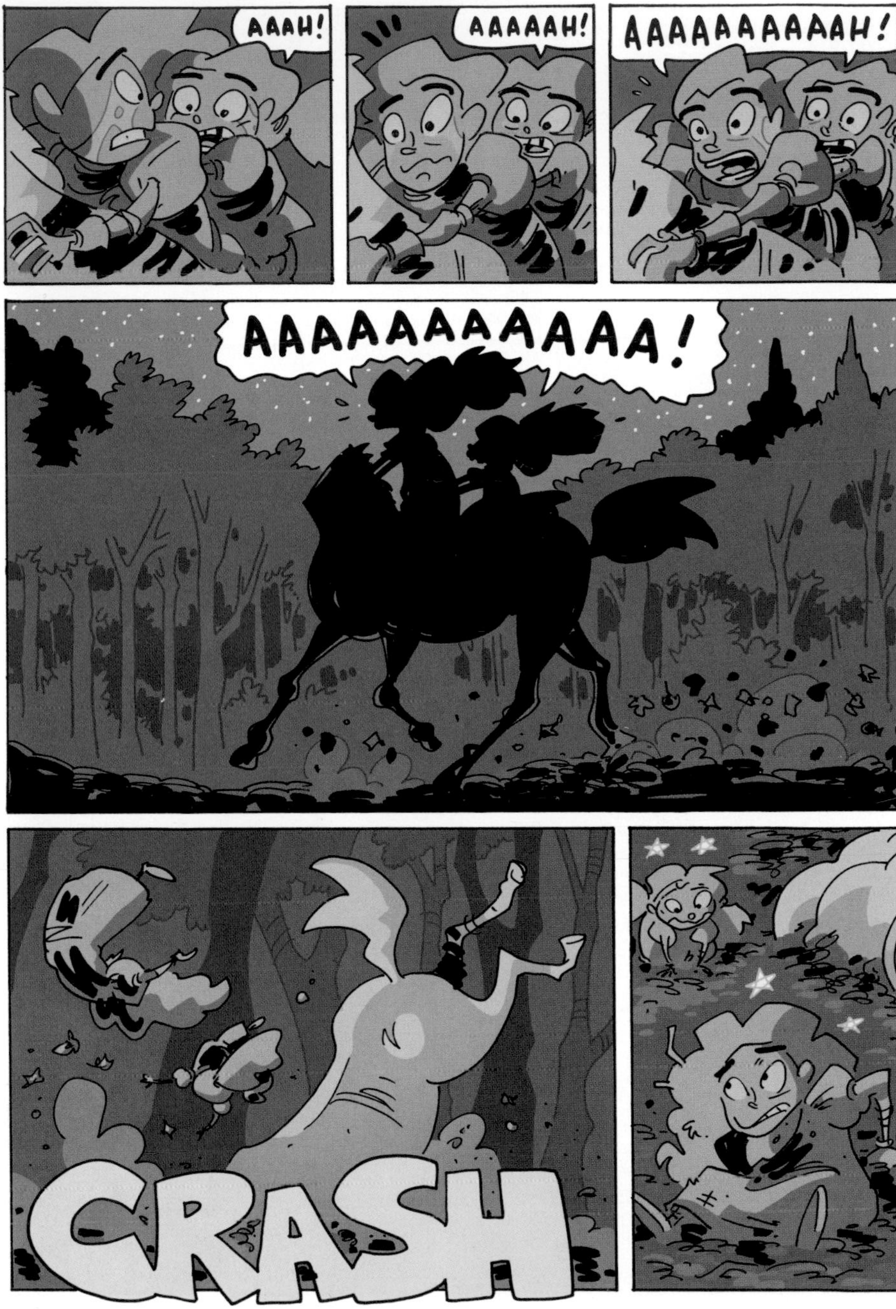
AAAH!
AAAAAH!
AAAAAAAAAAH!
AAAAAAAAAAAA!
CRASH

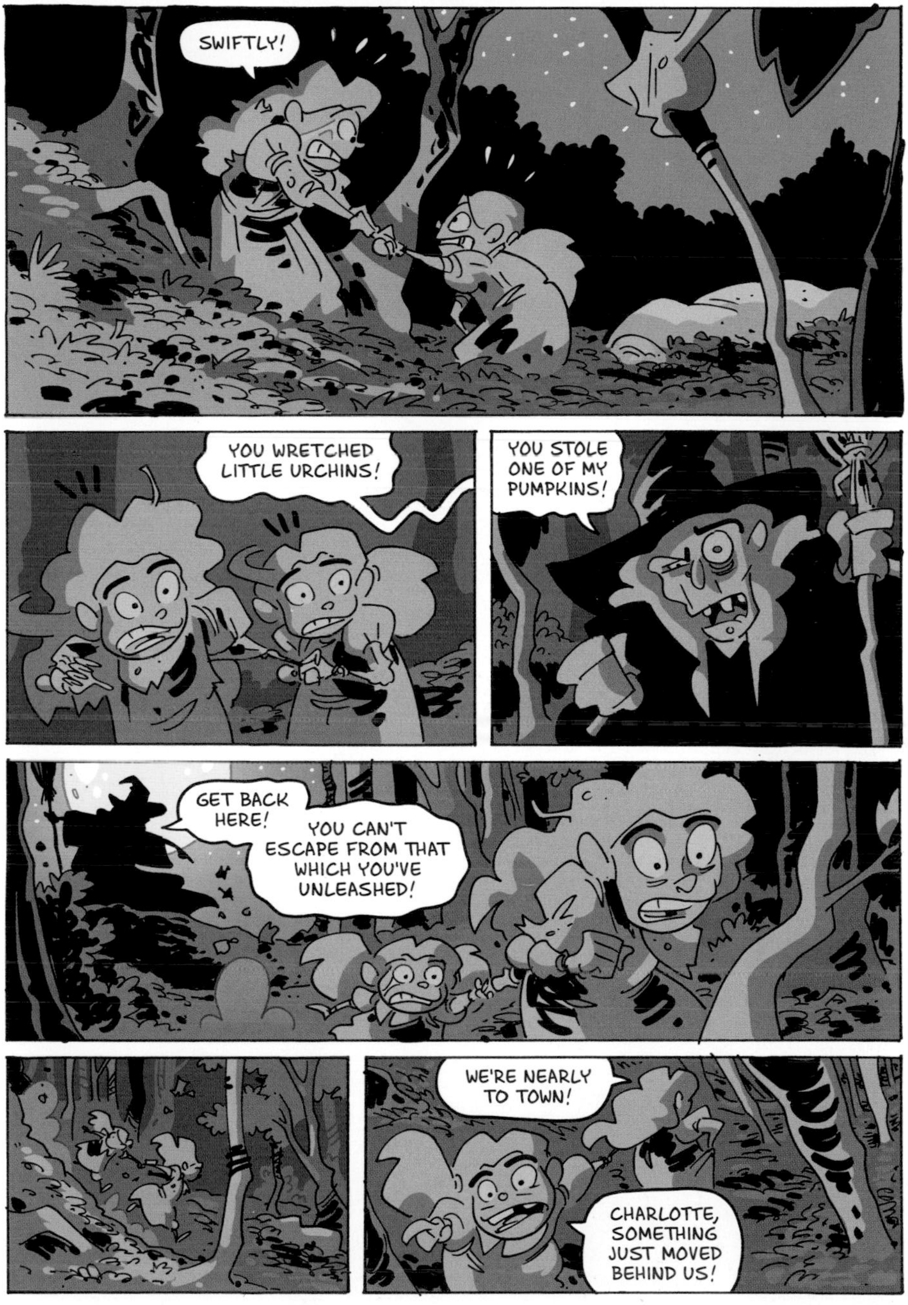
SWIFTLY!
YOU WRETCHED LITTLE URCHINS!
YOU STOLE ONE OF MY PUMPKINS!
GET BACK HERE!
YOU CAN'T ESCAPE FROM THAT WHICH YOU'VE UNLEASHED!
WE'RE NEARLY TO TOWN!
CHARLOTTE, SOMETHING JUST MOVED BEHIND US!

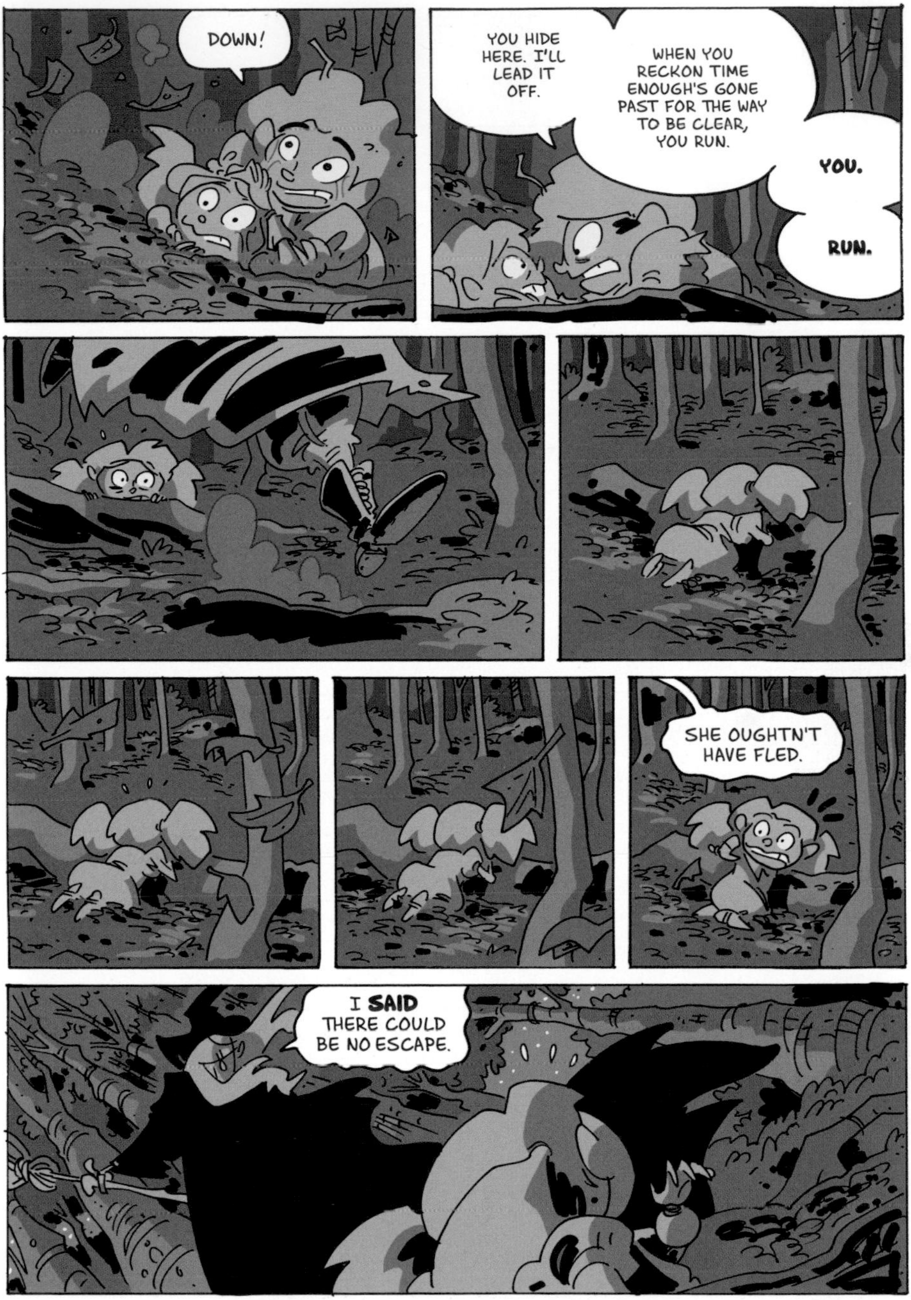
DOWN!
YOU HIDE HERE. I'LL LEAD IT OFF.
WHEN YOU RECKON TIME ENOUGH'S GONE PAST FOR THE WAY TO BE CLEAR, YOU RUN.
YOU.
RUN.
SHE OUGHTN'T HAVE FLED.
I SAID THERE COULD BE NO ESCAPE.

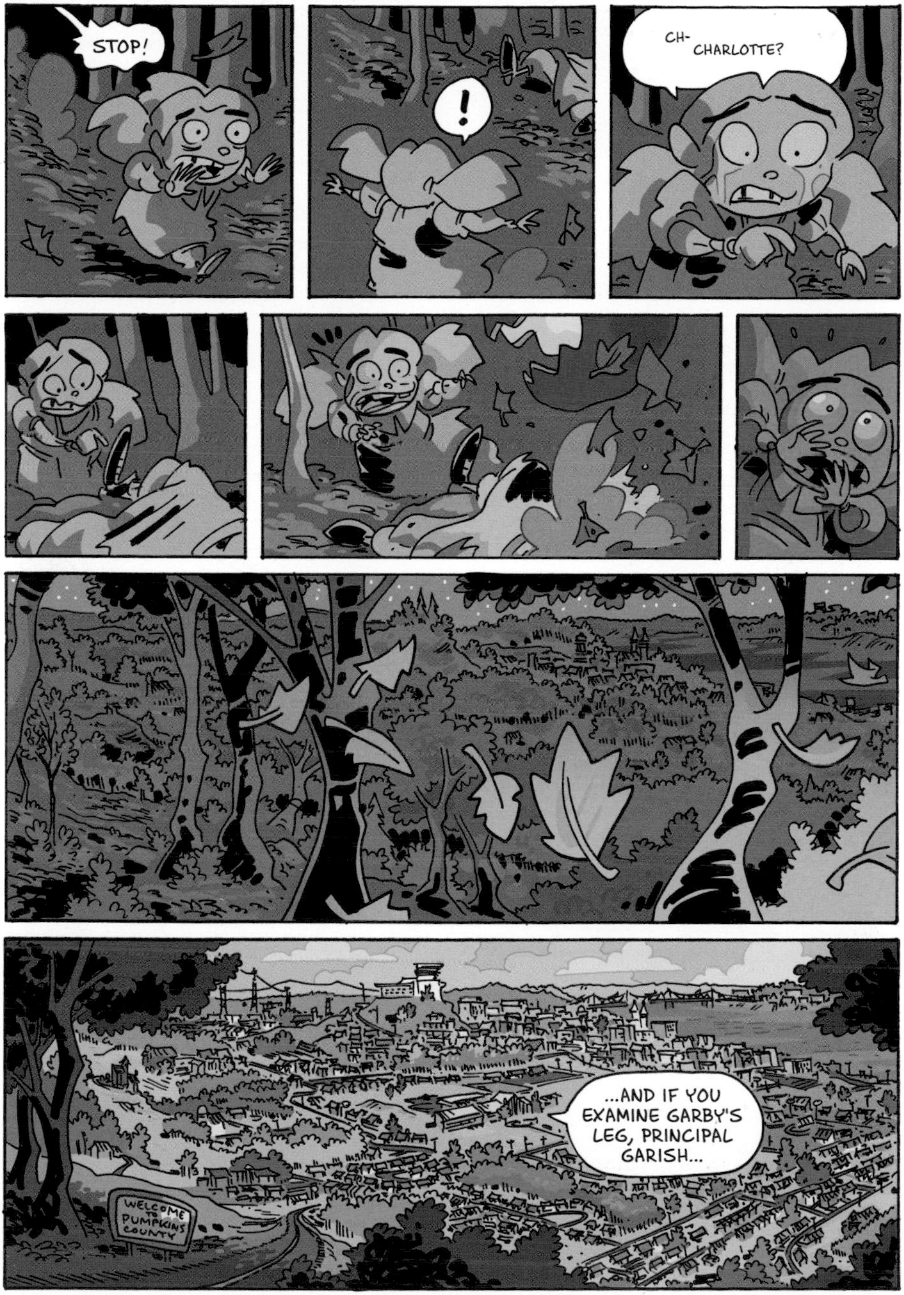
STOP!
!
CH-
CHARLOTTE?
...AND IF YOU EXAMINE GARBY'S LEG, PRINCIPAL GARISH...
WELCOME TO PUMPKINS COUNTY

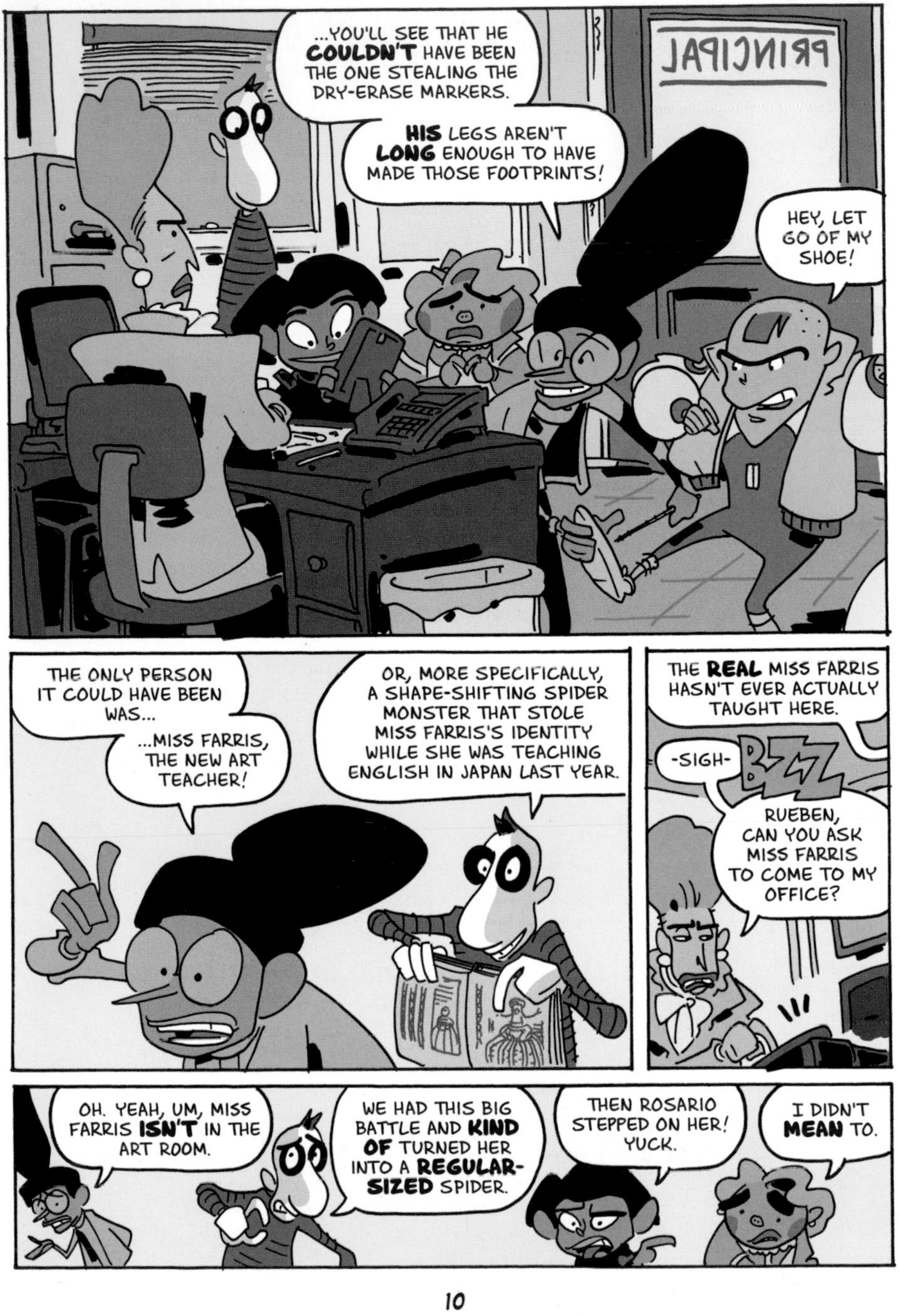

PRINCIPAL
...YOU'LL SEE THAT HE **COULDN'T** HAVE BEEN THE ONE STEALING THE DRY-ERASE MARKERS.
HIS LEGS AREN'T **LONG** ENOUGH TO HAVE MADE THOSE FOOTPRINTS!
HEY, LET GO OF MY SHOE!
THE ONLY PERSON IT COULD HAVE BEEN WAS...
...MISS FARRIS, THE NEW ART TEACHER!
OR, MORE SPECIFICALLY, A SHAPE-SHIFTING SPIDER MONSTER THAT STOLE MISS FARRIS'S IDENTITY WHILE SHE WAS TEACHING ENGLISH IN JAPAN LAST YEAR.
THE **REAL** MISS FARRIS HASN'T EVER ACTUALLY TAUGHT HERE.
-SIGH-
BZZZ
RUEBEN, CAN YOU ASK MISS FARRIS TO COME TO MY OFFICE?
OH. YEAH, UM, MISS FARRIS **ISN'T** IN THE ART ROOM.
WE HAD THIS BIG BATTLE AND **KIND OF** TURNED HER INTO A **REGULAR-SIZED** SPIDER.
THEN ROSARIO STEPPED ON HER! YUCK.
I DIDN'T **MEAN** TO.

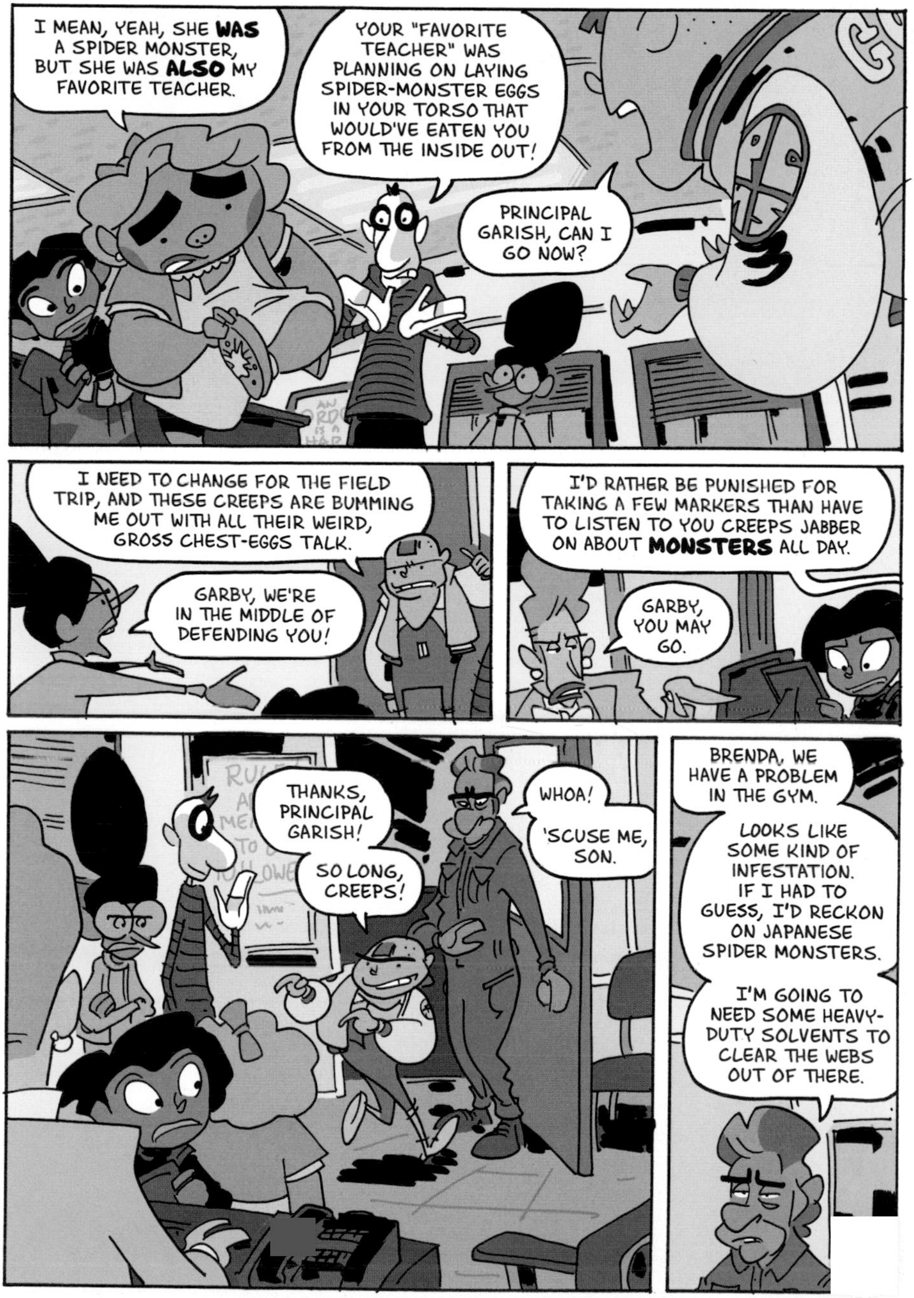

I MEAN, YEAH, SHE **WAS** A SPIDER MONSTER, BUT SHE WAS **ALSO** MY FAVORITE TEACHER.
YOUR "FAVORITE TEACHER" WAS PLANNING ON LAYING SPIDER-MONSTER EGGS IN YOUR TORSO THAT WOULD'VE EATEN YOU FROM THE INSIDE OUT!
PRINCIPAL GARISH, CAN I GO NOW?
I NEED TO CHANGE FOR THE FIELD TRIP, AND THESE CREEPS ARE BUMMING ME OUT WITH ALL THEIR WEIRD, GROSS CHEST-EGGS TALK.
GARBY, WE'RE IN THE MIDDLE OF DEFENDING YOU!
I'D RATHER BE PUNISHED FOR TAKING A FEW MARKERS THAN HAVE TO LISTEN TO YOU CREEPS JABBER ON ABOUT **MONSTERS** ALL DAY.
GARBY, YOU MAY GO.
THANKS, PRINCIPAL GARISH!
SO LONG, CREEPS!
WHOA!
'SCUSE ME, SON.
BRENDA, WE HAVE A PROBLEM IN THE GYM.
LOOKS LIKE SOME KIND OF INFESTATION. IF I HAD TO GUESS, I'D RECKON ON JAPANESE SPIDER MONSTERS.
I'M GOING TO NEED SOME HEAVY-DUTY SOLVENTS TO CLEAR THE WEBS OUT OF THERE.

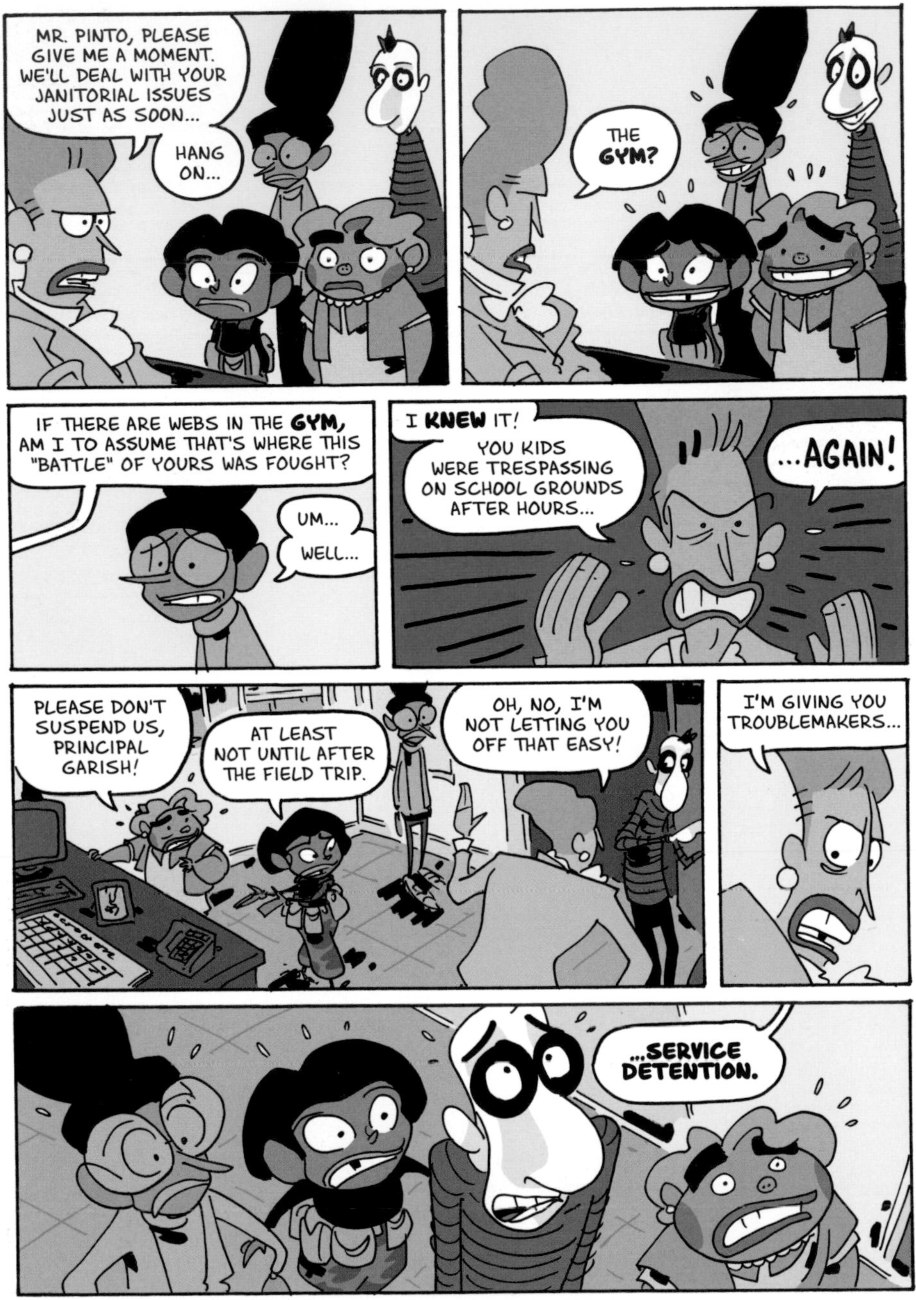
MR. PINTO, PLEASE GIVE ME A MOMENT. WE'LL DEAL WITH YOUR JANITORIAL ISSUES JUST AS SOON...
HANG ON...
THE **GYM?**
IF THERE ARE WEBS IN THE **GYM,** AM I TO ASSUME THAT'S WHERE THIS "BATTLE" OF YOURS WAS FOUGHT?
UM...
WELL...
I **KNEW** IT!
YOU KIDS WERE TRESPASSING ON SCHOOL GROUNDS AFTER HOURS...
...AGAIN!
PLEASE DON'T SUSPEND US, PRINCIPAL GARISH!
AT LEAST NOT UNTIL AFTER THE FIELD TRIP.
OH, NO, I'M NOT LETTING YOU OFF THAT EASY!
I'M GIVING YOU TROUBLEMAKERS...
...SERVICE DETENTION.

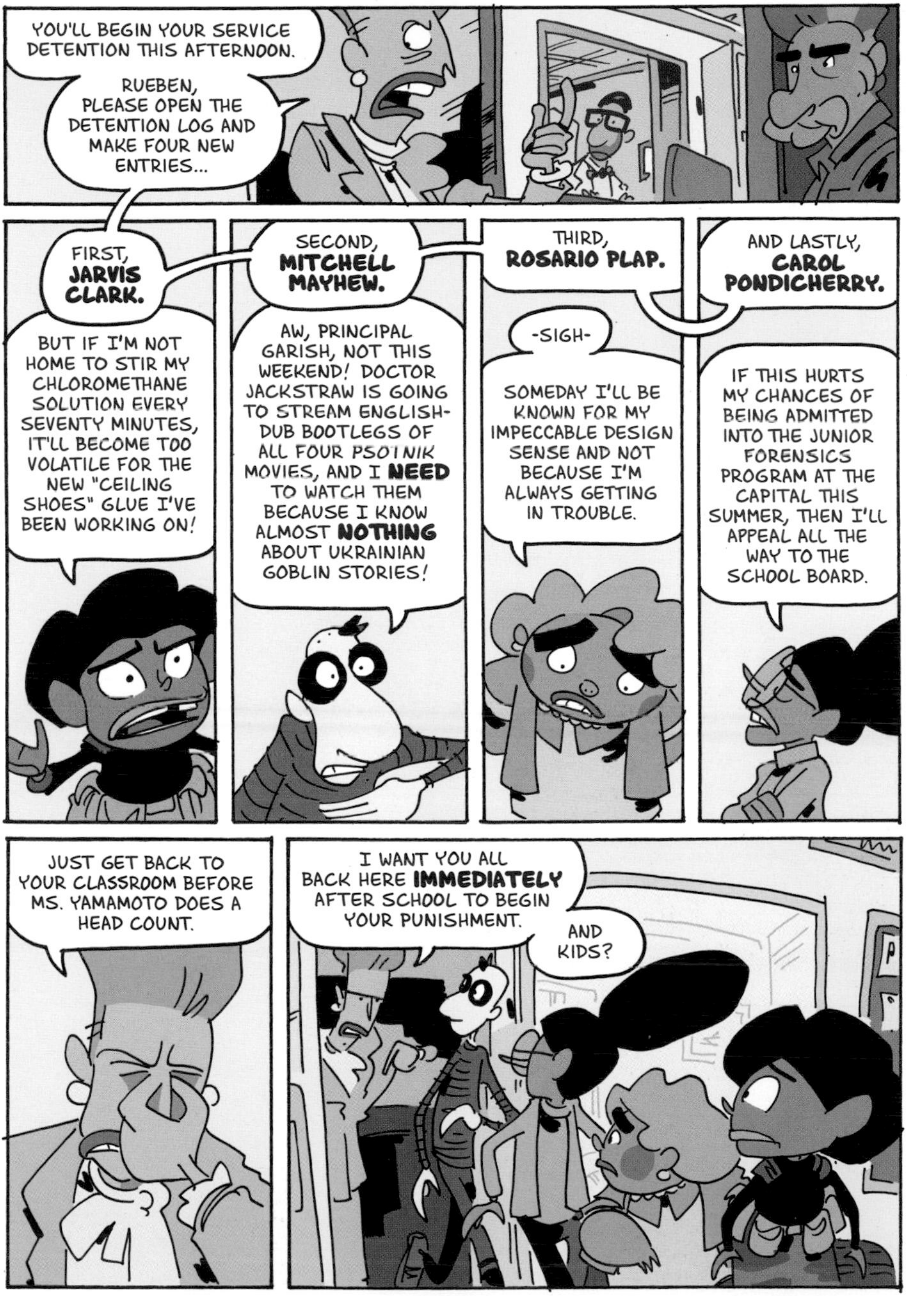
YOU'LL BEGIN YOUR SERVICE DETENTION THIS AFTERNOON.
RUEBEN, PLEASE OPEN THE DETENTION LOG AND MAKE FOUR NEW ENTRIES...
FIRST, **JARVIS CLARK.**
SECOND, **MITCHELL MAYHEW.**
THIRD, **ROSARIO PLAP.**
AND LASTLY, **CAROL PONDICHERRY.**
BUT IF I'M NOT HOME TO STIR MY CHLOROMETHANE SOLUTION EVERY SEVENTY MINUTES, IT'LL BECOME TOO VOLATILE FOR THE NEW "CEILING SHOES" GLUE I'VE BEEN WORKING ON!
AW, PRINCIPAL GARISH, NOT THIS WEEKEND! DOCTOR JACKSTRAW IS GOING TO STREAM ENGLISH-DUB BOOTLEGS OF ALL FOUR PSOTNIK MOVIES, AND I **NEED** TO WATCH THEM BECAUSE I KNOW ALMOST **NOTHING** ABOUT UKRAINIAN GOBLIN STORIES!
-SIGH-
SOMEDAY I'LL BE KNOWN FOR MY IMPECCABLE DESIGN SENSE AND NOT BECAUSE I'M ALWAYS GETTING IN TROUBLE.
IF THIS HURTS MY CHANCES OF BEING ADMITTED INTO THE JUNIOR FORENSICS PROGRAM AT THE CAPITAL THIS SUMMER, THEN I'LL APPEAL ALL THE WAY TO THE SCHOOL BOARD.
JUST GET BACK TO YOUR CLASSROOM BEFORE MS. YAMAMOTO DOES A HEAD COUNT.
I WANT YOU ALL BACK HERE **IMMEDIATELY** AFTER SCHOOL TO BEGIN YOUR PUNISHMENT.
AND KIDS?

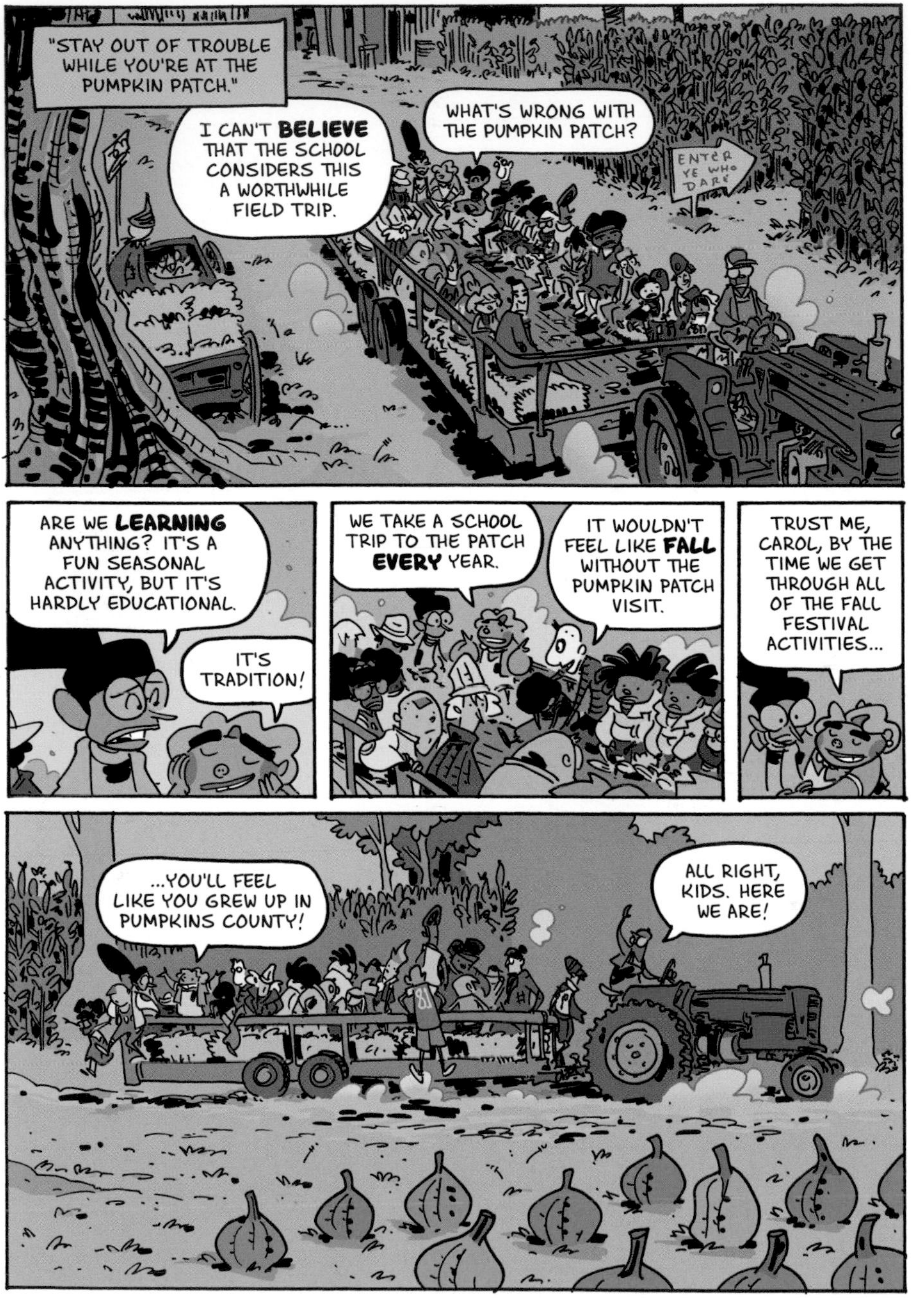
"STAY OUT OF TROUBLE WHILE YOU'RE AT THE PUMPKIN PATCH."
I CAN'T **BELIEVE** THAT THE SCHOOL CONSIDERS THIS A WORTHWHILE FIELD TRIP.
WHAT'S WRONG WITH THE PUMPKIN PATCH?
ENTER YE WHO DARE
ARE WE **LEARNING** ANYTHING? IT'S A FUN SEASONAL ACTIVITY, BUT IT'S HARDLY EDUCATIONAL.
IT'S TRADITION!
WE TAKE A SCHOOL TRIP TO THE PATCH **EVERY** YEAR.
IT WOULDN'T FEEL LIKE **FALL** WITHOUT THE PUMPKIN PATCH VISIT.
TRUST ME, CAROL, BY THE TIME WE GET THROUGH ALL OF THE FALL FESTIVAL ACTIVITIES...
...YOU'LL FEEL LIKE YOU GREW UP IN PUMPKINS COUNTY!
ALL RIGHT, KIDS. HERE WE ARE!

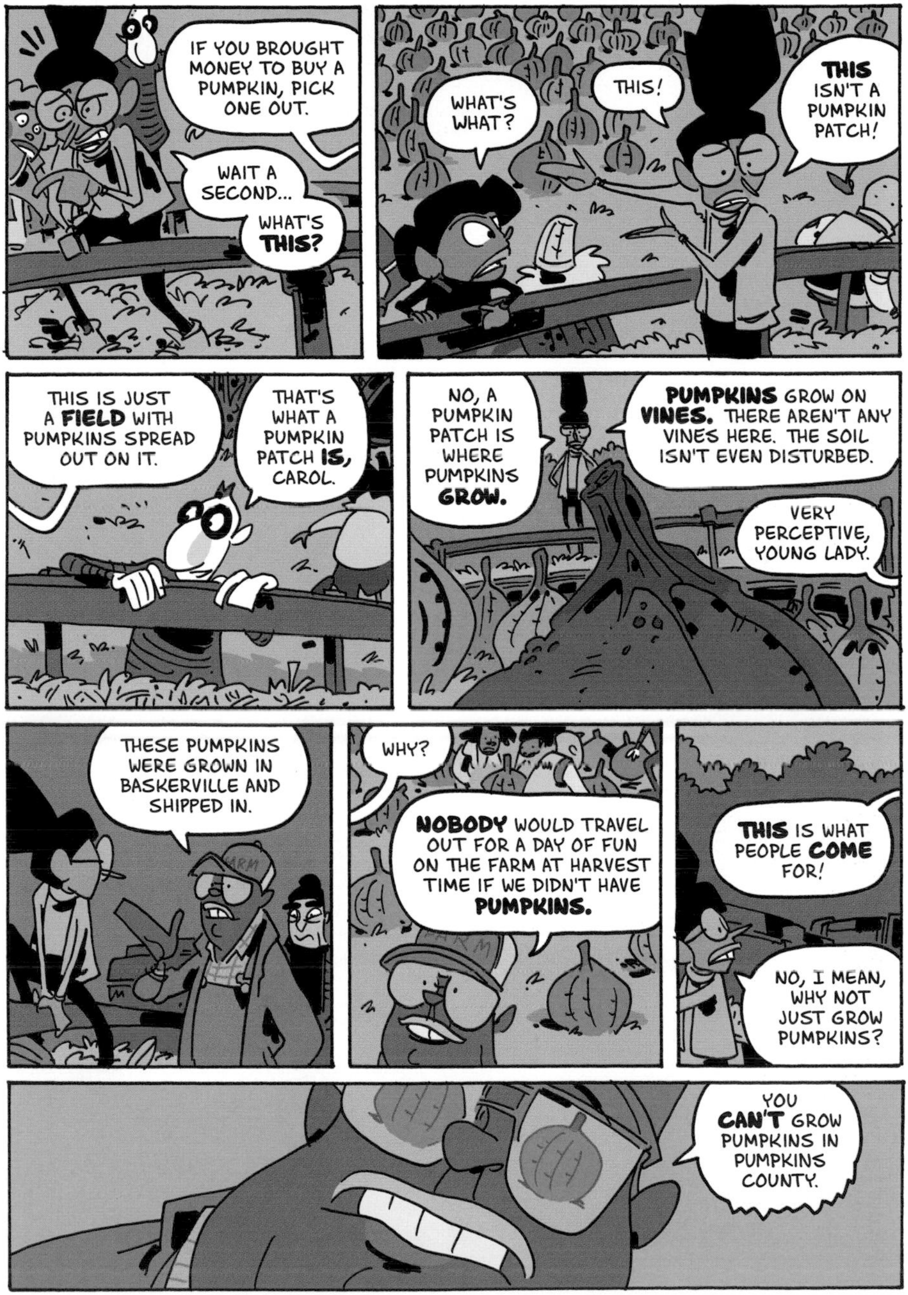
IF YOU BROUGHT MONEY TO BUY A PUMPKIN, PICK ONE OUT.
WAIT A SECOND...
WHAT'S **THIS?**
WHAT'S WHAT?
THIS!
THIS ISN'T A PUMPKIN PATCH!
THIS IS JUST A **FIELD** WITH PUMPKINS SPREAD OUT ON IT.
THAT'S WHAT A PUMPKIN PATCH **IS,** CAROL.
NO, A PUMPKIN PATCH IS WHERE PUMPKINS **GROW.**
PUMPKINS GROW ON **VINES.** THERE AREN'T ANY VINES HERE. THE SOIL ISN'T EVEN DISTURBED.
VERY PERCEPTIVE, YOUNG LADY.
THESE PUMPKINS WERE GROWN IN BASKERVILLE AND SHIPPED IN.
WHY?
NOBODY WOULD TRAVEL OUT FOR A DAY OF FUN ON THE FARM AT HARVEST TIME IF WE DIDN'T HAVE **PUMPKINS.**
THIS IS WHAT PEOPLE **COME** FOR!
NO, I MEAN, WHY NOT JUST GROW PUMPKINS?
YOU **CAN'T** GROW PUMPKINS IN PUMPKINS COUNTY.

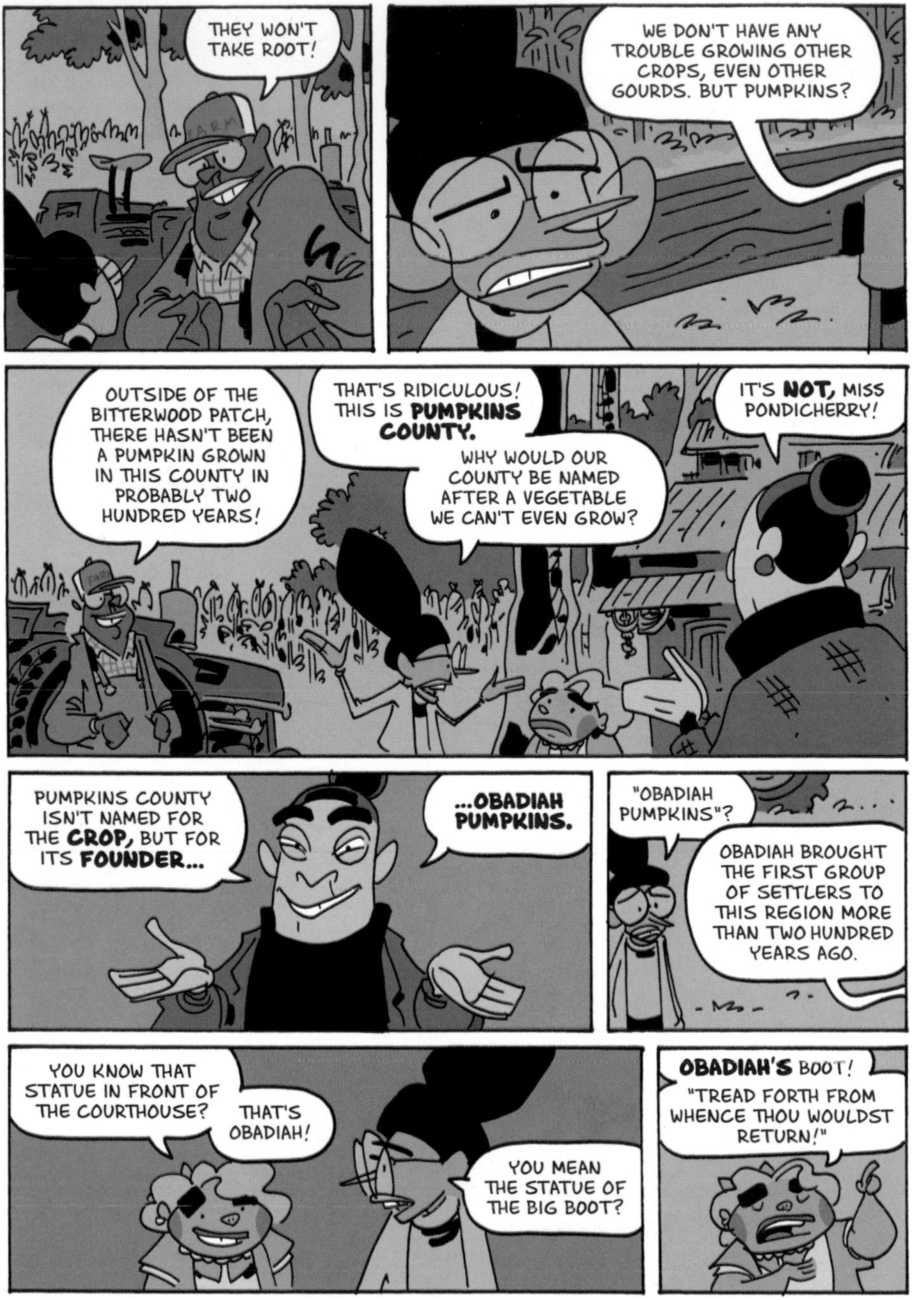
THEY WON'T TAKE ROOT!
WE DON'T HAVE ANY TROUBLE GROWING OTHER CROPS, EVEN OTHER GOURDS. BUT PUMPKINS?
OUTSIDE OF THE BITTERWOOD PATCH, THERE HASN'T BEEN A PUMPKIN GROWN IN THIS COUNTY IN PROBABLY TWO HUNDRED YEARS!
THAT'S RIDICULOUS! THIS IS **PUMPKINS COUNTY.**
WHY WOULD OUR COUNTY BE NAMED AFTER A VEGETABLE WE CAN'T EVEN GROW?
IT'S **NOT,** MISS PONDICHERRY!
PUMPKINS COUNTY ISN'T NAMED FOR THE **CROP,** BUT FOR ITS **FOUNDER...**
...OBADIAH PUMPKINS.
"OBADIAH PUMPKINS"?
OBADIAH BROUGHT THE FIRST GROUP OF SETTLERS TO THIS REGION MORE THAN TWO HUNDRED YEARS AGO.
YOU KNOW THAT STATUE IN FRONT OF THE COURTHOUSE?
THAT'S OBADIAH!
YOU MEAN THE STATUE OF THE BIG BOOT?
OBADIAH'S BOOT!
"TREAD FORTH FROM WHENCE THOU WOULDST RETURN!"

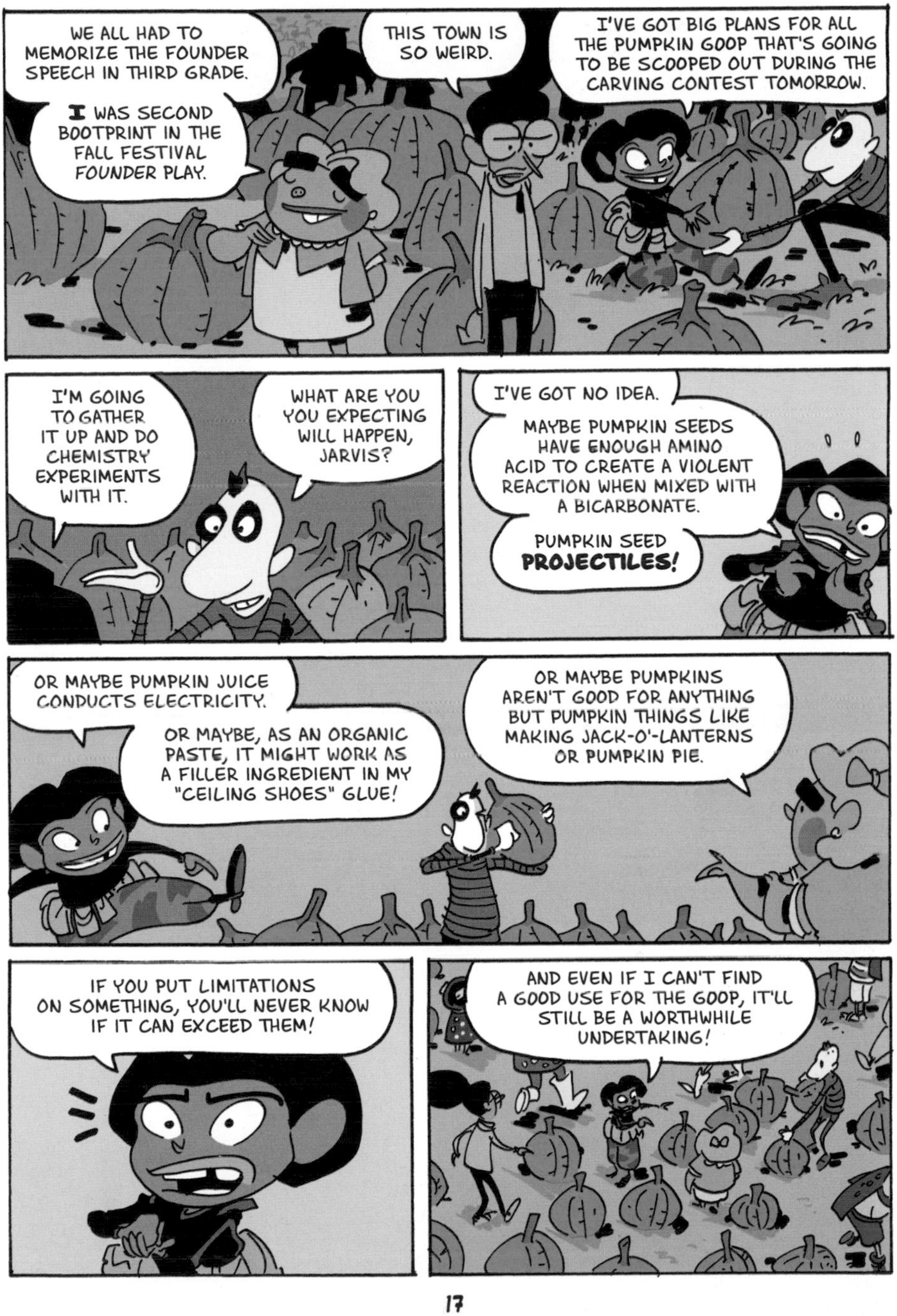

WE ALL HAD TO MEMORIZE THE FOUNDER SPEECH IN THIRD GRADE.
I WAS SECOND BOOTPRINT IN THE FALL FESTIVAL FOUNDER PLAY.
THIS TOWN IS SO WEIRD.
I'VE GOT BIG PLANS FOR ALL THE PUMPKIN GOOP THAT'S GOING TO BE SCOOPED OUT DURING THE CARVING CONTEST TOMORROW.
I'M GOING TO GATHER IT UP AND DO CHEMISTRY EXPERIMENTS WITH IT.
WHAT ARE YOU YOU EXPECTING WILL HAPPEN, JARVIS?
I'VE GOT NO IDEA.
MAYBE PUMPKIN SEEDS HAVE ENOUGH AMINO ACID TO CREATE A VIOLENT REACTION WHEN MIXED WITH A BICARBONATE.
PUMPKIN SEED PROJECTILES!
OR MAYBE PUMPKIN JUICE CONDUCTS ELECTRICITY.
OR MAYBE, AS AN ORGANIC PASTE, IT MIGHT WORK AS A FILLER INGREDIENT IN MY "CEILING SHOES" GLUE!
OR MAYBE PUMPKINS AREN'T GOOD FOR ANYTHING BUT PUMPKIN THINGS LIKE MAKING JACK-O'-LANTERNS OR PUMPKIN PIE.
IF YOU PUT LIMITATIONS ON SOMETHING, YOU'LL NEVER KNOW IF IT CAN EXCEED THEM!
AND EVEN IF I CAN'T FIND A GOOD USE FOR THE GOOP, IT'LL STILL BE A WORTHWHILE UNDERTAKING!

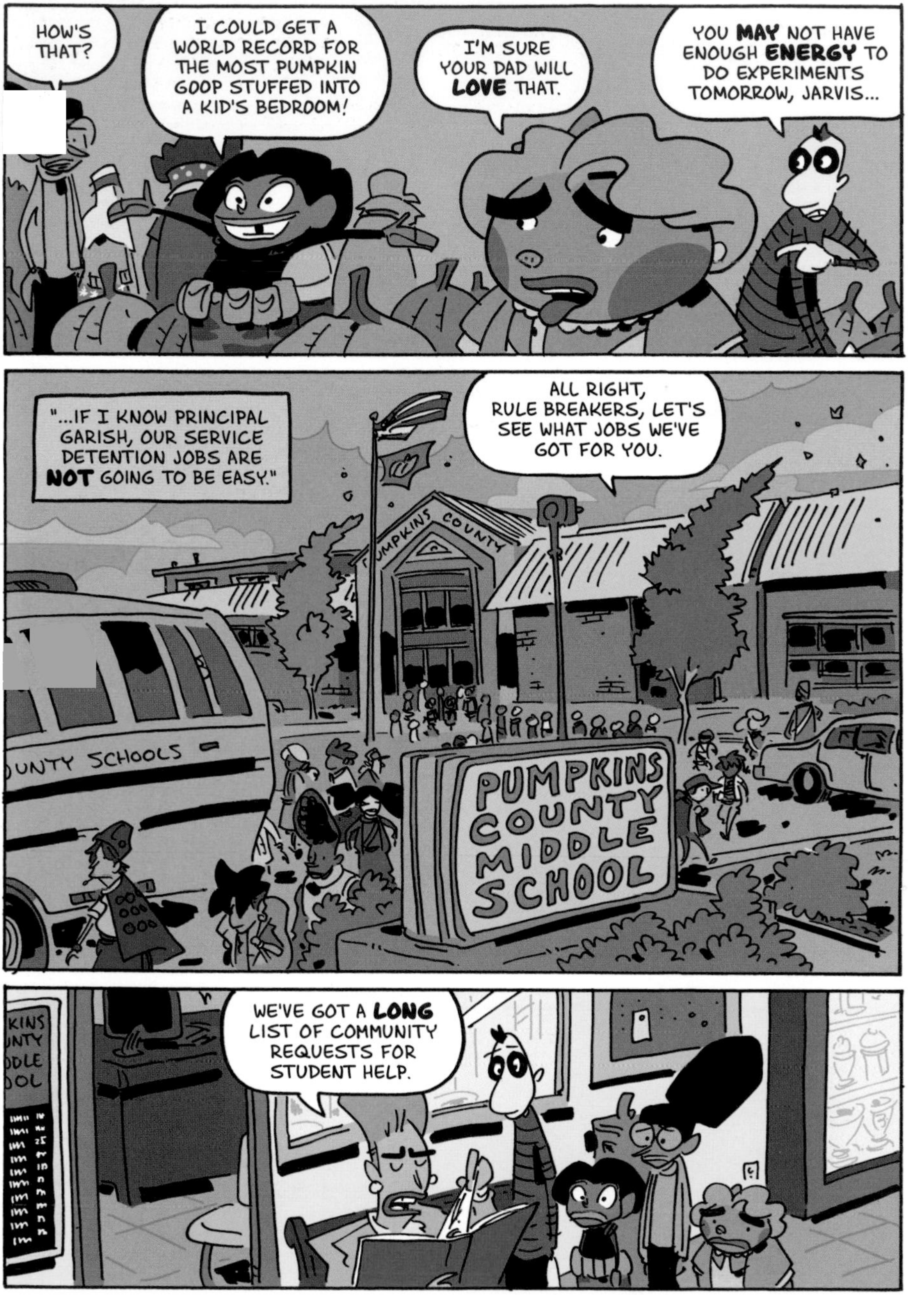
HOW'S THAT?
I COULD GET A WORLD RECORD FOR THE MOST PUMPKIN GOOP STUFFED INTO A KID'S BEDROOM!
I'M SURE YOUR DAD WILL **LOVE** THAT.
YOU **MAY** NOT HAVE ENOUGH **ENERGY** TO DO EXPERIMENTS TOMORROW, JARVIS...
"...IF I KNOW PRINCIPAL GARISH, OUR SERVICE DETENTION JOBS ARE **NOT** GOING TO BE EASY."
ALL RIGHT, RULE BREAKERS, LET'S SEE WHAT JOBS WE'VE GOT FOR YOU.
PUMPKINS COUNTY
PUMPKINS COUNTY MIDDLE SCHOOL
WE'VE GOT A **LONG** LIST OF COMMUNITY REQUESTS FOR STUDENT HELP.

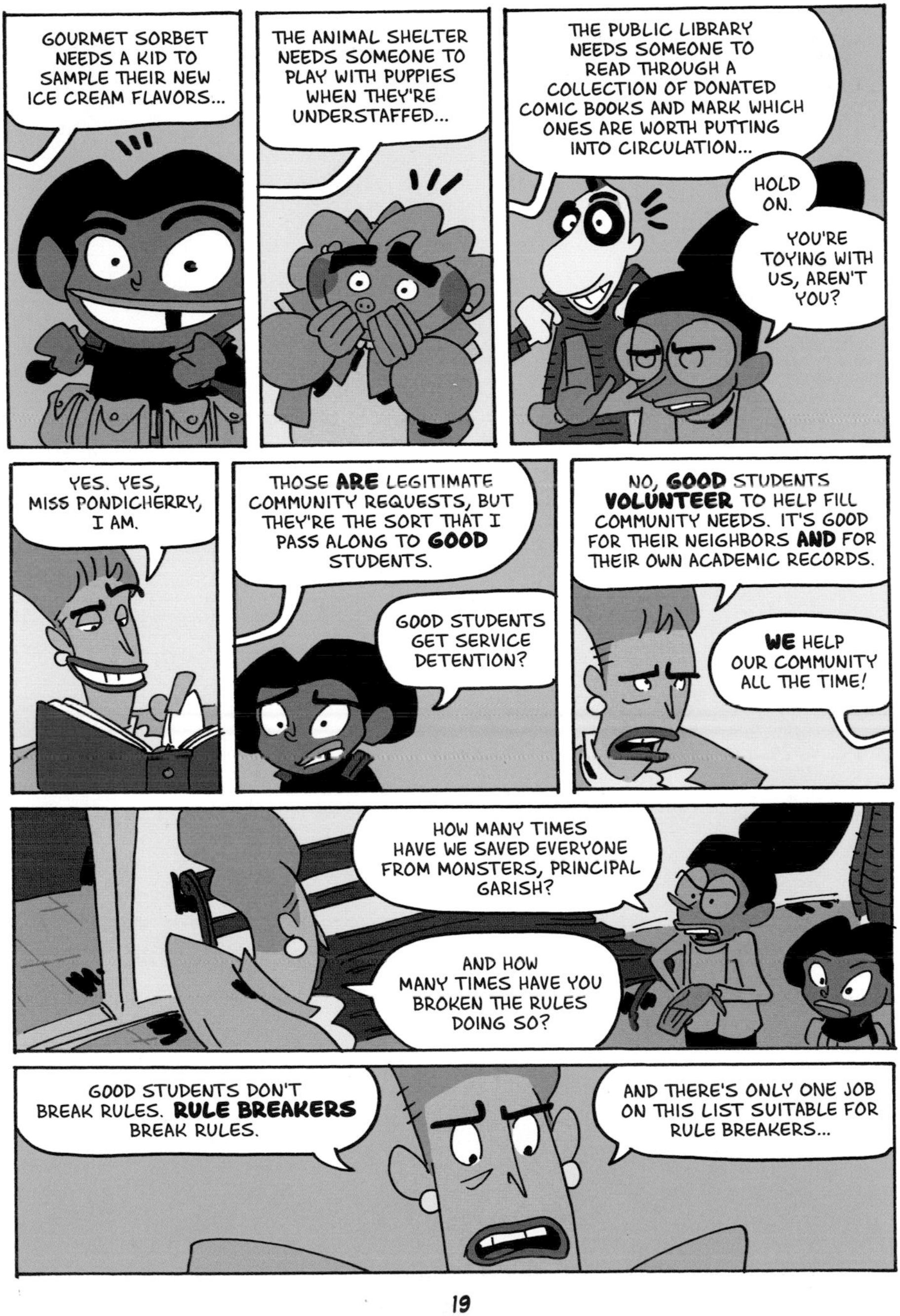
GOURMET SORBET NEEDS A KID TO SAMPLE THEIR NEW ICE CREAM FLAVORS...
THE ANIMAL SHELTER NEEDS SOMEONE TO PLAY WITH PUPPIES WHEN THEY'RE UNDERSTAFFED...
THE PUBLIC LIBRARY NEEDS SOMEONE TO READ THROUGH A COLLECTION OF DONATED COMIC BOOKS AND MARK WHICH ONES ARE WORTH PUTTING INTO CIRCULATION...
HOLD ON.
YOU'RE TOYING WITH US, AREN'T YOU?
YES. YES, MISS PONDICHERRY, I AM.
THOSE **ARE** LEGITIMATE COMMUNITY REQUESTS, BUT THEY'RE THE SORT THAT I PASS ALONG TO **GOOD** STUDENTS.
GOOD STUDENTS GET SERVICE DETENTION?
NO, **GOOD** STUDENTS **VOLUNTEER** TO HELP FILL COMMUNITY NEEDS. IT'S GOOD FOR THEIR NEIGHBORS **AND** FOR THEIR OWN ACADEMIC RECORDS.
WE HELP OUR COMMUNITY ALL THE TIME!
HOW MANY TIMES HAVE WE SAVED EVERYONE FROM MONSTERS, PRINCIPAL GARISH?
AND HOW MANY TIMES HAVE YOU BROKEN THE RULES DOING SO?
GOOD STUDENTS DON'T BREAK RULES. **RULE BREAKERS** BREAK RULES.
AND THERE'S ONLY ONE JOB ON THIS LIST SUITABLE FOR RULE BREAKERS...

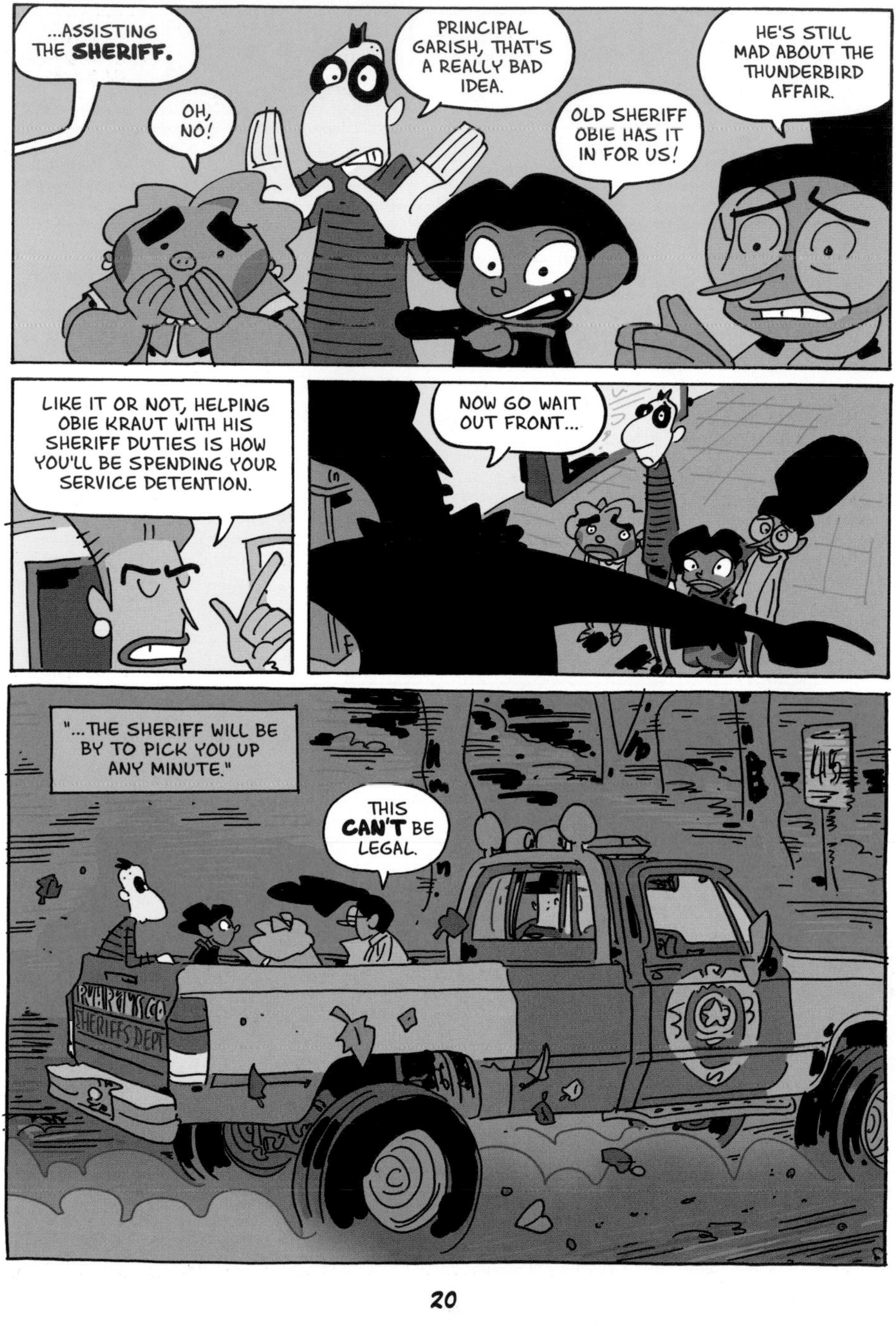
...ASSISTING THE **SHERIFF.**
OH, NO!
PRINCIPAL GARISH, THAT'S A REALLY BAD IDEA.
OLD SHERIFF OBIE HAS IT IN FOR US!
HE'S STILL MAD ABOUT THE THUNDERBIRD AFFAIR.
LIKE IT OR NOT, HELPING OBIE KRAUT WITH HIS SHERIFF DUTIES IS HOW YOU'LL BE SPENDING YOUR SERVICE DETENTION.
NOW GO WAIT OUT FRONT...
"...THE SHERIFF WILL BE BY TO PICK YOU UP ANY MINUTE."
THIS **CAN'T** BE LEGAL.
SHERIFFS DEPT

HEY, AT LEAST **YOU** GET TO SPEND THE WEEKEND DOING SOMETHING THAT GETS YOU EXCITED.

THIS ISN'T EXCITING!

BUT YOU'VE BEEN BUGGING SHERIFF OBIE TO LET YOU SHADOW HIM FOR **MONTHS!**

YEAH, WHEN HE'S **SOLVING CRIMES.**

BUT PROPERTY SEIZURE? YUCK.

PROPERTY SEIZURE IS AN UNPLEASANT BUT NECESSARY DUTY OF THE SHERIFF'S DEPARTMENT.

LAW ENFORCEMENT **ISN'T** JUST CRACKING CASES AND STOPPING BAD GUYS...

...AND WISHING IT WERE DOESN'T DO ANYBODY ANY GOOD.

NO HUNTING FISHING DRAGING

NO SOLICITING

GO AWAY

PUMPKINS CO SHERIFFS DEPT

NO TRESPASSING

KEEP OUT

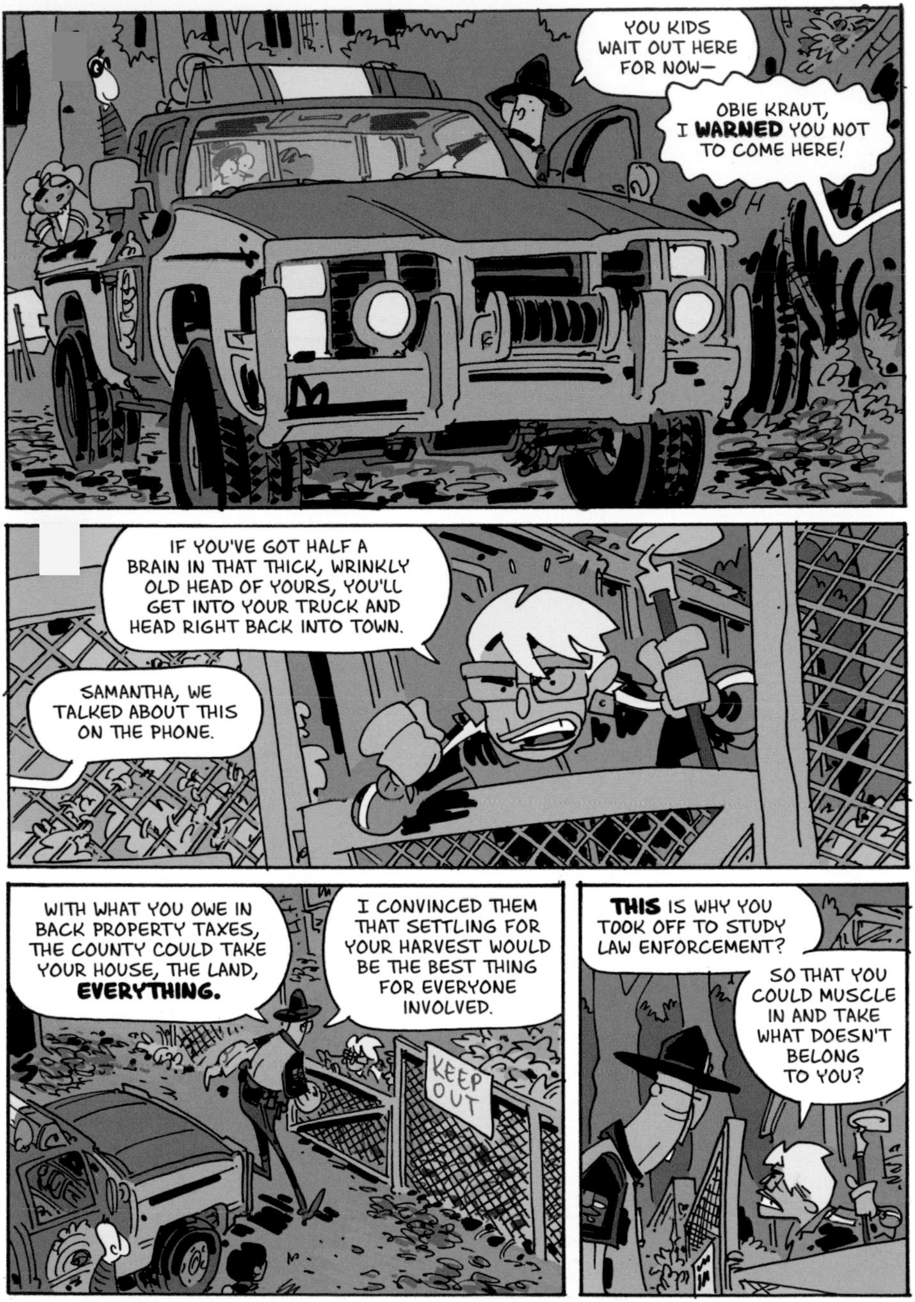
YOU KIDS WAIT OUT HERE FOR NOW—
OBIE KRAUT, I **WARNED** YOU NOT TO COME HERE!
IF YOU'VE GOT HALF A BRAIN IN THAT THICK, WRINKLY OLD HEAD OF YOURS, YOU'LL GET INTO YOUR TRUCK AND HEAD RIGHT BACK INTO TOWN.
SAMANTHA, WE TALKED ABOUT THIS ON THE PHONE.
WITH WHAT YOU OWE IN BACK PROPERTY TAXES, THE COUNTY COULD TAKE YOUR HOUSE, THE LAND, **EVERYTHING.**
I CONVINCED THEM THAT SETTLING FOR YOUR HARVEST WOULD BE THE BEST THING FOR EVERYONE INVOLVED.
KEEP OUT
THIS IS WHY YOU TOOK OFF TO STUDY LAW ENFORCEMENT?
SO THAT YOU COULD MUSCLE IN AND TAKE WHAT DOESN'T BELONG TO YOU?

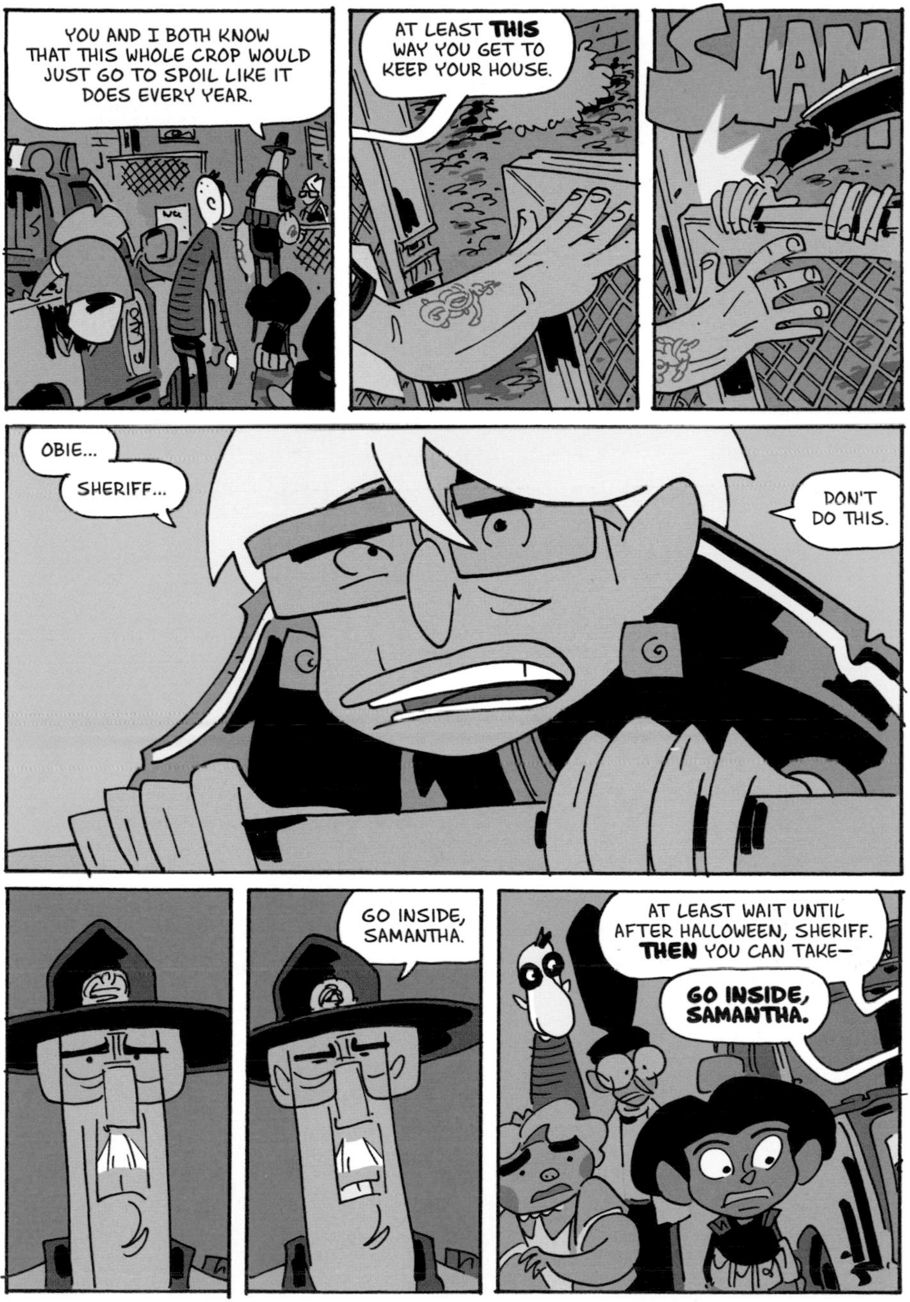
YOU AND I BOTH KNOW THAT THIS WHOLE CROP WOULD JUST GO TO SPOIL LIKE IT DOES EVERY YEAR.
AT LEAST **THIS** WAY YOU GET TO KEEP YOUR HOUSE.
SLAM
OBIE...
SHERIFF...
DON'T DO THIS.
GO INSIDE, SAMANTHA.
AT LEAST WAIT UNTIL AFTER HALLOWEEN, SHERIFF. **THEN** YOU CAN TAKE–
GO INSIDE, SAMANTHA.

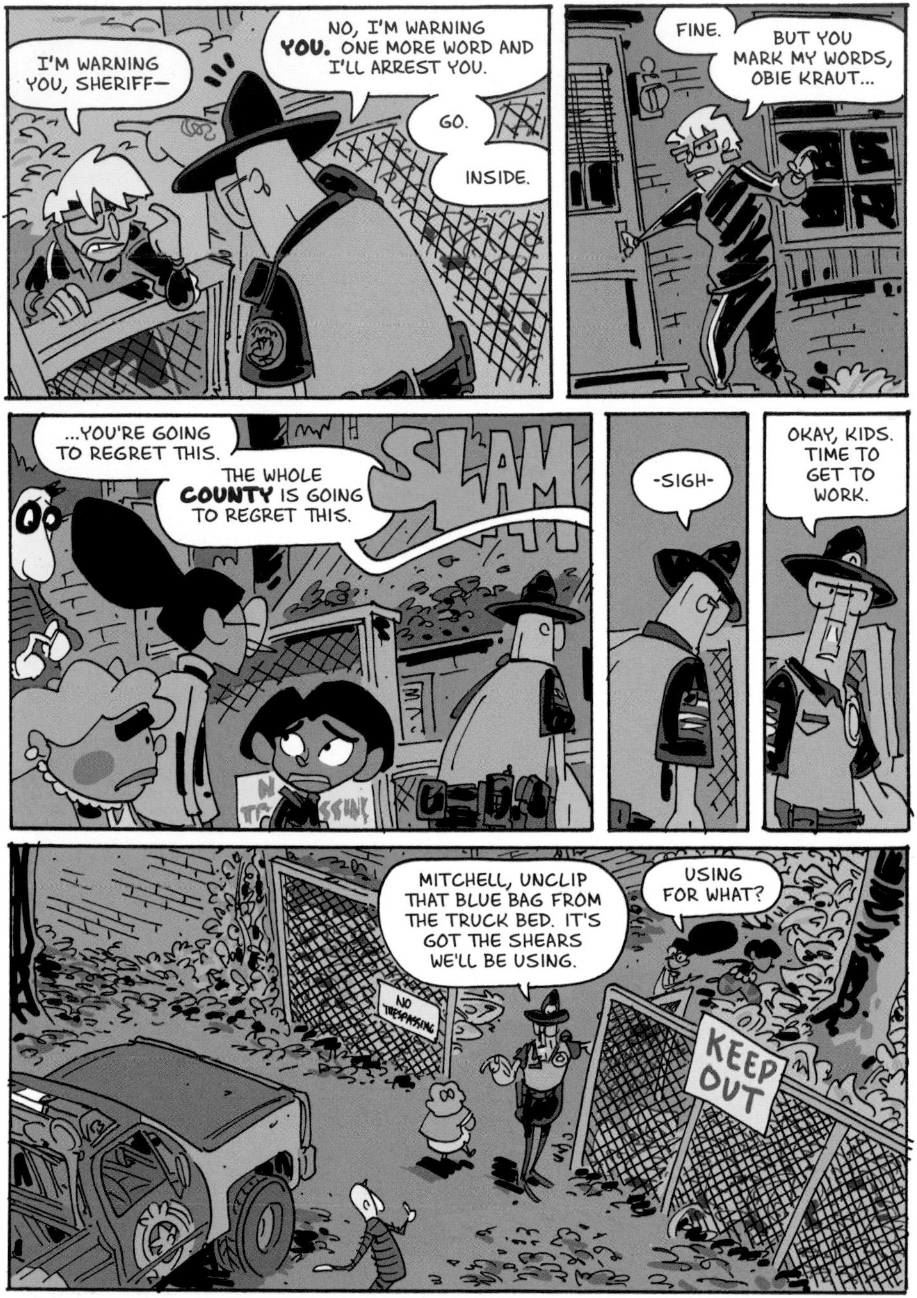
I'M WARNING YOU, SHERIFF—
NO, I'M WARNING YOU. ONE MORE WORD AND I'LL ARREST YOU.
GO.
INSIDE.
FINE.
BUT YOU MARK MY WORDS, OBIE KRAUT...
...YOU'RE GOING TO REGRET THIS.
THE WHOLE COUNTY IS GOING TO REGRET THIS.
SLAM
-SIGH-
OKAY, KIDS. TIME TO GET TO WORK.
MITCHELL, UNCLIP THAT BLUE BAG FROM THE TRUCK BED. IT'S GOT THE SHEARS WE'LL BE USING.
USING FOR WHAT?
NO TRESPASSING
KEEP OUT

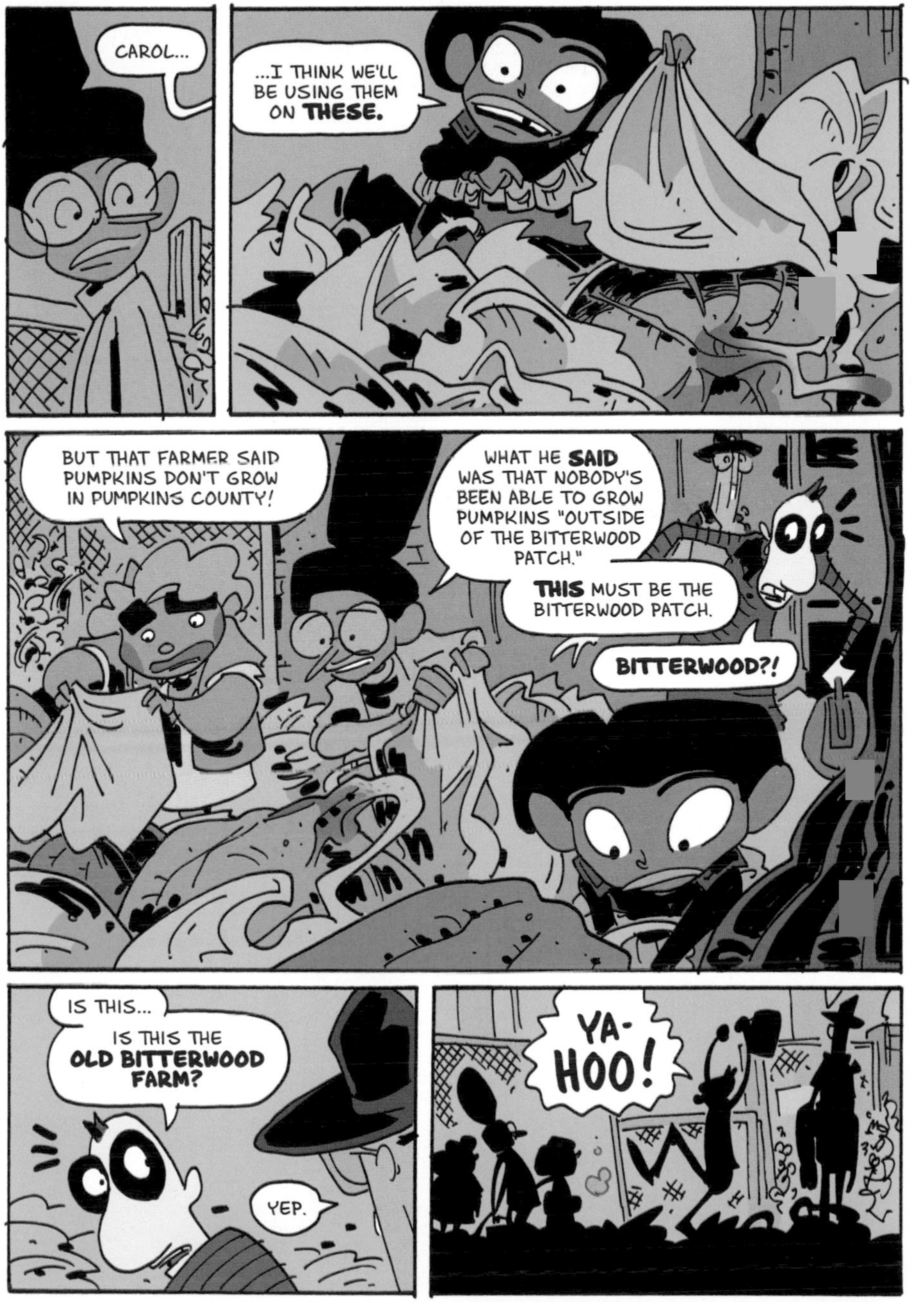
CAROL...
...I THINK WE'LL BE USING THEM ON **THESE.**
BUT THAT FARMER SAID PUMPKINS DON'T GROW IN PUMPKINS COUNTY!
WHAT HE **SAID** WAS THAT NOBODY'S BEEN ABLE TO GROW PUMPKINS "OUTSIDE OF THE BITTERWOOD PATCH."
THIS MUST BE THE BITTERWOOD PATCH.
BITTERWOOD?!
IS THIS...
IS THIS THE **OLD BITTERWOOD FARM?**
YEP.
YA-HOO!

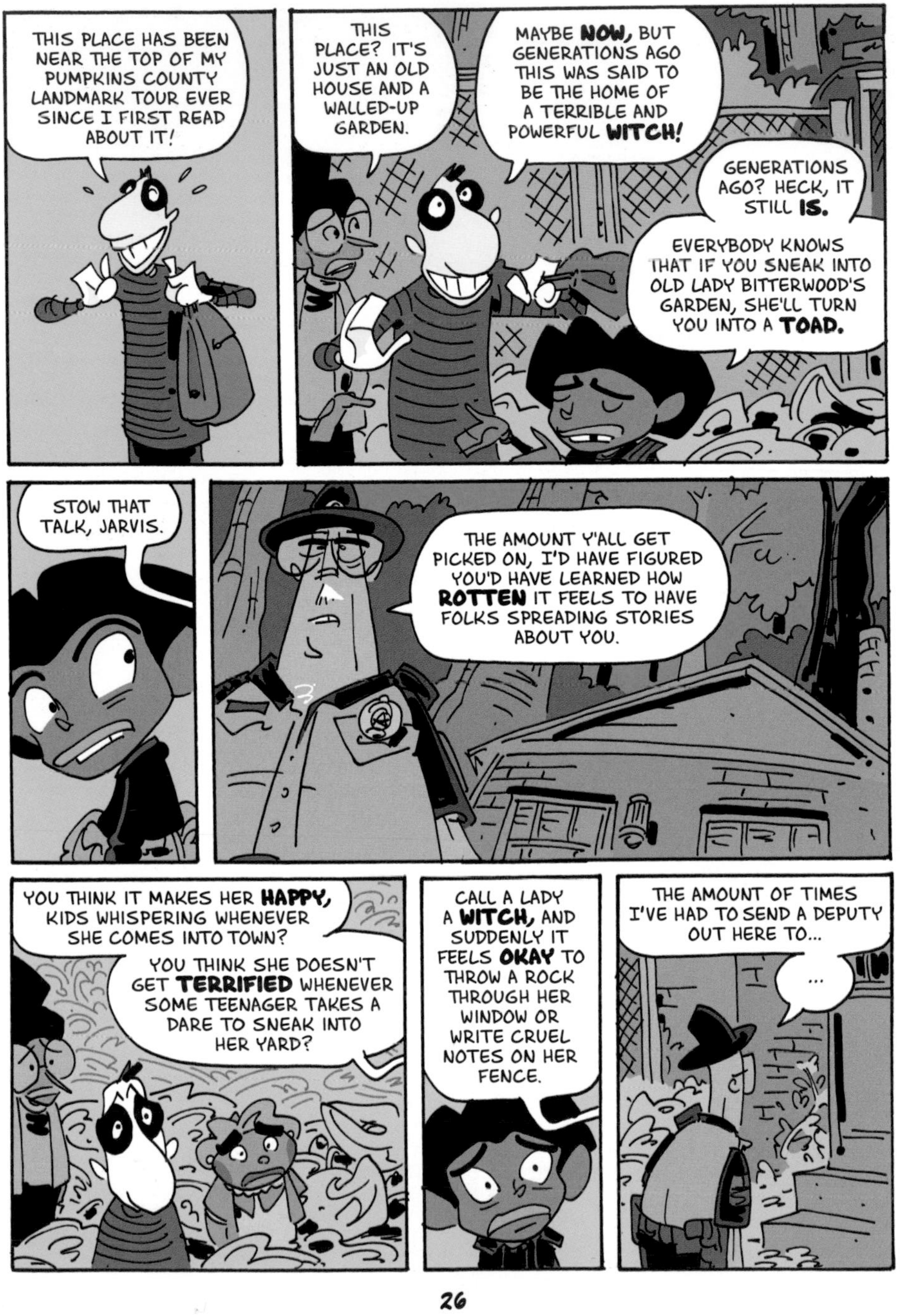
THIS PLACE HAS BEEN NEAR THE TOP OF MY PUMPKINS COUNTY LANDMARK TOUR EVER SINCE I FIRST READ ABOUT IT!
THIS PLACE? IT'S JUST AN OLD HOUSE AND A WALLED-UP GARDEN.
MAYBE NOW, BUT GENERATIONS AGO THIS WAS SAID TO BE THE HOME OF A TERRIBLE AND POWERFUL WITCH!
GENERATIONS AGO? HECK, IT STILL IS.
EVERYBODY KNOWS THAT IF YOU SNEAK INTO OLD LADY BITTERWOOD'S GARDEN, SHE'LL TURN YOU INTO A TOAD.
STOW THAT TALK, JARVIS.
THE AMOUNT Y'ALL GET PICKED ON, I'D HAVE FIGURED YOU'D HAVE LEARNED HOW ROTTEN IT FEELS TO HAVE FOLKS SPREADING STORIES ABOUT YOU.
YOU THINK IT MAKES HER HAPPY, KIDS WHISPERING WHENEVER SHE COMES INTO TOWN?
YOU THINK SHE DOESN'T GET TERRIFIED WHENEVER SOME TEENAGER TAKES A DARE TO SNEAK INTO HER YARD?
CALL A LADY A WITCH, AND SUDDENLY IT FEELS OKAY TO THROW A ROCK THROUGH HER WINDOW OR WRITE CRUEL NOTES ON HER FENCE.
THE AMOUNT OF TIMES I'VE HAD TO SEND A DEPUTY OUT HERE TO...
...

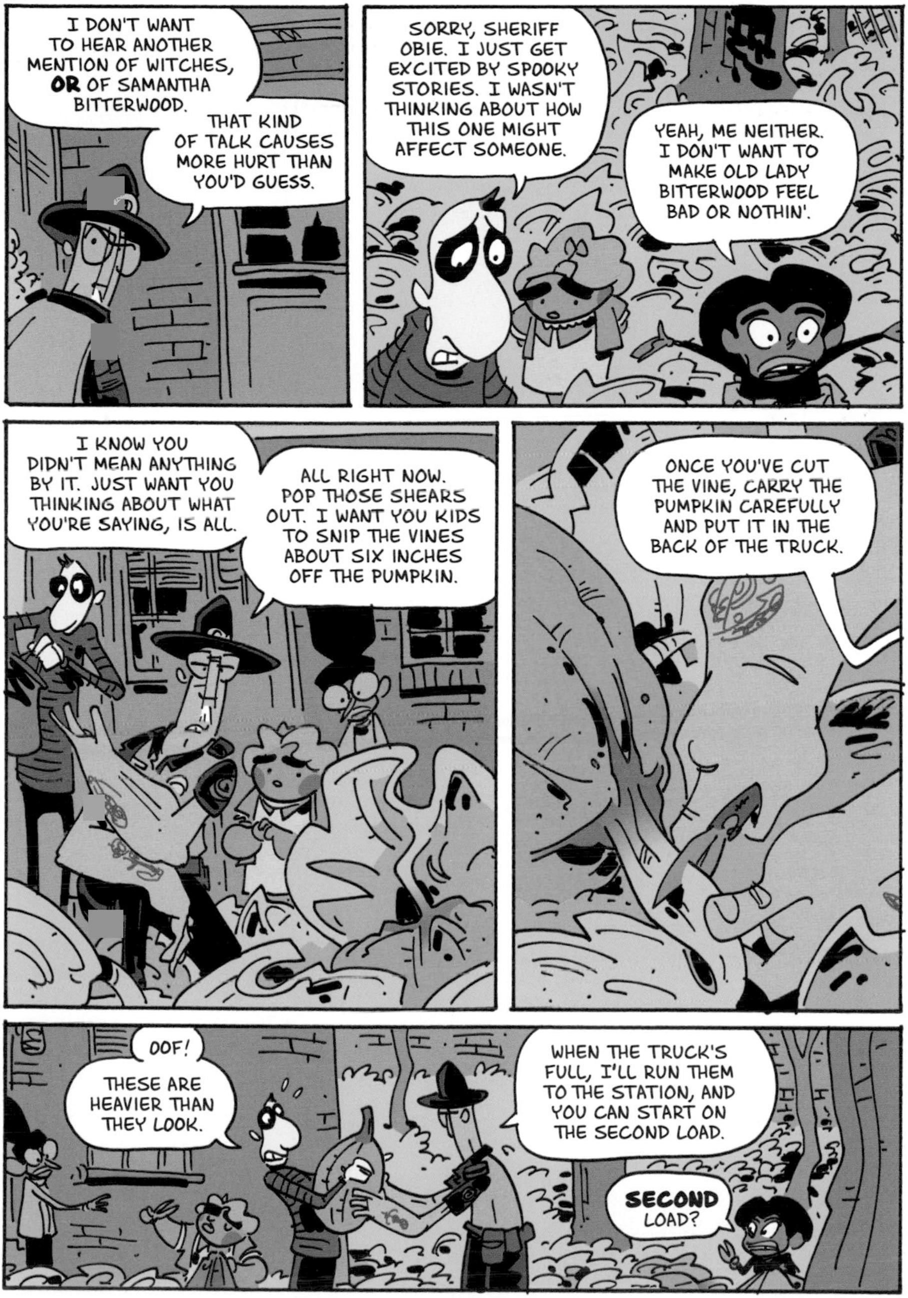

I DON'T WANT TO HEAR ANOTHER MENTION OF WITCHES, **OR** OF SAMANTHA BITTERWOOD.
THAT KIND OF TALK CAUSES MORE HURT THAN YOU'D GUESS.
SORRY, SHERIFF OBIE. I JUST GET EXCITED BY SPOOKY STORIES. I WASN'T THINKING ABOUT HOW THIS ONE MIGHT AFFECT SOMEONE.
YEAH, ME NEITHER. I DON'T WANT TO MAKE OLD LADY BITTERWOOD FEEL BAD OR NOTHIN'.
I KNOW YOU DIDN'T MEAN ANYTHING BY IT. JUST WANT YOU THINKING ABOUT WHAT YOU'RE SAYING, IS ALL.
ALL RIGHT NOW. POP THOSE SHEARS OUT. I WANT YOU KIDS TO SNIP THE VINES ABOUT SIX INCHES OFF THE PUMPKIN.
ONCE YOU'VE CUT THE VINE, CARRY THE PUMPKIN CAREFULLY AND PUT IT IN THE BACK OF THE TRUCK.
OOF!
THESE ARE HEAVIER THAN THEY LOOK.
WHEN THE TRUCK'S FULL, I'LL RUN THEM TO THE STATION, AND YOU CAN START ON THE SECOND LOAD.
SECOND LOAD?

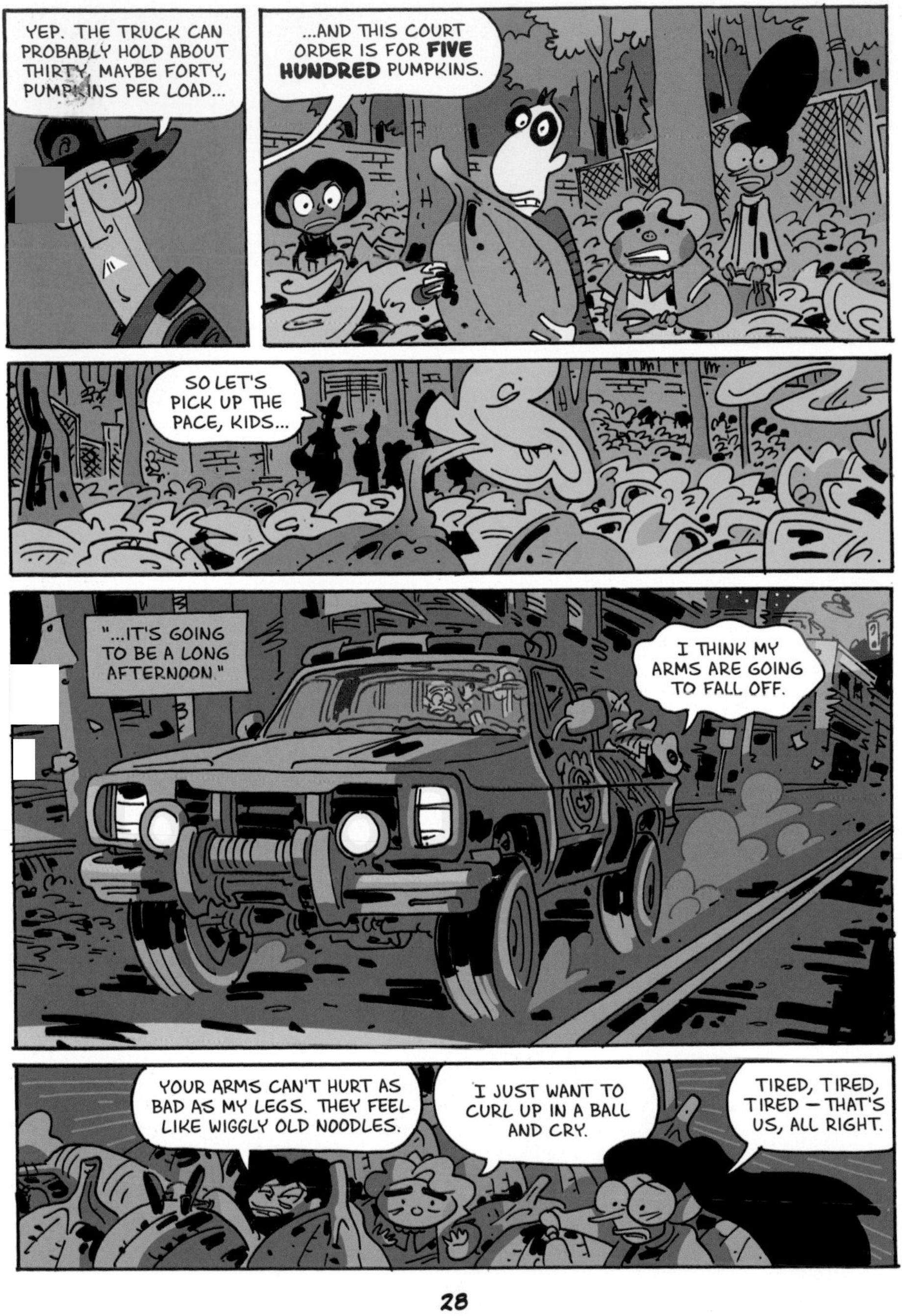
YEP. THE TRUCK CAN PROBABLY HOLD ABOUT THIRTY, MAYBE FORTY, PUMPKINS PER LOAD...
...AND THIS COURT ORDER IS FOR **FIVE HUNDRED** PUMPKINS.
SO LET'S PICK UP THE PACE, KIDS...
"...IT'S GOING TO BE A LONG AFTERNOON."
I THINK MY ARMS ARE GOING TO FALL OFF.
YOUR ARMS CAN'T HURT AS BAD AS MY LEGS. THEY FEEL LIKE WIGGLY OLD NOODLES.
I JUST WANT TO CURL UP IN A BALL AND CRY.
TIRED, TIRED, TIRED — THAT'S US, ALL RIGHT.

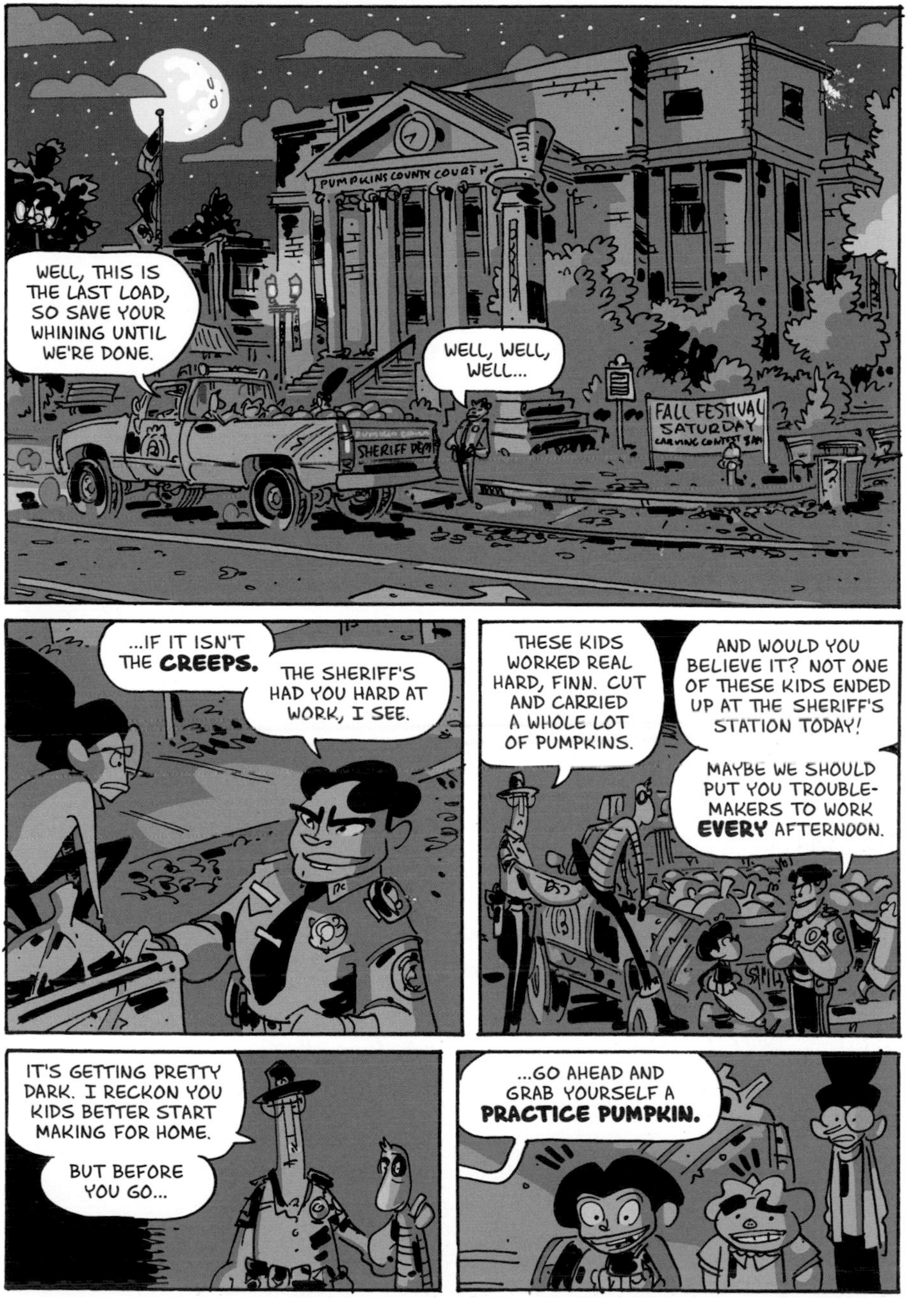
PUMPKINS COUNTY COURTH
WELL, THIS IS THE LAST LOAD, SO SAVE YOUR WHINING UNTIL WE'RE DONE.
WELL, WELL, WELL...
SHERIFF DEPT
FALL FESTIVAL SATURDAY CARVING CONTEST 8AM
...IF IT ISN'T THE **CREEPS.**
THE SHERIFF'S HAD YOU HARD AT WORK, I SEE.
THESE KIDS WORKED REAL HARD, FINN. CUT AND CARRIED A WHOLE LOT OF PUMPKINS.
AND WOULD YOU BELIEVE IT? NOT ONE OF THESE KIDS ENDED UP AT THE SHERIFF'S STATION TODAY!
MAYBE WE SHOULD PUT YOU TROUBLE-MAKERS TO WORK **EVERY** AFTERNOON.
IT'S GETTING PRETTY DARK. I RECKON YOU KIDS BETTER START MAKING FOR HOME.
BUT BEFORE YOU GO...
...GO AHEAD AND GRAB YOURSELF A **PRACTICE PUMPKIN.**

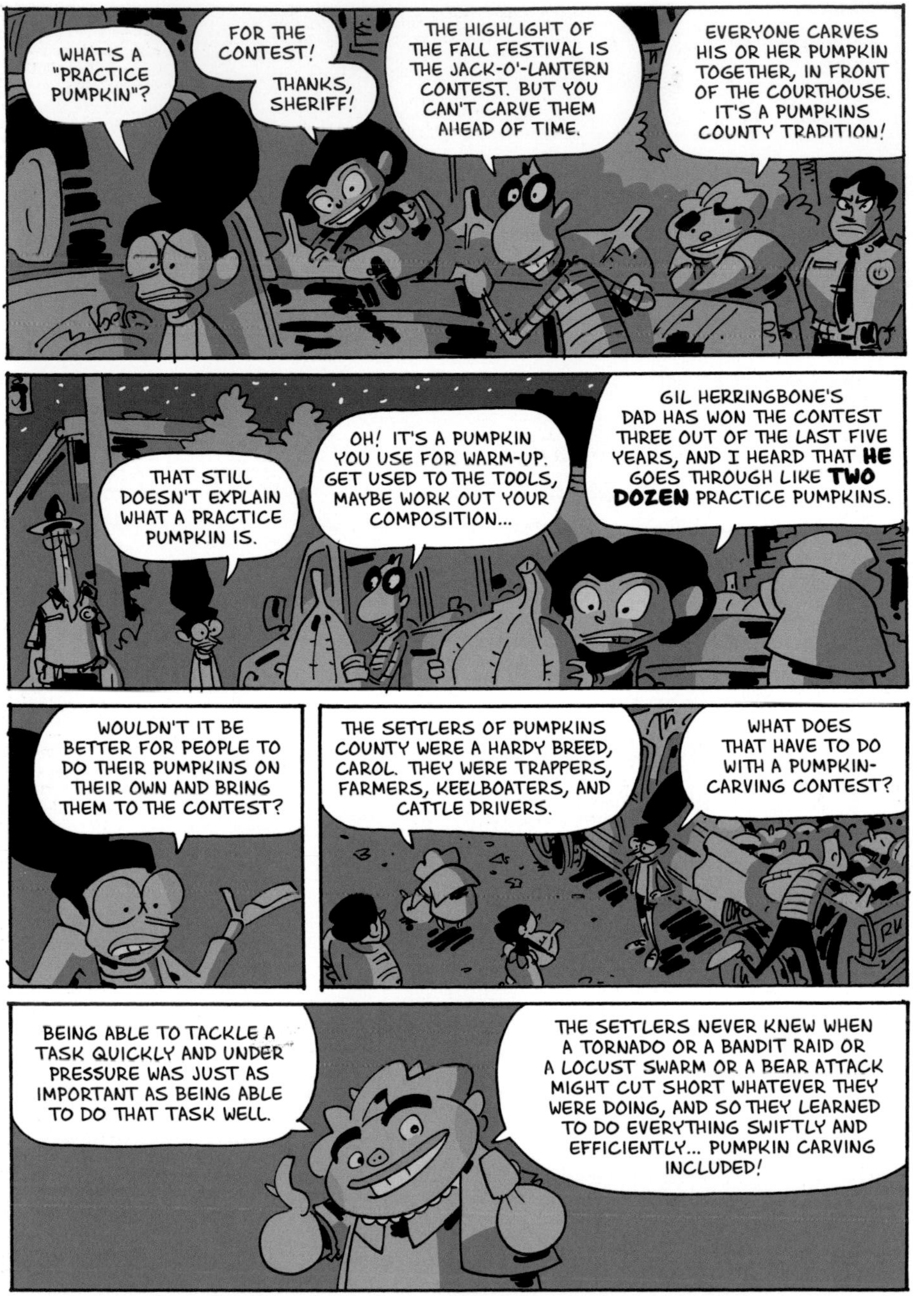
WHAT'S A "PRACTICE PUMPKIN"?
FOR THE CONTEST!
THANKS, SHERIFF!
THE HIGHLIGHT OF THE FALL FESTIVAL IS THE JACK-O'-LANTERN CONTEST. BUT YOU CAN'T CARVE THEM AHEAD OF TIME.
EVERYONE CARVES HIS OR HER PUMPKIN TOGETHER, IN FRONT OF THE COURTHOUSE. IT'S A PUMPKINS COUNTY TRADITION!
THAT STILL DOESN'T EXPLAIN WHAT A PRACTICE PUMPKIN IS.
OH! IT'S A PUMPKIN YOU USE FOR WARM-UP. GET USED TO THE TOOLS, MAYBE WORK OUT YOUR COMPOSITION...
GIL HERRINGBONE'S DAD HAS WON THE CONTEST THREE OUT OF THE LAST FIVE YEARS, AND I HEARD THAT **HE** GOES THROUGH LIKE **TWO DOZEN** PRACTICE PUMPKINS.
WOULDN'T IT BE BETTER FOR PEOPLE TO DO THEIR PUMPKINS ON THEIR OWN AND BRING THEM TO THE CONTEST?
THE SETTLERS OF PUMPKINS COUNTY WERE A HARDY BREED, CAROL. THEY WERE TRAPPERS, FARMERS, KEELBOATERS, AND CATTLE DRIVERS.
WHAT DOES THAT HAVE TO DO WITH A PUMPKIN-CARVING CONTEST?
BEING ABLE TO TACKLE A TASK QUICKLY AND UNDER PRESSURE WAS JUST AS IMPORTANT AS BEING ABLE TO DO THAT TASK WELL.
THE SETTLERS NEVER KNEW WHEN A TORNADO OR A BANDIT RAID OR A LOCUST SWARM OR A BEAR ATTACK MIGHT CUT SHORT WHATEVER THEY WERE DOING, AND SO THEY LEARNED TO DO EVERYTHING SWIFTLY AND EFFICIENTLY... PUMPKIN CARVING INCLUDED!

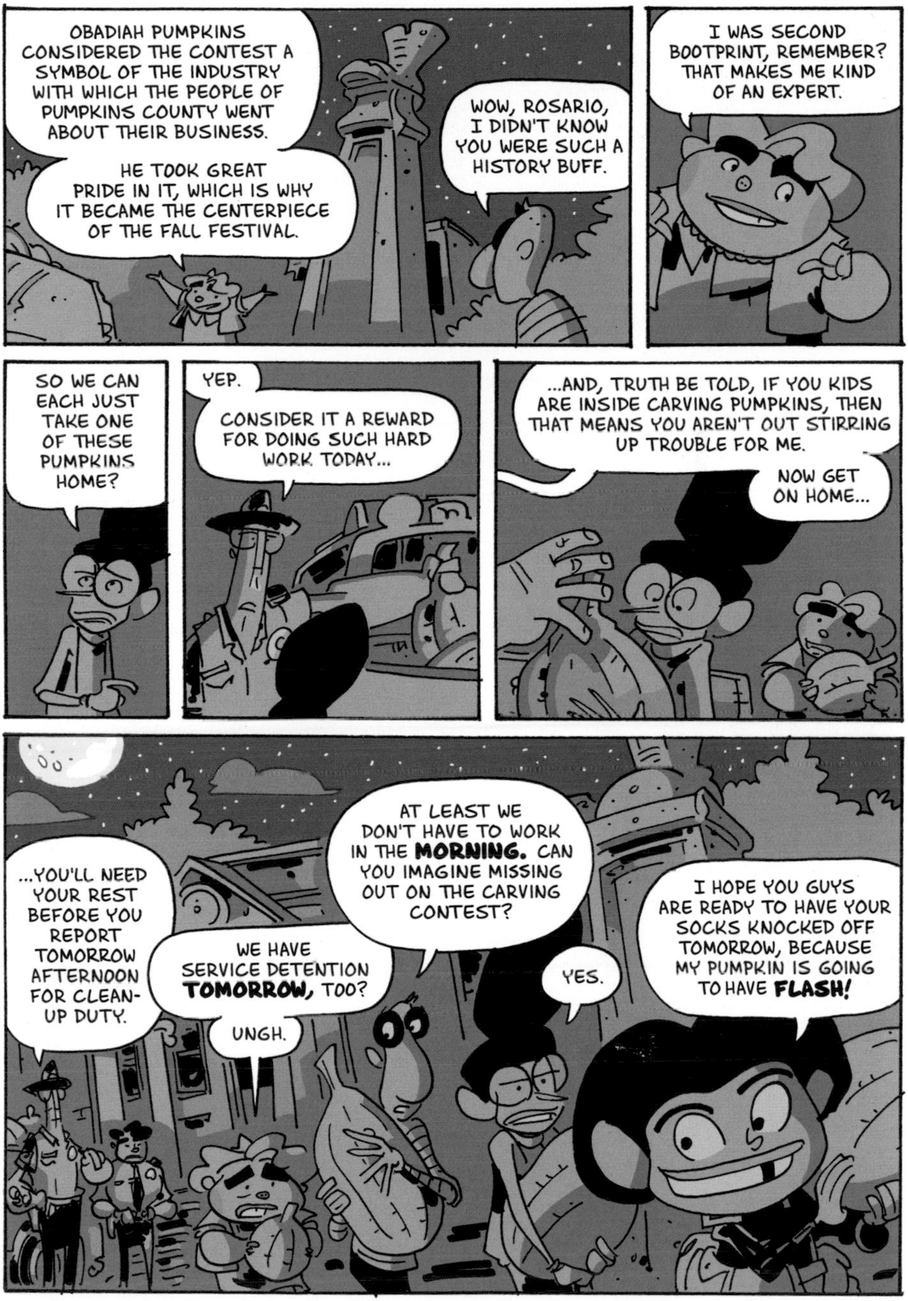
OBADIAH PUMPKINS CONSIDERED THE CONTEST A SYMBOL OF THE INDUSTRY WITH WHICH THE PEOPLE OF PUMPKINS COUNTY WENT ABOUT THEIR BUSINESS.
HE TOOK GREAT PRIDE IN IT, WHICH IS WHY IT BECAME THE CENTERPIECE OF THE FALL FESTIVAL.
WOW, ROSARIO, I DIDN'T KNOW YOU WERE SUCH A HISTORY BUFF.
I WAS SECOND BOOTPRINT, REMEMBER? THAT MAKES ME KIND OF AN EXPERT.
SO WE CAN EACH JUST TAKE ONE OF THESE PUMPKINS HOME?
YEP.
CONSIDER IT A REWARD FOR DOING SUCH HARD WORK TODAY...
...AND, TRUTH BE TOLD, IF YOU KIDS ARE INSIDE CARVING PUMPKINS, THEN THAT MEANS YOU AREN'T OUT STIRRING UP TROUBLE FOR ME.
NOW GET ON HOME...
...YOU'LL NEED YOUR REST BEFORE YOU REPORT TOMORROW AFTERNOON FOR CLEAN-UP DUTY.
WE HAVE SERVICE DETENTION **TOMORROW**, TOO?
UNGH.
AT LEAST WE DON'T HAVE TO WORK IN THE **MORNING.** CAN YOU IMAGINE MISSING OUT ON THE CARVING CONTEST?
YES.
I HOPE YOU GUYS ARE READY TO HAVE YOUR SOCKS KNOCKED OFF TOMORROW, BECAUSE MY PUMPKIN IS GOING TO HAVE **FLASH!**

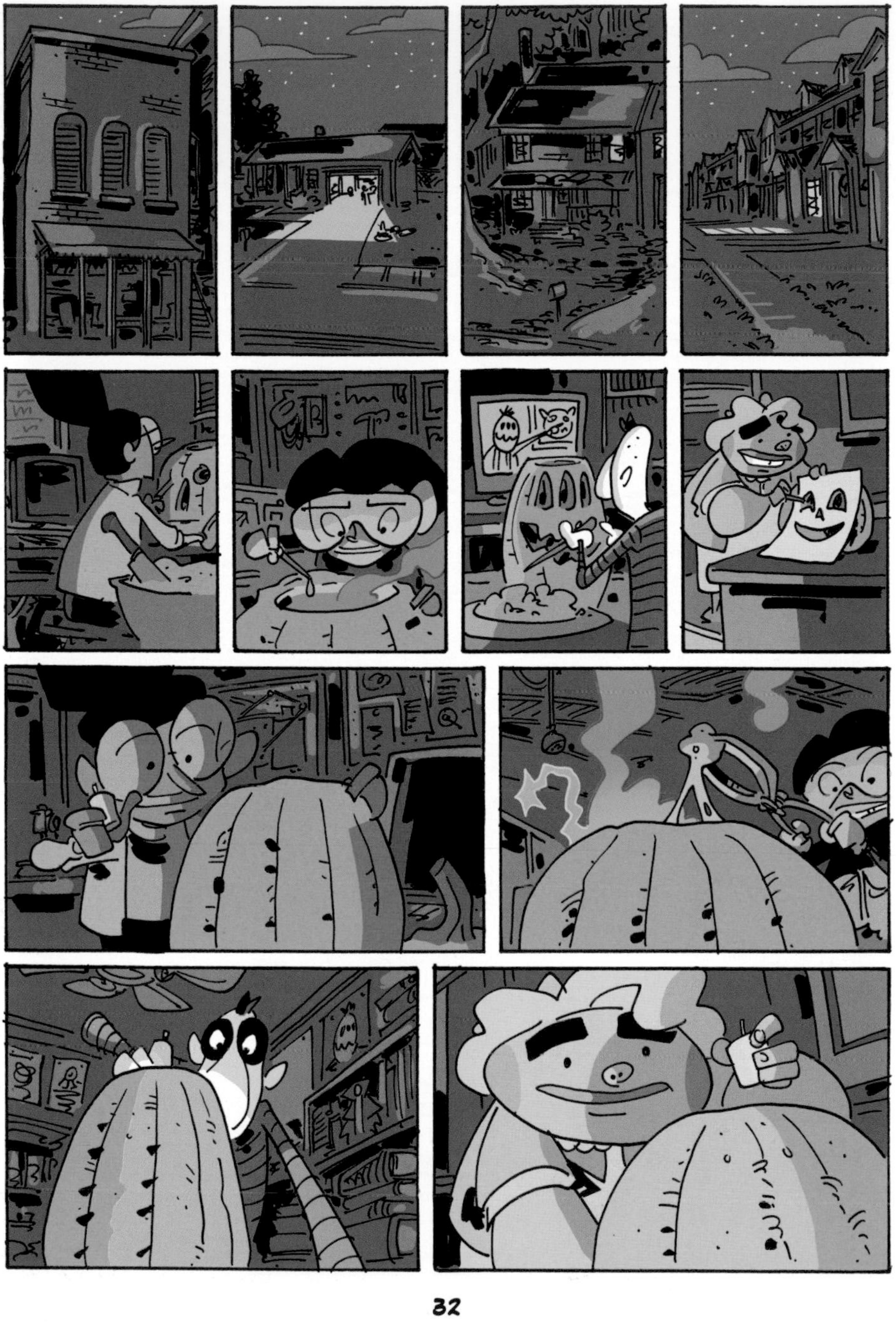

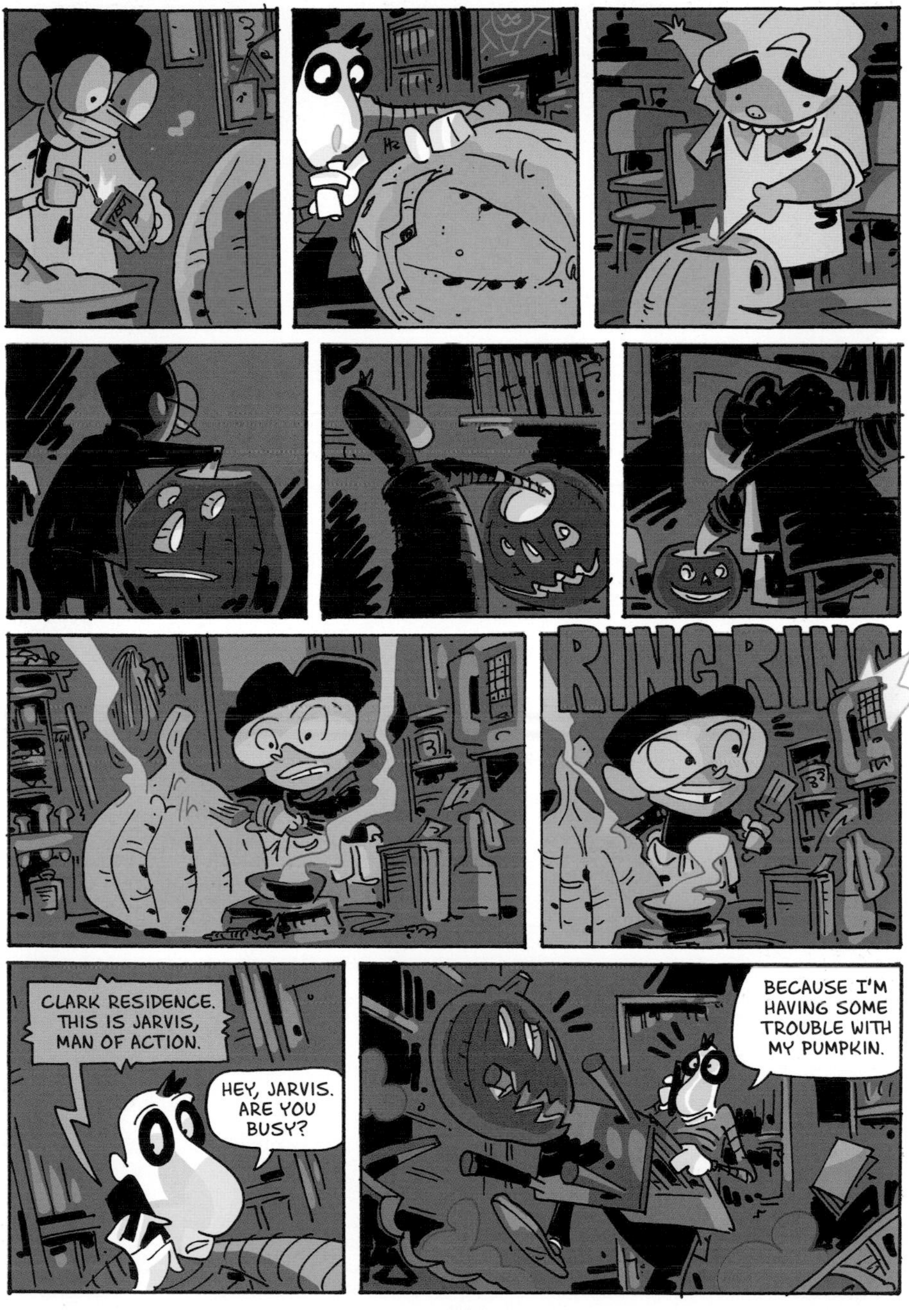
RING RING
CLARK RESIDENCE. THIS IS JARVIS, MAN OF ACTION.
HEY, JARVIS. ARE YOU BUSY?
BECAUSE I'M HAVING SOME TROUBLE WITH MY PUMPKIN.

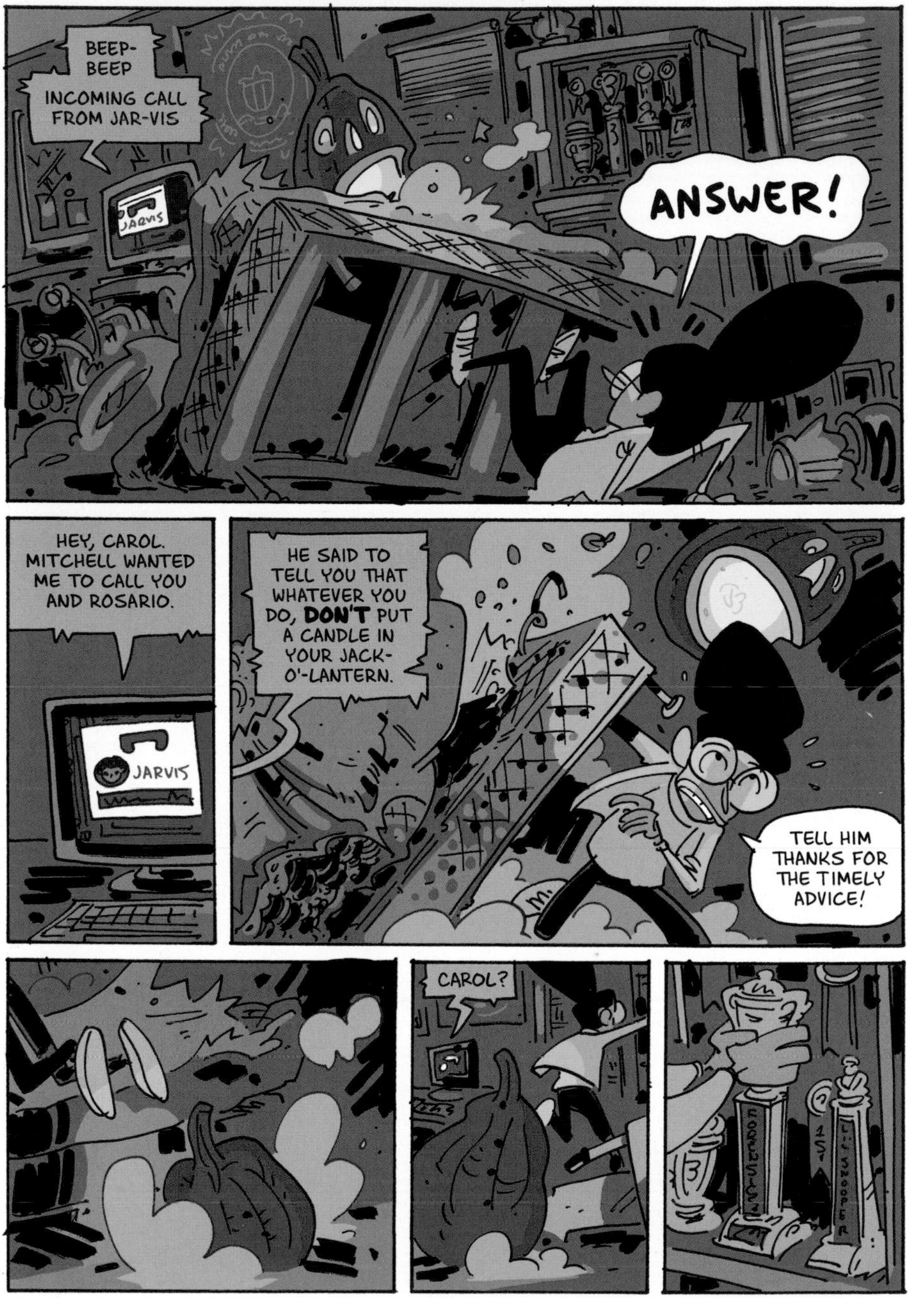
BEEP-BEEP
INCOMING CALL FROM JAR-VIS
JARVIS
ANSWER!
HEY, CAROL. MITCHELL WANTED ME TO CALL YOU AND ROSARIO.
JARVIS
HE SAID TO TELL YOU THAT WHATEVER YOU DO, DON'T PUT A CANDLE IN YOUR JACK-O'-LANTERN.
TELL HIM THANKS FOR THE TIMELY ADVICE!
CAROL?

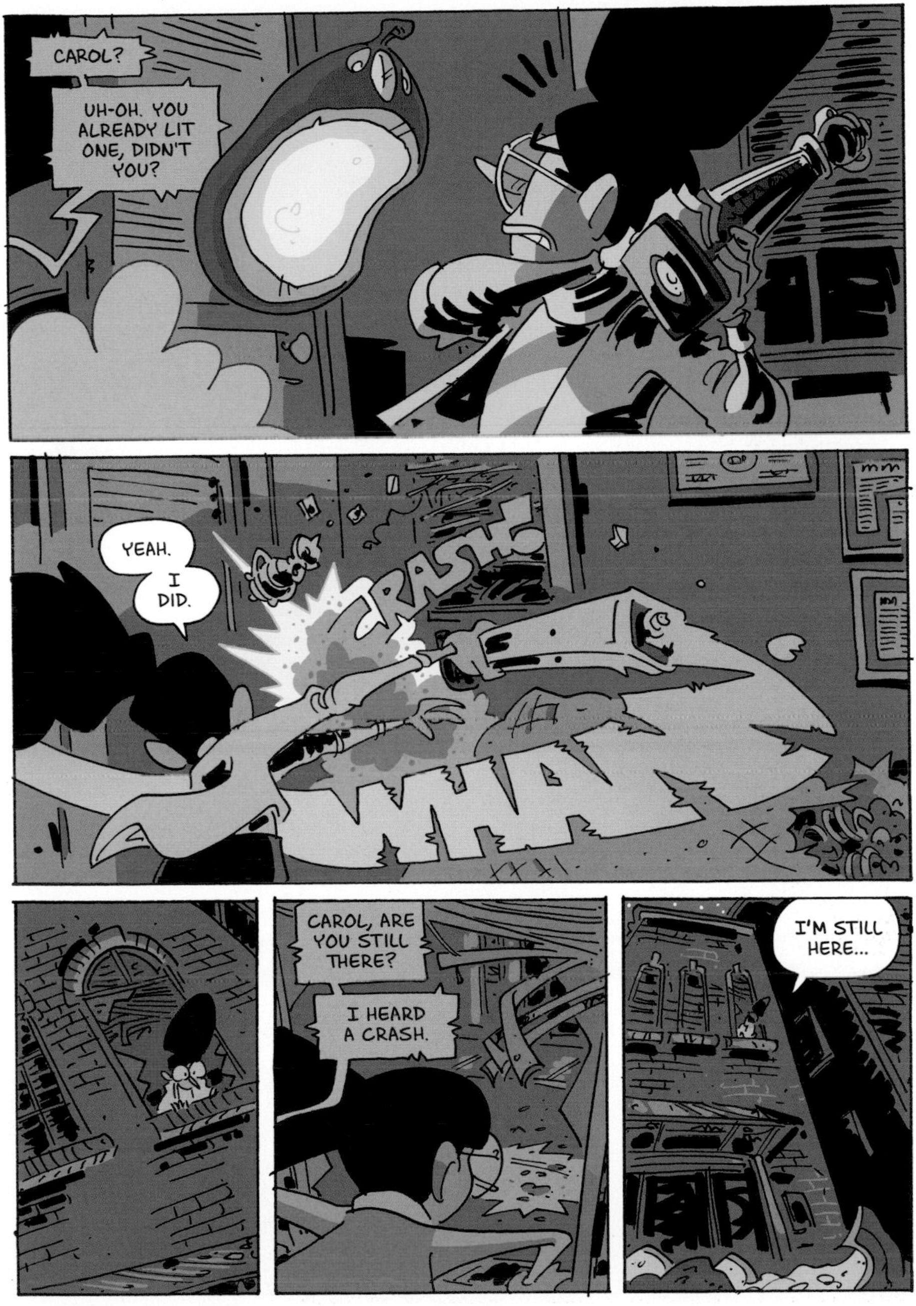
CAROL?
UH-OH. YOU ALREADY LIT ONE, DIDN'T YOU?
YEAH.
I DID.
CRASH!
WHA
CAROL, ARE YOU STILL THERE?
I HEARD A CRASH.
I'M STILL HERE...

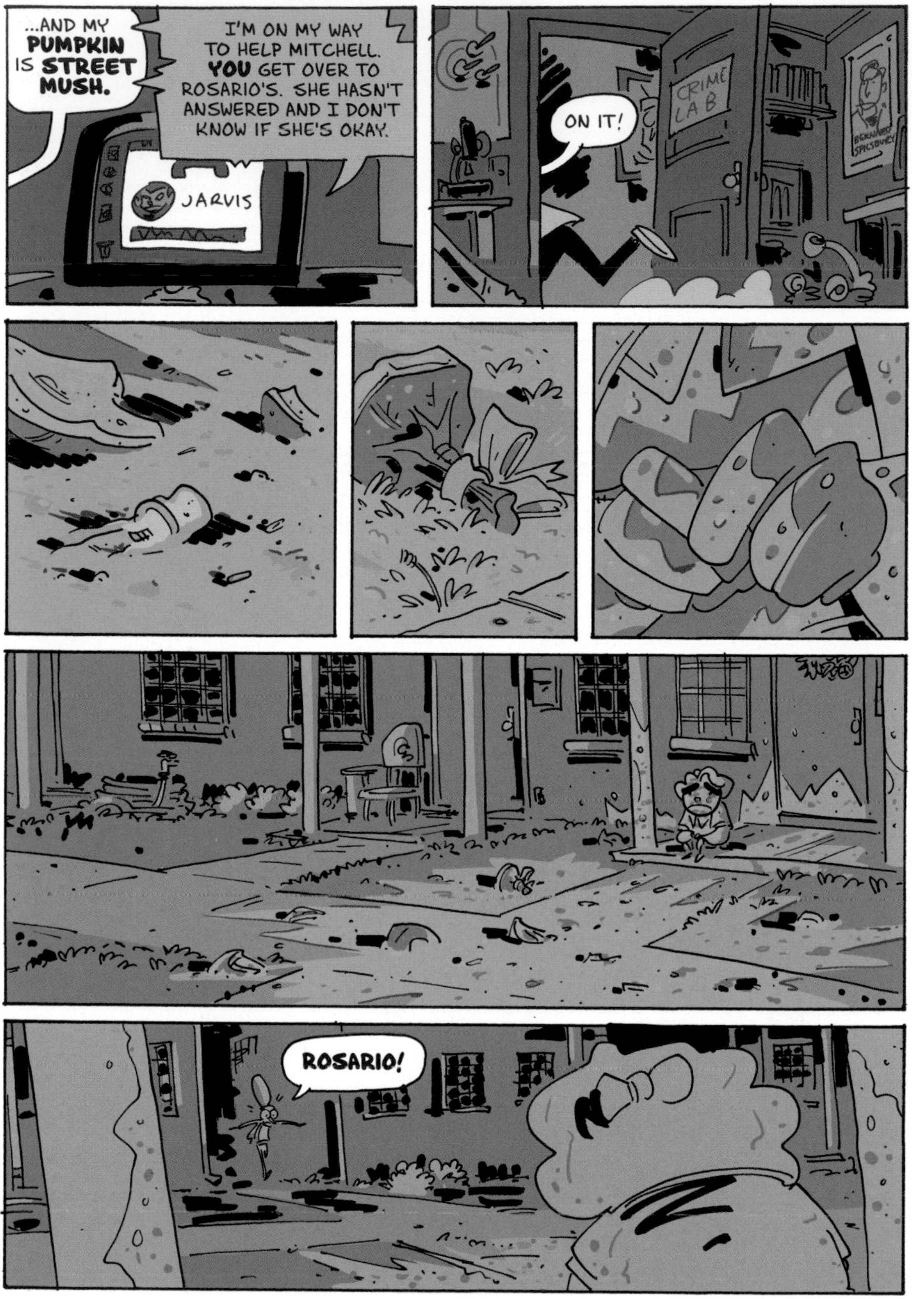
...AND MY PUMPKIN IS STREET MUSH.
I'M ON MY WAY TO HELP MITCHELL. YOU GET OVER TO ROSARIO'S. SHE HASN'T ANSWERED AND I DON'T KNOW IF SHE'S OKAY.
JARVIS
ON IT!
CRIME LAB
ROSARIO!

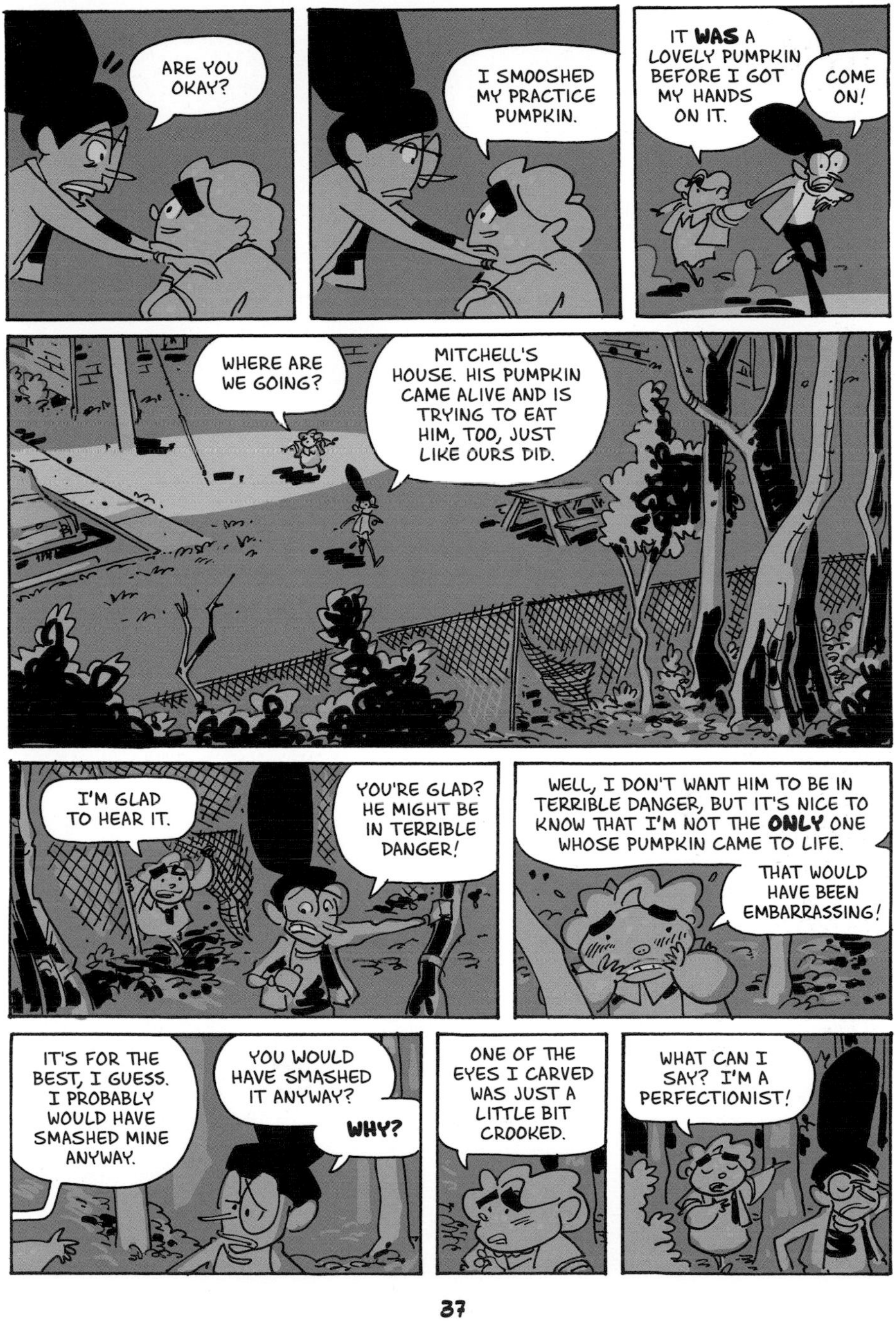
ARE YOU OKAY?
I SMOOSHED MY PRACTICE PUMPKIN.
IT WAS A LOVELY PUMPKIN BEFORE I GOT MY HANDS ON IT.
COME ON!
WHERE ARE WE GOING?
MITCHELL'S HOUSE. HIS PUMPKIN CAME ALIVE AND IS TRYING TO EAT HIM, TOO, JUST LIKE OURS DID.
I'M GLAD TO HEAR IT.
YOU'RE GLAD? HE MIGHT BE IN TERRIBLE DANGER!
WELL, I DON'T WANT HIM TO BE IN TERRIBLE DANGER, BUT IT'S NICE TO KNOW THAT I'M NOT THE ONLY ONE WHOSE PUMPKIN CAME TO LIFE.
THAT WOULD HAVE BEEN EMBARRASSING!
IT'S FOR THE BEST, I GUESS. I PROBABLY WOULD HAVE SMASHED MINE ANYWAY.
YOU WOULD HAVE SMASHED IT ANYWAY?
WHY?
ONE OF THE EYES I CARVED WAS JUST A LITTLE BIT CROOKED.
WHAT CAN I SAY? I'M A PERFECTIONIST!

MITCHELL!

HEY, FRIENDS! GOOD TO SEE YOU!

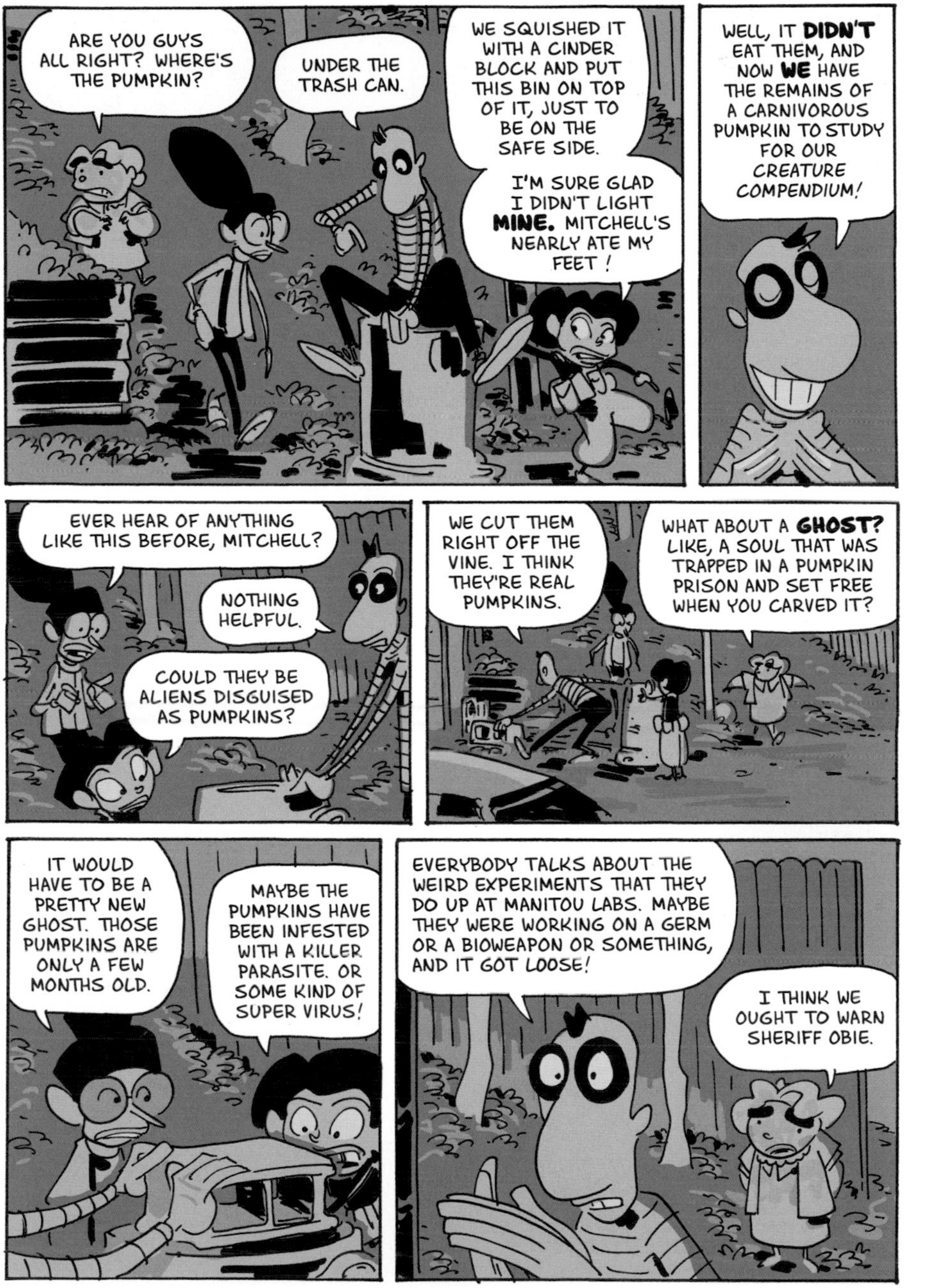

ARE YOU GUYS ALL RIGHT? WHERE'S THE PUMPKIN?
UNDER THE TRASH CAN.
WE SQUISHED IT WITH A CINDER BLOCK AND PUT THIS BIN ON TOP OF IT, JUST TO BE ON THE SAFE SIDE.
I'M SURE GLAD I DIDN'T LIGHT **MINE.** MITCHELL'S NEARLY ATE MY FEET!
WELL, IT **DIDN'T** EAT THEM, AND NOW **WE** HAVE THE REMAINS OF A CARNIVOROUS PUMPKIN TO STUDY FOR OUR CREATURE COMPENDIUM!
EVER HEAR OF ANYTHING LIKE THIS BEFORE, MITCHELL?
NOTHING HELPFUL.
COULD THEY BE ALIENS DISGUISED AS PUMPKINS?
WE CUT THEM RIGHT OFF THE VINE. I THINK THEY'RE REAL PUMPKINS.
WHAT ABOUT A **GHOST?** LIKE, A SOUL THAT WAS TRAPPED IN A PUMPKIN PRISON AND SET FREE WHEN YOU CARVED IT?
IT WOULD HAVE TO BE A PRETTY NEW GHOST. THOSE PUMPKINS ARE ONLY A FEW MONTHS OLD.
MAYBE THE PUMPKINS HAVE BEEN INFESTED WITH A KILLER PARASITE. OR SOME KIND OF SUPER VIRUS!
EVERYBODY TALKS ABOUT THE WEIRD EXPERIMENTS THAT THEY DO UP AT MANITOU LABS. MAYBE THEY WERE WORKING ON A GERM OR A BIOWEAPON OR SOMETHING, AND IT GOT LOOSE!
I THINK WE OUGHT TO WARN SHERIFF OBIE.

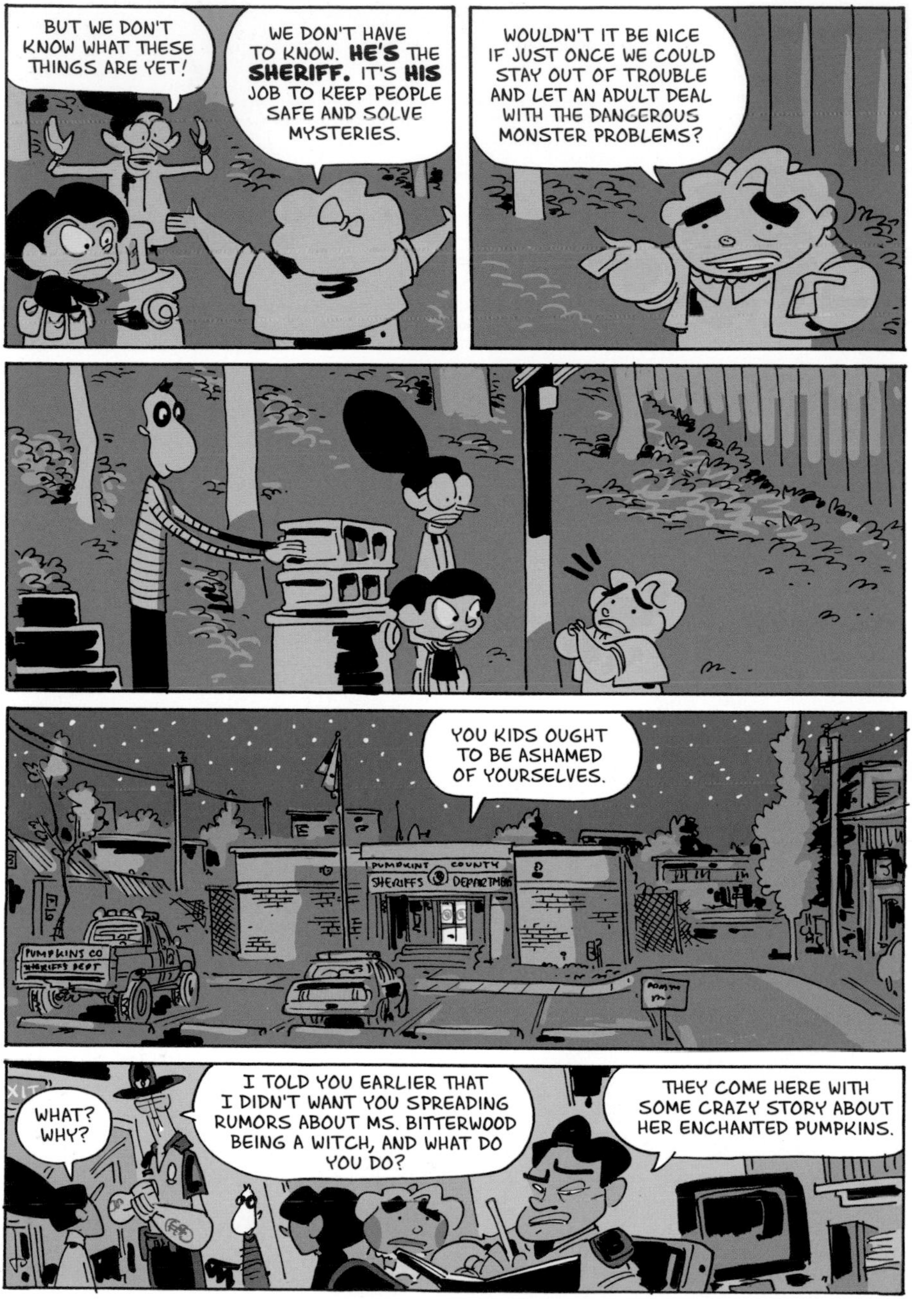
BUT WE DON'T KNOW WHAT THESE THINGS ARE YET!
WE DON'T HAVE TO KNOW. **HE'S** THE **SHERIFF.** IT'S **HIS** JOB TO KEEP PEOPLE SAFE AND SOLVE MYSTERIES.
WOULDN'T IT BE NICE IF JUST ONCE WE COULD STAY OUT OF TROUBLE AND LET AN ADULT DEAL WITH THE DANGEROUS MONSTER PROBLEMS?
YOU KIDS OUGHT TO BE ASHAMED OF YOURSELVES.
PUMPKINT COUNTY SHERIFFS DEPARTMENT
PUMPKINS CO SHERIFFS DEPT
WHAT? WHY?
I TOLD YOU EARLIER THAT I DIDN'T WANT YOU SPREADING RUMORS ABOUT MS. BITTERWOOD BEING A WITCH, AND WHAT DO YOU DO?
THEY COME HERE WITH SOME CRAZY STORY ABOUT HER ENCHANTED PUMPKINS.

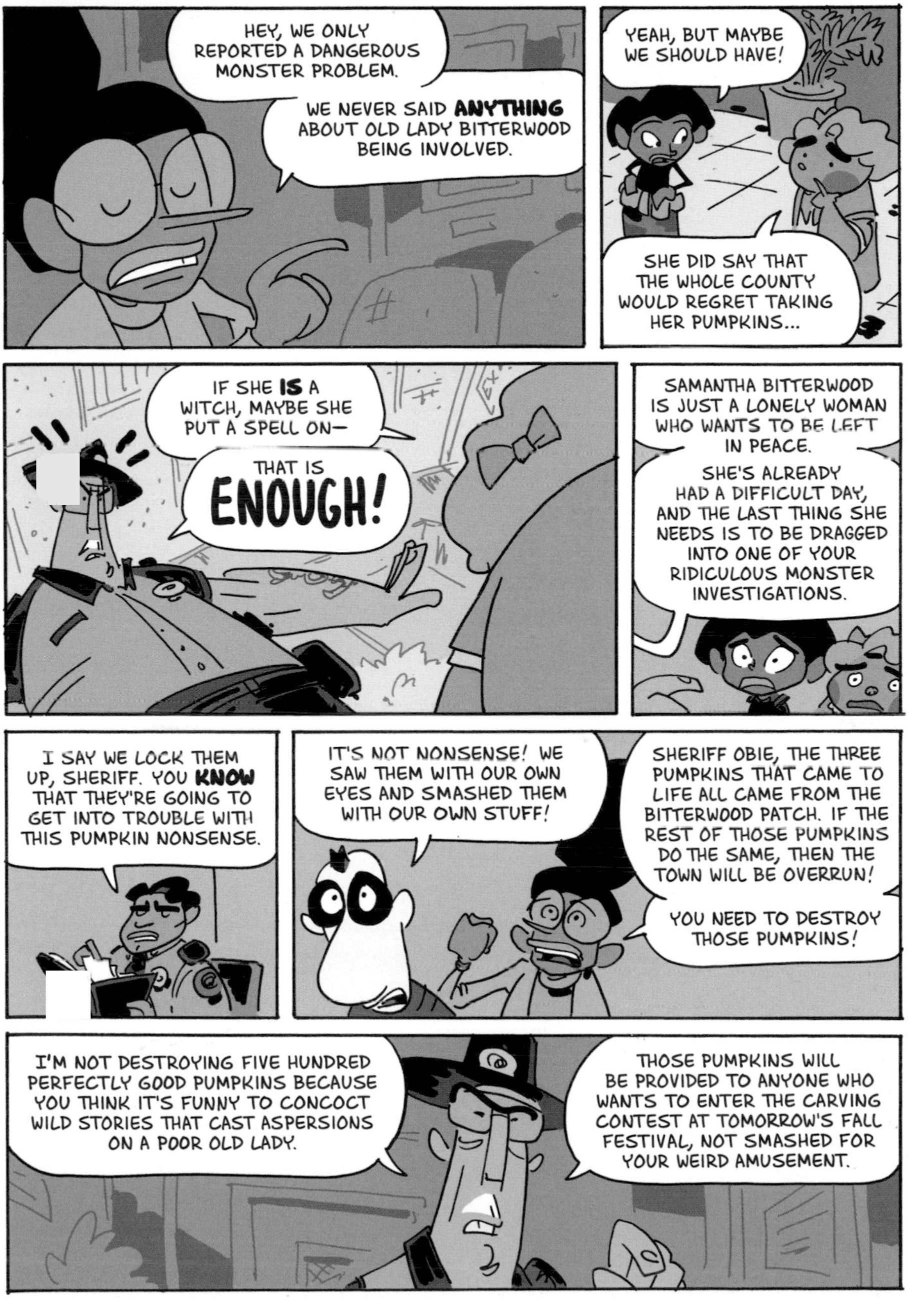

HEY, WE ONLY REPORTED A DANGEROUS MONSTER PROBLEM.
WE NEVER SAID **ANYTHING** ABOUT OLD LADY BITTERWOOD BEING INVOLVED.
YEAH, BUT MAYBE WE SHOULD HAVE!
SHE DID SAY THAT THE WHOLE COUNTY WOULD REGRET TAKING HER PUMPKINS...
IF SHE **IS** A WITCH, MAYBE SHE PUT A SPELL ON—
THAT IS ENOUGH!
SAMANTHA BITTERWOOD IS JUST A LONELY WOMAN WHO WANTS TO BE LEFT IN PEACE.
SHE'S ALREADY HAD A DIFFICULT DAY, AND THE LAST THING SHE NEEDS IS TO BE DRAGGED INTO ONE OF YOUR RIDICULOUS MONSTER INVESTIGATIONS.
I SAY WE LOCK THEM UP, SHERIFF. YOU **KNOW** THAT THEY'RE GOING TO GET INTO TROUBLE WITH THIS PUMPKIN NONSENSE.
IT'S NOT NONSENSE! WE SAW THEM WITH OUR OWN EYES AND SMASHED THEM WITH OUR OWN STUFF!
SHERIFF OBIE, THE THREE PUMPKINS THAT CAME TO LIFE ALL CAME FROM THE BITTERWOOD PATCH. IF THE REST OF THOSE PUMPKINS DO THE SAME, THEN THE TOWN WILL BE OVERRUN!
YOU NEED TO DESTROY THOSE PUMPKINS!
I'M NOT DESTROYING FIVE HUNDRED PERFECTLY GOOD PUMPKINS BECAUSE YOU THINK IT'S FUNNY TO CONCOCT WILD STORIES THAT CAST ASPERSIONS ON A POOR OLD LADY.
THOSE PUMPKINS WILL BE PROVIDED TO ANYONE WHO WANTS TO ENTER THE CARVING CONTEST AT TOMORROW'S FALL FESTIVAL, NOT SMASHED FOR YOUR WEIRD AMUSEMENT.

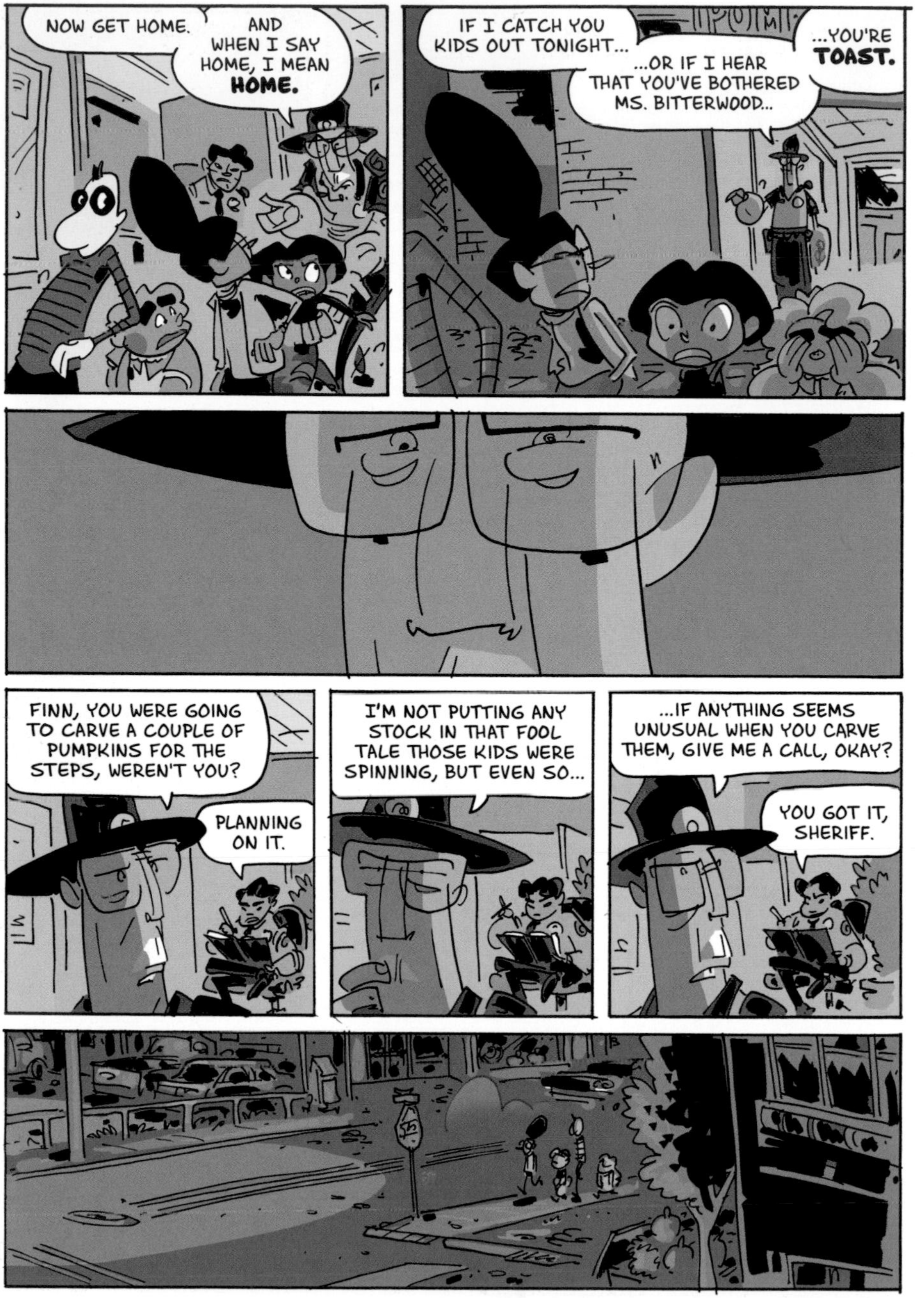
NOW GET HOME.
AND WHEN I SAY HOME, I MEAN **HOME.**
IF I CATCH YOU KIDS OUT TONIGHT...
...OR IF I HEAR THAT YOU'VE BOTHERED MS. BITTERWOOD...
...YOU'RE **TOAST.**
FINN, YOU WERE GOING TO CARVE A COUPLE OF PUMPKINS FOR THE STEPS, WEREN'T YOU?
PLANNING ON IT.
I'M NOT PUTTING ANY STOCK IN THAT FOOL TALE THOSE KIDS WERE SPINNING, BUT EVEN SO...
...IF ANYTHING SEEMS UNUSUAL WHEN YOU CARVE THEM, GIVE ME A CALL, OKAY?
YOU GOT IT, SHERIFF.

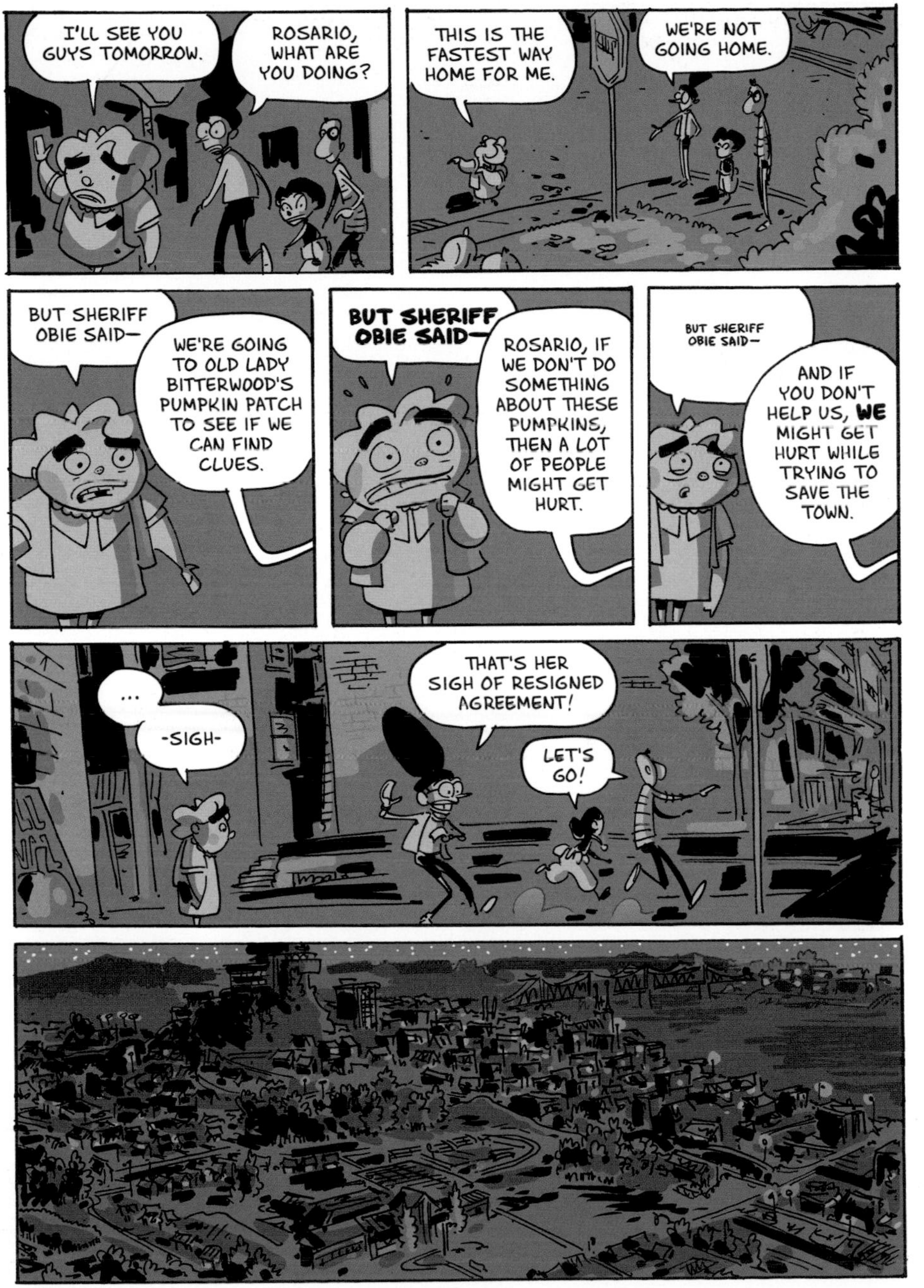
I'LL SEE YOU GUYS TOMORROW.
ROSARIO, WHAT ARE YOU DOING?
THIS IS THE FASTEST WAY HOME FOR ME.
WE'RE NOT GOING HOME.
BUT SHERIFF OBIE SAID—
WE'RE GOING TO OLD LADY BITTERWOOD'S PUMPKIN PATCH TO SEE IF WE CAN FIND CLUES.
BUT SHERIFF OBIE SAID—
ROSARIO, IF WE DON'T DO SOMETHING ABOUT THESE PUMPKINS, THEN A LOT OF PEOPLE MIGHT GET HURT.
BUT SHERIFF OBIE SAID—
AND IF YOU DON'T HELP US, WE MIGHT GET HURT WHILE TRYING TO SAVE THE TOWN.
...
-SIGH-
THAT'S HER SIGH OF RESIGNED AGREEMENT!
LET'S GO!

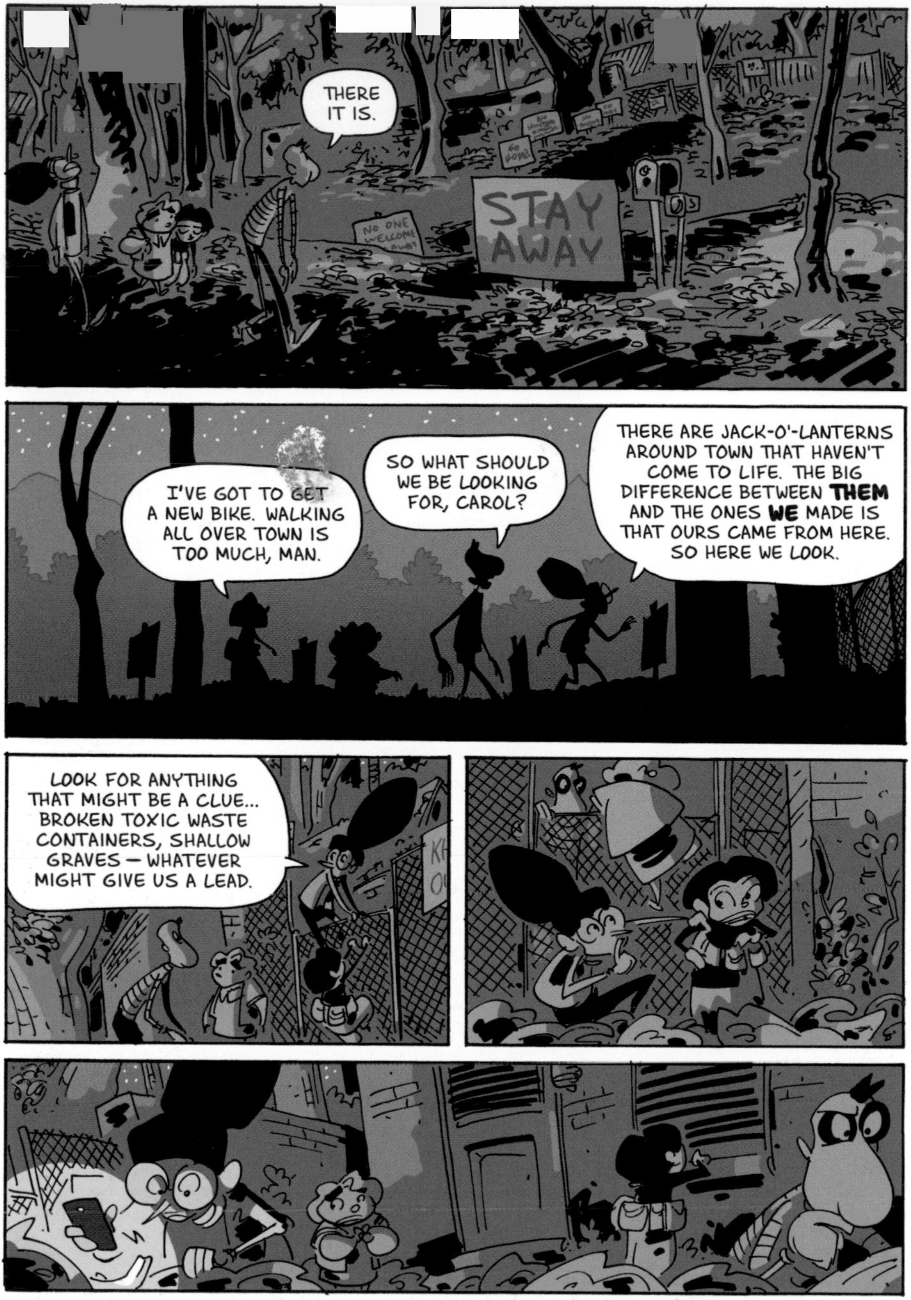
THERE IT IS.
STAY AWAY
I'VE GOT TO GET A NEW BIKE. WALKING ALL OVER TOWN IS TOO MUCH, MAN.
SO WHAT SHOULD WE BE LOOKING FOR, CAROL?
THERE ARE JACK-O'-LANTERNS AROUND TOWN THAT HAVEN'T COME TO LIFE. THE BIG DIFFERENCE BETWEEN **THEM** AND THE ONES **WE** MADE IS THAT OURS CAME FROM HERE. SO HERE WE LOOK.
LOOK FOR ANYTHING THAT MIGHT BE A CLUE... BROKEN TOXIC WASTE CONTAINERS, SHALLOW GRAVES — WHATEVER MIGHT GIVE US A LEAD.

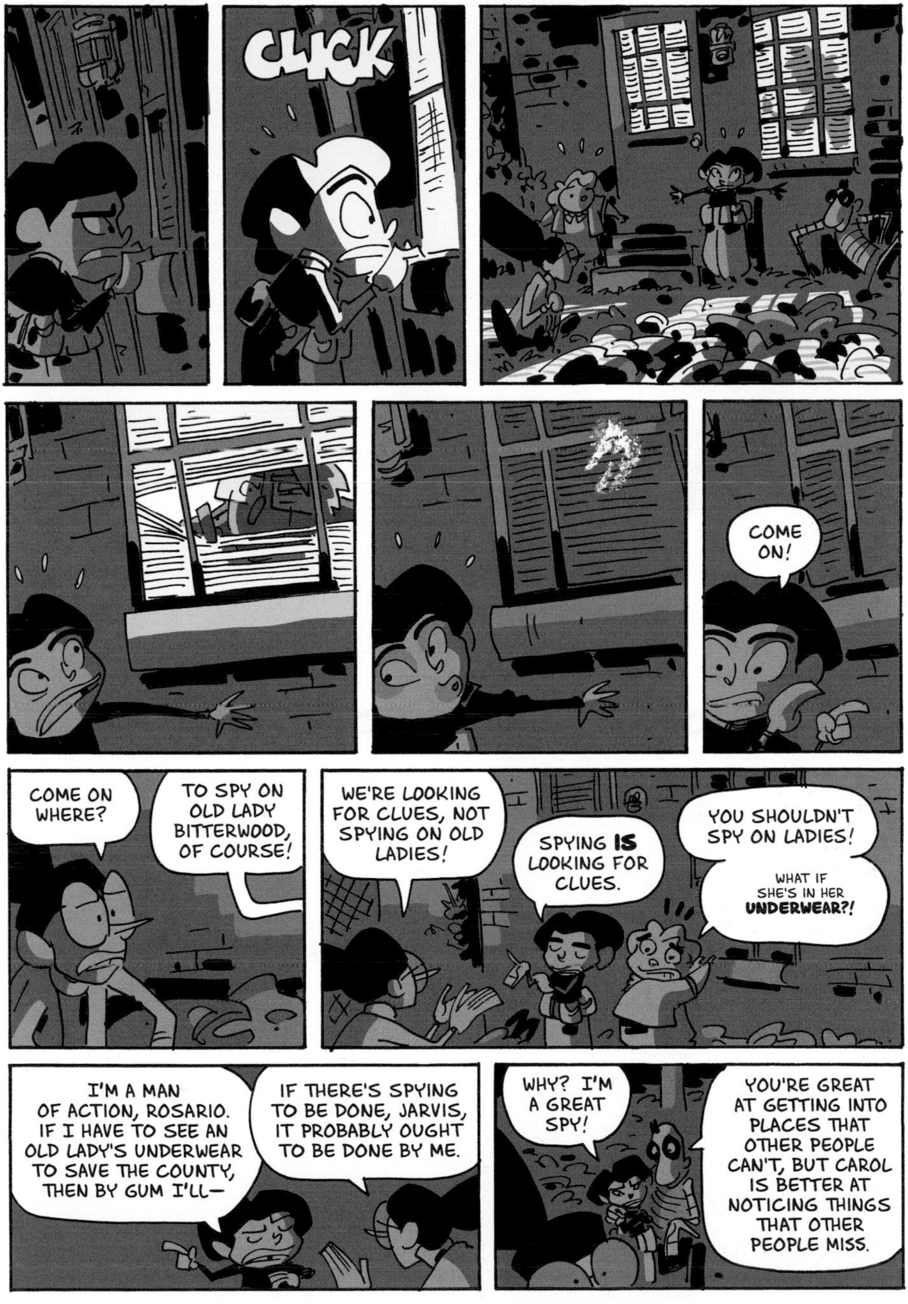
CLICK
COME ON!
COME ON WHERE?
TO SPY ON OLD LADY BITTERWOOD, OF COURSE!
WE'RE LOOKING FOR CLUES, NOT SPYING ON OLD LADIES!
SPYING IS LOOKING FOR CLUES.
YOU SHOULDN'T SPY ON LADIES!
WHAT IF SHE'S IN HER UNDERWEAR?!
I'M A MAN OF ACTION, ROSARIO. IF I HAVE TO SEE AN OLD LADY'S UNDERWEAR TO SAVE THE COUNTY, THEN BY GUM I'LL—
IF THERE'S SPYING TO BE DONE, JARVIS, IT PROBABLY OUGHT TO BE DONE BY ME.
WHY? I'M A GREAT SPY!
YOU'RE GREAT AT GETTING INTO PLACES THAT OTHER PEOPLE CAN'T, BUT CAROL IS BETTER AT NOTICING THINGS THAT OTHER PEOPLE MISS.

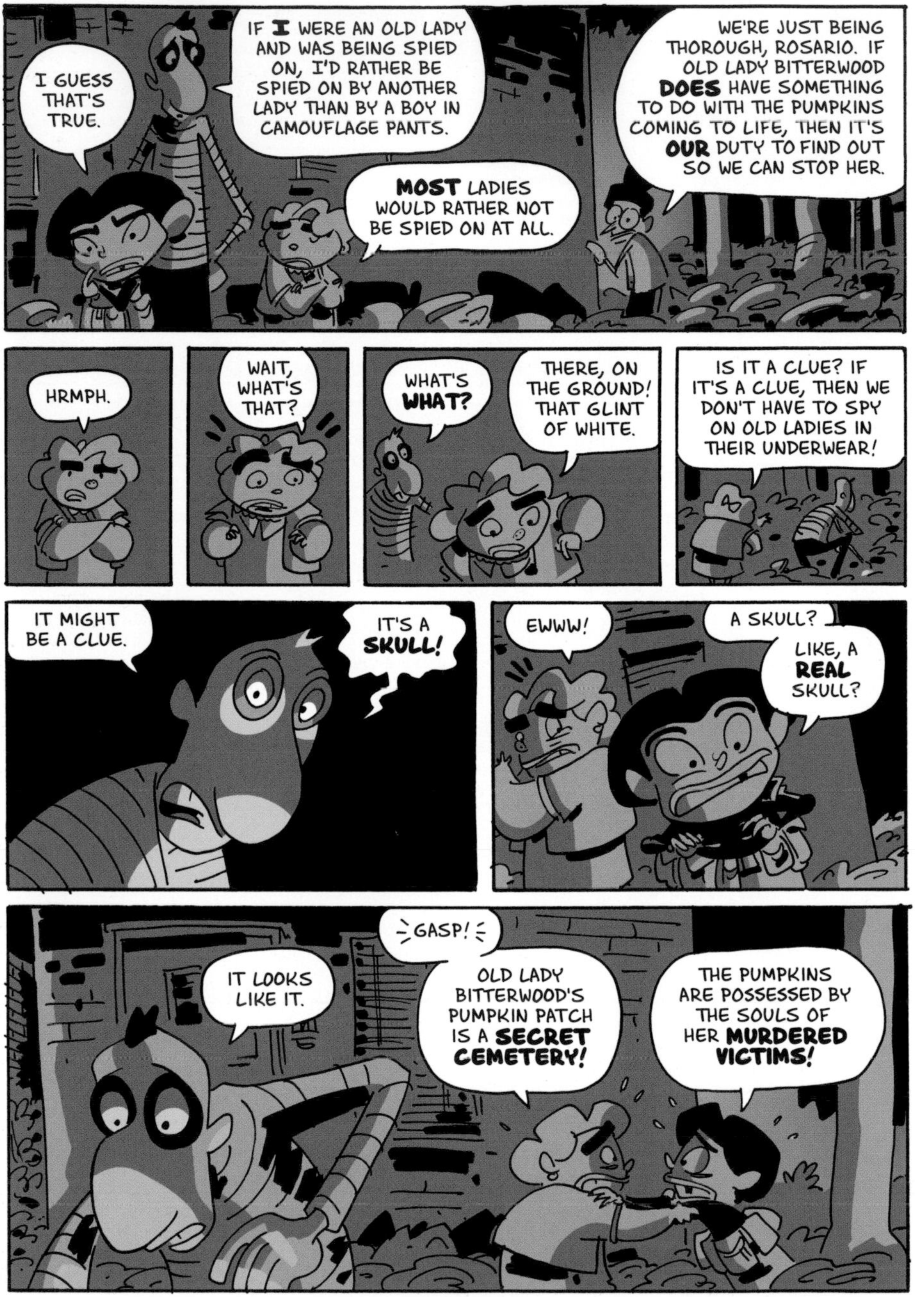
I GUESS THAT'S TRUE.
IF **I** WERE AN OLD LADY AND WAS BEING SPIED ON, I'D RATHER BE SPIED ON BY ANOTHER LADY THAN BY A BOY IN CAMOUFLAGE PANTS.
MOST LADIES WOULD RATHER NOT BE SPIED ON AT ALL.
WE'RE JUST BEING THOROUGH, ROSARIO. IF OLD LADY BITTERWOOD **DOES** HAVE SOMETHING TO DO WITH THE PUMPKINS COMING TO LIFE, THEN IT'S **OUR** DUTY TO FIND OUT SO WE CAN STOP HER.
HRMPH.
WAIT, WHAT'S THAT?
WHAT'S **WHAT?**
THERE, ON THE GROUND! THAT GLINT OF WHITE.
IS IT A CLUE? IF IT'S A CLUE, THEN WE DON'T HAVE TO SPY ON OLD LADIES IN THEIR UNDERWEAR!
IT MIGHT BE A CLUE.
IT'S A **SKULL!**
EWWW!
A SKULL?
LIKE, A **REAL** SKULL?
GASP!
IT LOOKS LIKE IT.
OLD LADY BITTERWOOD'S PUMPKIN PATCH IS A **SECRET CEMETERY!**
THE PUMPKINS ARE POSSESSED BY THE SOULS OF HER **MURDERED VICTIMS!**

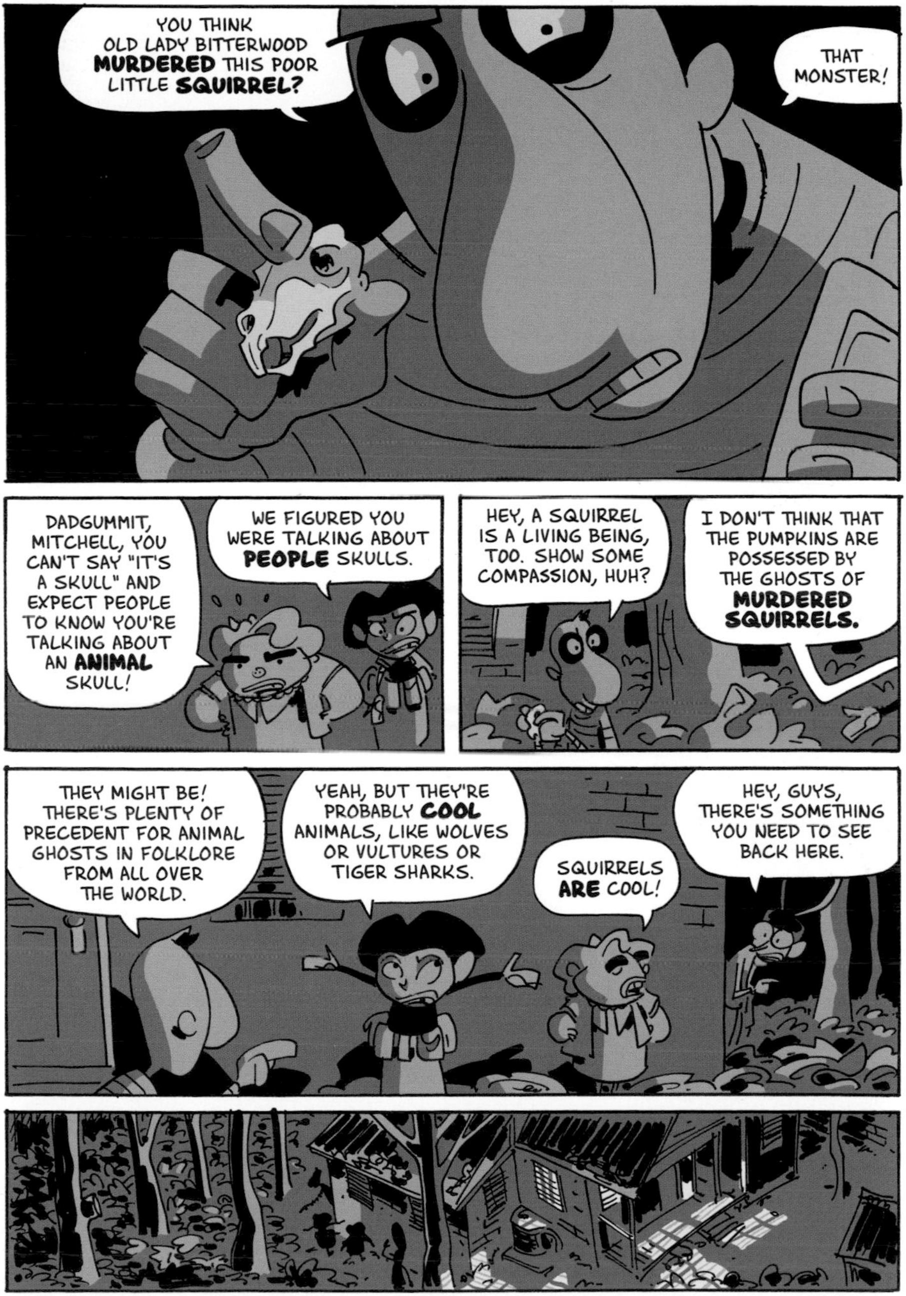
YOU THINK OLD LADY BITTERWOOD **MURDERED** THIS POOR LITTLE **SQUIRREL?**
THAT MONSTER!
DADGUMMIT, MITCHELL, YOU CAN'T SAY "IT'S A SKULL" AND EXPECT PEOPLE TO KNOW YOU'RE TALKING ABOUT AN **ANIMAL** SKULL!
WE FIGURED YOU WERE TALKING ABOUT **PEOPLE** SKULLS.
HEY, A SQUIRREL IS A LIVING BEING, TOO. SHOW SOME COMPASSION, HUH?
I DON'T THINK THAT THE PUMPKINS ARE POSSESSED BY THE GHOSTS OF **MURDERED SQUIRRELS.**
THEY MIGHT BE! THERE'S PLENTY OF PRECEDENT FOR ANIMAL GHOSTS IN FOLKLORE FROM ALL OVER THE WORLD.
YEAH, BUT THEY'RE PROBABLY **COOL** ANIMALS, LIKE WOLVES OR VULTURES OR TIGER SHARKS.
SQUIRRELS **ARE** COOL!
HEY, GUYS, THERE'S SOMETHING YOU NEED TO SEE BACK HERE.

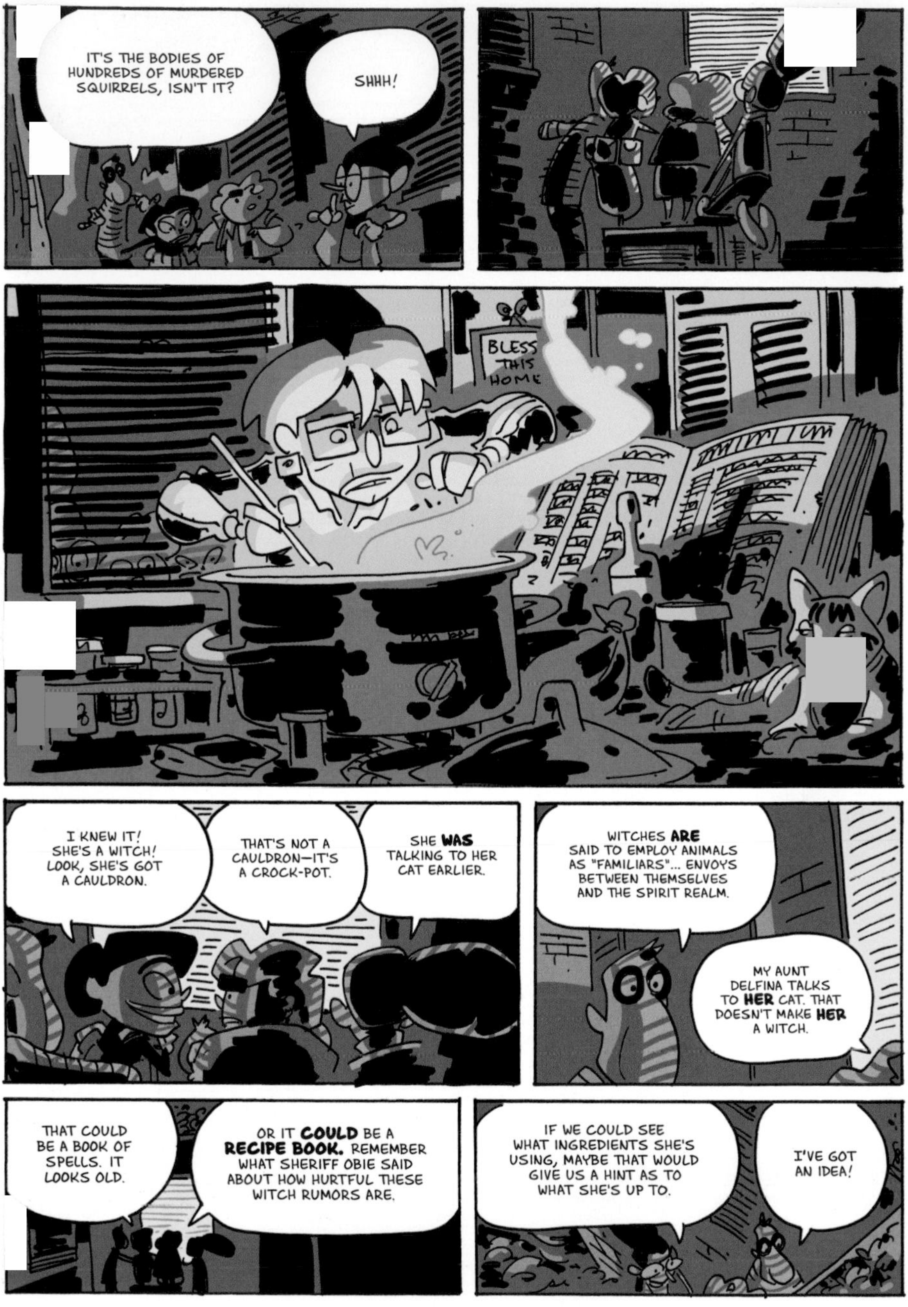
IT'S THE BODIES OF HUNDREDS OF MURDERED SQUIRRELS, ISN'T IT?
SHHH!
BLESS THIS HOME
I KNEW IT! SHE'S A WITCH! LOOK, SHE'S GOT A CAULDRON.
THAT'S NOT A CAULDRON—IT'S A CROCK-POT.
SHE WAS TALKING TO HER CAT EARLIER.
WITCHES ARE SAID TO EMPLOY ANIMALS AS "FAMILIARS"... ENVOYS BETWEEN THEMSELVES AND THE SPIRIT REALM.
MY AUNT DELFINA TALKS TO HER CAT. THAT DOESN'T MAKE HER A WITCH.
THAT COULD BE A BOOK OF SPELLS. IT LOOKS OLD.
OR IT COULD BE A RECIPE BOOK. REMEMBER WHAT SHERIFF OBIE SAID ABOUT HOW HURTFUL THESE WITCH RUMORS ARE.
IF WE COULD SEE WHAT INGREDIENTS SHE'S USING, MAYBE THAT WOULD GIVE US A HINT AS TO WHAT SHE'S UP TO.
I'VE GOT AN IDEA!

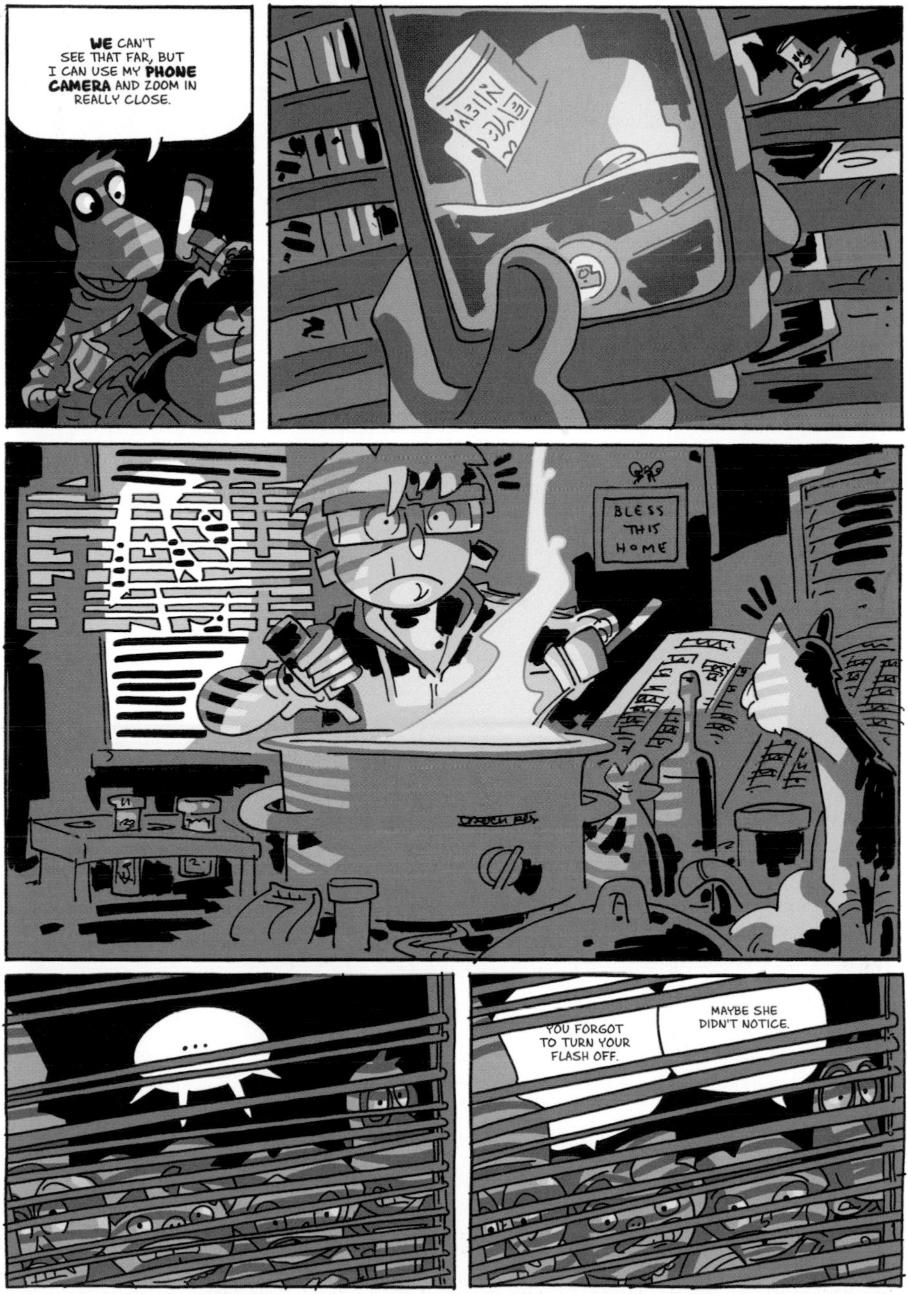
WE CAN'T SEE THAT FAR, BUT I CAN USE MY PHONE CAMERA AND ZOOM IN REALLY CLOSE.
BLESS THIS HOME
...
YOU FORGOT TO TURN YOUR FLASH OFF.
MAYBE SHE DIDN'T NOTICE.

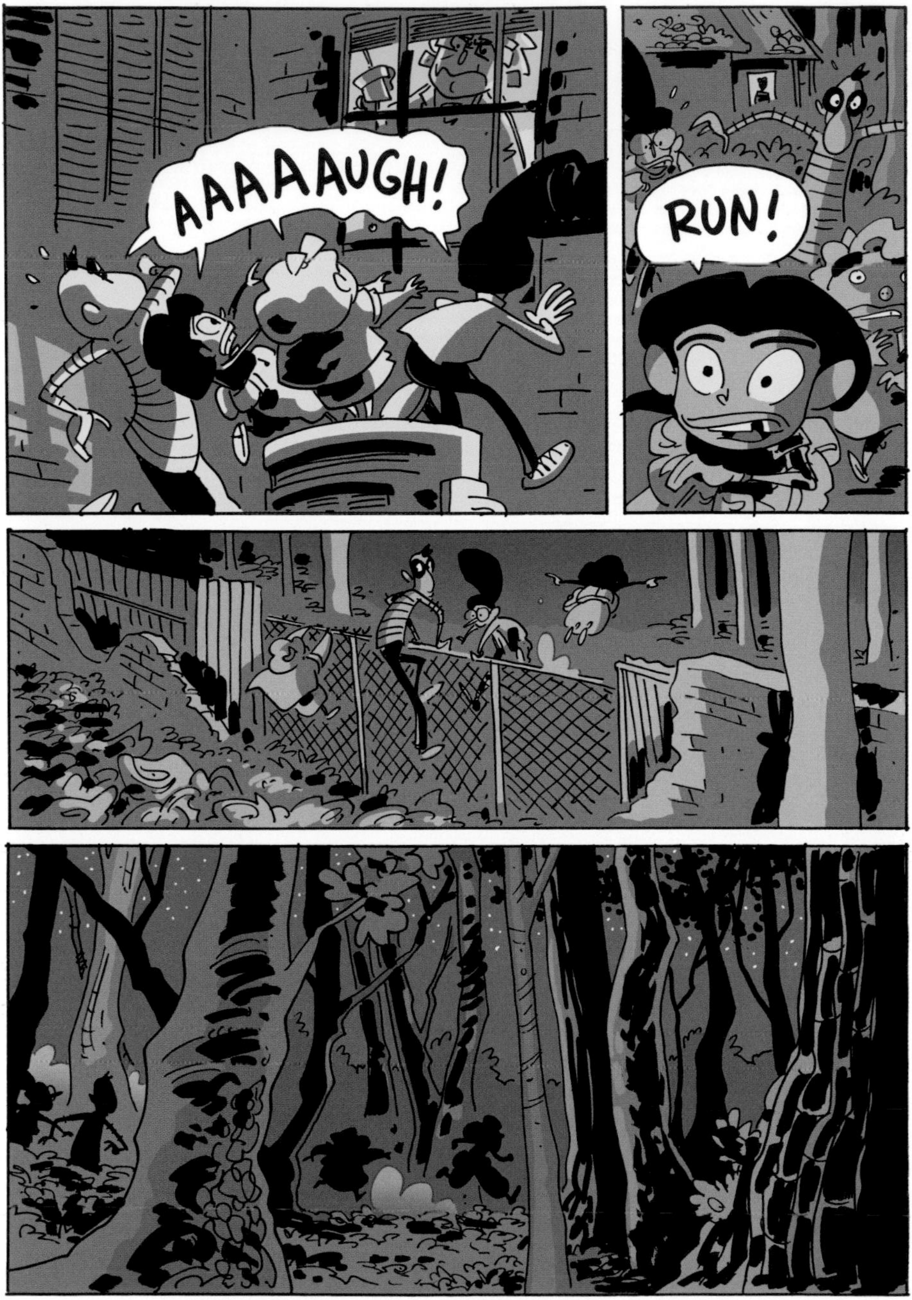
AAAAAUGH!
RUN!

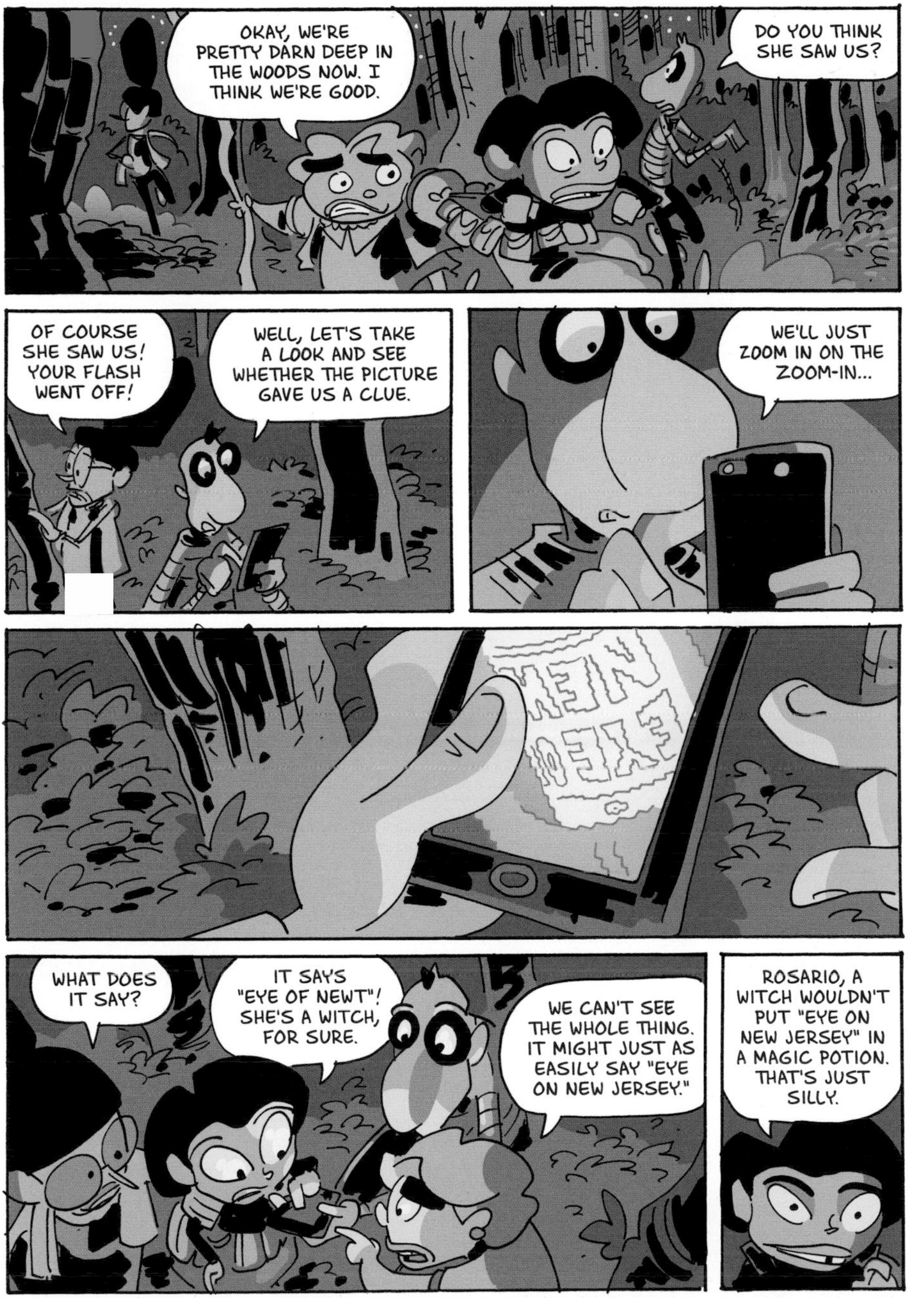
OKAY, WE'RE PRETTY DARN DEEP IN THE WOODS NOW. I THINK WE'RE GOOD.
DO YOU THINK SHE SAW US?
OF COURSE SHE SAW US! YOUR FLASH WENT OFF!
WELL, LET'S TAKE A LOOK AND SEE WHETHER THE PICTURE GAVE US A CLUE.
WE'LL JUST ZOOM IN ON THE ZOOM-IN...
WHAT DOES IT SAY?
IT SAYS "EYE OF NEWT"! SHE'S A WITCH, FOR SURE.
WE CAN'T SEE THE WHOLE THING. IT MIGHT JUST AS EASILY SAY "EYE ON NEW JERSEY."
ROSARIO, A WITCH WOULDN'T PUT "EYE ON NEW JERSEY" IN A MAGIC POTION. THAT'S JUST SILLY.

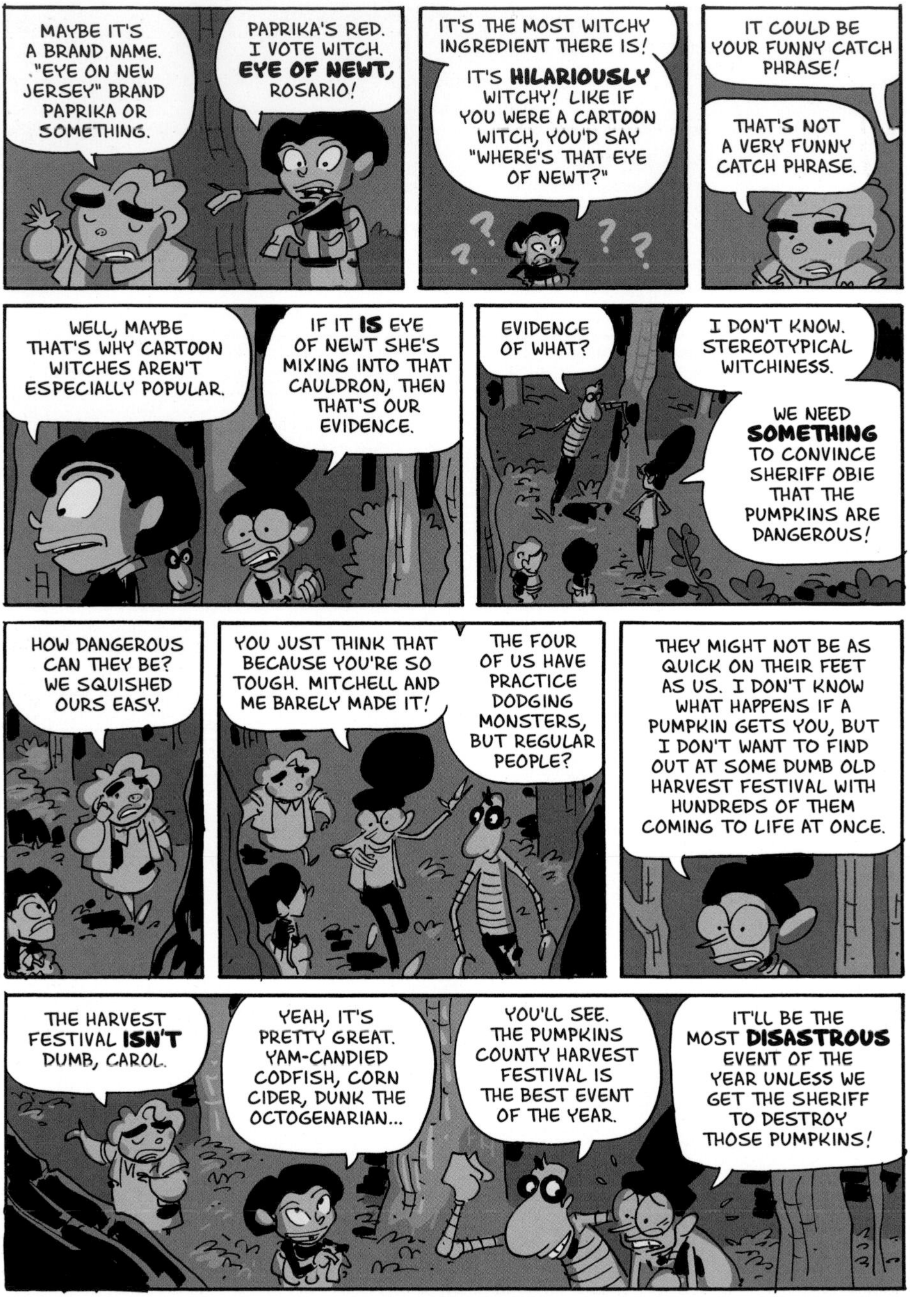
MAYBE IT'S A BRAND NAME. "EYE ON NEW JERSEY" BRAND PAPRIKA OR SOMETHING.
PAPRIKA'S RED. I VOTE WITCH. EYE OF NEWT, ROSARIO!
IT'S THE MOST WITCHY INGREDIENT THERE IS!
IT'S HILARIOUSLY WITCHY! LIKE IF YOU WERE A CARTOON WITCH, YOU'D SAY "WHERE'S THAT EYE OF NEWT?"
IT COULD BE YOUR FUNNY CATCH PHRASE!
THAT'S NOT A VERY FUNNY CATCH PHRASE.
WELL, MAYBE THAT'S WHY CARTOON WITCHES AREN'T ESPECIALLY POPULAR.
IF IT IS EYE OF NEWT SHE'S MIXING INTO THAT CAULDRON, THEN THAT'S OUR EVIDENCE.
EVIDENCE OF WHAT?
I DON'T KNOW. STEREOTYPICAL WITCHINESS.
WE NEED SOMETHING TO CONVINCE SHERIFF OBIE THAT THE PUMPKINS ARE DANGEROUS!
HOW DANGEROUS CAN THEY BE? WE SQUISHED OURS EASY.
YOU JUST THINK THAT BECAUSE YOU'RE SO TOUGH. MITCHELL AND ME BARELY MADE IT!
THE FOUR OF US HAVE PRACTICE DODGING MONSTERS, BUT REGULAR PEOPLE?
THEY MIGHT NOT BE AS QUICK ON THEIR FEET AS US. I DON'T KNOW WHAT HAPPENS IF A PUMPKIN GETS YOU, BUT I DON'T WANT TO FIND OUT AT SOME DUMB OLD HARVEST FESTIVAL WITH HUNDREDS OF THEM COMING TO LIFE AT ONCE.
THE HARVEST FESTIVAL ISN'T DUMB, CAROL.
YEAH, IT'S PRETTY GREAT. YAM-CANDIED CODFISH, CORN CIDER, DUNK THE OCTOGENARIAN...
YOU'LL SEE. THE PUMPKINS COUNTY HARVEST FESTIVAL IS THE BEST EVENT OF THE YEAR.
IT'LL BE THE MOST DISASTROUS EVENT OF THE YEAR UNLESS WE GET THE SHERIFF TO DESTROY THOSE PUMPKINS!

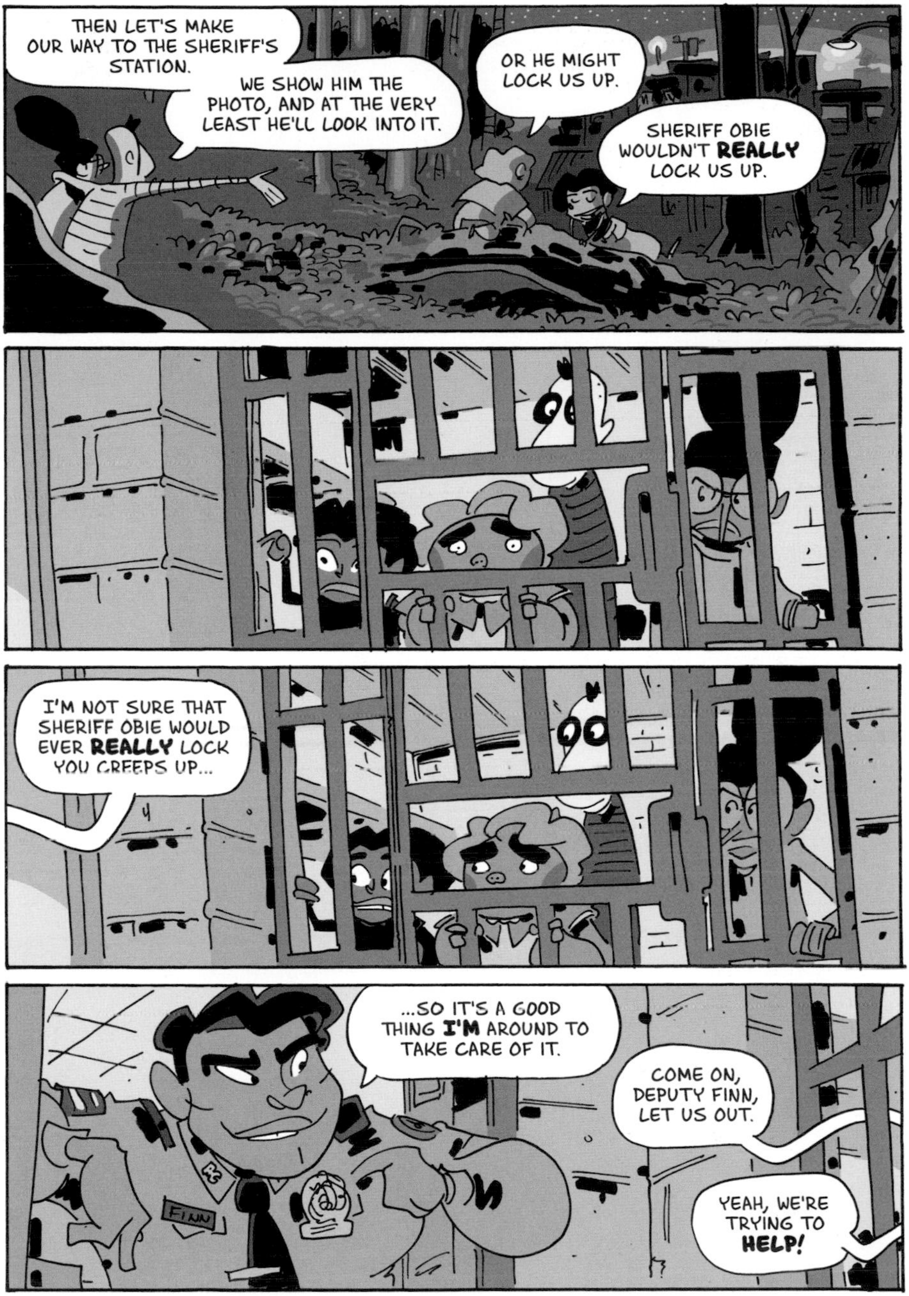
THEN LET'S MAKE OUR WAY TO THE SHERIFF'S STATION.
WE SHOW HIM THE PHOTO, AND AT THE VERY LEAST HE'LL LOOK INTO IT.
OR HE MIGHT LOCK US UP.
SHERIFF OBIE WOULDN'T **REALLY** LOCK US UP.
I'M NOT SURE THAT SHERIFF OBIE WOULD EVER **REALLY** LOCK YOU CREEPS UP...
...SO IT'S A GOOD THING **I'M** AROUND TO TAKE CARE OF IT.
FINN
COME ON, DEPUTY FINN, LET US OUT.
YEAH, WE'RE TRYING TO **HELP!**

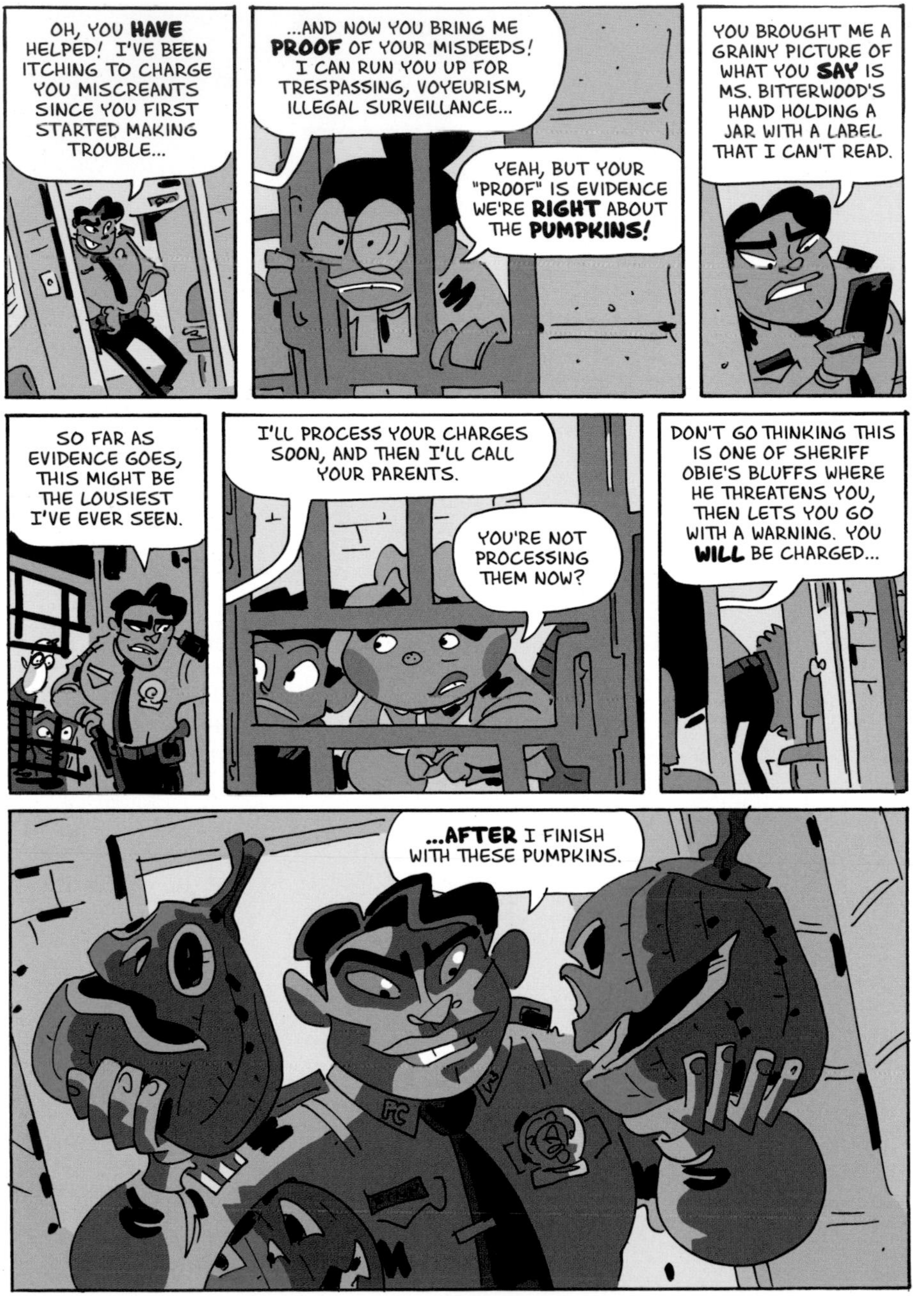
OH, YOU **HAVE** HELPED! I'VE BEEN ITCHING TO CHARGE YOU MISCREANTS SINCE YOU FIRST STARTED MAKING TROUBLE...
...AND NOW YOU BRING ME **PROOF** OF YOUR MISDEEDS! I CAN RUN YOU UP FOR TRESPASSING, VOYEURISM, ILLEGAL SURVEILLANCE...
YEAH, BUT YOUR "PROOF" IS EVIDENCE WE'RE **RIGHT** ABOUT THE **PUMPKINS!**
YOU BROUGHT ME A GRAINY PICTURE OF WHAT YOU **SAY** IS MS. BITTERWOOD'S HAND HOLDING A JAR WITH A LABEL THAT I CAN'T READ.
SO FAR AS EVIDENCE GOES, THIS MIGHT BE THE LOUSIEST I'VE EVER SEEN.
I'LL PROCESS YOUR CHARGES SOON, AND THEN I'LL CALL YOUR PARENTS.
YOU'RE NOT PROCESSING THEM NOW?
DON'T GO THINKING THIS IS ONE OF SHERIFF OBIE'S BLUFFS WHERE HE THREATENS YOU, THEN LETS YOU GO WITH A WARNING. YOU **WILL** BE CHARGED...
...**AFTER** I FINISH WITH THESE PUMPKINS.

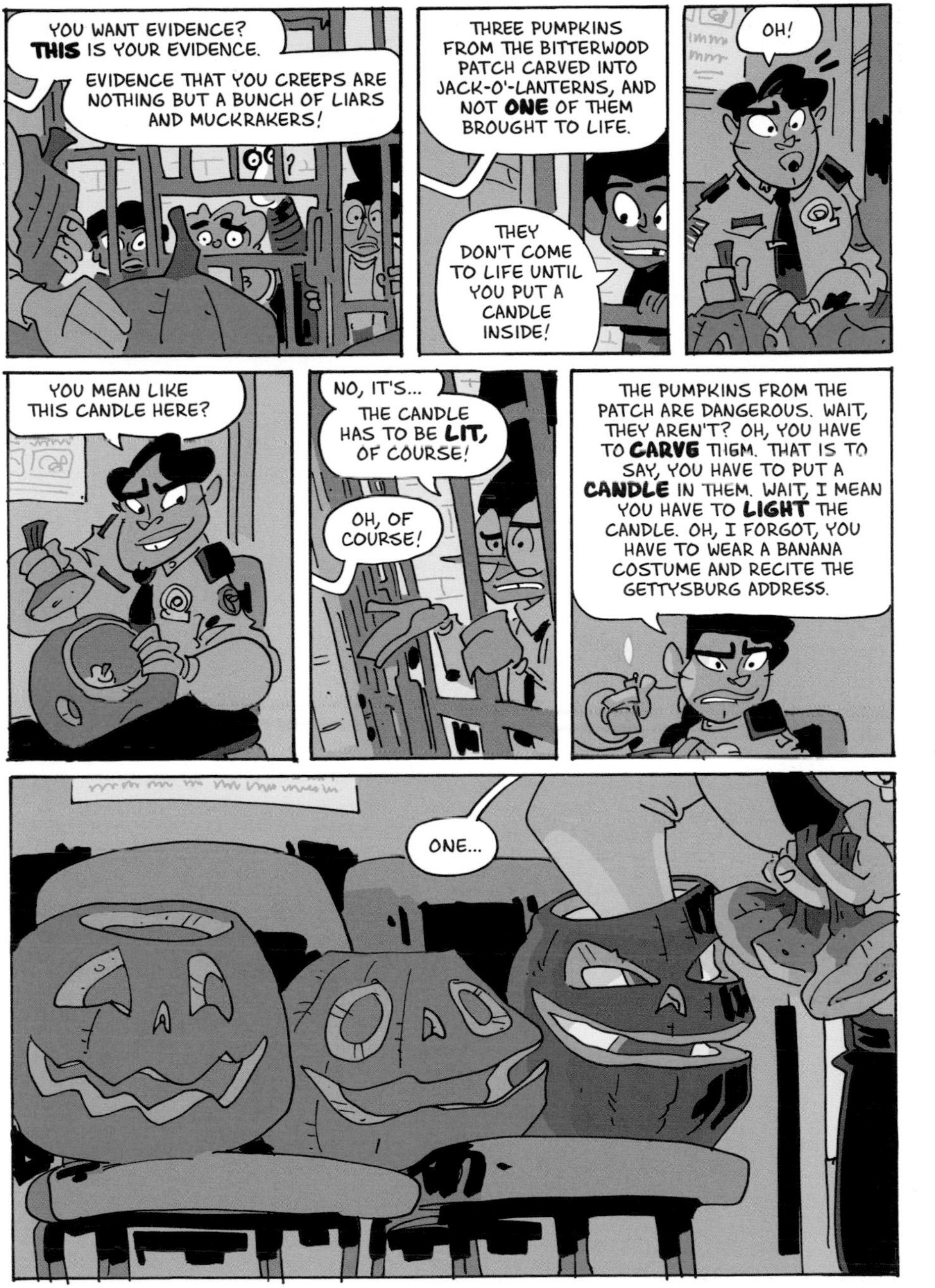

YOU WANT EVIDENCE? THIS IS YOUR EVIDENCE.
EVIDENCE THAT YOU CREEPS ARE NOTHING BUT A BUNCH OF LIARS AND MUCKRAKERS!
THREE PUMPKINS FROM THE BITTERWOOD PATCH CARVED INTO JACK-O'-LANTERNS, AND NOT ONE OF THEM BROUGHT TO LIFE.
THEY DON'T COME TO LIFE UNTIL YOU PUT A CANDLE INSIDE!
OH!
YOU MEAN LIKE THIS CANDLE HERE?
NO, IT'S...
THE CANDLE HAS TO BE LIT, OF COURSE!
OH, OF COURSE!
THE PUMPKINS FROM THE PATCH ARE DANGEROUS. WAIT, THEY AREN'T? OH, YOU HAVE TO CARVE THEM. THAT IS TO SAY, YOU HAVE TO PUT A CANDLE IN THEM. WAIT, I MEAN YOU HAVE TO LIGHT THE CANDLE. OH, I FORGOT, YOU HAVE TO WEAR A BANANA COSTUME AND RECITE THE GETTYSBURG ADDRESS.
ONE...

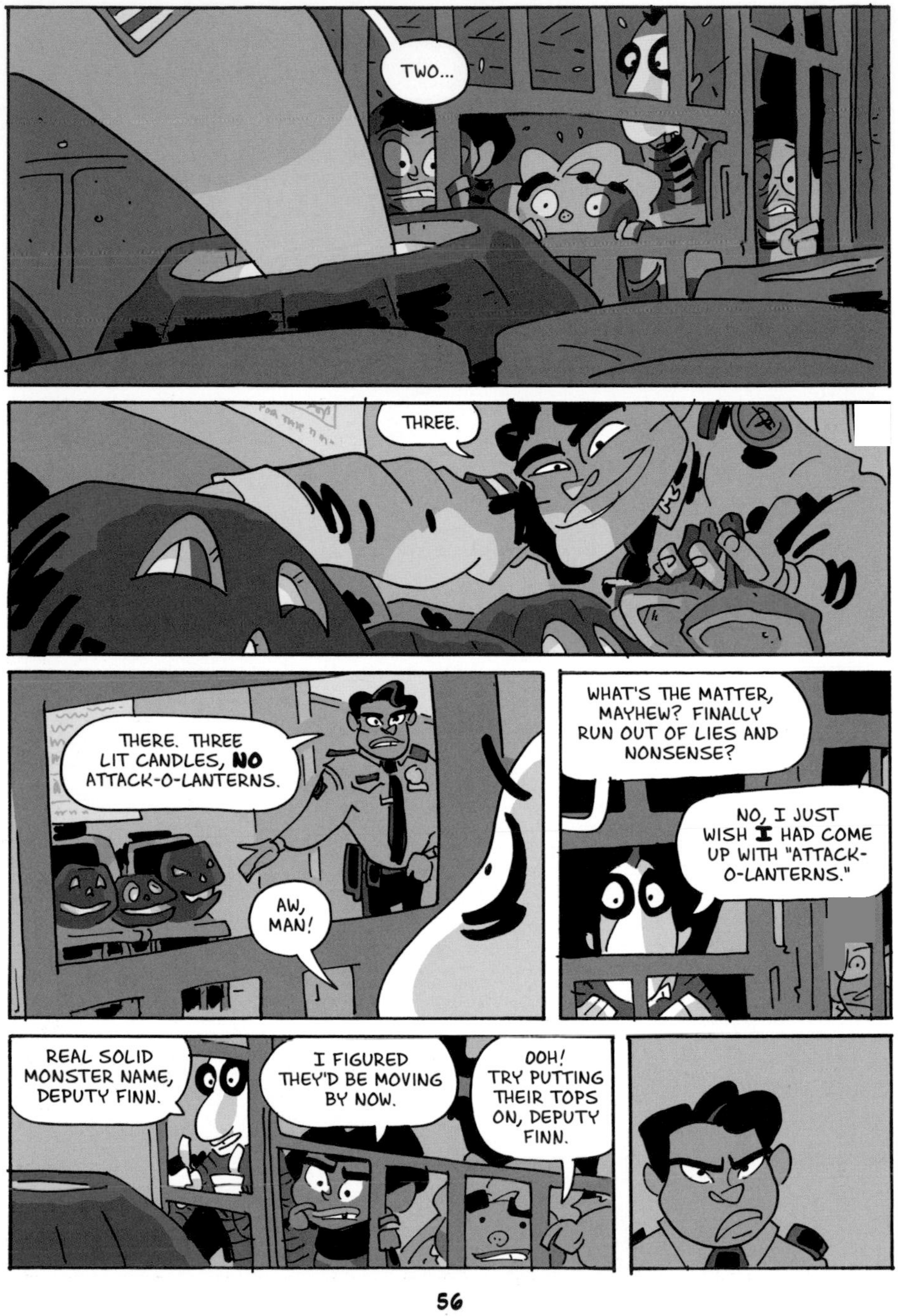
TWO...
THREE.
THERE. THREE LIT CANDLES, NO ATTACK-O-LANTERNS.
AW, MAN!
WHAT'S THE MATTER, MAYHEW? FINALLY RUN OUT OF LIES AND NONSENSE?
NO, I JUST WISH I HAD COME UP WITH "ATTACK-O-LANTERNS."
REAL SOLID MONSTER NAME, DEPUTY FINN.
I FIGURED THEY'D BE MOVING BY NOW.
OOH! TRY PUTTING THEIR TOPS ON, DEPUTY FINN.

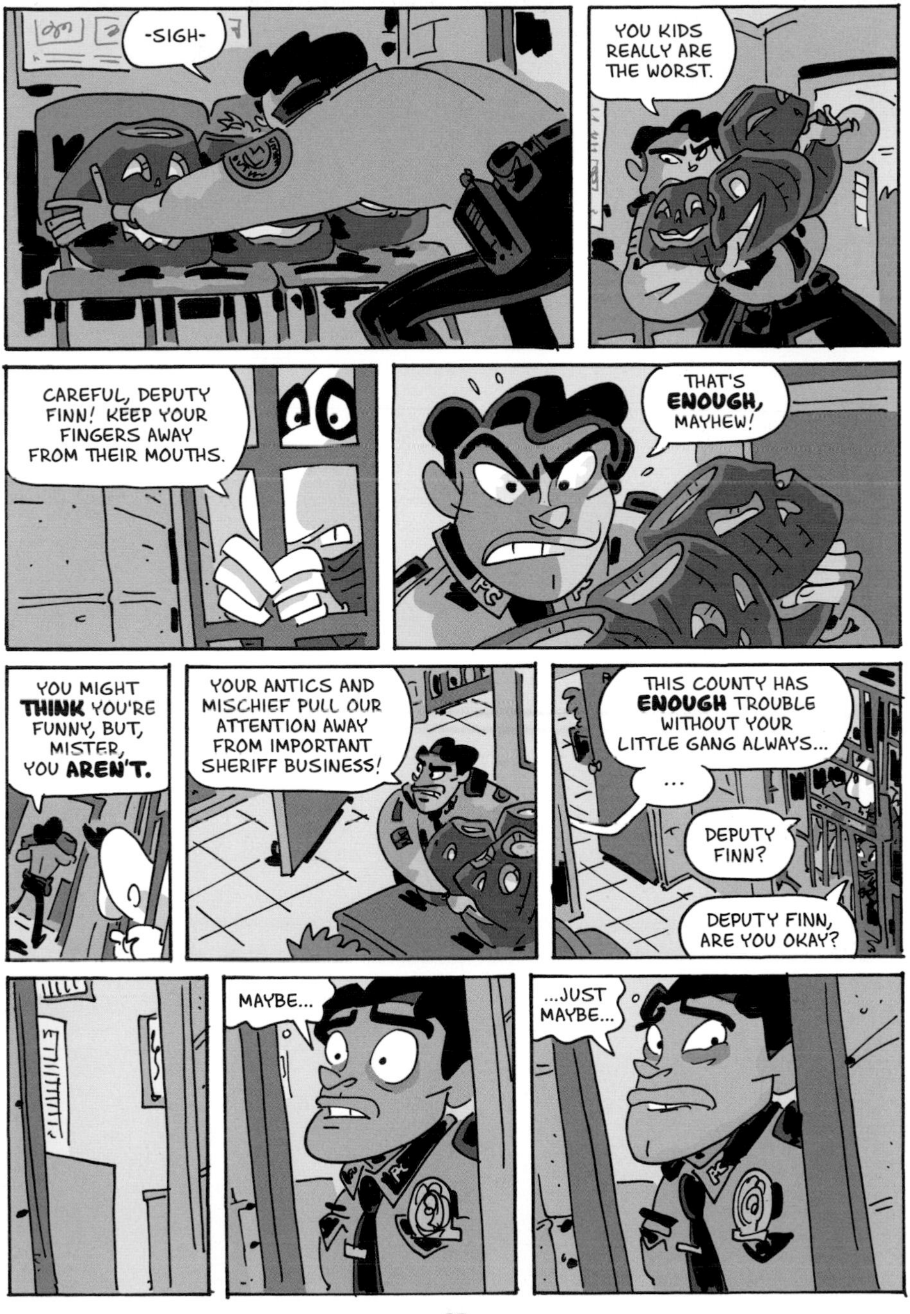
-SIGH-
YOU KIDS REALLY ARE THE WORST.
CAREFUL, DEPUTY FINN! KEEP YOUR FINGERS AWAY FROM THEIR MOUTHS.
THAT'S **ENOUGH,** MAYHEW!
YOU MIGHT **THINK** YOU'RE FUNNY, BUT, MISTER, YOU **AREN'T.**
YOUR ANTICS AND MISCHIEF PULL OUR ATTENTION AWAY FROM IMPORTANT SHERIFF BUSINESS!
THIS COUNTY HAS **ENOUGH** TROUBLE WITHOUT YOUR LITTLE GANG ALWAYS...
...
DEPUTY FINN?
DEPUTY FINN, ARE YOU OKAY?
MAYBE...
...JUST MAYBE...

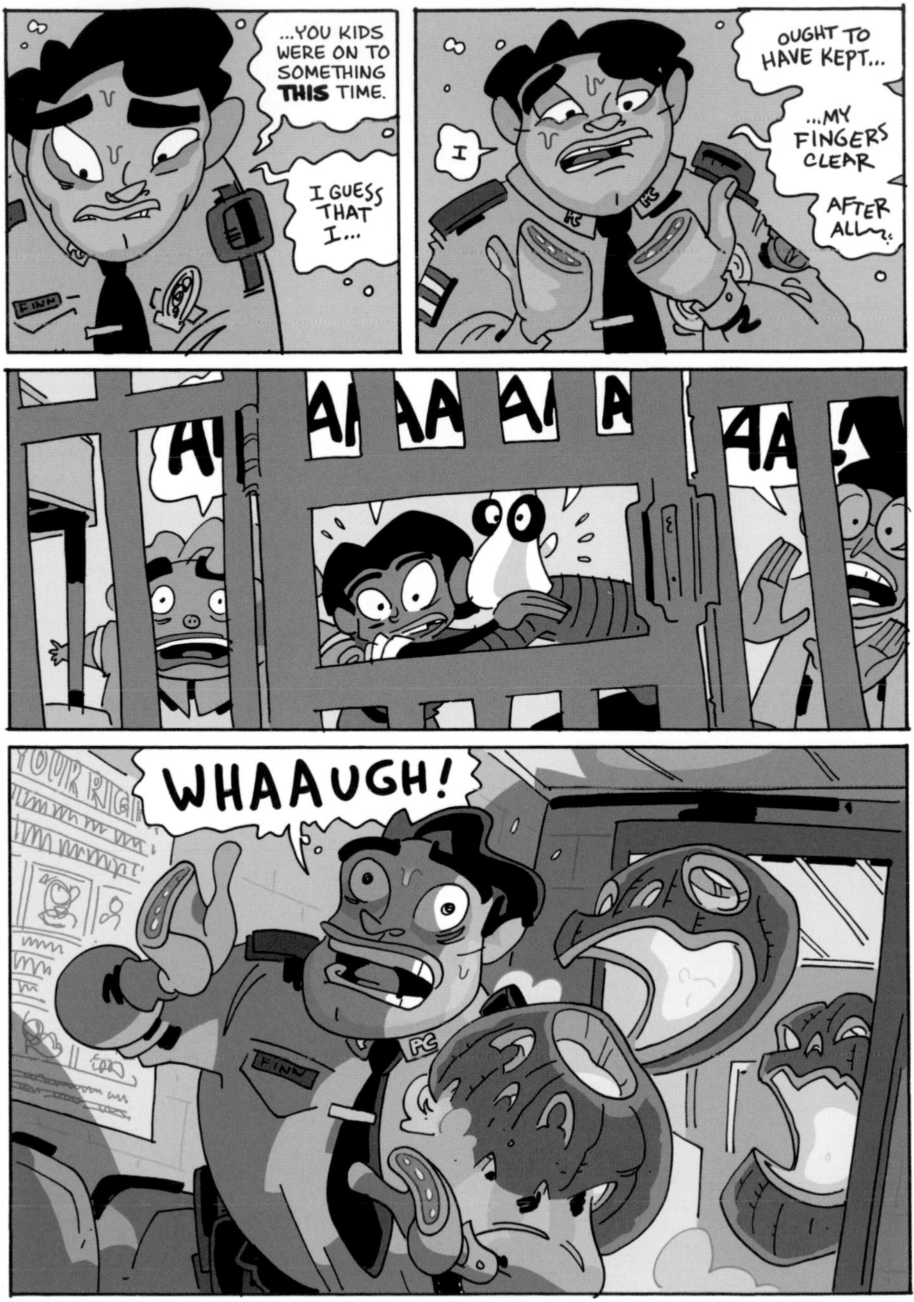
...YOU KIDS WERE ON TO SOMETHING THIS TIME.
I GUESS THAT I...
I
OUGHT TO HAVE KEPT...
...MY FINGERS CLEAR
AFTER ALL
FINN
WHAAUGH!
FINN
PC

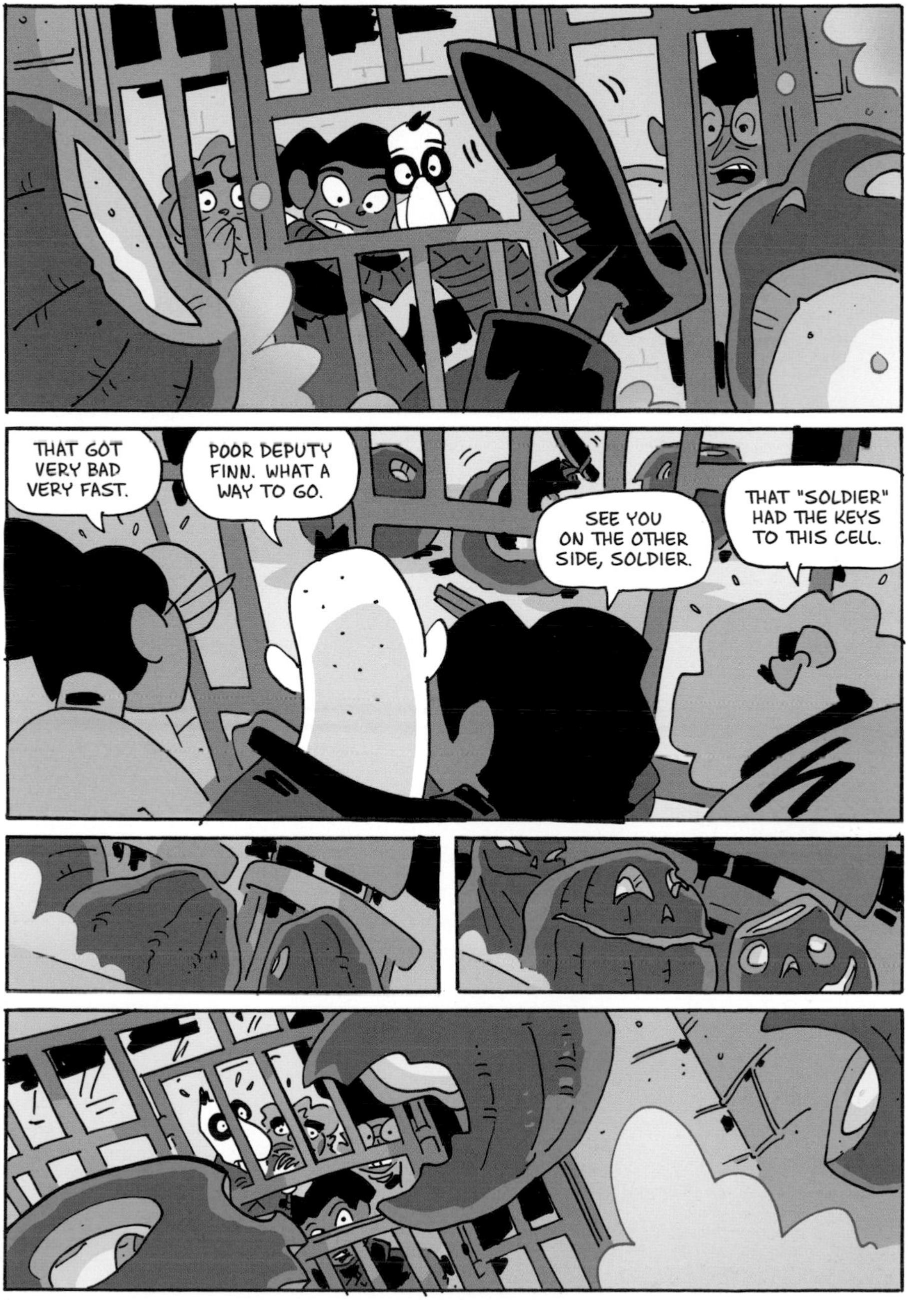
THAT GOT VERY BAD VERY FAST.
POOR DEPUTY FINN. WHAT A WAY TO GO.
SEE YOU ON THE OTHER SIDE, SOLDIER.
THAT "SOLDIER" HAD THE KEYS TO THIS CELL.

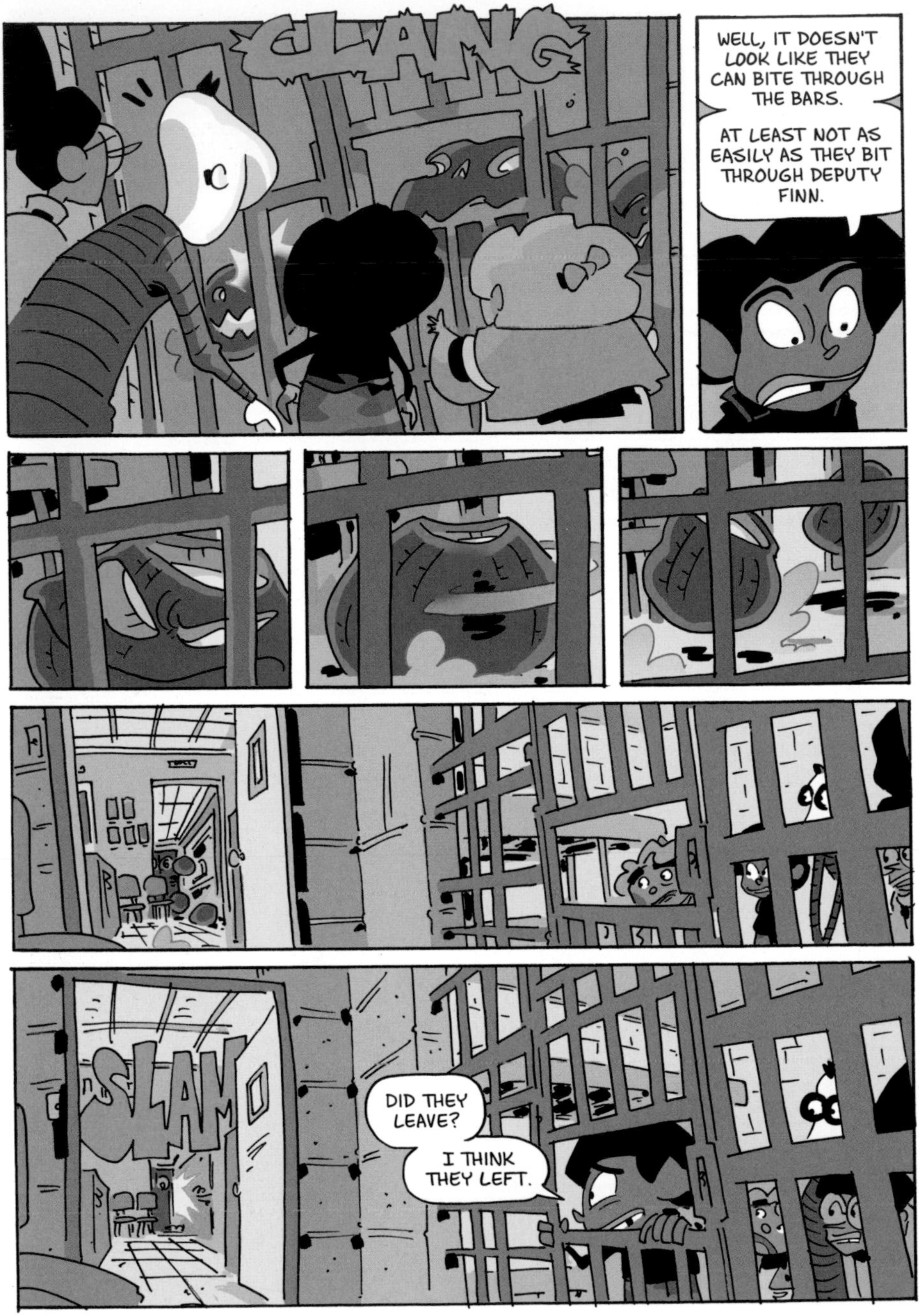
CLANG
WELL, IT DOESN'T LOOK LIKE THEY CAN BITE THROUGH THE BARS.
AT LEAST NOT AS EASILY AS THEY BIT THROUGH DEPUTY FINN.
SLAM
DID THEY LEAVE?
I THINK THEY LEFT.

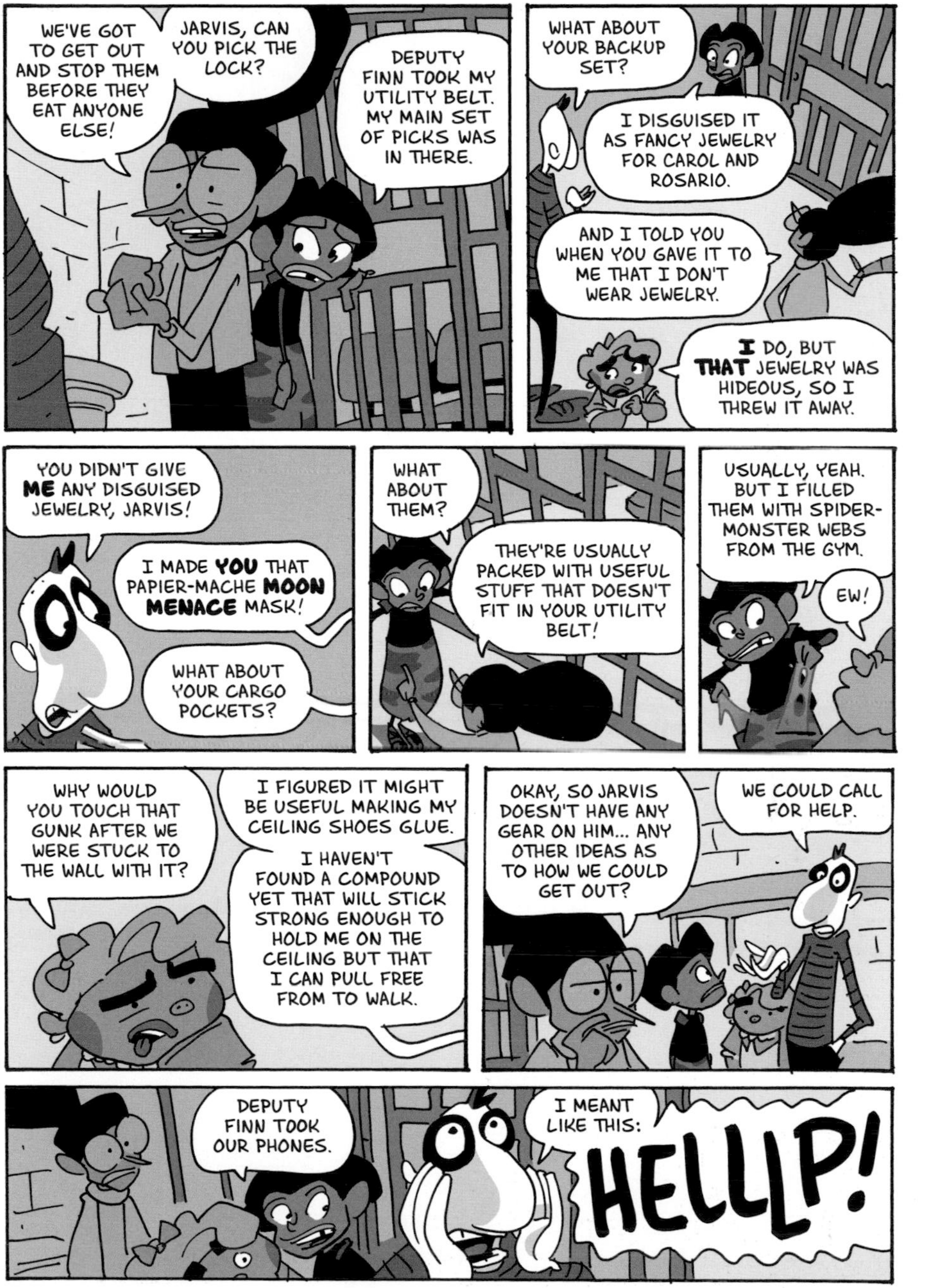
WE'VE GOT TO GET OUT AND STOP THEM BEFORE THEY EAT ANYONE ELSE!
JARVIS, CAN YOU PICK THE LOCK?
DEPUTY FINN TOOK MY UTILITY BELT. MY MAIN SET OF PICKS WAS IN THERE.
WHAT ABOUT YOUR BACKUP SET?
I DISGUISED IT AS FANCY JEWELRY FOR CAROL AND ROSARIO.
AND I TOLD YOU WHEN YOU GAVE IT TO ME THAT I DON'T WEAR JEWELRY.
I DO, BUT THAT JEWELRY WAS HIDEOUS, SO I THREW IT AWAY.
YOU DIDN'T GIVE ME ANY DISGUISED JEWELRY, JARVIS!
I MADE YOU THAT PAPIER-MACHE MOON MENACE MASK!
WHAT ABOUT YOUR CARGO POCKETS?
WHAT ABOUT THEM?
THEY'RE USUALLY PACKED WITH USEFUL STUFF THAT DOESN'T FIT IN YOUR UTILITY BELT!
USUALLY, YEAH. BUT I FILLED THEM WITH SPIDER-MONSTER WEBS FROM THE GYM.
EW!
WHY WOULD YOU TOUCH THAT GUNK AFTER WE WERE STUCK TO THE WALL WITH IT?
I FIGURED IT MIGHT BE USEFUL MAKING MY CEILING SHOES GLUE.
I HAVEN'T FOUND A COMPOUND YET THAT WILL STICK STRONG ENOUGH TO HOLD ME ON THE CEILING BUT THAT I CAN PULL FREE FROM TO WALK.
OKAY, SO JARVIS DOESN'T HAVE ANY GEAR ON HIM... ANY OTHER IDEAS AS TO HOW WE COULD GET OUT?
WE COULD CALL FOR HELP.
DEPUTY FINN TOOK OUR PHONES.
I MEANT LIKE THIS:
HELLLP!

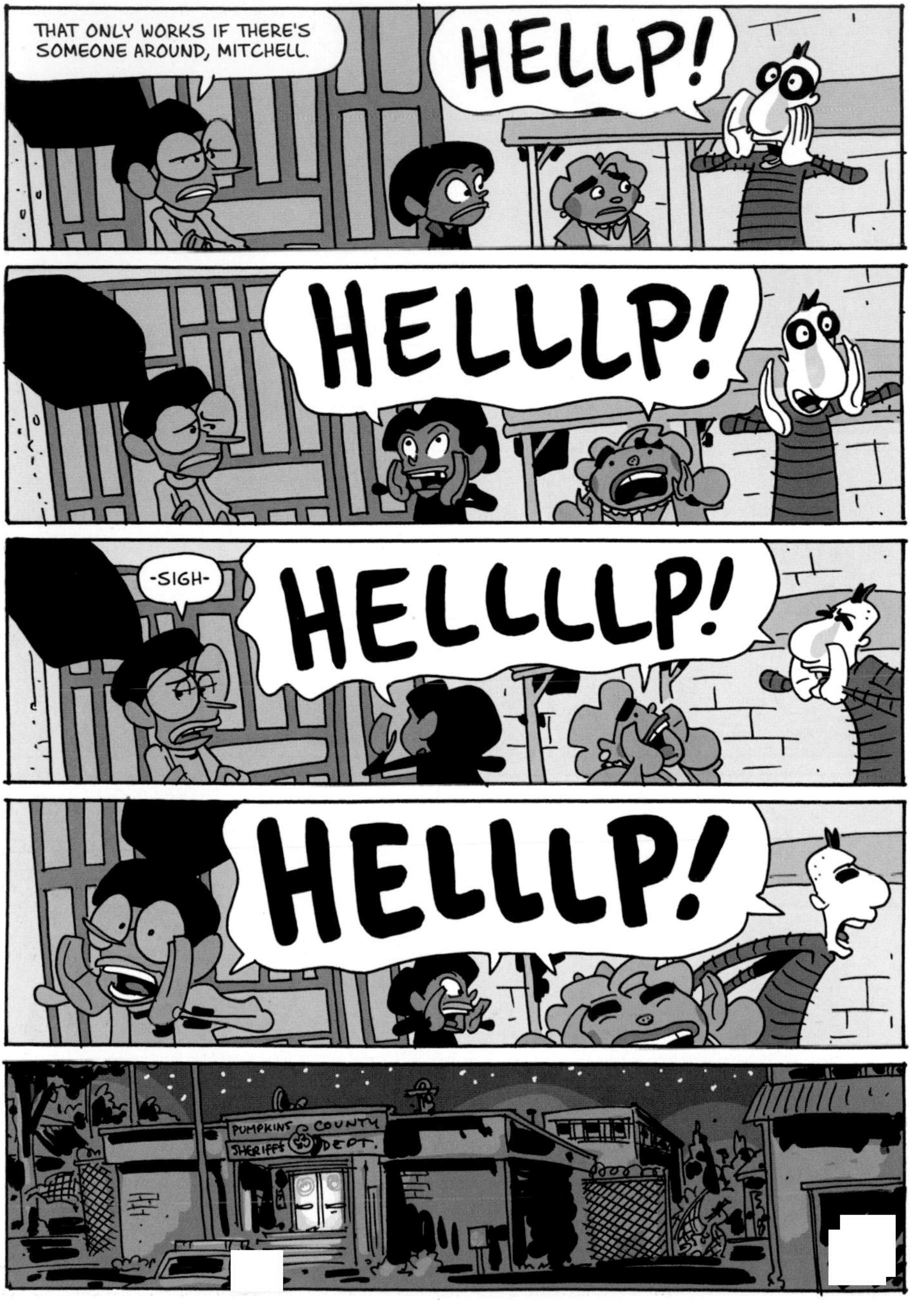
THAT ONLY WORKS IF THERE'S SOMEONE AROUND, MITCHELL.
HELLP!
HELLLP!
-SIGH-
HELLLLP!
HELLLP!
PUMPKINS COUNTY
SHERIFF'S DEPT.

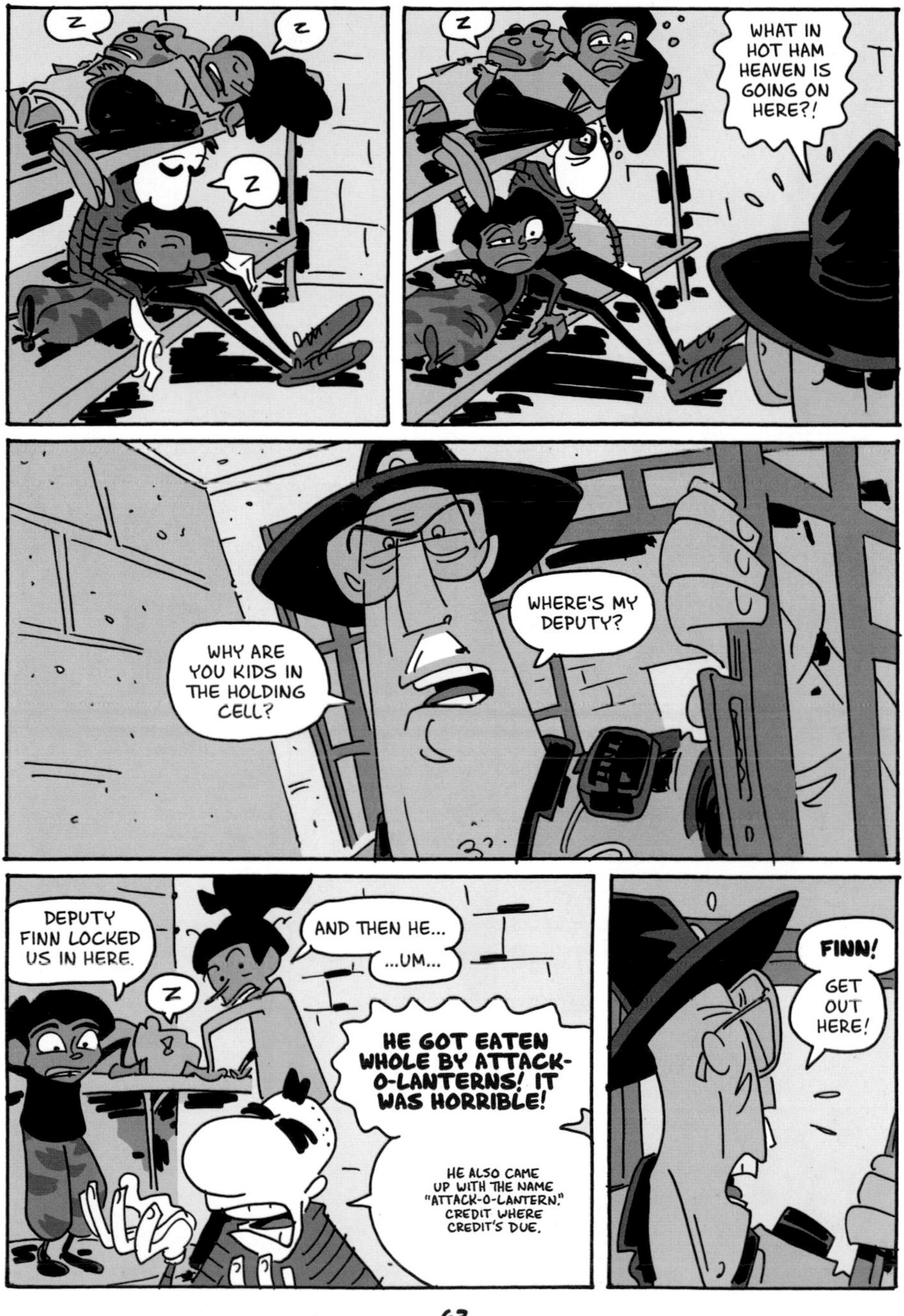
Z
Z
Z
Z
WHAT IN HOT HAM HEAVEN IS GOING ON HERE?!
WHERE'S MY DEPUTY?
WHY ARE YOU KIDS IN THE HOLDING CELL?
DEPUTY FINN LOCKED US IN HERE.
Z
AND THEN HE...
...UM...
HE GOT EATEN WHOLE BY ATTACK-O-LANTERNS! IT WAS HORRIBLE!
HE ALSO CAME UP WITH THE NAME "ATTACK-O-LANTERN." CREDIT WHERE CREDIT'S DUE.
FINN!
GET OUT HERE!

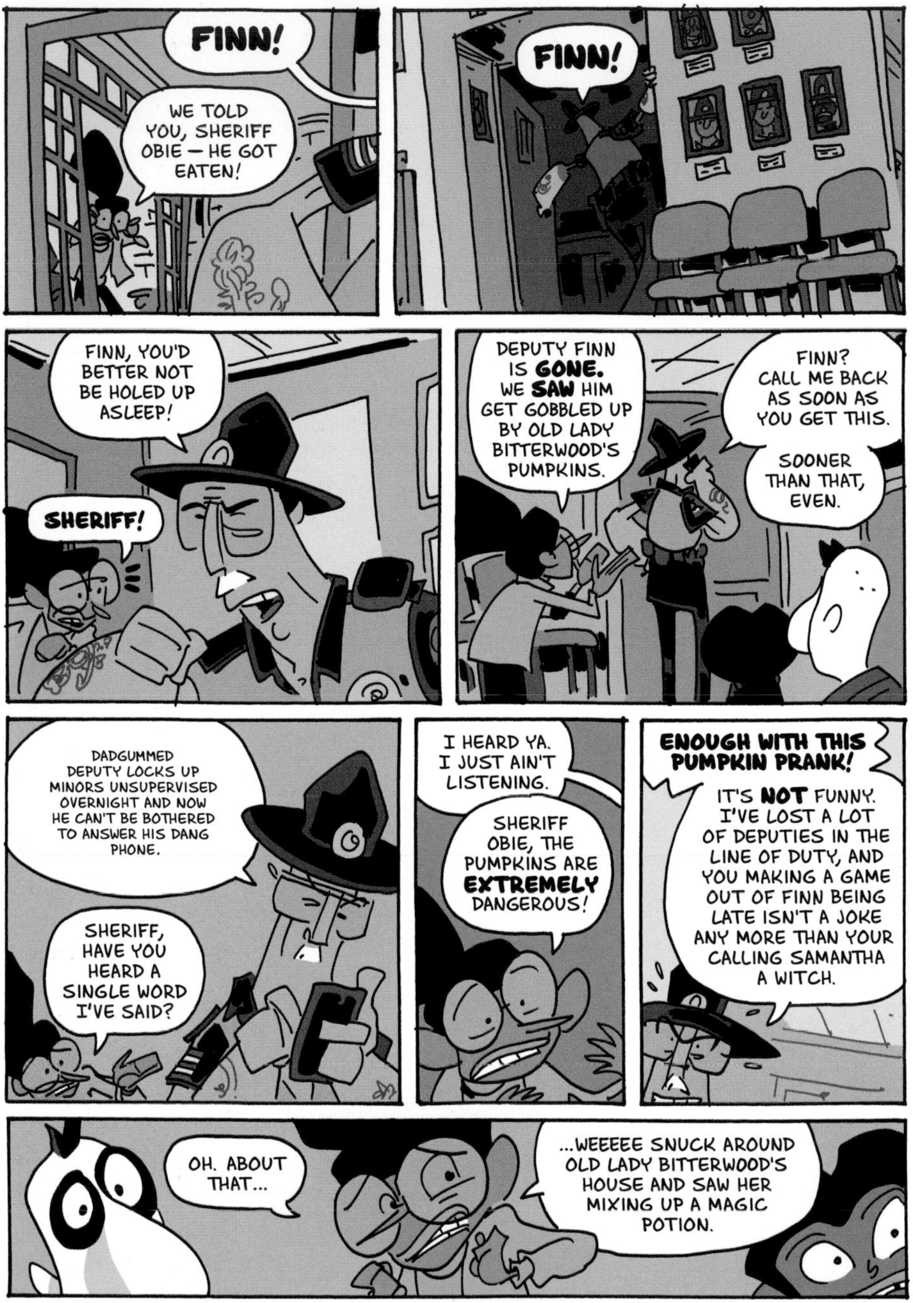
FINN!
WE TOLD YOU, SHERIFF OBIE — HE GOT EATEN!
FINN!
FINN, YOU'D BETTER NOT BE HOLED UP ASLEEP!
SHERIFF!
DEPUTY FINN IS GONE. WE SAW HIM GET GOBBLED UP BY OLD LADY BITTERWOOD'S PUMPKINS.
FINN? CALL ME BACK AS SOON AS YOU GET THIS.
SOONER THAN THAT, EVEN.
DADGUMMED DEPUTY LOCKS UP MINORS UNSUPERVISED OVERNIGHT AND NOW HE CAN'T BE BOTHERED TO ANSWER HIS DANG PHONE.
SHERIFF, HAVE YOU HEARD A SINGLE WORD I'VE SAID?
I HEARD YA. I JUST AIN'T LISTENING.
SHERIFF OBIE, THE PUMPKINS ARE EXTREMELY DANGEROUS!
ENOUGH WITH THIS PUMPKIN PRANK!
IT'S NOT FUNNY. I'VE LOST A LOT OF DEPUTIES IN THE LINE OF DUTY, AND YOU MAKING A GAME OUT OF FINN BEING LATE ISN'T A JOKE ANY MORE THAN YOUR CALLING SAMANTHA A WITCH.
OH. ABOUT THAT...
...WEEEEE SNUCK AROUND OLD LADY BITTERWOOD'S HOUSE AND SAW HER MIXING UP A MAGIC POTION.

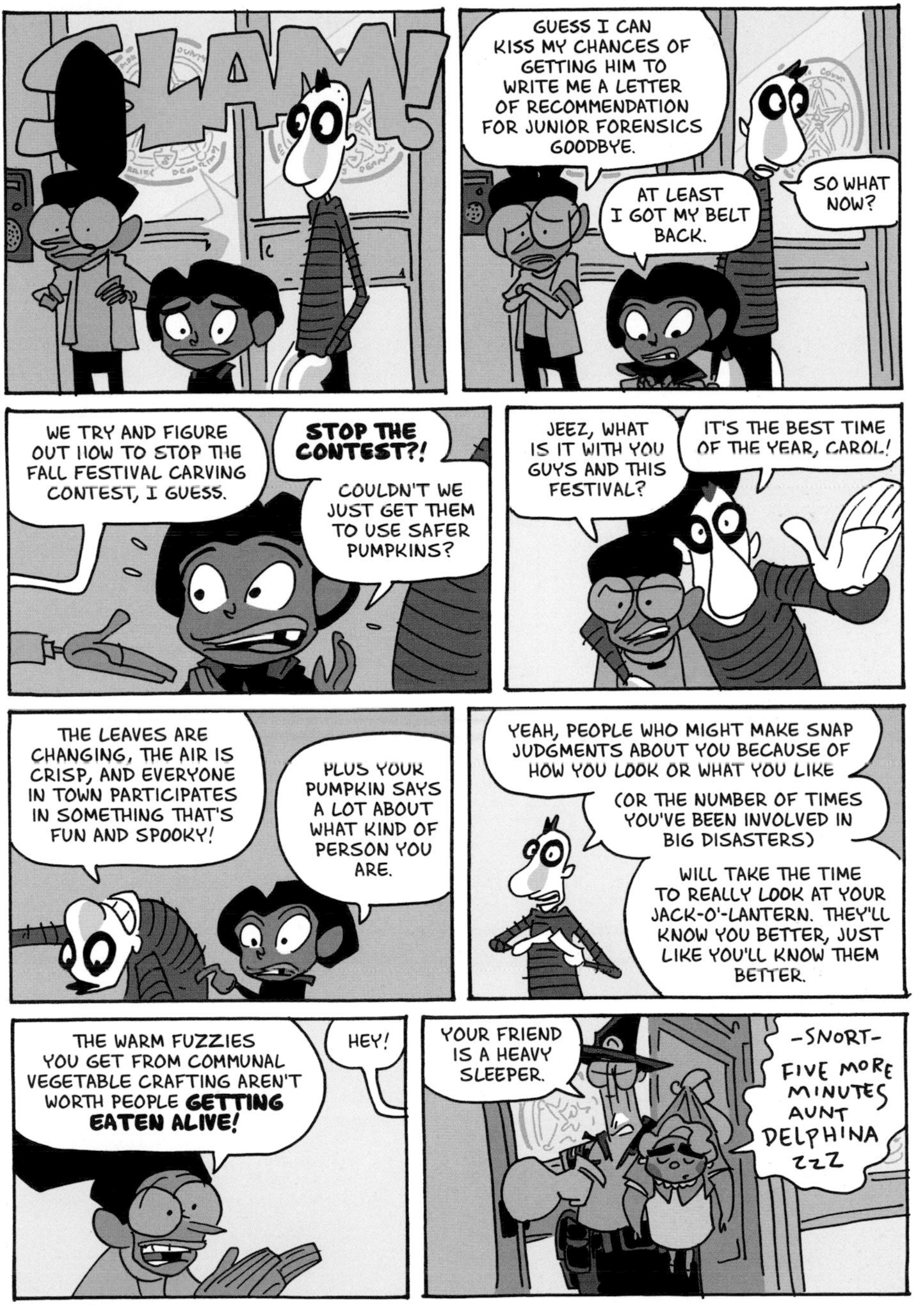
SLAM!
GUESS I CAN KISS MY CHANCES OF GETTING HIM TO WRITE ME A LETTER OF RECOMMENDATION FOR JUNIOR FORENSICS GOODBYE.
AT LEAST I GOT MY BELT BACK.
SO WHAT NOW?
WE TRY AND FIGURE OUT HOW TO STOP THE FALL FESTIVAL CARVING CONTEST, I GUESS.
STOP THE CONTEST?!
COULDN'T WE JUST GET THEM TO USE SAFER PUMPKINS?
JEEZ, WHAT IS IT WITH YOU GUYS AND THIS FESTIVAL?
IT'S THE BEST TIME OF THE YEAR, CAROL!
THE LEAVES ARE CHANGING, THE AIR IS CRISP, AND EVERYONE IN TOWN PARTICIPATES IN SOMETHING THAT'S FUN AND SPOOKY!
PLUS YOUR PUMPKIN SAYS A LOT ABOUT WHAT KIND OF PERSON YOU ARE.
YEAH, PEOPLE WHO MIGHT MAKE SNAP JUDGMENTS ABOUT YOU BECAUSE OF HOW YOU LOOK OR WHAT YOU LIKE
(OR THE NUMBER OF TIMES YOU'VE BEEN INVOLVED IN BIG DISASTERS)
WILL TAKE THE TIME TO REALLY LOOK AT YOUR JACK-O'-LANTERN. THEY'LL KNOW YOU BETTER, JUST LIKE YOU'LL KNOW THEM BETTER.
THE WARM FUZZIES YOU GET FROM COMMUNAL VEGETABLE CRAFTING AREN'T WORTH PEOPLE GETTING EATEN ALIVE!
HEY!
YOUR FRIEND IS A HEAVY SLEEPER.
-SNORT-
FIVE MORE MINUTES AUNT DELPHINA zzZ

YOU KIDS HAVE NO IDEA HOW LUCKY YOU ARE RIGHT NOW.

IF I WEREN'T SADDLED WITH THE FESTIVAL AND TRYING TO FIND MY DEPUTY, YOU'D BE IN A WORLD OF TROUBLE.

HECK, YOU **ARE** IN A WORLD OF TROUBLE. I'M GOING TO HAVE PRINCIPAL GARISH EXTEND YOUR SERVICE DETENTION INDEFINITELY.

NOW GET DOWN TO THE SQUARE AND GET WORKING. THERE'S A LOT OF PUMPKIN GOOP TO GATHER UP TODAY, AND I WANT YOU TAKING CARE OF IT **FIRST THING,** YOU GOT ME?

AWW, SHERIFF OBIE, YOU CAN'T MAKE US WORK DURING THE CONTEST!

MITCHELL, THE CONTEST IS THE LOWEST PRIORITY RIGHT NOW!

I'M DOING ALL THAT I CAN TO KEEP YOU STINKERS FROM PERMANENTLY RUINING YOUR LIVES.

I DON'T WANT TO PUT YOU IN THE SYSTEM. I DON'T WANT TO SEND YOU OFF TO A JUVENILE DETENTION CENTER. I DON'T WANT YOU YANKED OUT OF SCHOOL OR TAKEN FROM YOUR FAMILIES.

I GIVE YOU CHANCE AFTER CHANCE AFTER CHANCE TO SHAPE UP, AND YOU JUST KEEP PULLING THESE STUNTS.

NO MORE CHANCES. YOU TOW THE LINE FROM HERE ON OUT OR I'LL TREAT YOU LIKE I WOULD ANY OTHER LAWBREAKER, KIDS OR NOT.

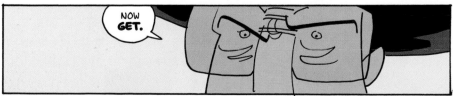

NOW **GET.**

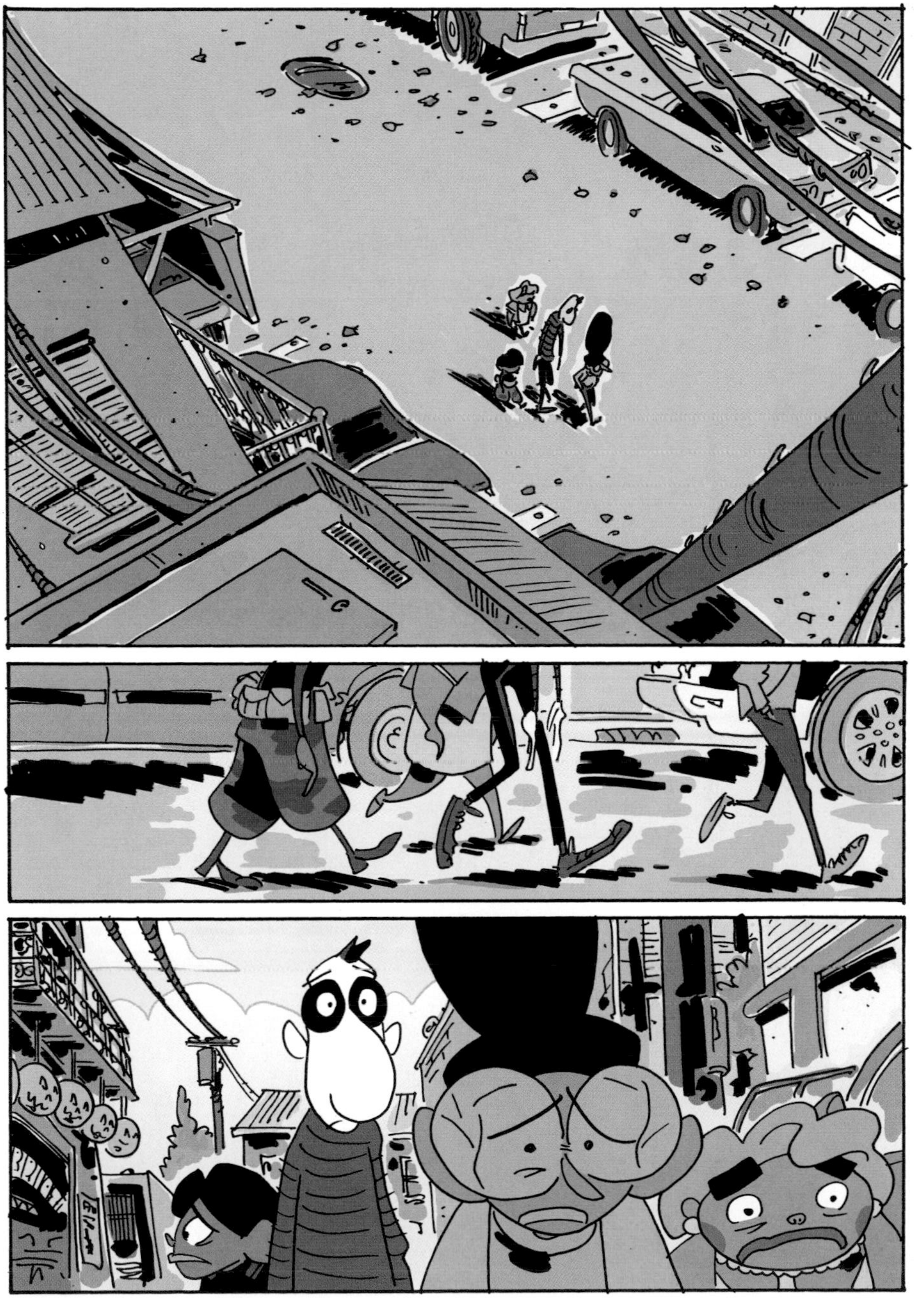

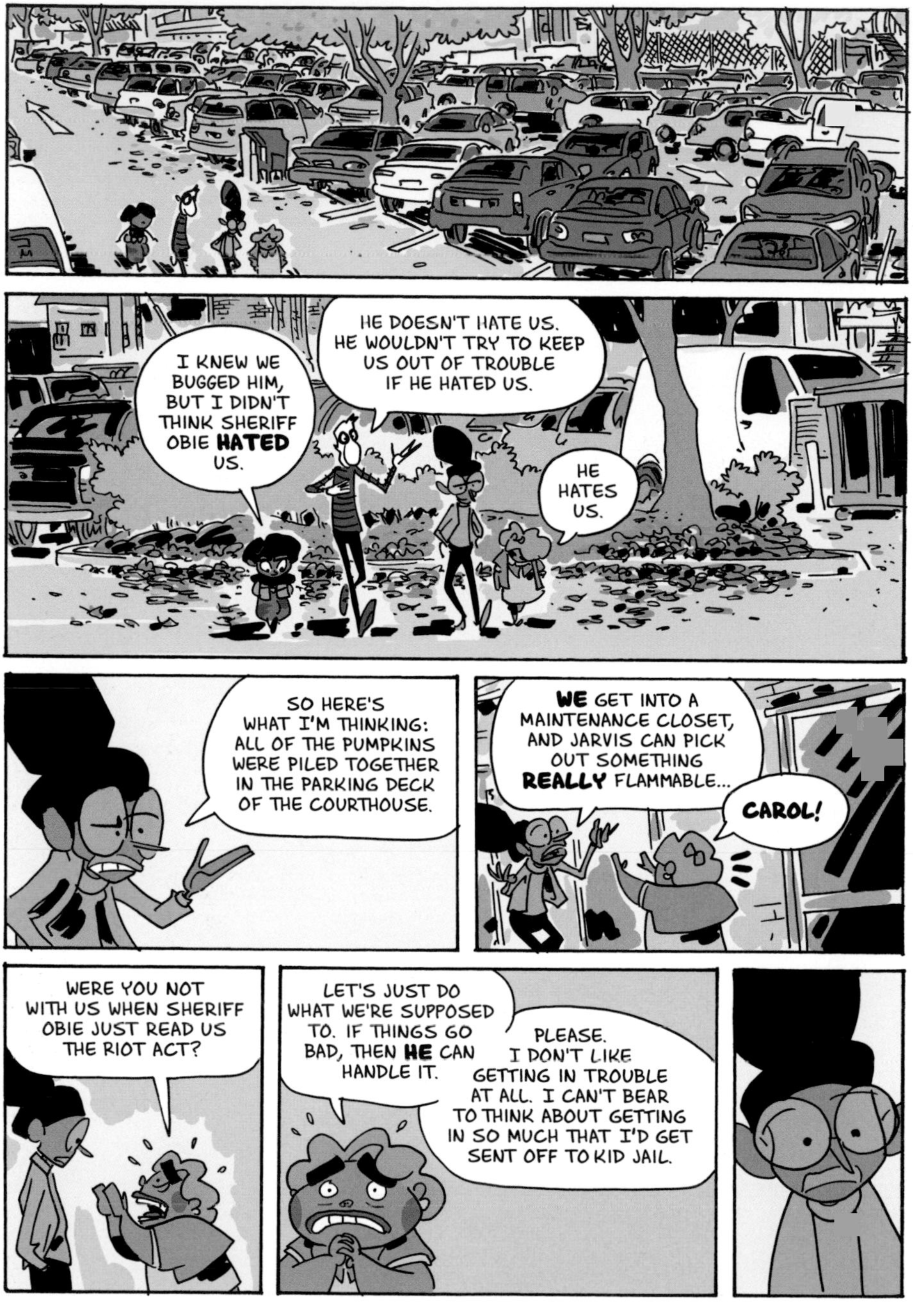
I KNEW WE BUGGED HIM, BUT I DIDN'T THINK SHERIFF OBIE **HATED** US.
HE DOESN'T HATE US. HE WOULDN'T TRY TO KEEP US OUT OF TROUBLE IF HE HATED US.
HE HATES US.
SO HERE'S WHAT I'M THINKING: ALL OF THE PUMPKINS WERE PILED TOGETHER IN THE PARKING DECK OF THE COURTHOUSE.
WE GET INTO A MAINTENANCE CLOSET, AND JARVIS CAN PICK OUT SOMETHING **REALLY** FLAMMABLE...
CAROL!
WERE YOU NOT WITH US WHEN SHERIFF OBIE JUST READ US THE RIOT ACT?
LET'S JUST DO WHAT WE'RE SUPPOSED TO. IF THINGS GO BAD, THEN **HE** CAN HANDLE IT.
PLEASE. I DON'T LIKE GETTING IN TROUBLE AT ALL. I CAN'T BEAR TO THINK ABOUT GETTING IN SO MUCH THAT I'D GET SENT OFF TO KID JAIL.

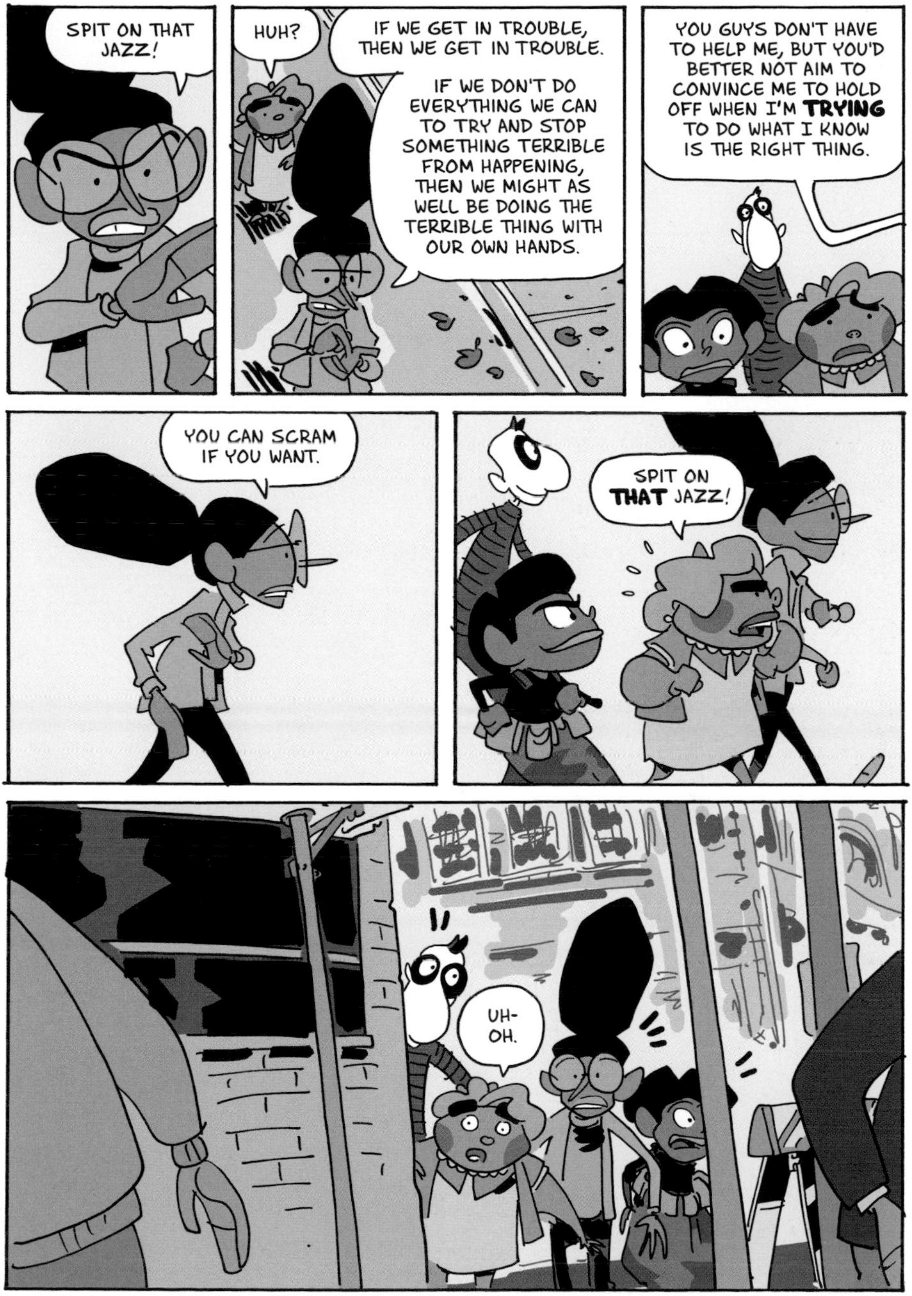
SPIT ON THAT JAZZ!
HUH?
IF WE GET IN TROUBLE, THEN WE GET IN TROUBLE.
IF WE DON'T DO EVERYTHING WE CAN TO TRY AND STOP SOMETHING TERRIBLE FROM HAPPENING, THEN WE MIGHT AS WELL BE DOING THE TERRIBLE THING WITH OUR OWN HANDS.
YOU GUYS DON'T HAVE TO HELP ME, BUT YOU'D BETTER NOT AIM TO CONVINCE ME TO HOLD OFF WHEN I'M **TRYING** TO DO WHAT I KNOW IS THE RIGHT THING.
YOU CAN SCRAM IF YOU WANT.
SPIT ON **THAT** JAZZ!
UH-OH.

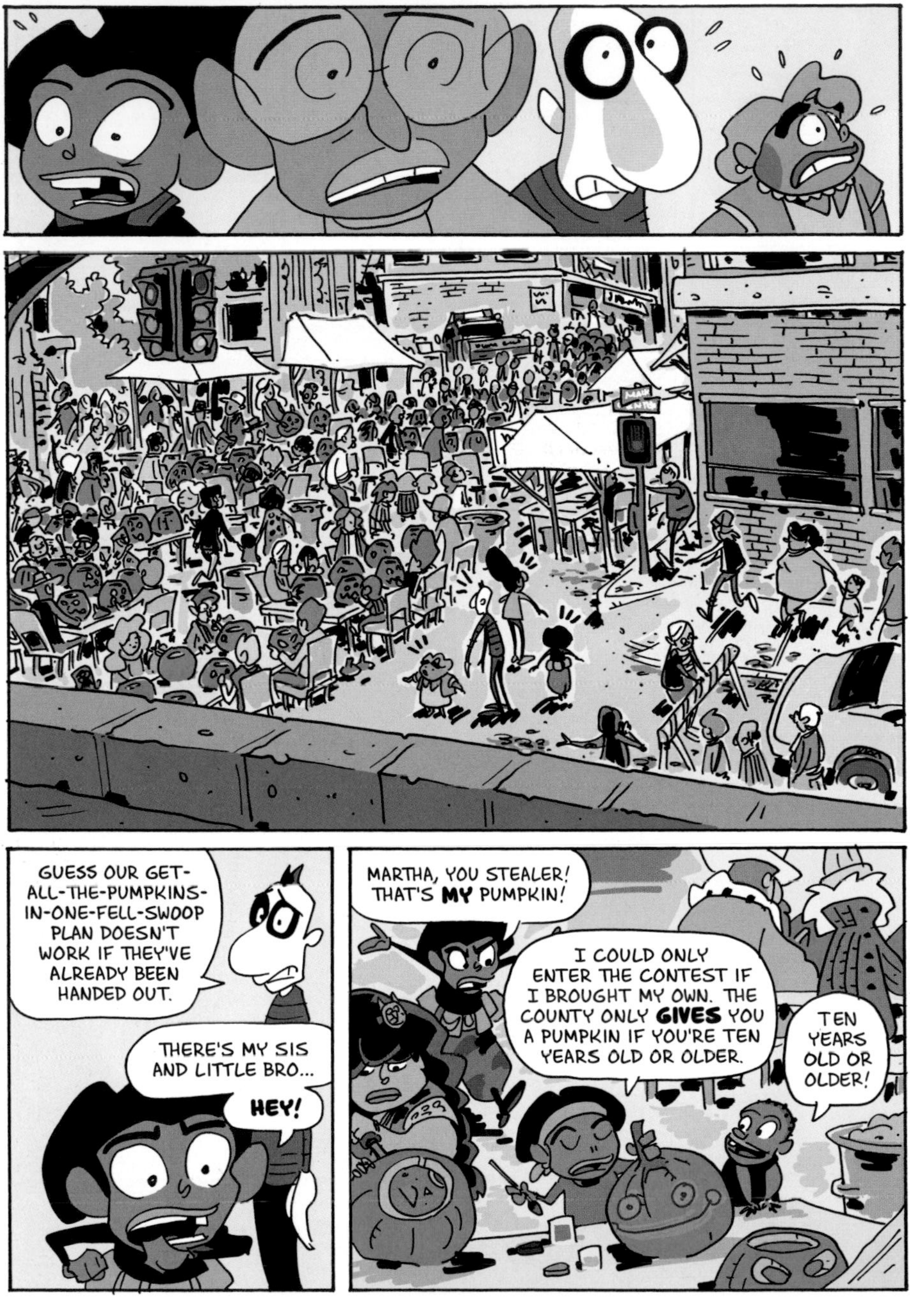
GUESS OUR GET-ALL-THE-PUMPKINS-IN-ONE-FELL-SWOOP PLAN DOESN'T WORK IF THEY'VE ALREADY BEEN HANDED OUT.
THERE'S MY SIS AND LITTLE BRO...
HEY!
MARTHA, YOU STEALER! THAT'S MY PUMPKIN!
I COULD ONLY ENTER THE CONTEST IF I BROUGHT MY OWN. THE COUNTY ONLY GIVES YOU A PUMPKIN IF YOU'RE TEN YEARS OLD OR OLDER.
TEN YEARS OLD OR OLDER!

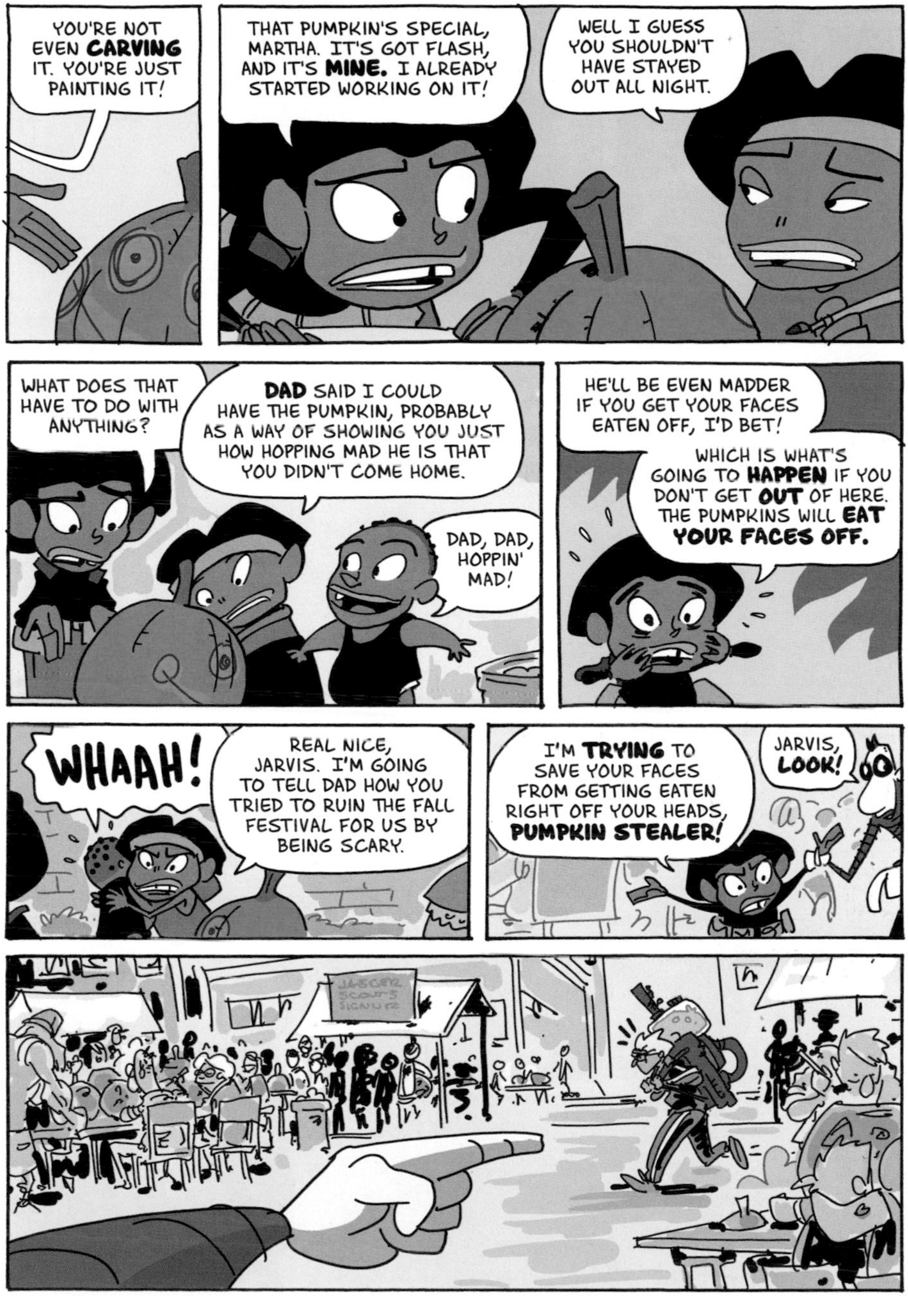
YOU'RE NOT EVEN **CARVING** IT. YOU'RE JUST PAINTING IT!
THAT PUMPKIN'S SPECIAL, MARTHA. IT'S GOT FLASH, AND IT'S **MINE.** I ALREADY STARTED WORKING ON IT!
WELL I GUESS YOU SHOULDN'T HAVE STAYED OUT ALL NIGHT.
WHAT DOES THAT HAVE TO DO WITH ANYTHING?
DAD SAID I COULD HAVE THE PUMPKIN, PROBABLY AS A WAY OF SHOWING YOU JUST HOW HOPPING MAD HE IS THAT YOU DIDN'T COME HOME.
DAD, DAD, HOPPIN' MAD!
HE'LL BE EVEN MADDER IF YOU GET YOUR FACES EATEN OFF, I'D BET!
WHICH IS WHAT'S GOING TO **HAPPEN** IF YOU DON'T GET **OUT** OF HERE. THE PUMPKINS WILL **EAT YOUR FACES OFF.**
WHAAH!
REAL NICE, JARVIS. I'M GOING TO TELL DAD HOW YOU TRIED TO RUIN THE FALL FESTIVAL FOR US BY BEING SCARY.
I'M **TRYING** TO SAVE YOUR FACES FROM GETTING EATEN RIGHT OFF YOUR HEADS, **PUMPKIN STEALER!**
JARVIS, **LOOK!**

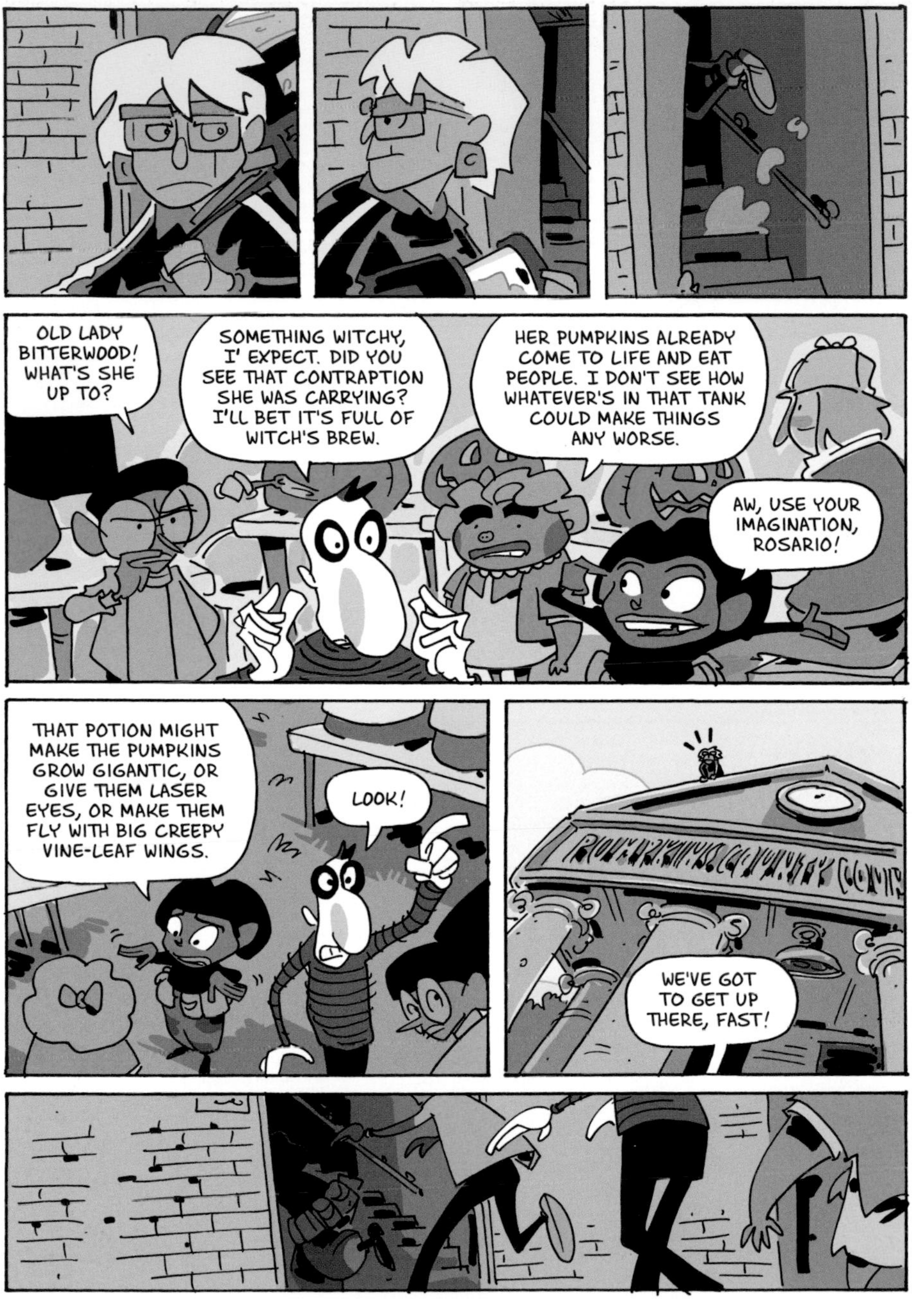
OLD LADY BITTERWOOD! WHAT'S SHE UP TO?
SOMETHING WITCHY, I' EXPECT. DID YOU SEE THAT CONTRAPTION SHE WAS CARRYING? I'LL BET IT'S FULL OF WITCH'S BREW.
HER PUMPKINS ALREADY COME TO LIFE AND EAT PEOPLE. I DON'T SEE HOW WHATEVER'S IN THAT TANK COULD MAKE THINGS ANY WORSE.
AW, USE YOUR IMAGINATION, ROSARIO!
THAT POTION MIGHT MAKE THE PUMPKINS GROW GIGANTIC, OR GIVE THEM LASER EYES, OR MAKE THEM FLY WITH BIG CREEPY VINE-LEAF WINGS.
LOOK!
WE'VE GOT TO GET UP THERE, FAST!

WHIRRRRRRRRRRR...?

WHAT IS THAT THING?

I DON'T KNOW, BUT I WANT ONE!

IT LOOKS LIKE SOMEBODY CROSSED A YARD SPRAYER WITH A LEAF BLOWER.

WHIRRRRRRACH VROMM

OOF!

ALL RIGHT...

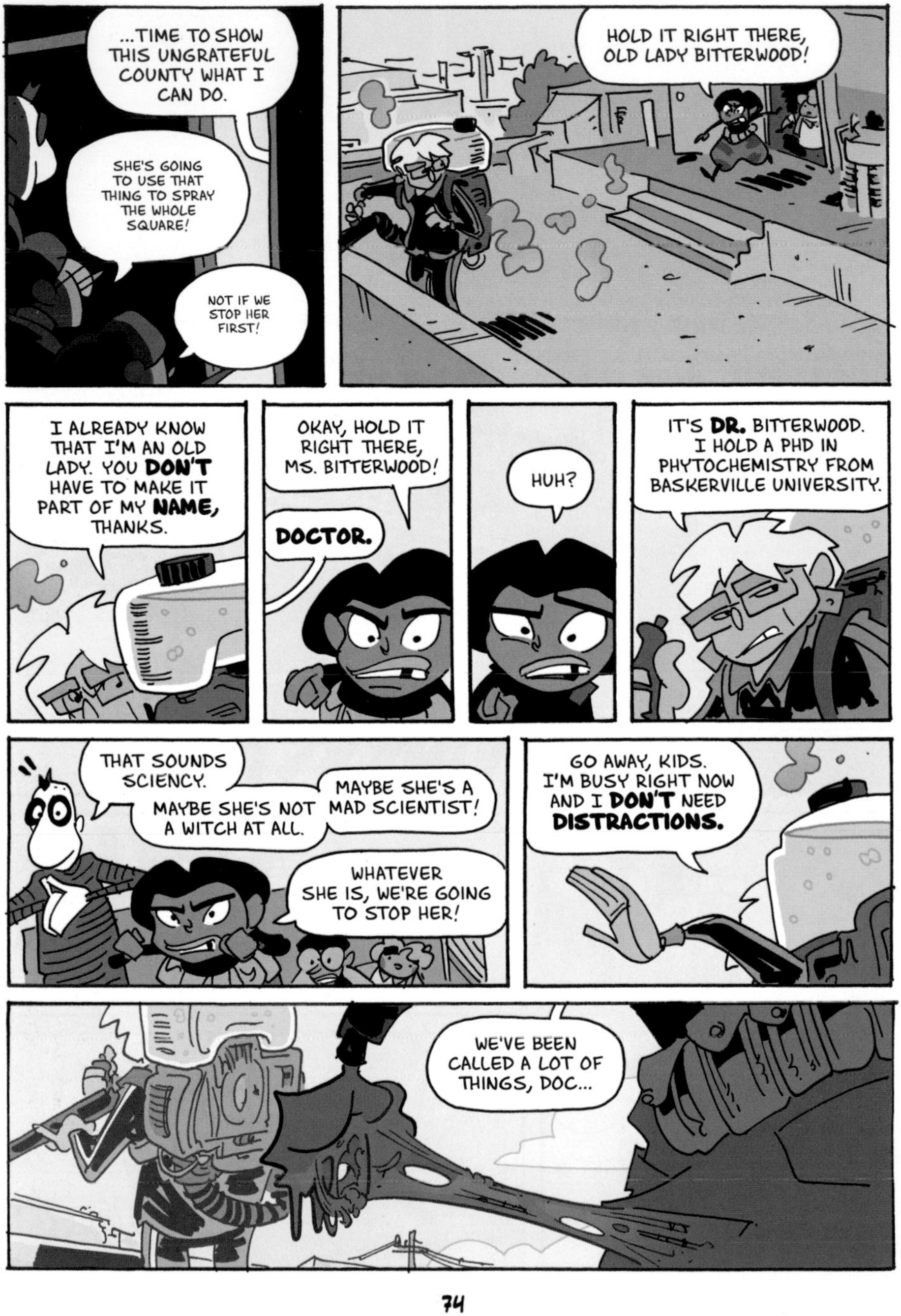
...TIME TO SHOW THIS UNGRATEFUL COUNTY WHAT I CAN DO.
SHE'S GOING TO USE THAT THING TO SPRAY THE WHOLE SQUARE!
NOT IF WE STOP HER FIRST!
HOLD IT RIGHT THERE, OLD LADY BITTERWOOD!
I ALREADY KNOW THAT I'M AN OLD LADY. YOU DON'T HAVE TO MAKE IT PART OF MY NAME, THANKS.
OKAY, HOLD IT RIGHT THERE, MS. BITTERWOOD!
DOCTOR.
HUH?
IT'S DR. BITTERWOOD. I HOLD A PHD IN PHYTOCHEMISTRY FROM BASKERVILLE UNIVERSITY.
THAT SOUNDS SCIENCY.
MAYBE SHE'S NOT A WITCH AT ALL.
MAYBE SHE'S A MAD SCIENTIST!
WHATEVER SHE IS, WE'RE GOING TO STOP HER!
GO AWAY, KIDS. I'M BUSY RIGHT NOW AND I DON'T NEED DISTRACTIONS.
WE'VE BEEN CALLED A LOT OF THINGS, DOC...

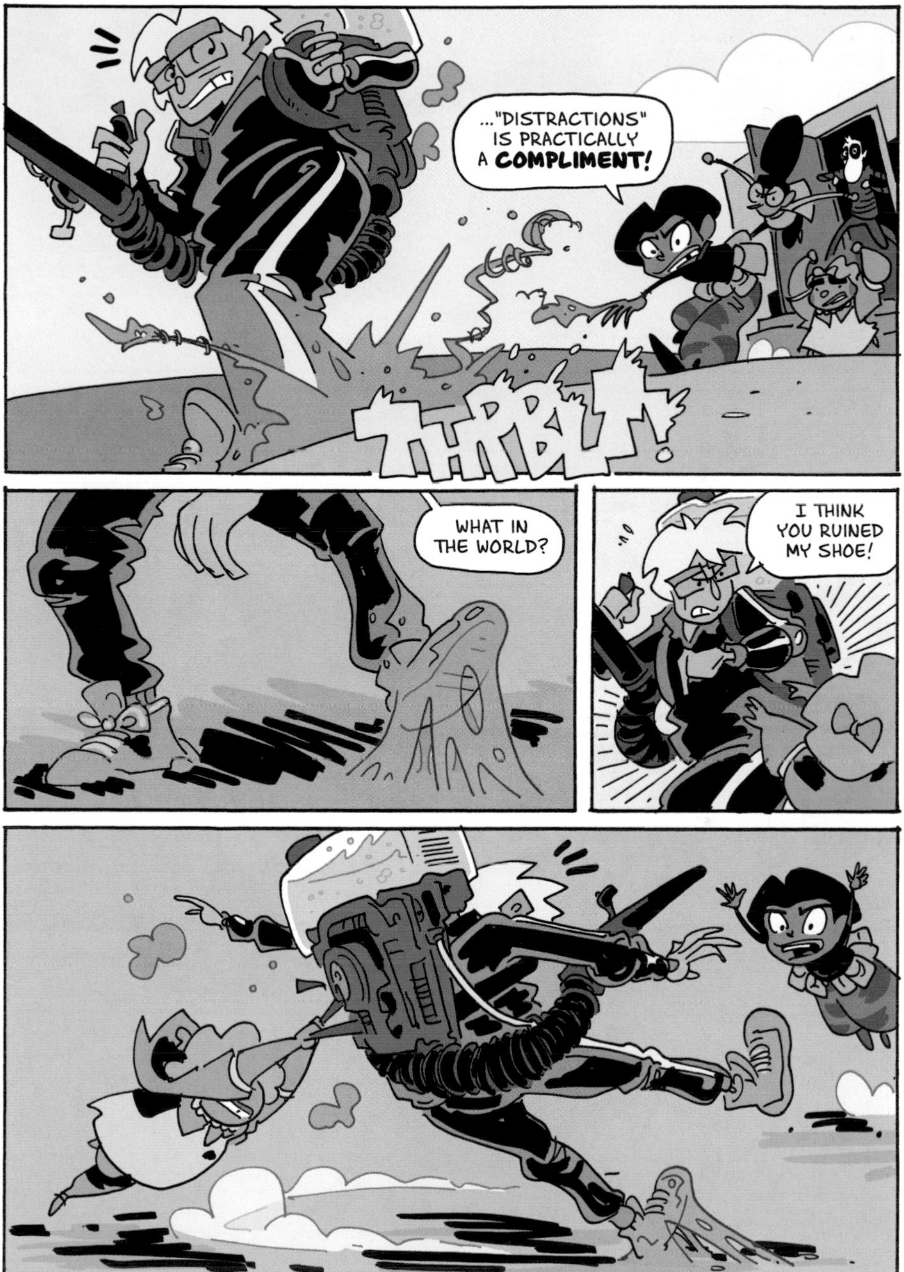
..."DISTRACTIONS" IS PRACTICALLY A **COMPLIMENT**!
THRBLT!
WHAT IN THE WORLD?
I THINK YOU RUINED MY SHOE!

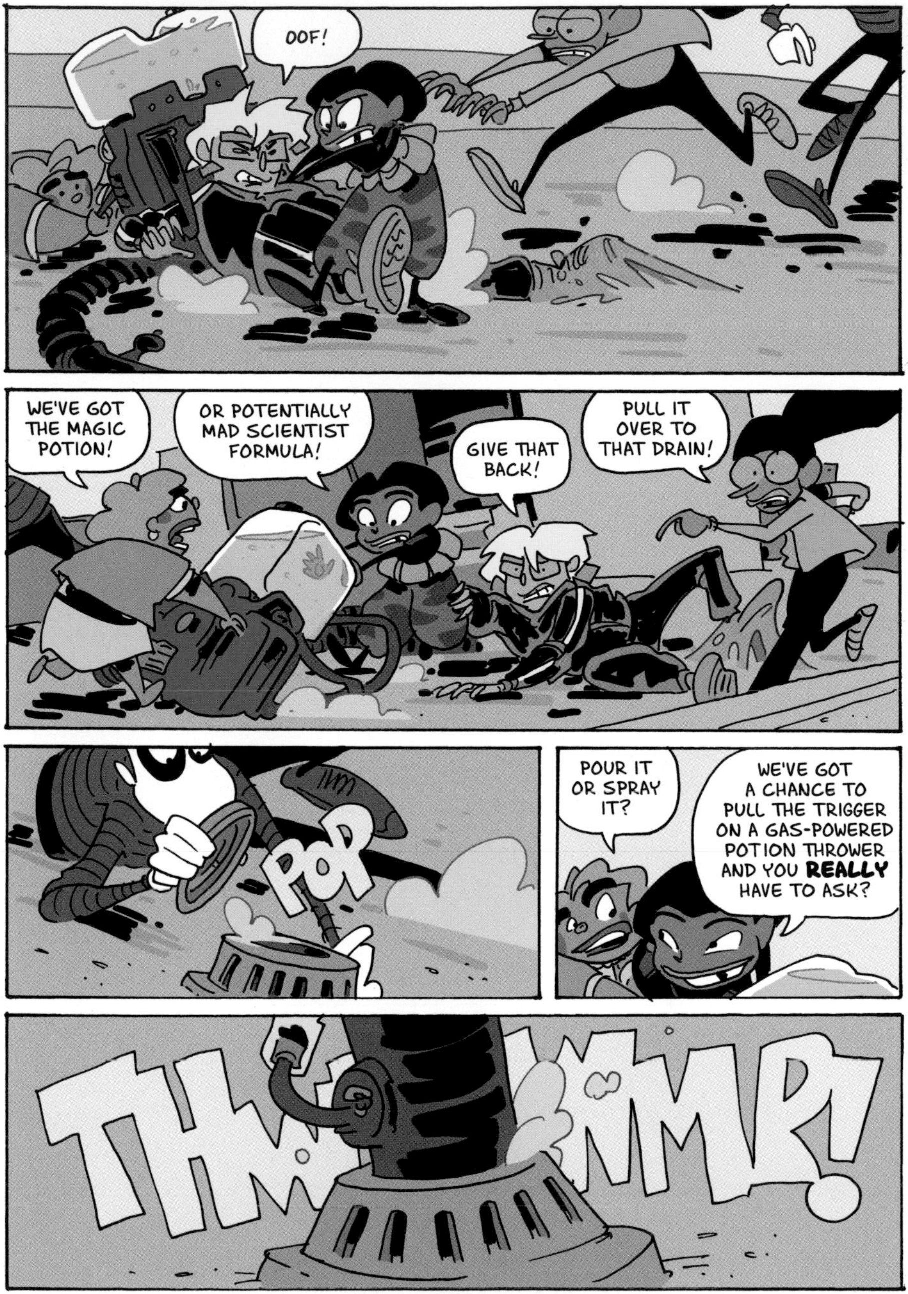
OOF!
WE'VE GOT THE MAGIC POTION!
OR POTENTIALLY MAD SCIENTIST FORMULA!
GIVE THAT BACK!
PULL IT OVER TO THAT DRAIN!
POP
POUR IT OR SPRAY IT?
WE'VE GOT A CHANCE TO PULL THE TRIGGER ON A GAS-POWERED POTION THROWER AND YOU **REALLY** HAVE TO ASK?
THWMMP!

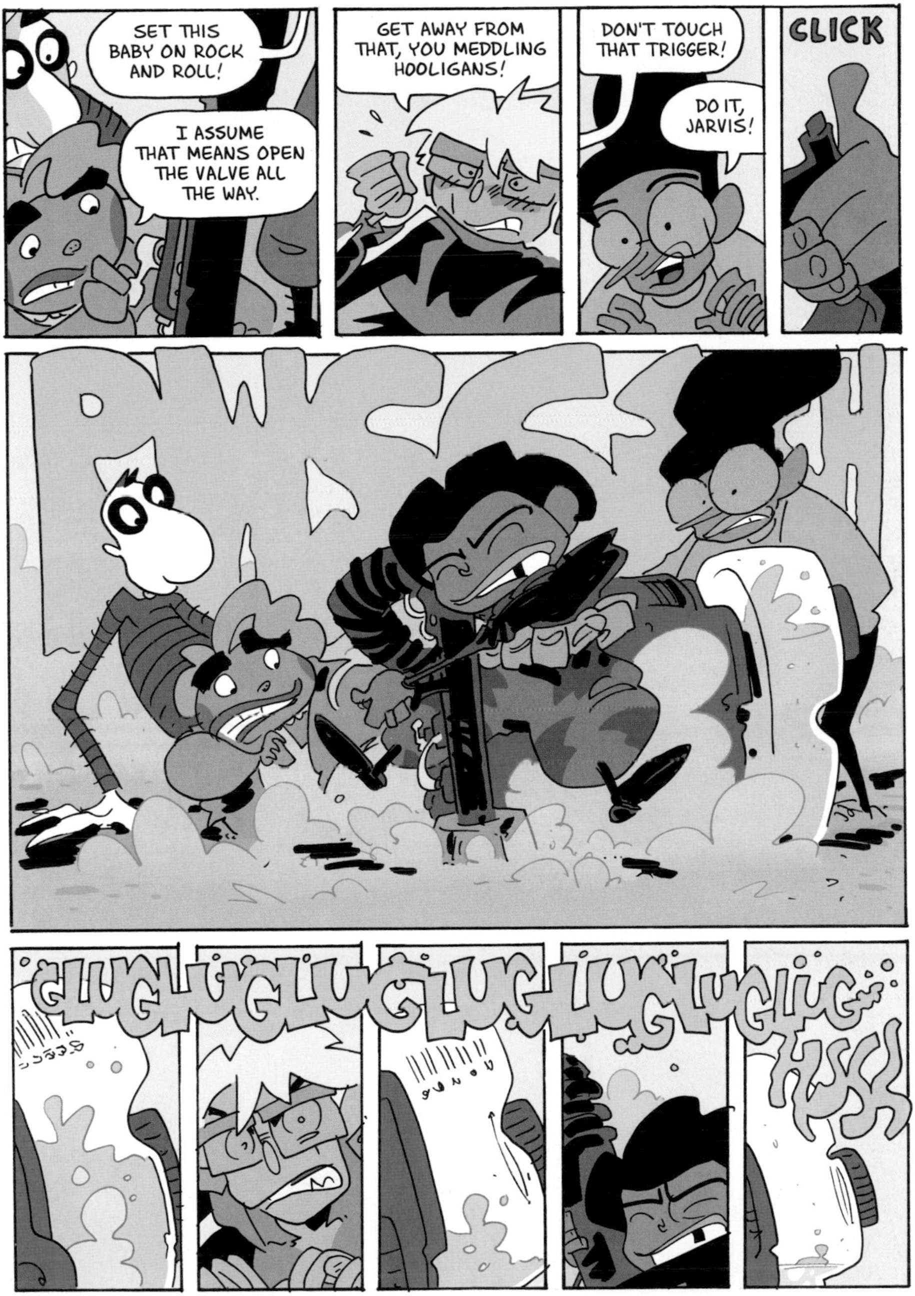
SET THIS BABY ON ROCK AND ROLL!
I ASSUME THAT MEANS OPEN THE VALVE ALL THE WAY.
GET AWAY FROM THAT, YOU MEDDLING HOOLIGANS!
DON'T TOUCH THAT TRIGGER!
DO IT, JARVIS!
CLICK
GLUGLUGLUGLUGLUGLUGLUGLUG
HSSS

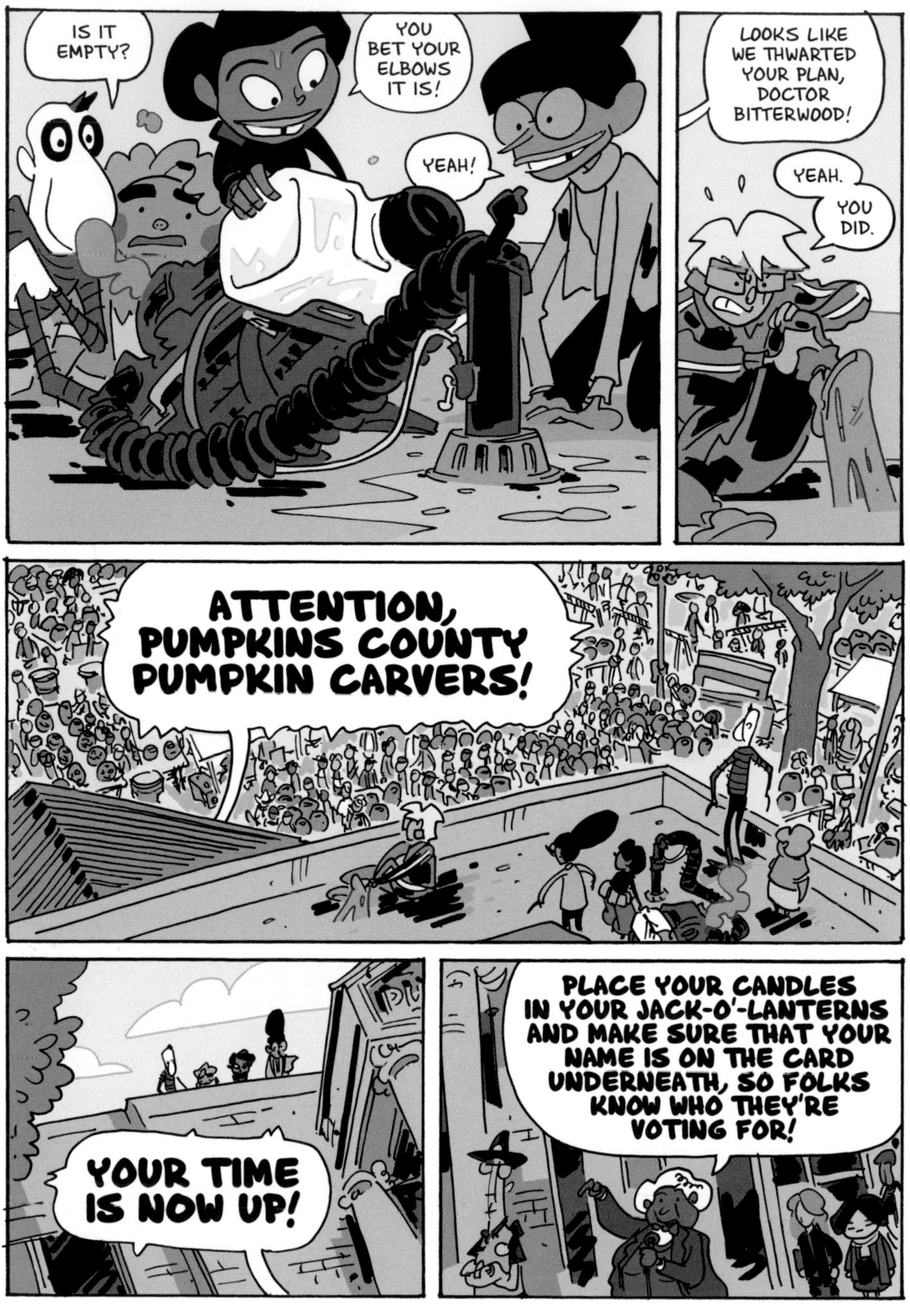
IS IT EMPTY?
YOU BET YOUR ELBOWS IT IS!
YEAH!
LOOKS LIKE WE THWARTED YOUR PLAN, DOCTOR BITTERWOOD!
YEAH.
YOU DID.
ATTENTION, PUMPKINS COUNTY PUMPKIN CARVERS!
YOUR TIME IS NOW UP!
PLACE YOUR CANDLES IN YOUR JACK-O'-LANTERNS AND MAKE SURE THAT YOUR NAME IS ON THE CARD UNDERNEATH, SO FOLKS KNOW WHO THEY'RE VOTING FOR!

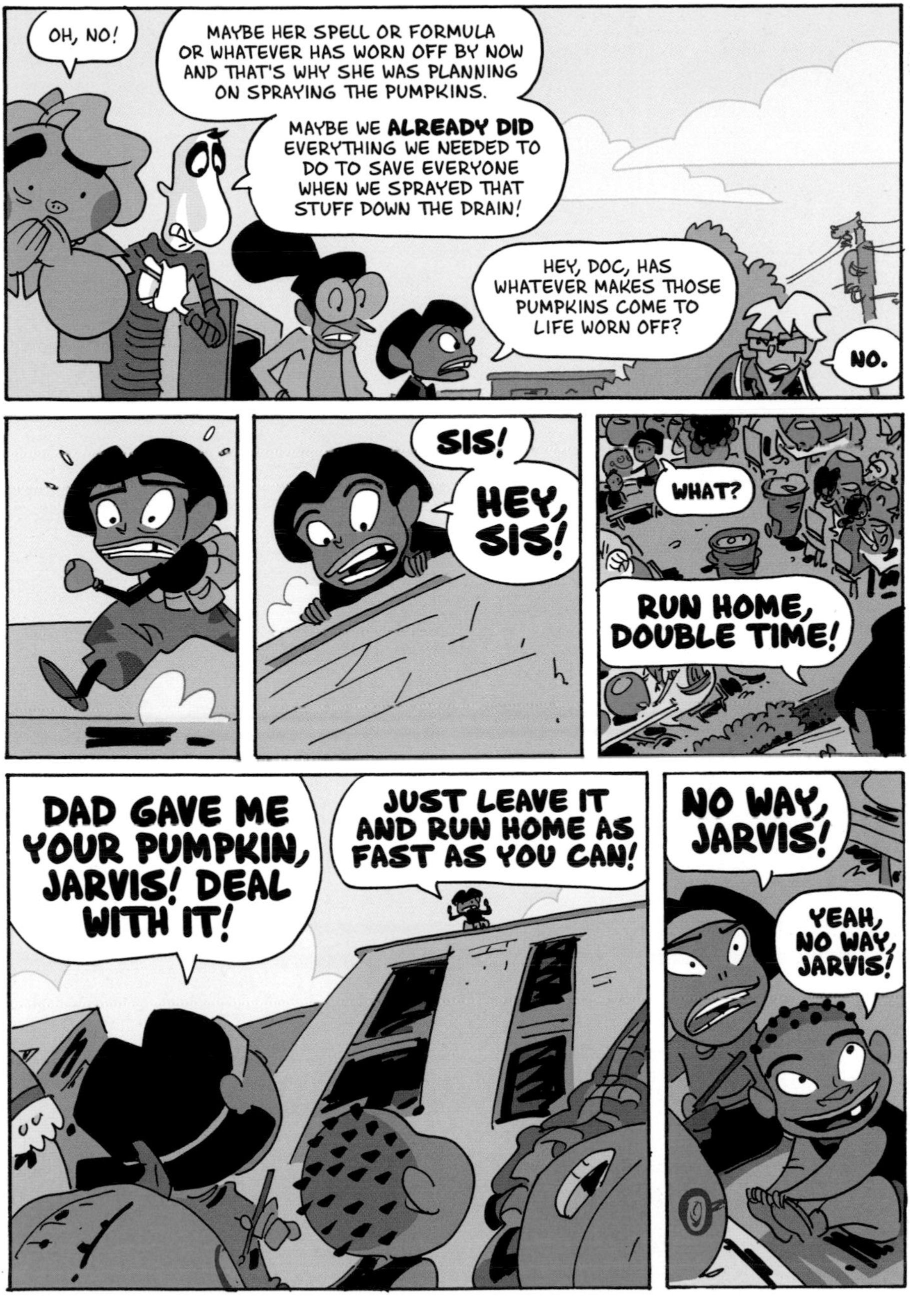
OH, NO!
MAYBE HER SPELL OR FORMULA OR WHATEVER HAS WORN OFF BY NOW AND THAT'S WHY SHE WAS PLANNING ON SPRAYING THE PUMPKINS.
MAYBE WE **ALREADY DID** EVERYTHING WE NEEDED TO DO TO SAVE EVERYONE WHEN WE SPRAYED THAT STUFF DOWN THE DRAIN!
HEY, DOC, HAS WHATEVER MAKES THOSE PUMPKINS COME TO LIFE WORN OFF?
NO.
SIS!
HEY, SIS!
WHAT?
RUN HOME, DOUBLE TIME!
DAD GAVE ME YOUR PUMPKIN, JARVIS! DEAL WITH IT!
JUST LEAVE IT AND RUN HOME AS FAST AS YOU CAN!
NO WAY, JARVIS!
YEAH, NO WAY, JARVIS!

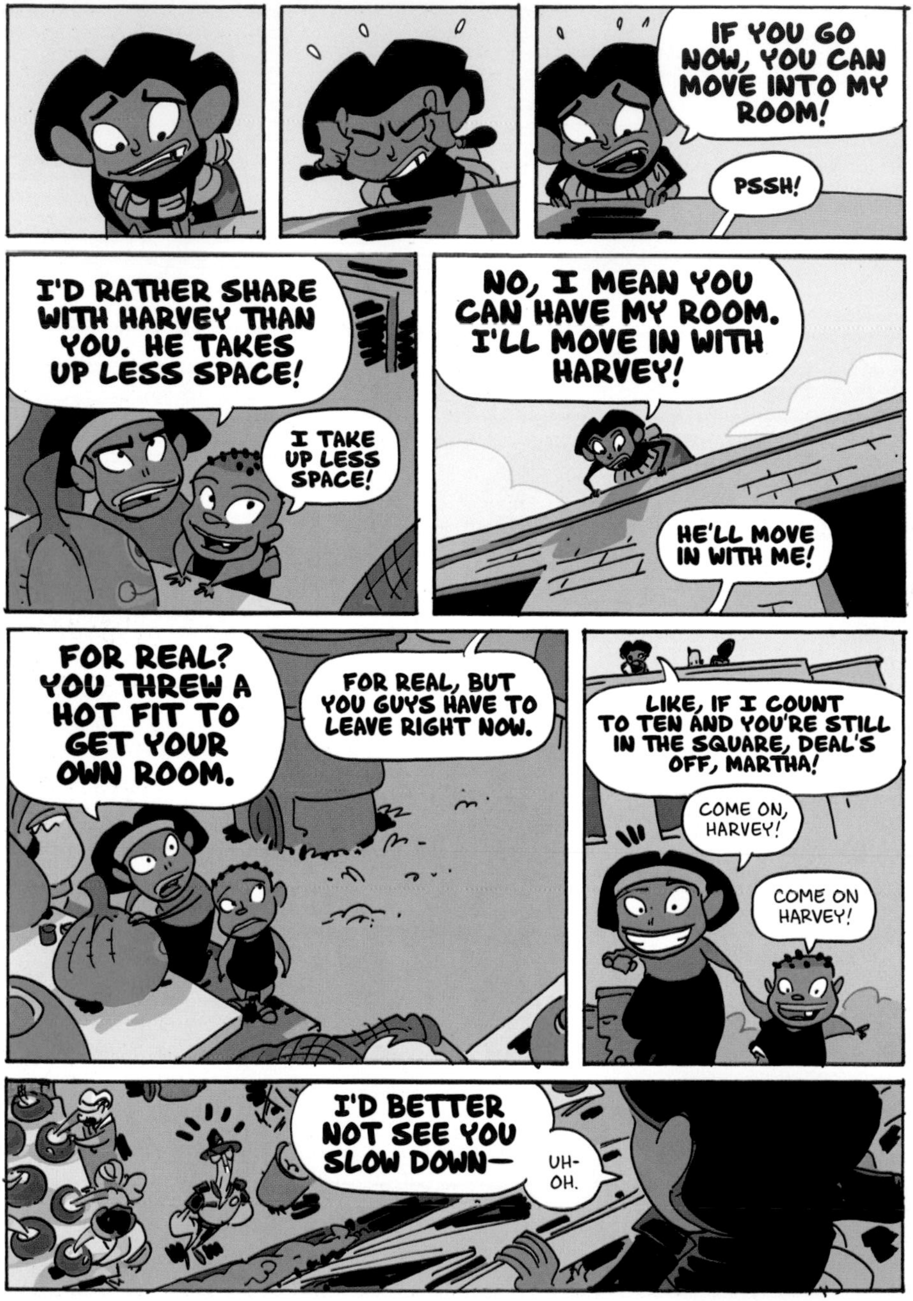
IF YOU GO NOW, YOU CAN MOVE INTO MY ROOM!
PSSH!
I'D RATHER SHARE WITH HARVEY THAN YOU. HE TAKES UP LESS SPACE!
I TAKE UP LESS SPACE!
NO, I MEAN YOU CAN HAVE MY ROOM. I'LL MOVE IN WITH HARVEY!
HE'LL MOVE IN WITH ME!
FOR REAL? YOU THREW A HOT FIT TO GET YOUR OWN ROOM.
FOR REAL, BUT YOU GUYS HAVE TO LEAVE RIGHT NOW.
LIKE, IF I COUNT TO TEN AND YOU'RE STILL IN THE SQUARE, DEAL'S OFF, MARTHA!
COME ON, HARVEY!
COME ON HARVEY!
I'D BETTER NOT SEE YOU SLOW DOWN—
UH-OH.

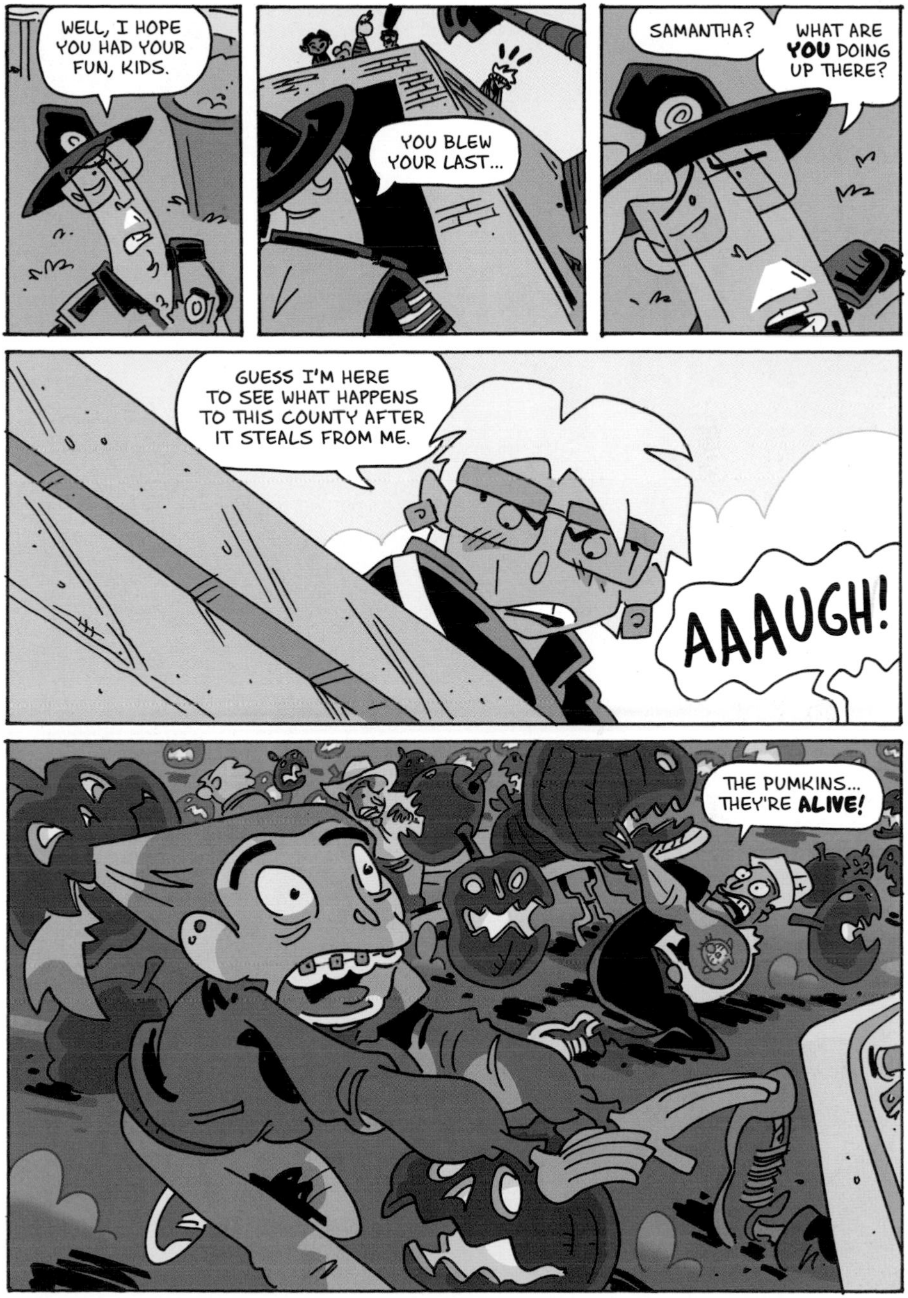
WELL, I HOPE YOU HAD YOUR FUN, KIDS.
YOU BLEW YOUR LAST...
SAMANTHA?
WHAT ARE **YOU** DOING UP THERE?
GUESS I'M HERE TO SEE WHAT HAPPENS TO THIS COUNTY AFTER IT STEALS FROM ME.
AAAUGH!
THE PUMKINS... THEY'RE **ALIVE!**

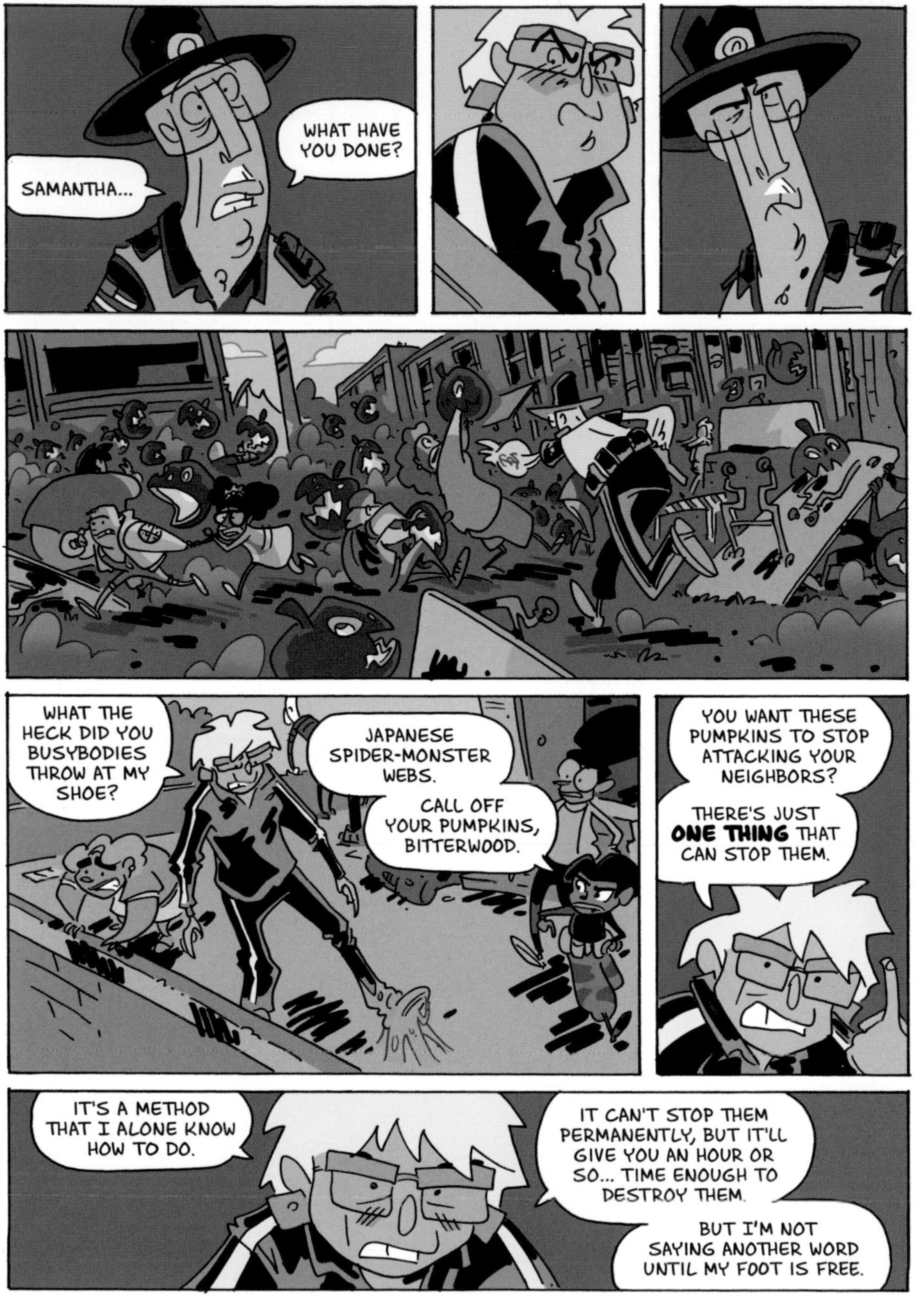
SAMANTHA...
WHAT HAVE YOU DONE?
WHAT THE HECK DID YOU BUSYBODIES THROW AT MY SHOE?
JAPANESE SPIDER-MONSTER WEBS.
CALL OFF YOUR PUMPKINS, BITTERWOOD.
YOU WANT THESE PUMPKINS TO STOP ATTACKING YOUR NEIGHBORS?
THERE'S JUST **ONE THING** THAT CAN STOP THEM.
IT'S A METHOD THAT I ALONE KNOW HOW TO DO.
IT CAN'T STOP THEM PERMANENTLY, BUT IT'LL GIVE YOU AN HOUR OR SO... TIME ENOUGH TO DESTROY THEM.
BUT I'M NOT SAYING ANOTHER WORD UNTIL MY FOOT IS FREE.

TRY THE LACES.

THIS ISN'T BUDGING.

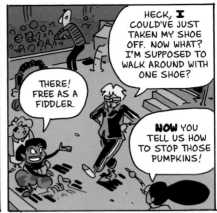

HECK, **I** COULD'VE JUST TAKEN MY SHOE OFF. NOW WHAT? I'M SUPPOSED TO WALK AROUND WITH ONE SHOE?

THERE! FREE AS A FIDDLER.

NOW YOU TELL US HOW TO STOP THOSE PUMPKINS!

THERE'S A **MAGIC POTION** THAT I KNOW HOW TO BREW.

MAGIC POTION? I KNEW IT! SHE **IS** A WITCH!

SAY SOMETHING ABOUT IT, SKINNY MISTER, AND SEE WHAT HAPPENS.

THIS POTION — HOW LONG DOES IT TAKE TO MAKE?

WE'RE NOT DOING MUCH GOOD HERE ON THE ROOF.

LET'S DO THE TALKING WHILE WE'RE WALKING, HUH?

THE POTION DOESN'T TAKE VERY LONG TO MAKE, BUT IT **DOES** REQUIRE SOME INCREDIBLY RARE, TOUGH-TO-FIND INGREDIENTS.

I'VE HAD THE FORESIGHT TO SPEND THE LAST **THIRTY YEARS** COLLECTING THOSE INGREDIENTS. I'M PROUD TO SAY THAT I WAS ABLE TO GET MY HANDS ON ALL OF THEM.

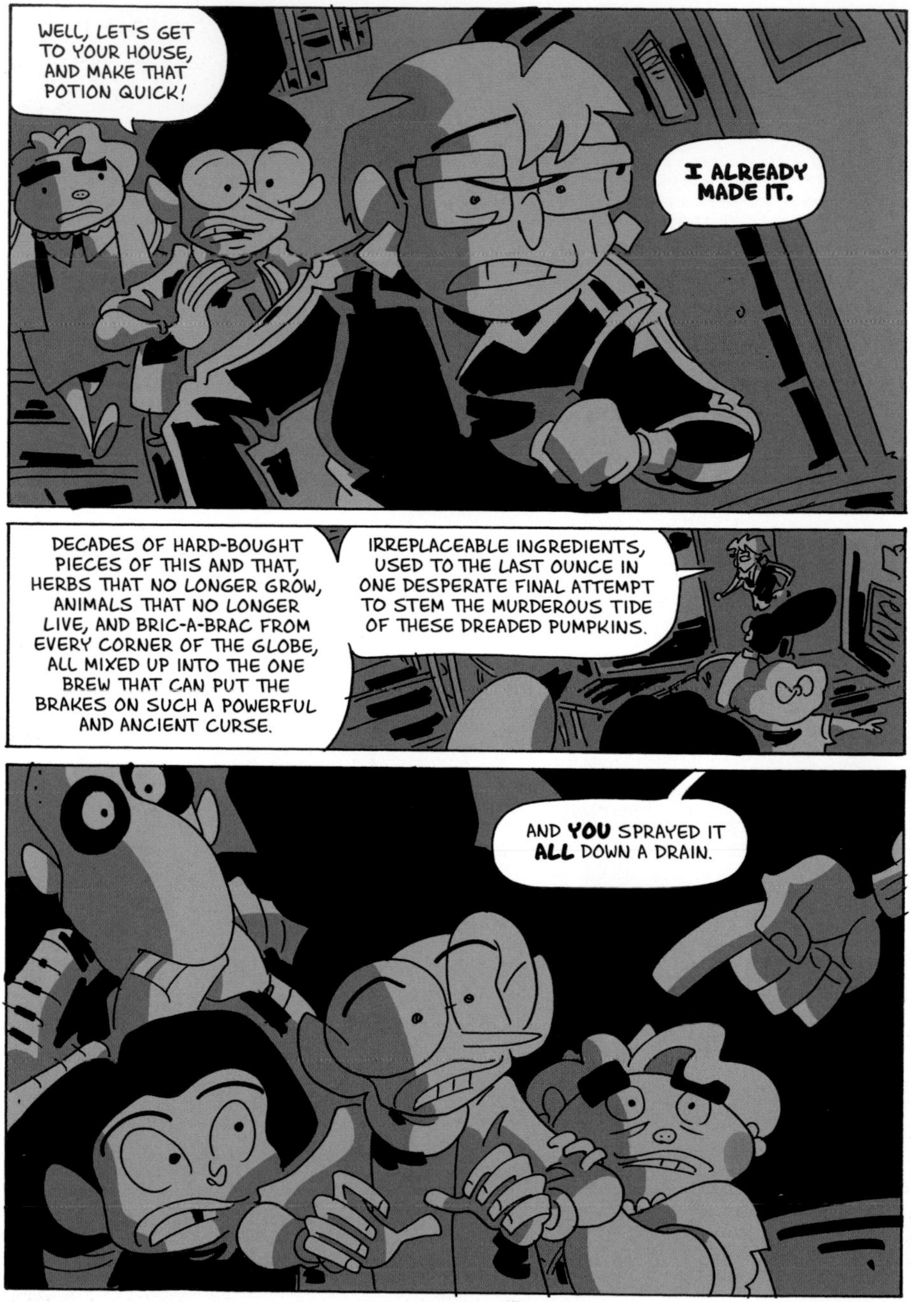
WELL, LET'S GET TO YOUR HOUSE, AND MAKE THAT POTION QUICK!
I ALREADY MADE IT.
DECADES OF HARD-BOUGHT PIECES OF THIS AND THAT, HERBS THAT NO LONGER GROW, ANIMALS THAT NO LONGER LIVE, AND BRIC-A-BRAC FROM EVERY CORNER OF THE GLOBE, ALL MIXED UP INTO THE ONE BREW THAT CAN PUT THE BRAKES ON SUCH A POWERFUL AND ANCIENT CURSE.
IRREPLACEABLE INGREDIENTS, USED TO THE LAST OUNCE IN ONE DESPERATE FINAL ATTEMPT TO STEM THE MURDEROUS TIDE OF THESE DREADED PUMPKINS.
AND **YOU** SPRAYED IT **ALL** DOWN A DRAIN.

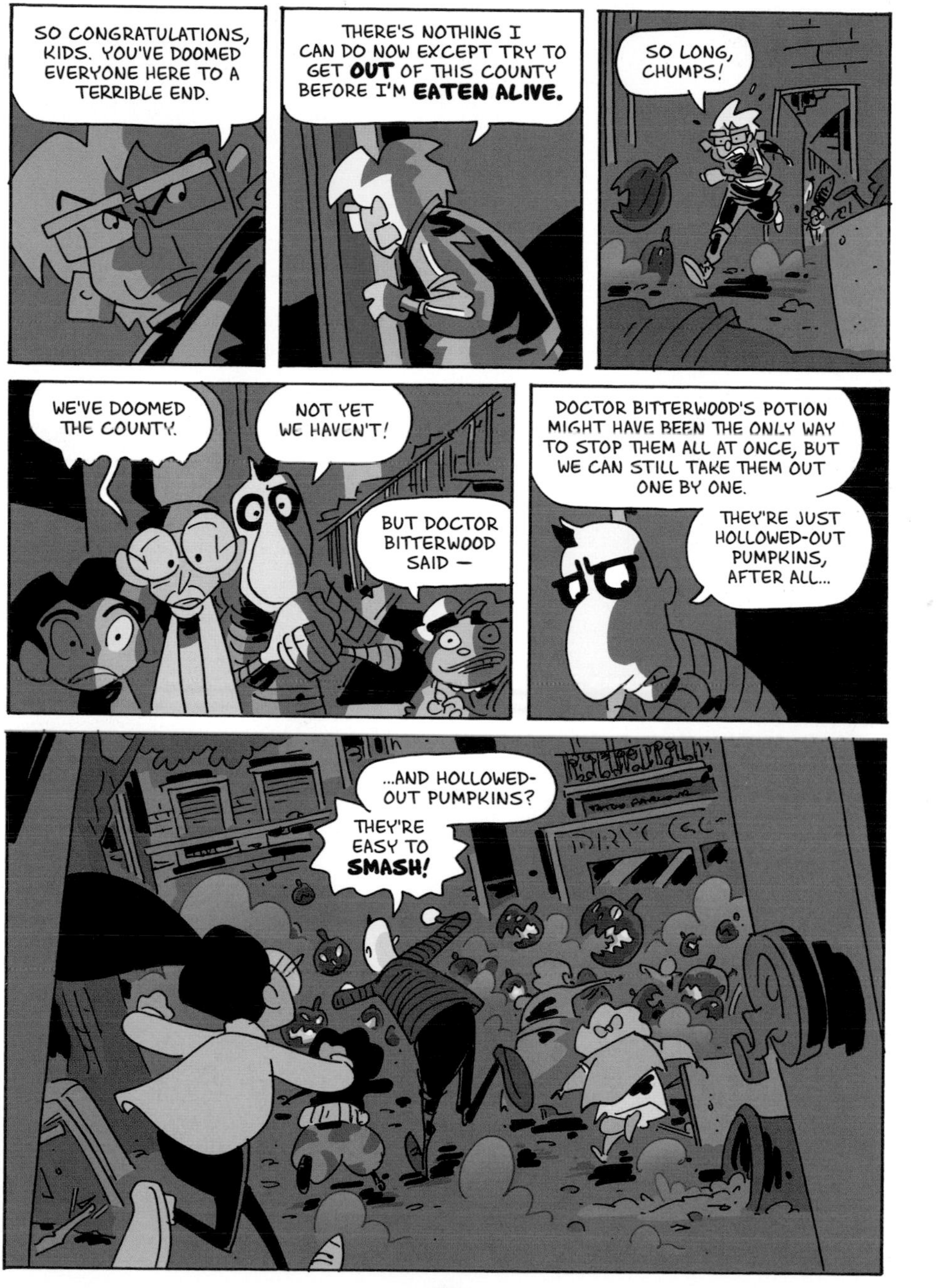
SO CONGRATULATIONS, KIDS. YOU'VE DOOMED EVERYONE HERE TO A TERRIBLE END.
THERE'S NOTHING I CAN DO NOW EXCEPT TRY TO GET **OUT** OF THIS COUNTY BEFORE I'M **EATEN ALIVE.**
SO LONG, CHUMPS!
WE'VE DOOMED THE COUNTY.
NOT YET WE HAVEN'T!
BUT DOCTOR BITTERWOOD SAID —
DOCTOR BITTERWOOD'S POTION MIGHT HAVE BEEN THE ONLY WAY TO STOP THEM ALL AT ONCE, BUT WE CAN STILL TAKE THEM OUT ONE BY ONE.
THEY'RE JUST HOLLOWED-OUT PUMPKINS, AFTER ALL...
...AND HOLLOWED-OUT PUMPKINS?
THEY'RE EASY TO **SMASH!**

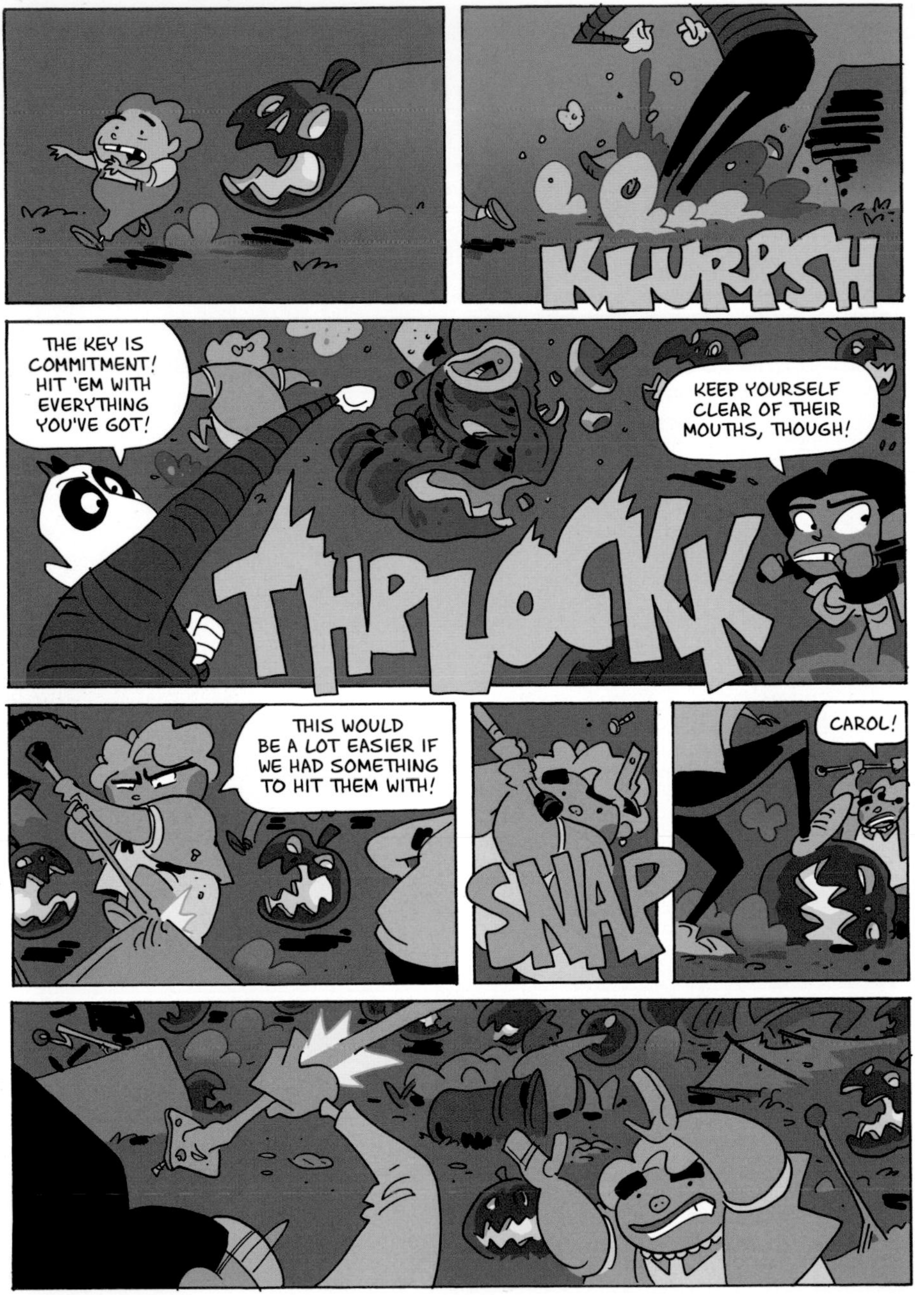
KLURPSH
THE KEY IS COMMITMENT! HIT 'EM WITH EVERYTHING YOU'VE GOT!
KEEP YOURSELF CLEAR OF THEIR MOUTHS, THOUGH!
THPLOCKK
THIS WOULD BE A LOT EASIER IF WE HAD SOMETHING TO HIT THEM WITH!
SNAP
CAROL!

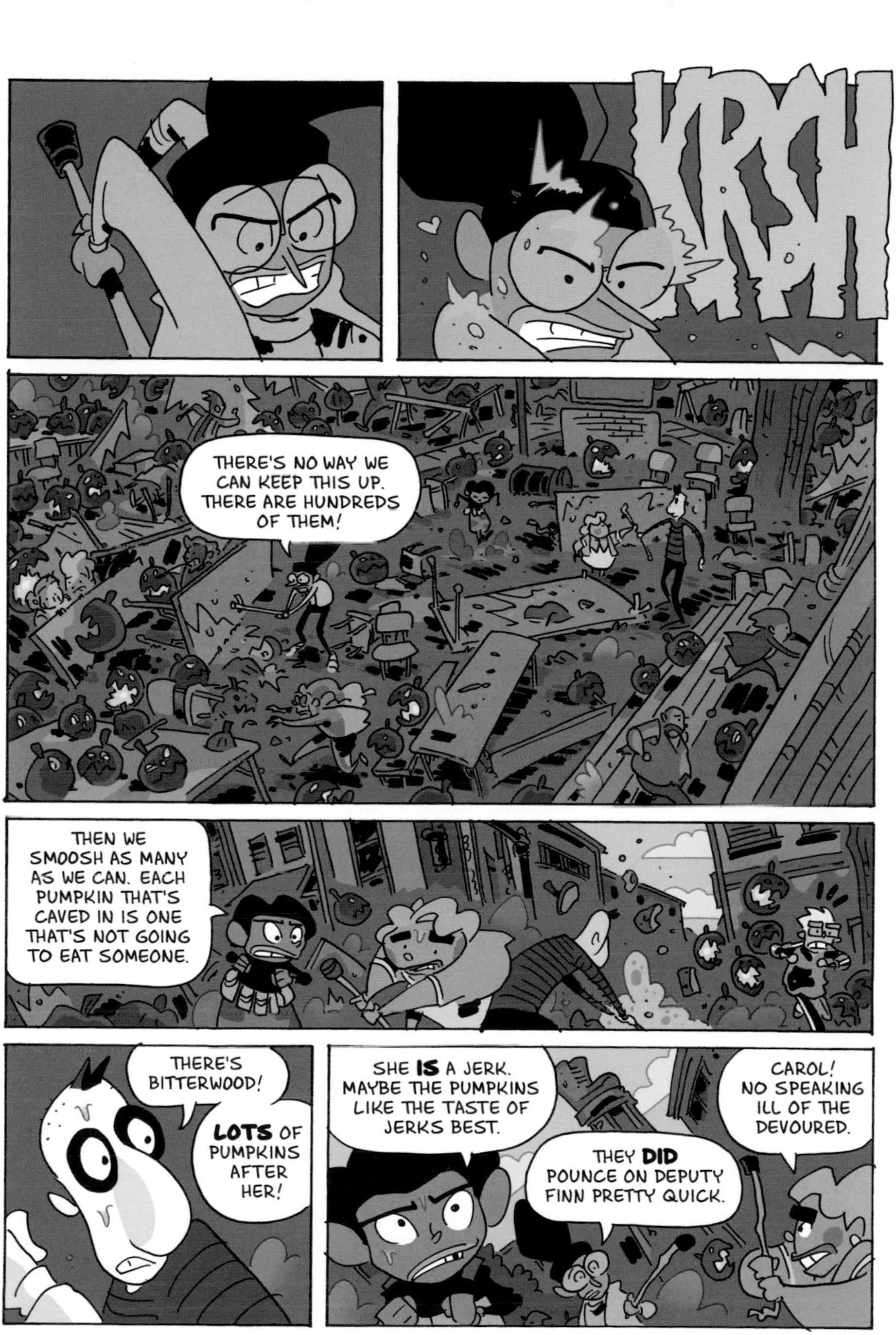
KRSH
THERE'S NO WAY WE CAN KEEP THIS UP. THERE ARE HUNDREDS OF THEM!
THEN WE SMOOSH AS MANY AS WE CAN. EACH PUMPKIN THAT'S CAVED IN IS ONE THAT'S NOT GOING TO EAT SOMEONE.
THERE'S BITTERWOOD!
LOTS OF PUMPKINS AFTER HER!
SHE IS A JERK. MAYBE THE PUMPKINS LIKE THE TASTE OF JERKS BEST.
CAROL! NO SPEAKING ILL OF THE DEVOURED.
THEY DID POUNCE ON DEPUTY FINN PRETTY QUICK.

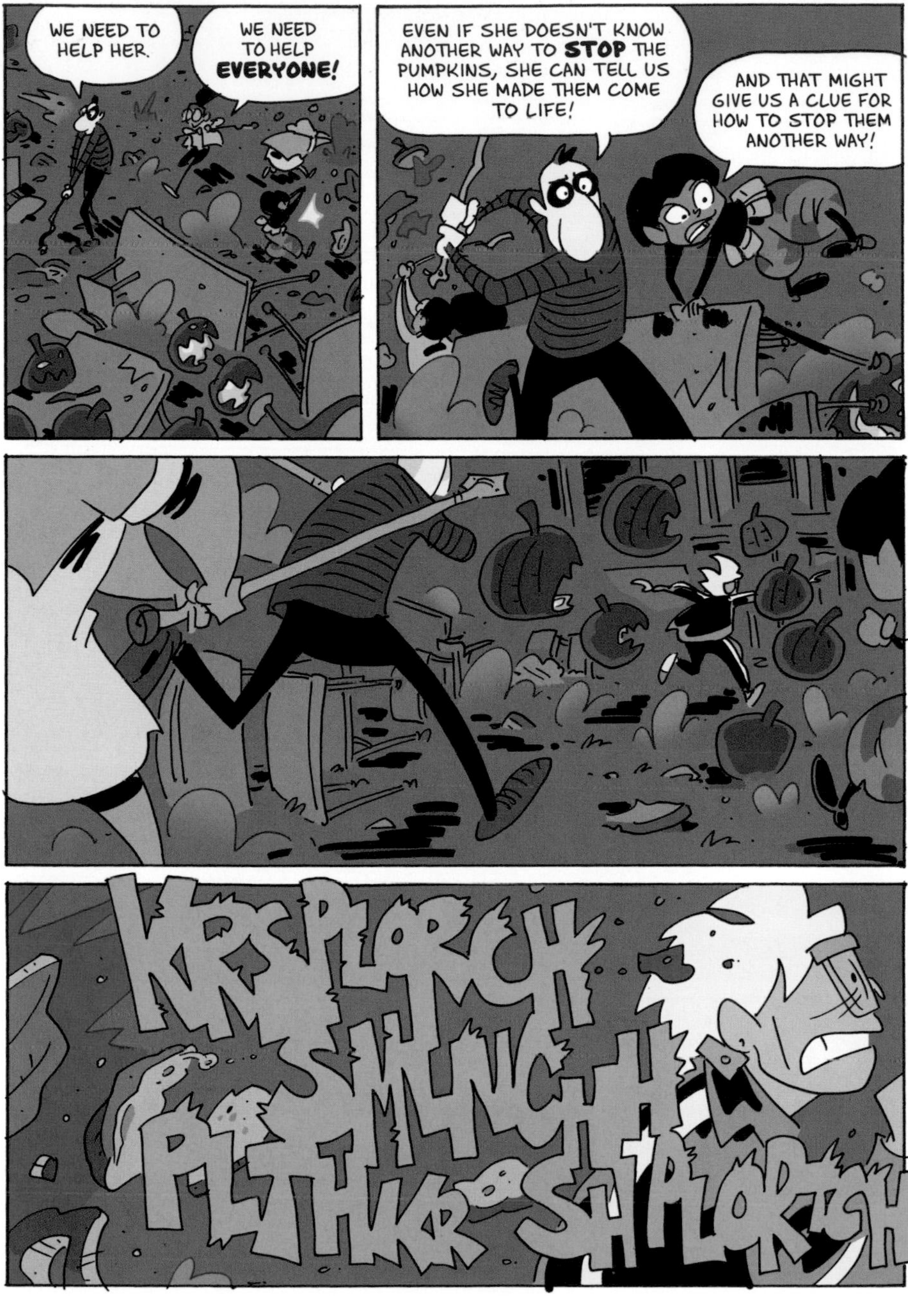
WE NEED TO HELP HER.
WE NEED TO HELP EVERYONE!
EVEN IF SHE DOESN'T KNOW ANOTHER WAY TO STOP THE PUMPKINS, SHE CAN TELL US HOW SHE MADE THEM COME TO LIFE!
AND THAT MIGHT GIVE US A CLUE FOR HOW TO STOP THEM ANOTHER WAY!
KRSPLORCH
SMUNCH
PLTHUKR
SHPLORCH

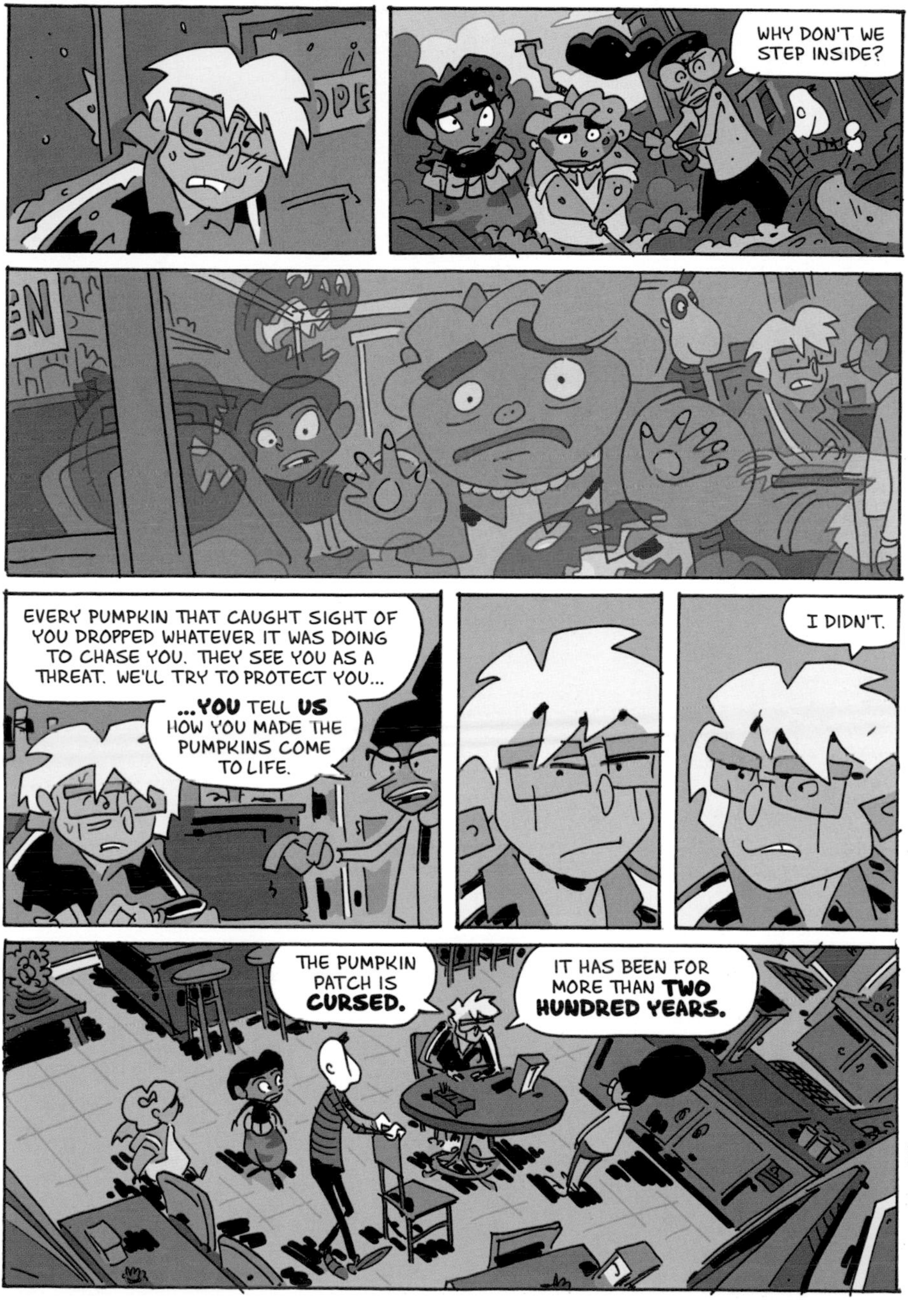
WHY DON'T WE STEP INSIDE?
EVERY PUMPKIN THAT CAUGHT SIGHT OF YOU DROPPED WHATEVER IT WAS DOING TO CHASE YOU. THEY SEE YOU AS A THREAT. WE'LL TRY TO PROTECT YOU...
...YOU TELL US HOW YOU MADE THE PUMPKINS COME TO LIFE.
I DIDN'T.
THE PUMPKIN PATCH IS CURSED.
IT HAS BEEN FOR MORE THAN TWO HUNDRED YEARS.

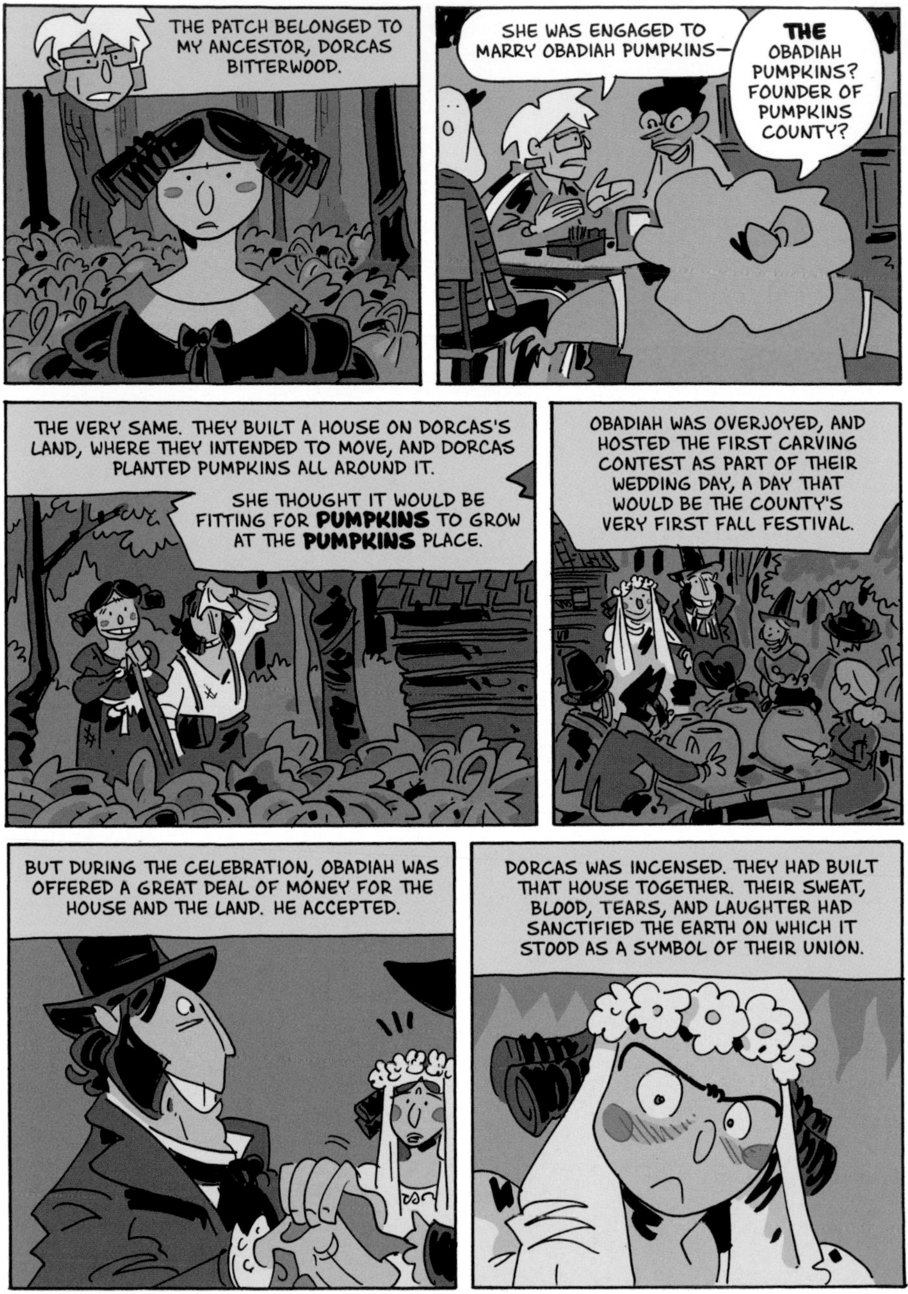

THE PATCH BELONGED TO MY ANCESTOR, DORCAS BITTERWOOD.
SHE WAS ENGAGED TO MARRY OBADIAH PUMPKINS—
THE OBADIAH PUMPKINS? FOUNDER OF PUMPKINS COUNTY?
THE VERY SAME. THEY BUILT A HOUSE ON DORCAS'S LAND, WHERE THEY INTENDED TO MOVE, AND DORCAS PLANTED PUMPKINS ALL AROUND IT.
SHE THOUGHT IT WOULD BE FITTING FOR PUMPKINS TO GROW AT THE PUMPKINS PLACE.
OBADIAH WAS OVERJOYED, AND HOSTED THE FIRST CARVING CONTEST AS PART OF THEIR WEDDING DAY, A DAY THAT WOULD BE THE COUNTY'S VERY FIRST FALL FESTIVAL.
BUT DURING THE CELEBRATION, OBADIAH WAS OFFERED A GREAT DEAL OF MONEY FOR THE HOUSE AND THE LAND. HE ACCEPTED.
DORCAS WAS INCENSED. THEY HAD BUILT THAT HOUSE TOGETHER. THEIR SWEAT, BLOOD, TEARS, AND LAUGHTER HAD SANCTIFIED THE EARTH ON WHICH IT STOOD AS A SYMBOL OF THEIR UNION.

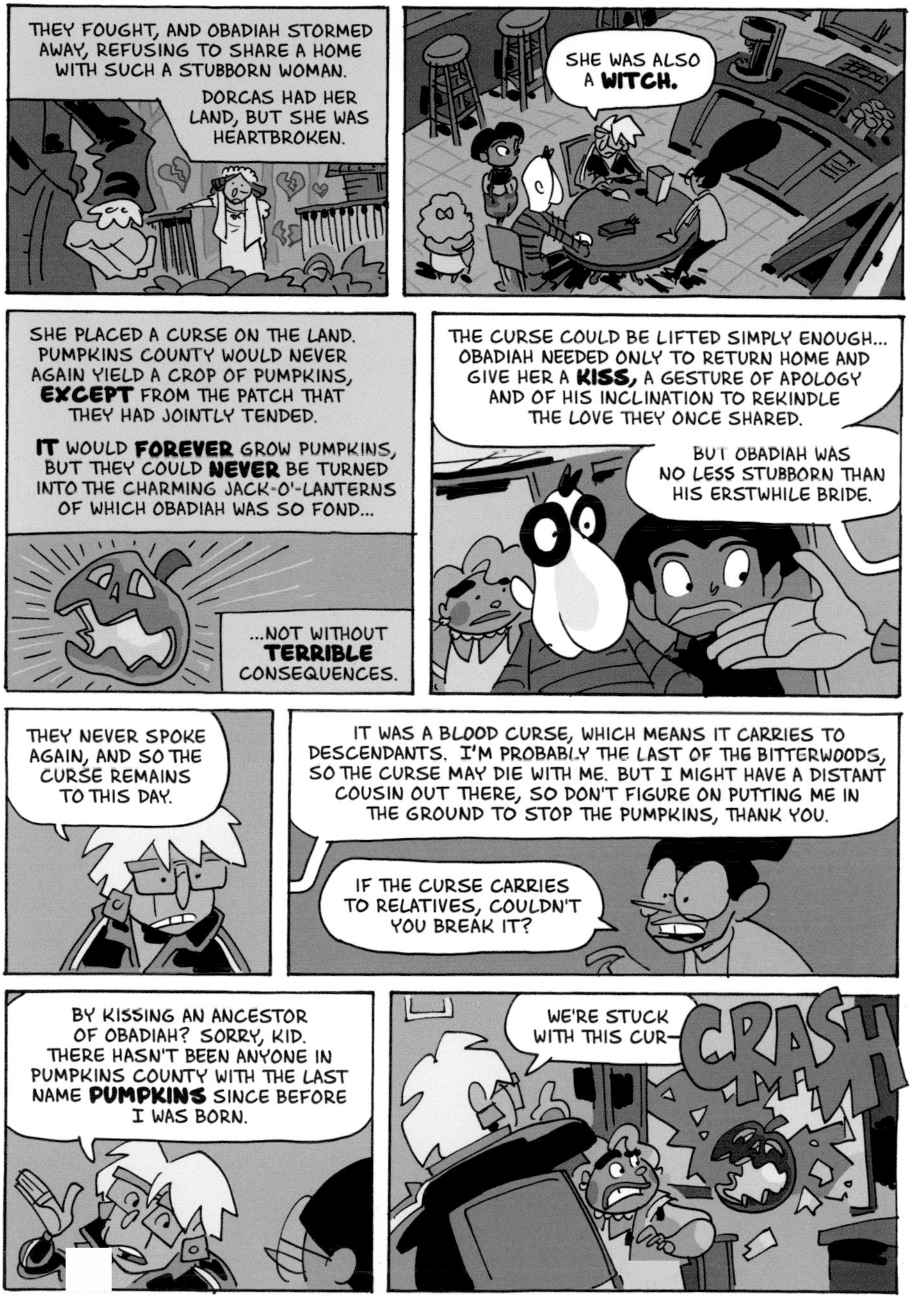
THEY FOUGHT, AND OBADIAH STORMED AWAY, REFUSING TO SHARE A HOME WITH SUCH A STUBBORN WOMAN.
DORCAS HAD HER LAND, BUT SHE WAS HEARTBROKEN.
SHE WAS ALSO A WITCH.
SHE PLACED A CURSE ON THE LAND. PUMPKINS COUNTY WOULD NEVER AGAIN YIELD A CROP OF PUMPKINS, EXCEPT FROM THE PATCH THAT THEY HAD JOINTLY TENDED.
IT WOULD FOREVER GROW PUMPKINS, BUT THEY COULD NEVER BE TURNED INTO THE CHARMING JACK-O'-LANTERNS OF WHICH OBADIAH WAS SO FOND...
...NOT WITHOUT TERRIBLE CONSEQUENCES.
THE CURSE COULD BE LIFTED SIMPLY ENOUGH... OBADIAH NEEDED ONLY TO RETURN HOME AND GIVE HER A KISS, A GESTURE OF APOLOGY AND OF HIS INCLINATION TO REKINDLE THE LOVE THEY ONCE SHARED.
BUT OBADIAH WAS NO LESS STUBBORN THAN HIS ERSTWHILE BRIDE.
THEY NEVER SPOKE AGAIN, AND SO THE CURSE REMAINS TO THIS DAY.
IT WAS A BLOOD CURSE, WHICH MEANS IT CARRIES TO DESCENDANTS. I'M PROBABLY THE LAST OF THE BITTERWOODS, SO THE CURSE MAY DIE WITH ME. BUT I MIGHT HAVE A DISTANT COUSIN OUT THERE, SO DON'T FIGURE ON PUTTING ME IN THE GROUND TO STOP THE PUMPKINS, THANK YOU.
IF THE CURSE CARRIES TO RELATIVES, COULDN'T YOU BREAK IT?
BY KISSING AN ANCESTOR OF OBADIAH? SORRY, KID. THERE HASN'T BEEN ANYONE IN PUMPKINS COUNTY WITH THE LAST NAME PUMPKINS SINCE BEFORE I WAS BORN.
WE'RE STUCK WITH THIS CUR—
CRASH

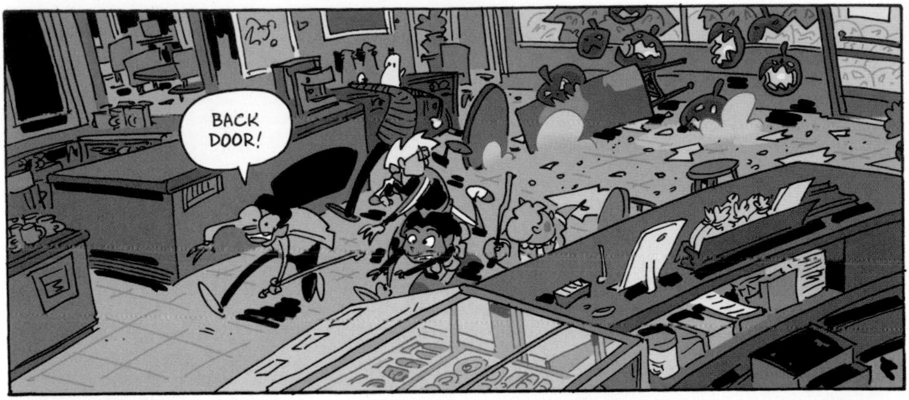
BACK DOOR!

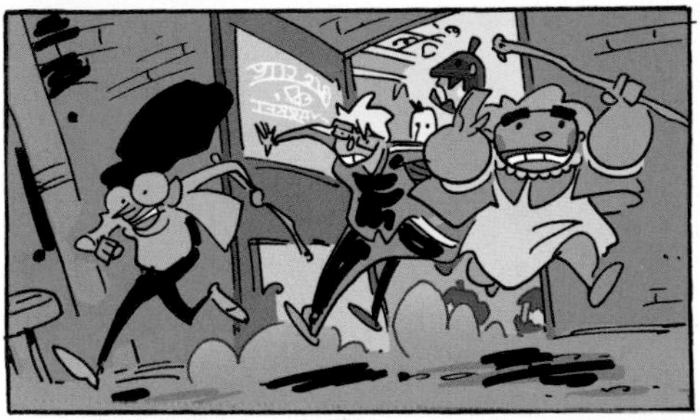

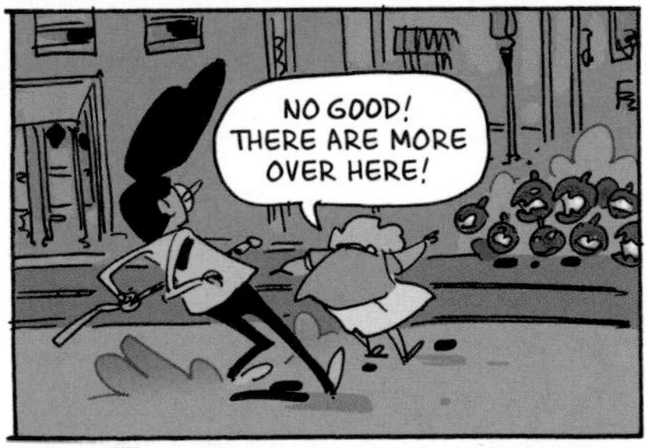
NO GOOD! THERE ARE MORE OVER HERE!

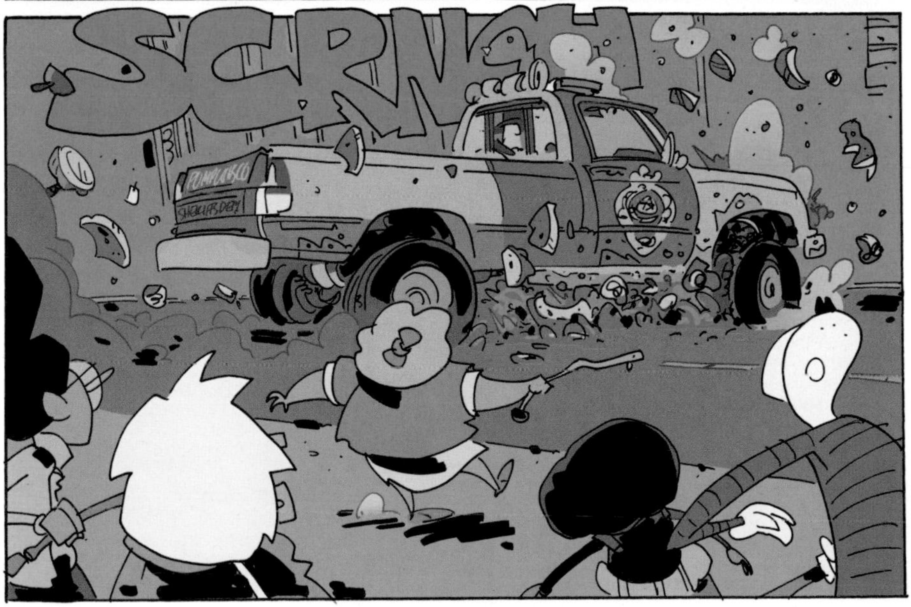
SCRNCH

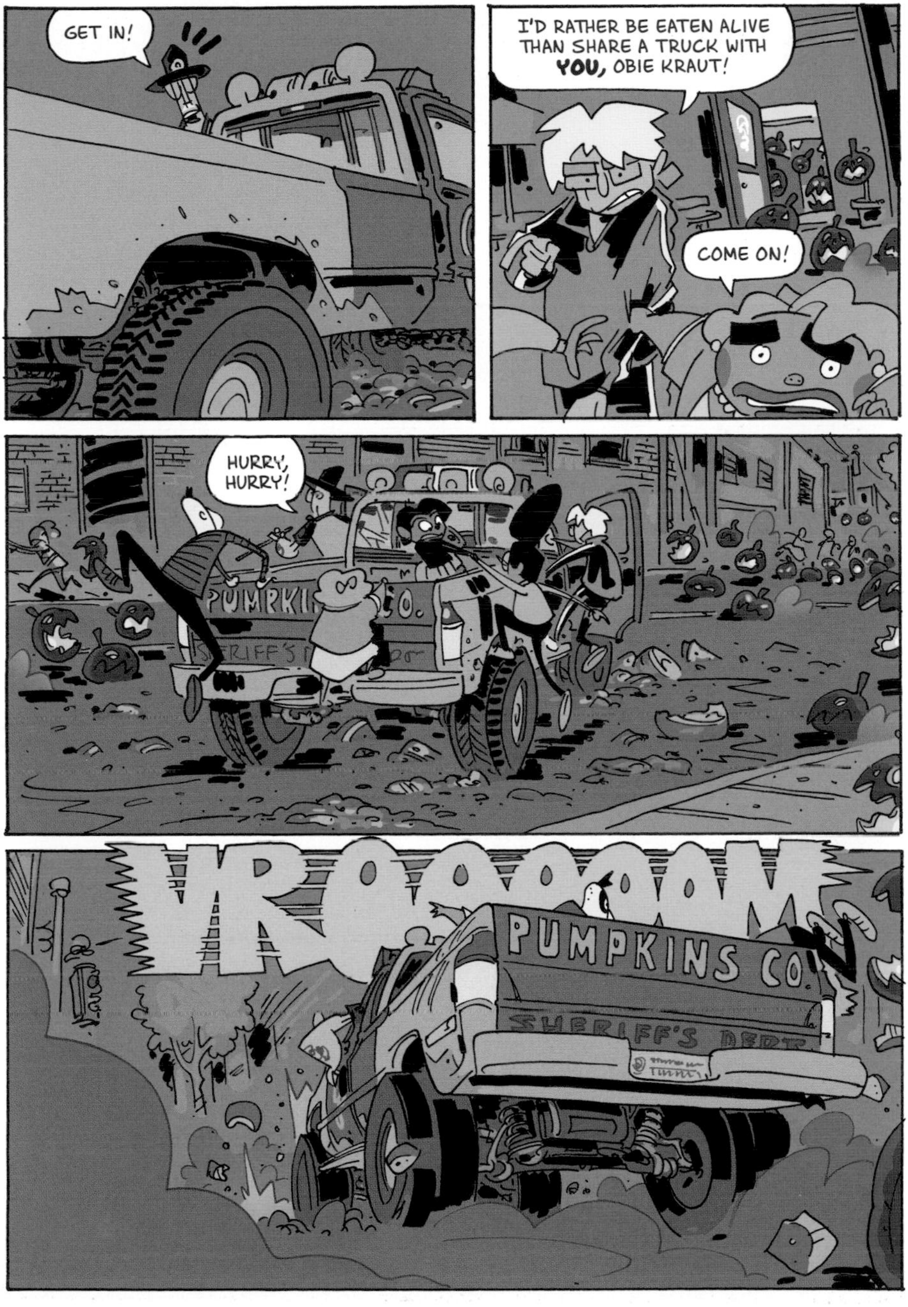
GET IN!
I'D RATHER BE EATEN ALIVE THAN SHARE A TRUCK WITH **YOU,** OBIE KRAUT!
COME ON!
HURRY, HURRY!
PUMPKINS CO.
VROOOOOM
PUMPKINS CO.
SHERIFF'S DEPT.

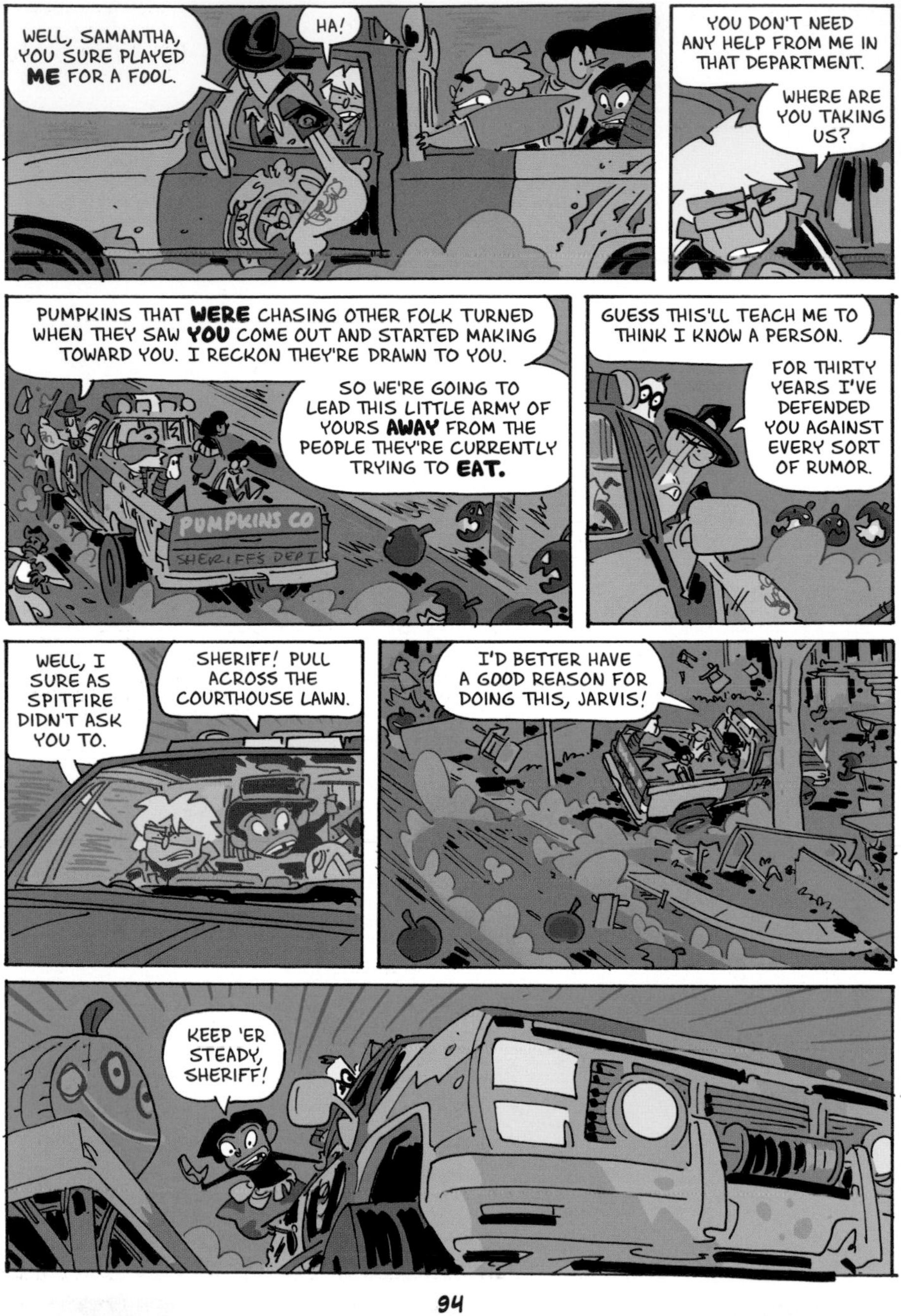

WELL, SAMANTHA, YOU SURE PLAYED **ME** FOR A FOOL.
HA!
YOU DON'T NEED ANY HELP FROM ME IN THAT DEPARTMENT.
WHERE ARE YOU TAKING US?
PUMPKINS THAT **WERE** CHASING OTHER FOLK TURNED WHEN THEY SAW **YOU** COME OUT AND STARTED MAKING TOWARD YOU. I RECKON THEY'RE DRAWN TO YOU.
SO WE'RE GOING TO LEAD THIS LITTLE ARMY OF YOURS **AWAY** FROM THE PEOPLE THEY'RE CURRENTLY TRYING TO **EAT.**
PUMPKINS CO
SHERIFF'S DEPT
GUESS THIS'LL TEACH ME TO THINK I KNOW A PERSON.
FOR THIRTY YEARS I'VE DEFENDED YOU AGAINST EVERY SORT OF RUMOR.
WELL, I SURE AS SPITFIRE DIDN'T ASK YOU TO.
SHERIFF! PULL ACROSS THE COURTHOUSE LAWN.
I'D BETTER HAVE A GOOD REASON FOR DOING THIS, JARVIS!
KEEP 'ER STEADY, SHERIFF!

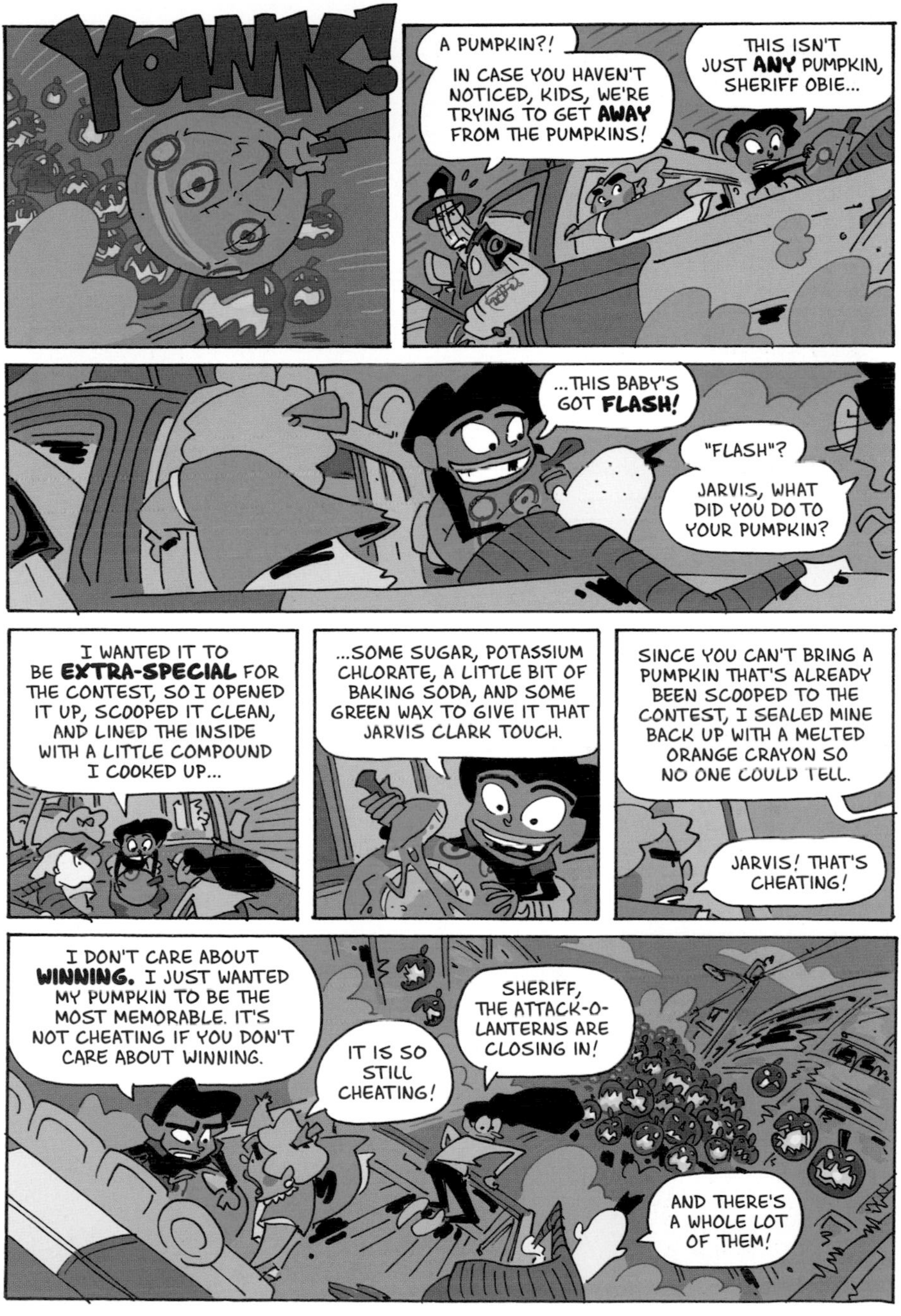
YOINK!
A PUMPKIN?!
IN CASE YOU HAVEN'T NOTICED, KIDS, WE'RE TRYING TO GET **AWAY** FROM THE PUMPKINS!
THIS ISN'T JUST **ANY** PUMPKIN, SHERIFF OBIE...
...THIS BABY'S GOT **FLASH!**
"FLASH"?
JARVIS, WHAT DID YOU DO TO YOUR PUMPKIN?
I WANTED IT TO BE **EXTRA-SPECIAL** FOR THE CONTEST, SO I OPENED IT UP, SCOOPED IT CLEAN, AND LINED THE INSIDE WITH A LITTLE COMPOUND I COOKED UP...
...SOME SUGAR, POTASSIUM CHLORATE, A LITTLE BIT OF BAKING SODA, AND SOME GREEN WAX TO GIVE IT THAT JARVIS CLARK TOUCH.
SINCE YOU CAN'T BRING A PUMPKIN THAT'S ALREADY BEEN SCOOPED TO THE CONTEST, I SEALED MINE BACK UP WITH A MELTED ORANGE CRAYON SO NO ONE COULD TELL.
JARVIS! THAT'S CHEATING!
I DON'T CARE ABOUT **WINNING.** I JUST WANTED MY PUMPKIN TO BE THE MOST MEMORABLE. IT'S NOT CHEATING IF YOU DON'T CARE ABOUT WINNING.
IT IS SO STILL CHEATING!
SHERIFF, THE ATTACK-O-LANTERNS ARE CLOSING IN!
AND THERE'S A WHOLE LOT OF THEM!

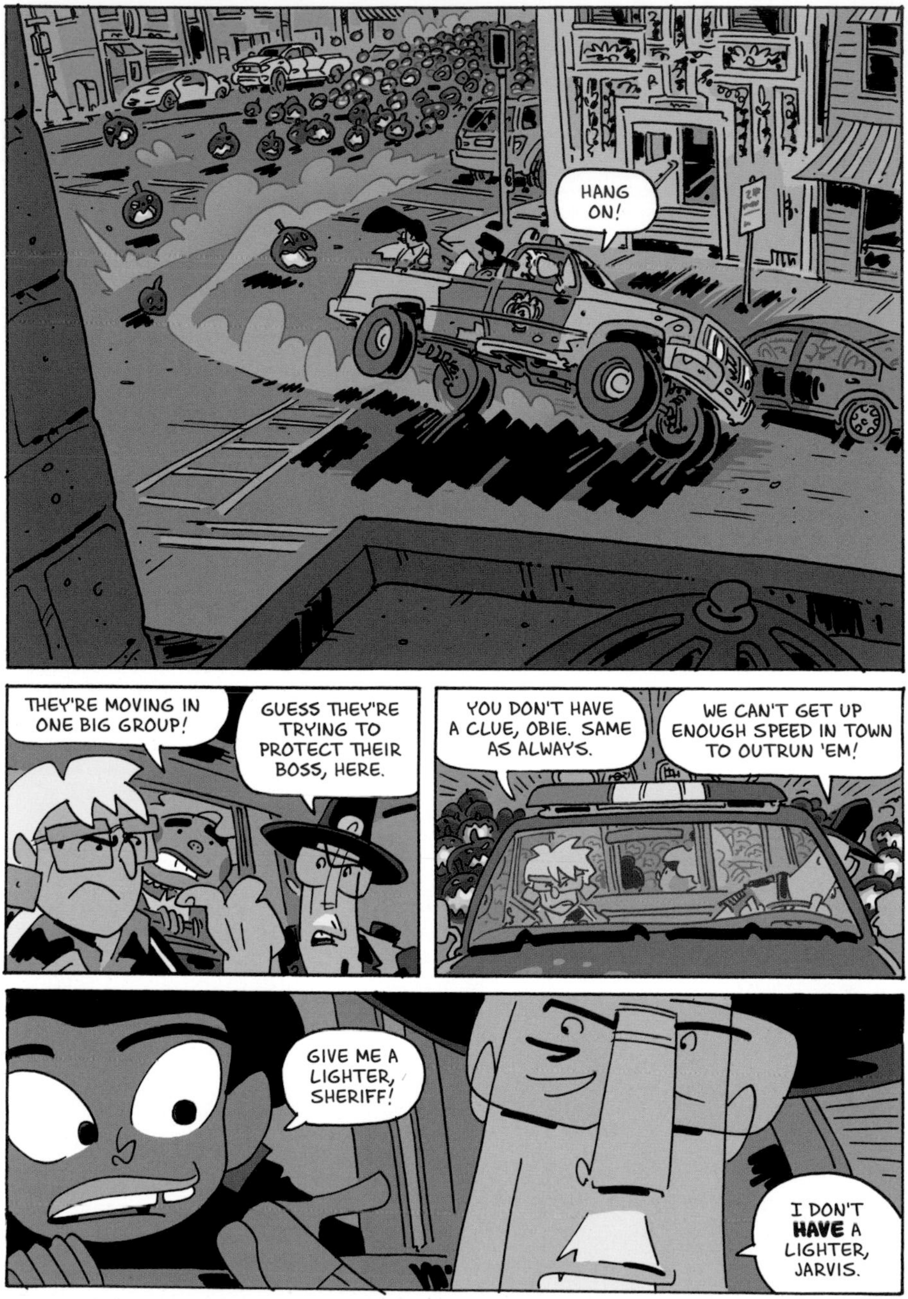
HANG ON!
THEY'RE MOVING IN ONE BIG GROUP!
GUESS THEY'RE TRYING TO PROTECT THEIR BOSS, HERE.
YOU DON'T HAVE A CLUE, OBIE. SAME AS ALWAYS.
WE CAN'T GET UP ENOUGH SPEED IN TOWN TO OUTRUN 'EM!
GIVE ME A LIGHTER, SHERIFF!
I DON'T **HAVE** A LIGHTER, JARVIS.

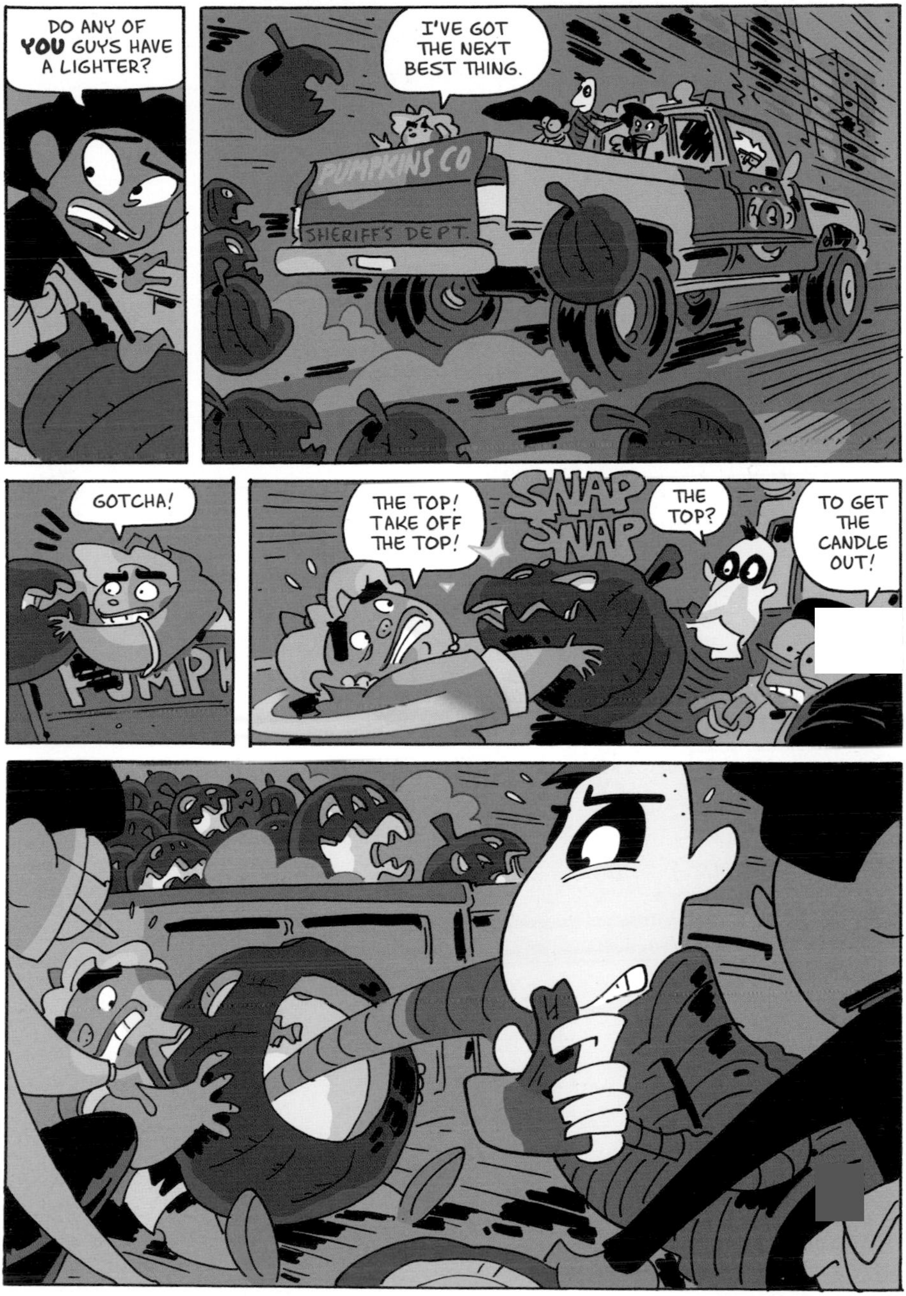

DO ANY OF **YOU** GUYS HAVE A LIGHTER?
I'VE GOT THE NEXT BEST THING.
PUMPKINS CO
SHERIFF'S DEPT.
3
GOTCHA!
PUMPK
THE TOP! TAKE OFF THE TOP!
SNAP SNAP
THE TOP?
TO GET THE CANDLE OUT!

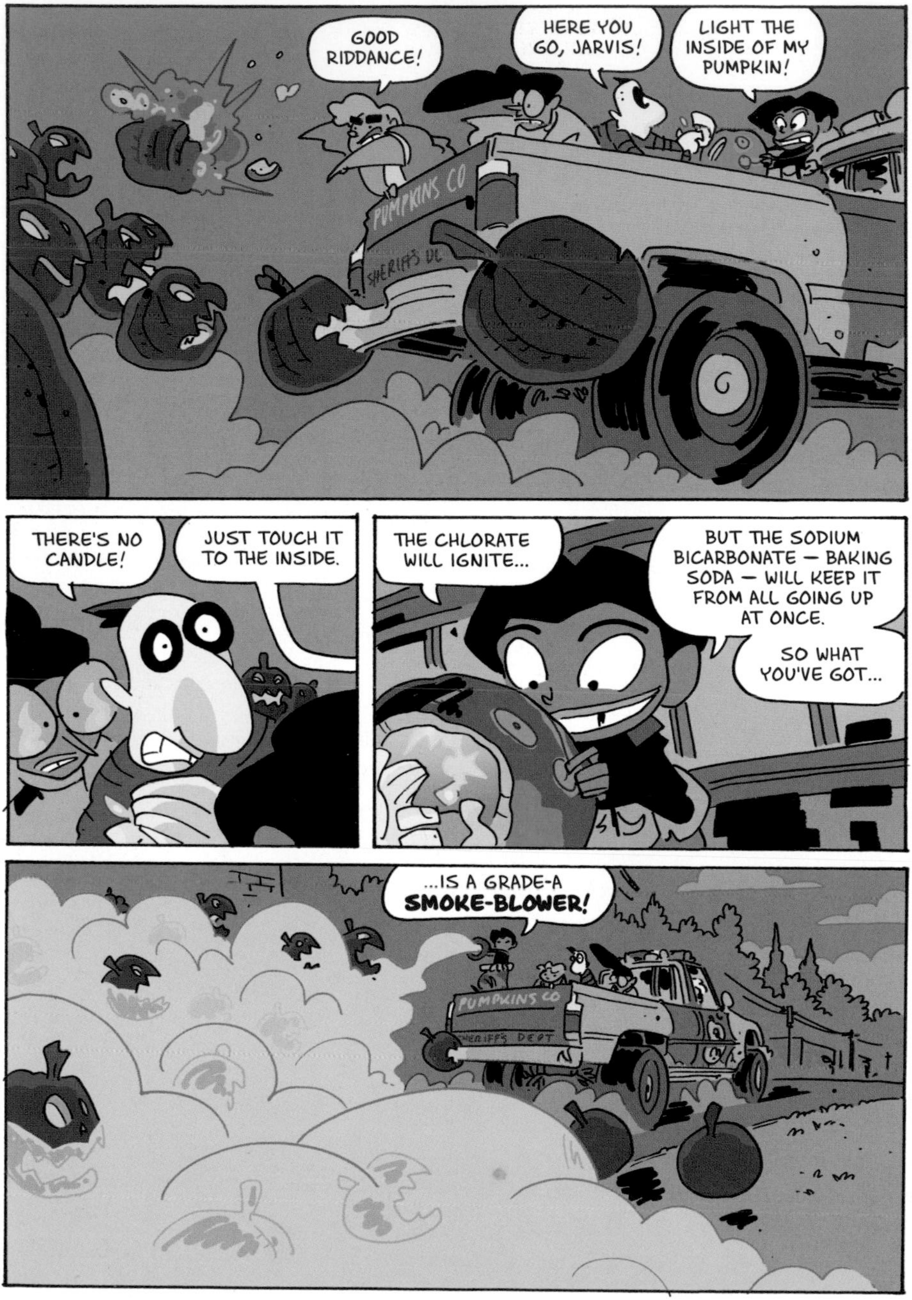
GOOD RIDDANCE!
HERE YOU GO, JARVIS!
LIGHT THE INSIDE OF MY PUMPKIN!
PUMPKINS CO
SHERIFF'S DEPT
THERE'S NO CANDLE!
JUST TOUCH IT TO THE INSIDE.
THE CHLORATE WILL IGNITE...
BUT THE SODIUM BICARBONATE — BAKING SODA — WILL KEEP IT FROM ALL GOING UP AT ONCE.
SO WHAT YOU'VE GOT...
...IS A GRADE-A **SMOKE-BLOWER!**
PUMPKINS CO
SHERIFF'S DEPT

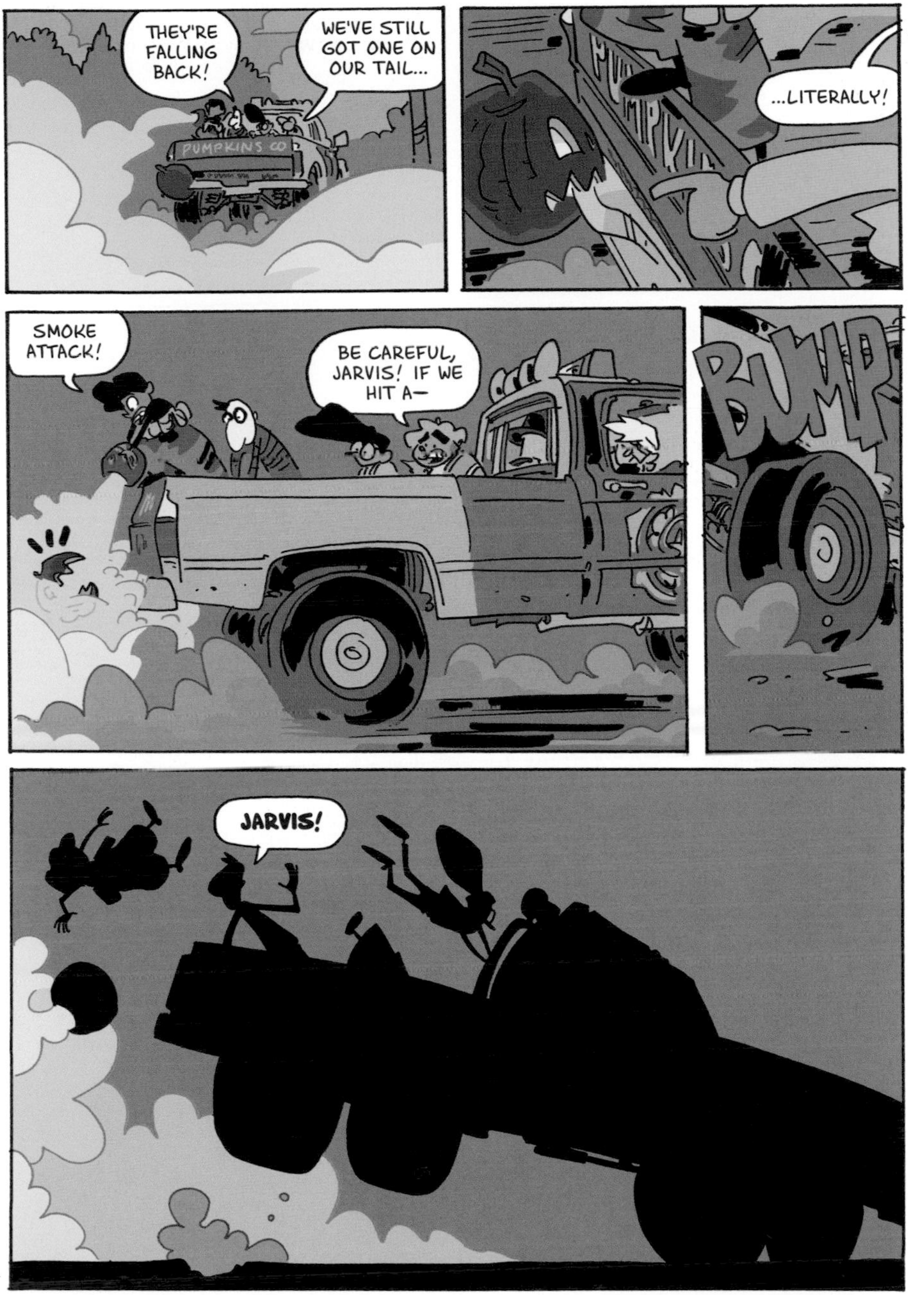
THEY'RE FALLING BACK!
WE'VE STILL GOT ONE ON OUR TAIL...
PUMPKINS CO
...LITERALLY!
SMOKE ATTACK!
BE CAREFUL, JARVIS! IF WE HIT A—
BUMP
JARVIS!

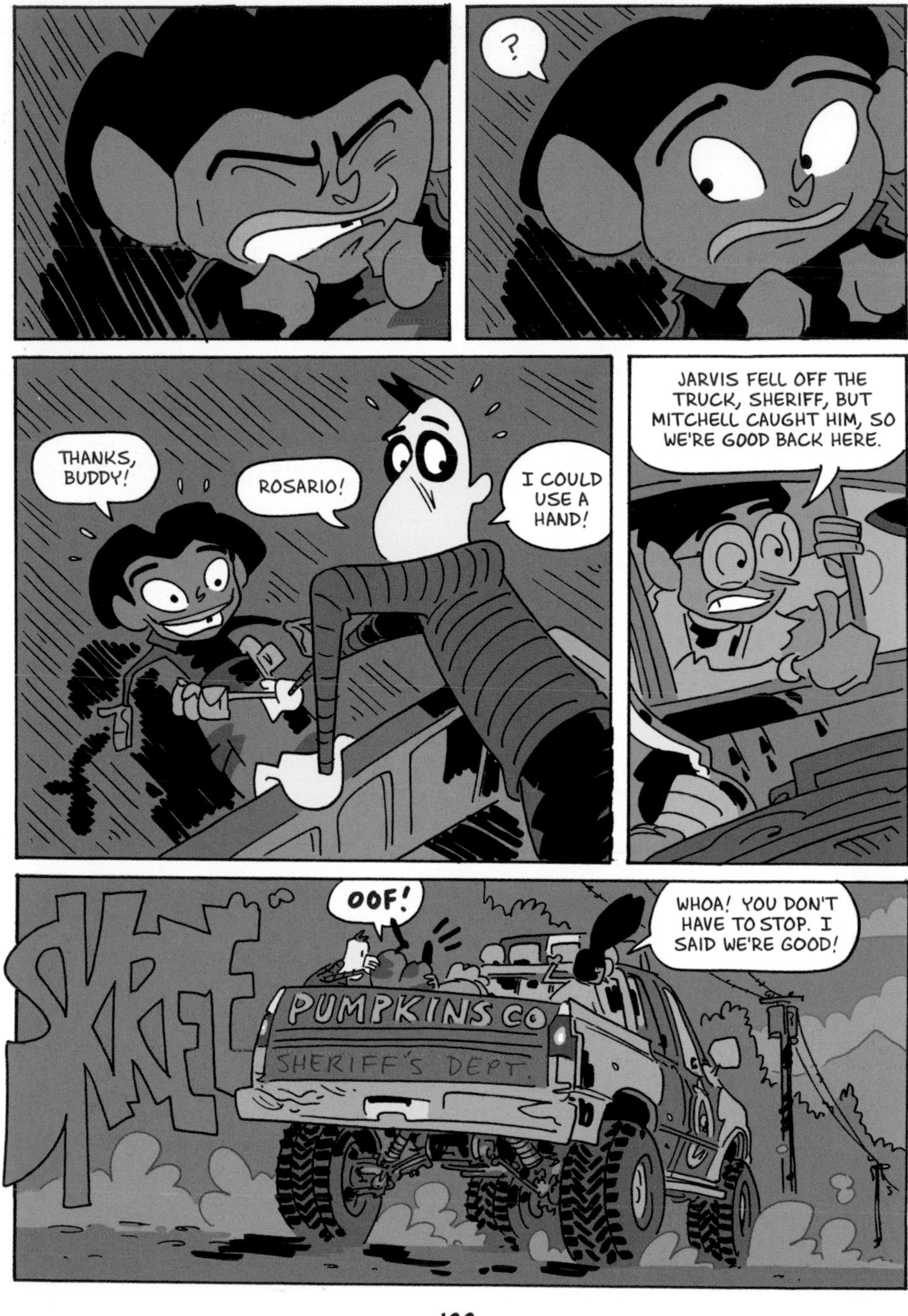
?
THANKS, BUDDY!
ROSARIO!
I COULD USE A HAND!
JARVIS FELL OFF THE TRUCK, SHERIFF, BUT MITCHELL CAUGHT HIM, SO WE'RE GOOD BACK HERE.
SKREE
OOF!
WHOA! YOU DON'T HAVE TO STOP. I SAID WE'RE GOOD!
PUMPKINS CO
SHERIFF'S DEPT.

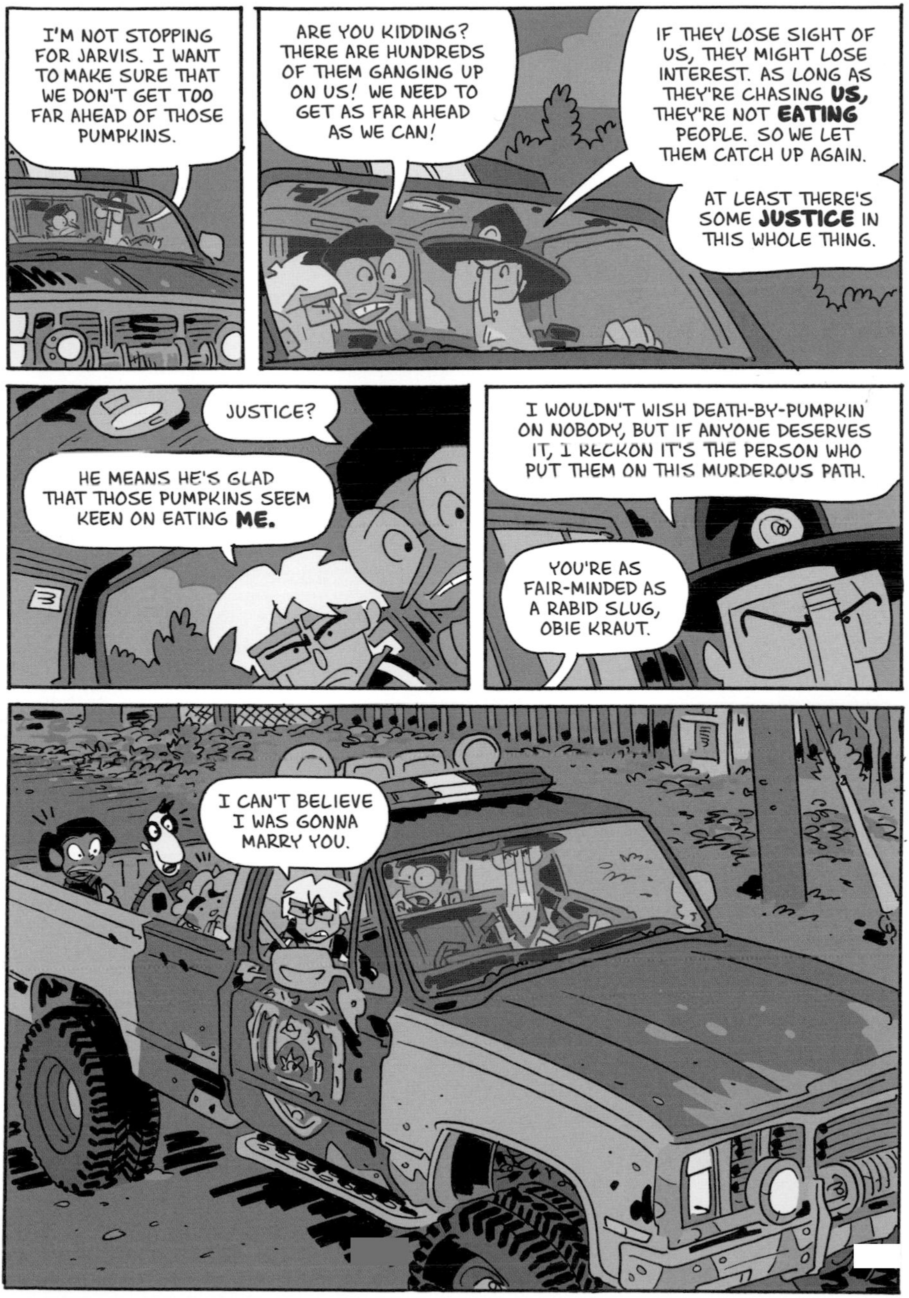
I'M NOT STOPPING FOR JARVIS. I WANT TO MAKE SURE THAT WE DON'T GET TOO FAR AHEAD OF THOSE PUMPKINS.
ARE YOU KIDDING? THERE ARE HUNDREDS OF THEM GANGING UP ON US! WE NEED TO GET AS FAR AHEAD AS WE CAN!
IF THEY LOSE SIGHT OF US, THEY MIGHT LOSE INTEREST. AS LONG AS THEY'RE CHASING **US,** THEY'RE NOT **EATING** PEOPLE. SO WE LET THEM CATCH UP AGAIN.
AT LEAST THERE'S SOME **JUSTICE** IN THIS WHOLE THING.
JUSTICE?
HE MEANS HE'S GLAD THAT THOSE PUMPKINS SEEM KEEN ON EATING **ME.**
I WOULDN'T WISH DEATH-BY-PUMPKIN ON NOBODY, BUT IF ANYONE DESERVES IT, I RECKON IT'S THE PERSON WHO PUT THEM ON THIS MURDEROUS PATH.
YOU'RE AS FAIR-MINDED AS A RABID SLUG, OBIE KRAUT.
I CAN'T BELIEVE I WAS GONNA MARRY YOU.

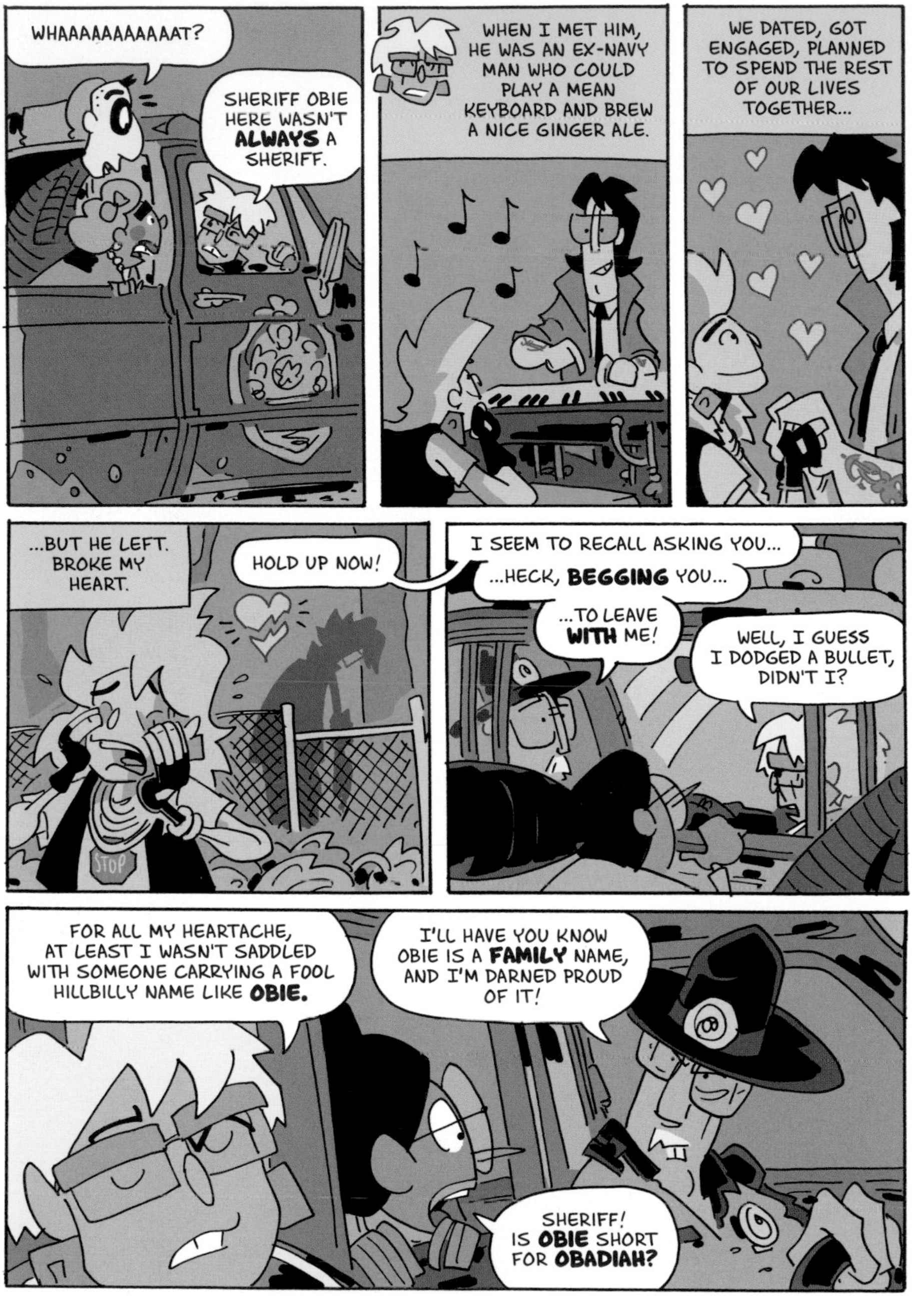
WHAAAAAAAAAAAT?
SHERIFF OBIE HERE WASN'T ALWAYS A SHERIFF.
WHEN I MET HIM, HE WAS AN EX-NAVY MAN WHO COULD PLAY A MEAN KEYBOARD AND BREW A NICE GINGER ALE.
WE DATED, GOT ENGAGED, PLANNED TO SPEND THE REST OF OUR LIVES TOGETHER...
...BUT HE LEFT. BROKE MY HEART.
HOLD UP NOW!
STOP
I SEEM TO RECALL ASKING YOU...
...HECK, BEGGING YOU...
...TO LEAVE WITH ME!
WELL, I GUESS I DODGED A BULLET, DIDN'T I?
FOR ALL MY HEARTACHE, AT LEAST I WASN'T SADDLED WITH SOMEONE CARRYING A FOOL HILLBILLY NAME LIKE OBIE.
I'LL HAVE YOU KNOW OBIE IS A FAMILY NAME, AND I'M DARNED PROUD OF IT!
SHERIFF! IS OBIE SHORT FOR OBADIAH?

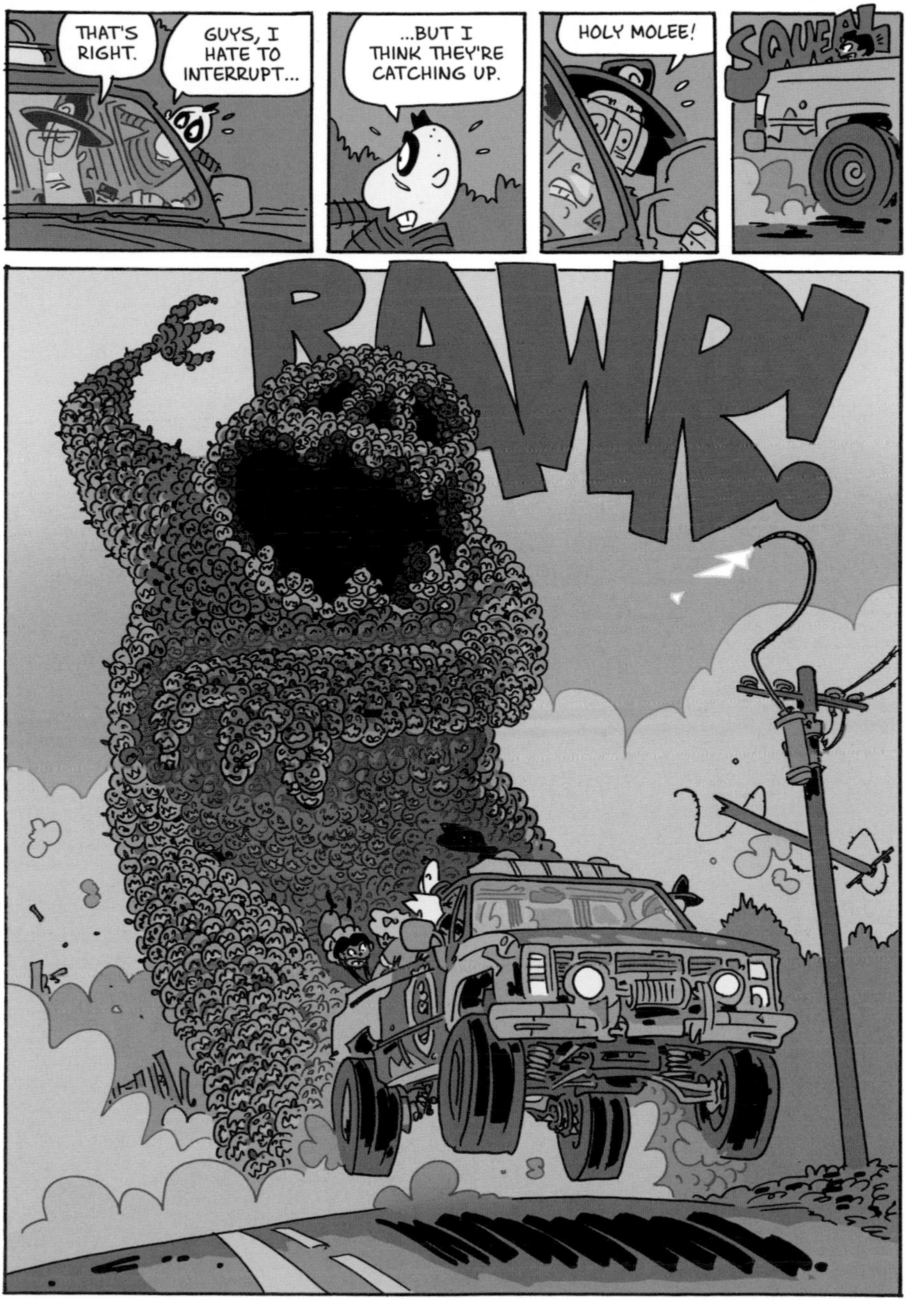
THAT'S RIGHT.
GUYS, I HATE TO INTERRUPT...
...BUT I THINK THEY'RE CATCHING UP.
HOLY MOLEE!
SQUEAL
RAWR!

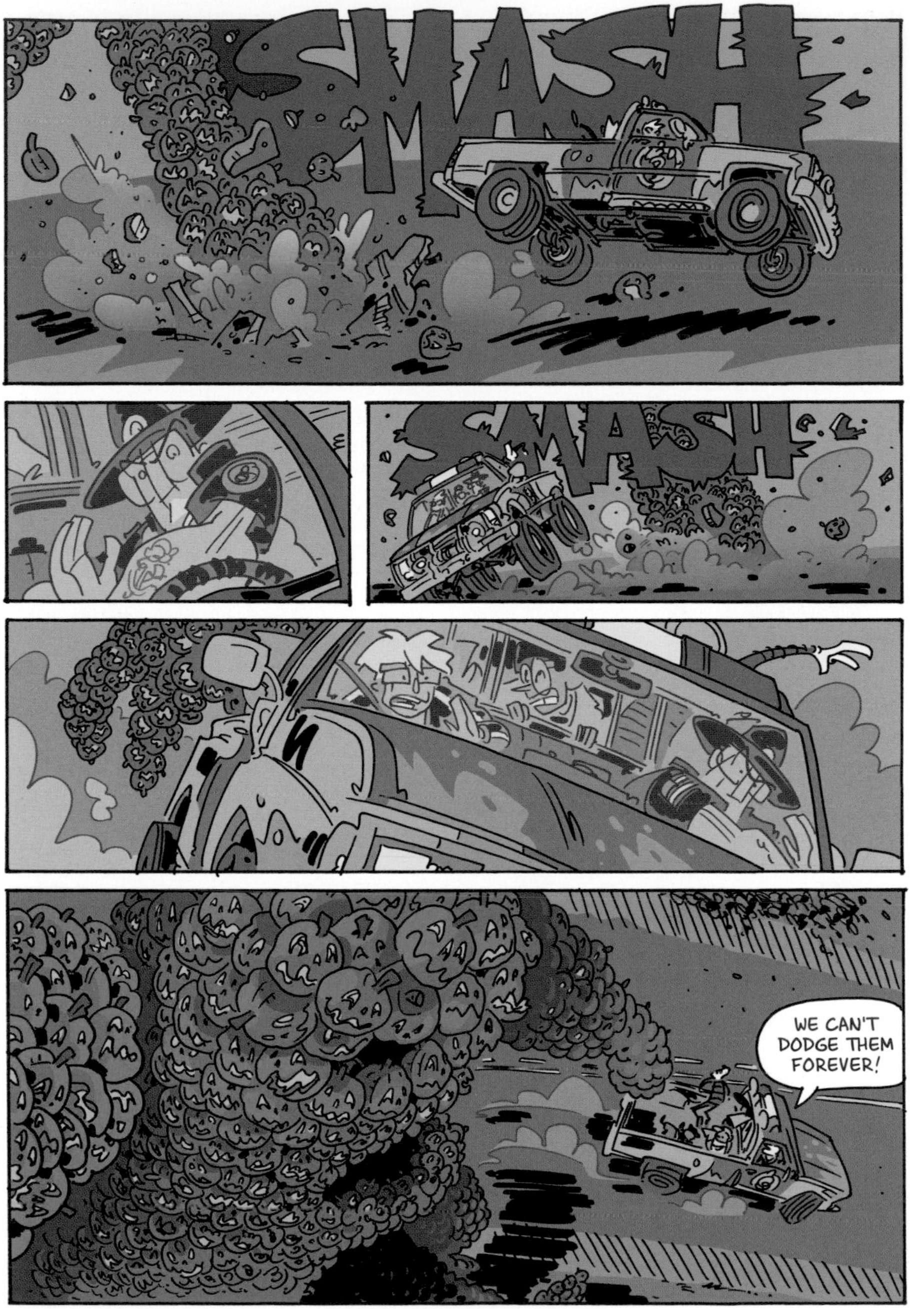
SMASH
SMASH
WE CAN'T DODGE THEM FOREVER!

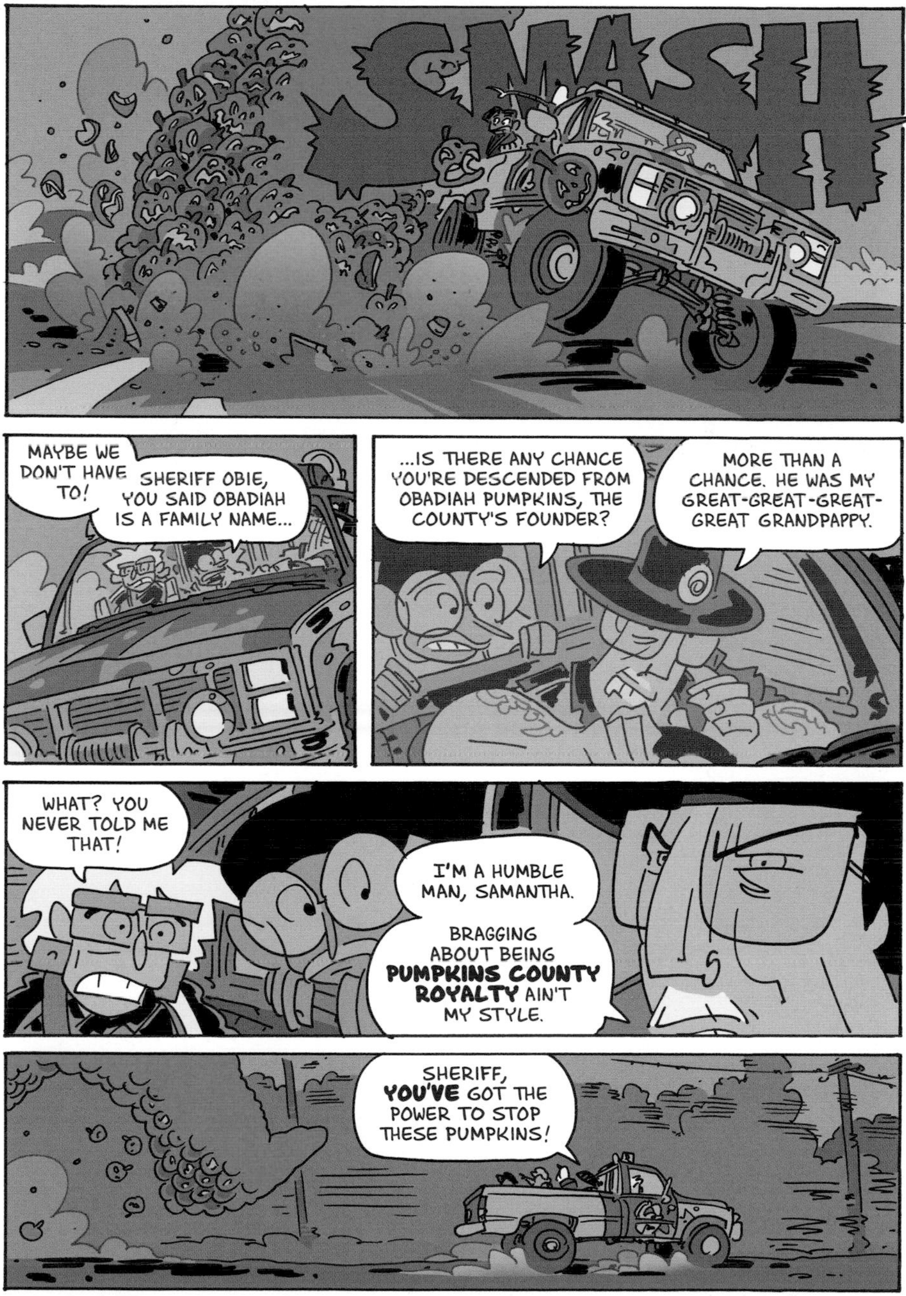
SMASH
MAYBE WE DON'T HAVE TO!
SHERIFF OBIE, YOU SAID OBADIAH IS A FAMILY NAME...
...IS THERE ANY CHANCE YOU'RE DESCENDED FROM OBADIAH PUMPKINS, THE COUNTY'S FOUNDER?
MORE THAN A CHANCE. HE WAS MY GREAT-GREAT-GREAT-GREAT GRANDPAPPY.
WHAT? YOU NEVER TOLD ME THAT!
I'M A HUMBLE MAN, SAMANTHA.
BRAGGING ABOUT BEING **PUMPKINS COUNTY ROYALTY** AIN'T MY STYLE.
SHERIFF, **YOU'VE** GOT THE POWER TO STOP THESE PUMPKINS!

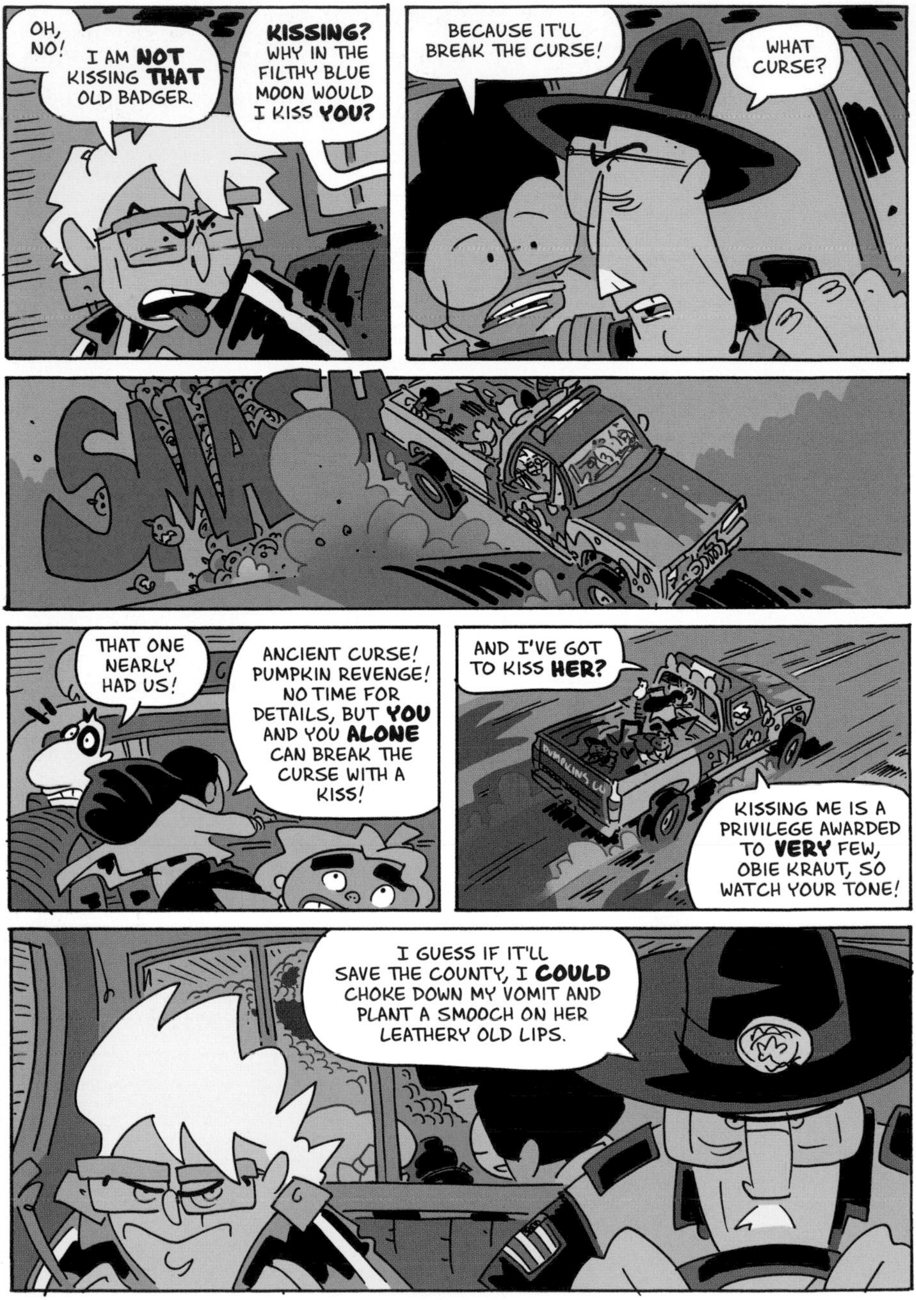
OH, NO!
I AM NOT KISSING THAT OLD BADGER.
KISSING? WHY IN THE FILTHY BLUE MOON WOULD I KISS YOU?
BECAUSE IT'LL BREAK THE CURSE!
WHAT CURSE?
SMASH
THAT ONE NEARLY HAD US!
ANCIENT CURSE! PUMPKIN REVENGE! NO TIME FOR DETAILS, BUT YOU AND YOU ALONE CAN BREAK THE CURSE WITH A KISS!
AND I'VE GOT TO KISS HER?
KISSING ME IS A PRIVILEGE AWARDED TO VERY FEW, OBIE KRAUT, SO WATCH YOUR TONE!
I GUESS IF IT'LL SAVE THE COUNTY, I COULD CHOKE DOWN MY VOMIT AND PLANT A SMOOCH ON HER LEATHERY OLD LIPS.

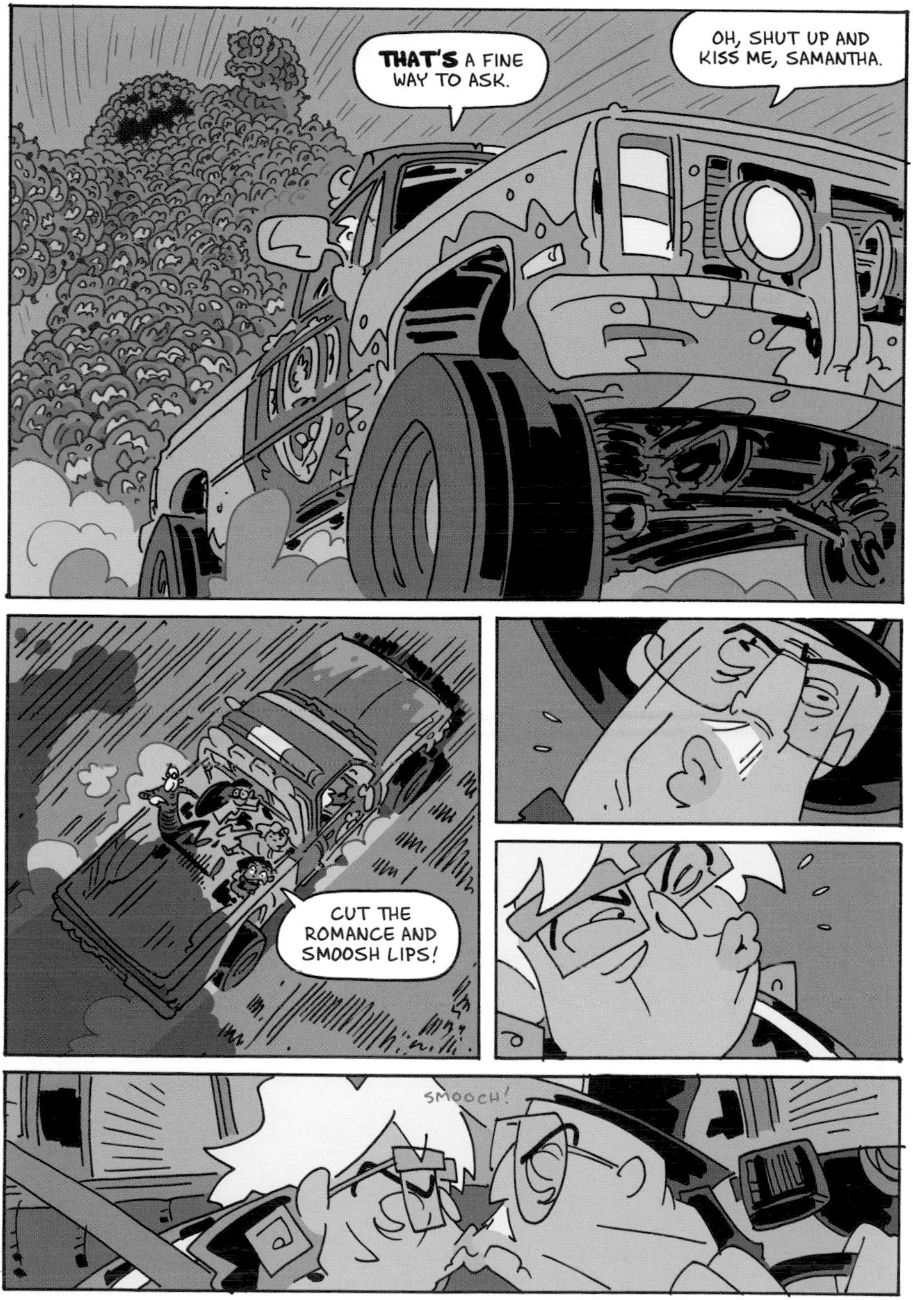
THAT'S A FINE WAY TO ASK.
OH, SHUT UP AND KISS ME, SAMANTHA.
CUT THE ROMANCE AND SMOOSH LIPS!
SMOOCH!

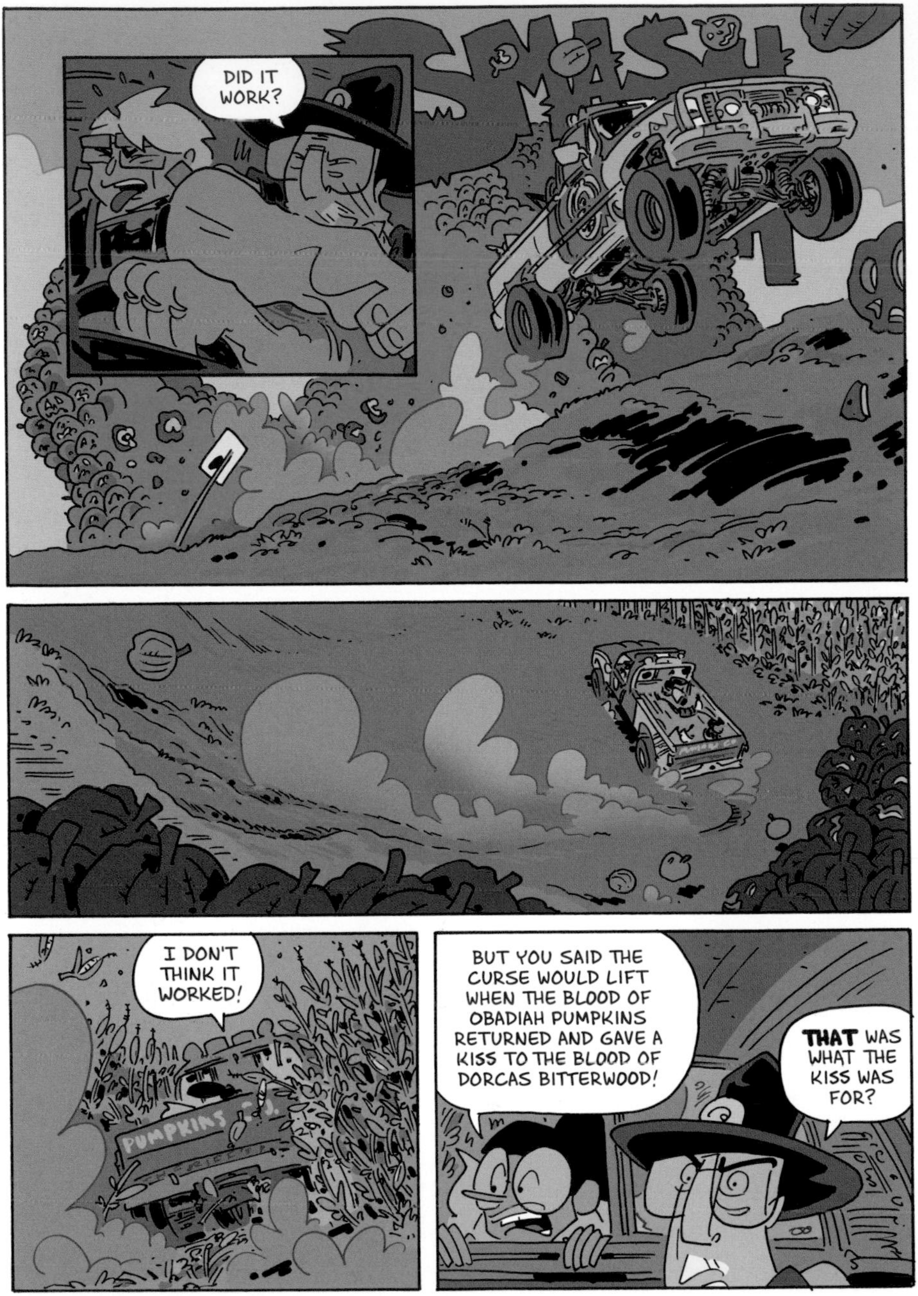

SMASH
DID IT WORK?
I DON'T THINK IT WORKED!
PUMPKINS CO.
BUT YOU SAID THE CURSE WOULD LIFT WHEN THE BLOOD OF OBADIAH PUMPKINS RETURNED AND GAVE A KISS TO THE BLOOD OF DORCAS BITTERWOOD!
THAT WAS WHAT THE KISS WAS FOR?

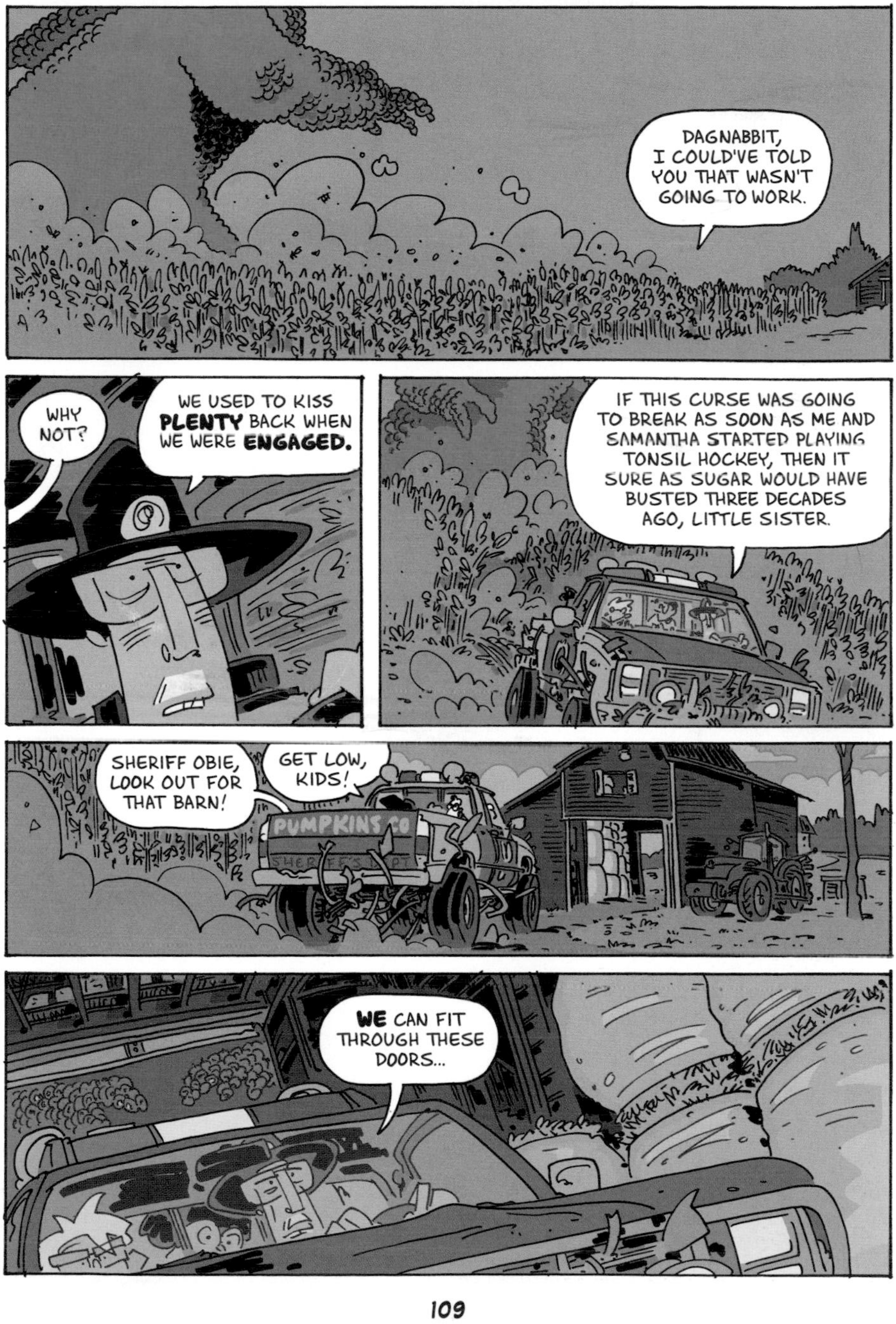
DAGNABBIT, I COULD'VE TOLD YOU THAT WASN'T GOING TO WORK.
WHY NOT?
WE USED TO KISS **PLENTY** BACK WHEN WE WERE **ENGAGED.**
IF THIS CURSE WAS GOING TO BREAK AS SOON AS ME AND SAMANTHA STARTED PLAYING TONSIL HOCKEY, THEN IT SURE AS SUGAR WOULD HAVE BUSTED THREE DECADES AGO, LITTLE SISTER.
SHERIFF OBIE, LOOK OUT FOR THAT BARN!
GET LOW, KIDS!
PUMPKINS CO
SHERIFF'S DEPT
WE CAN FIT THROUGH THESE DOORS...

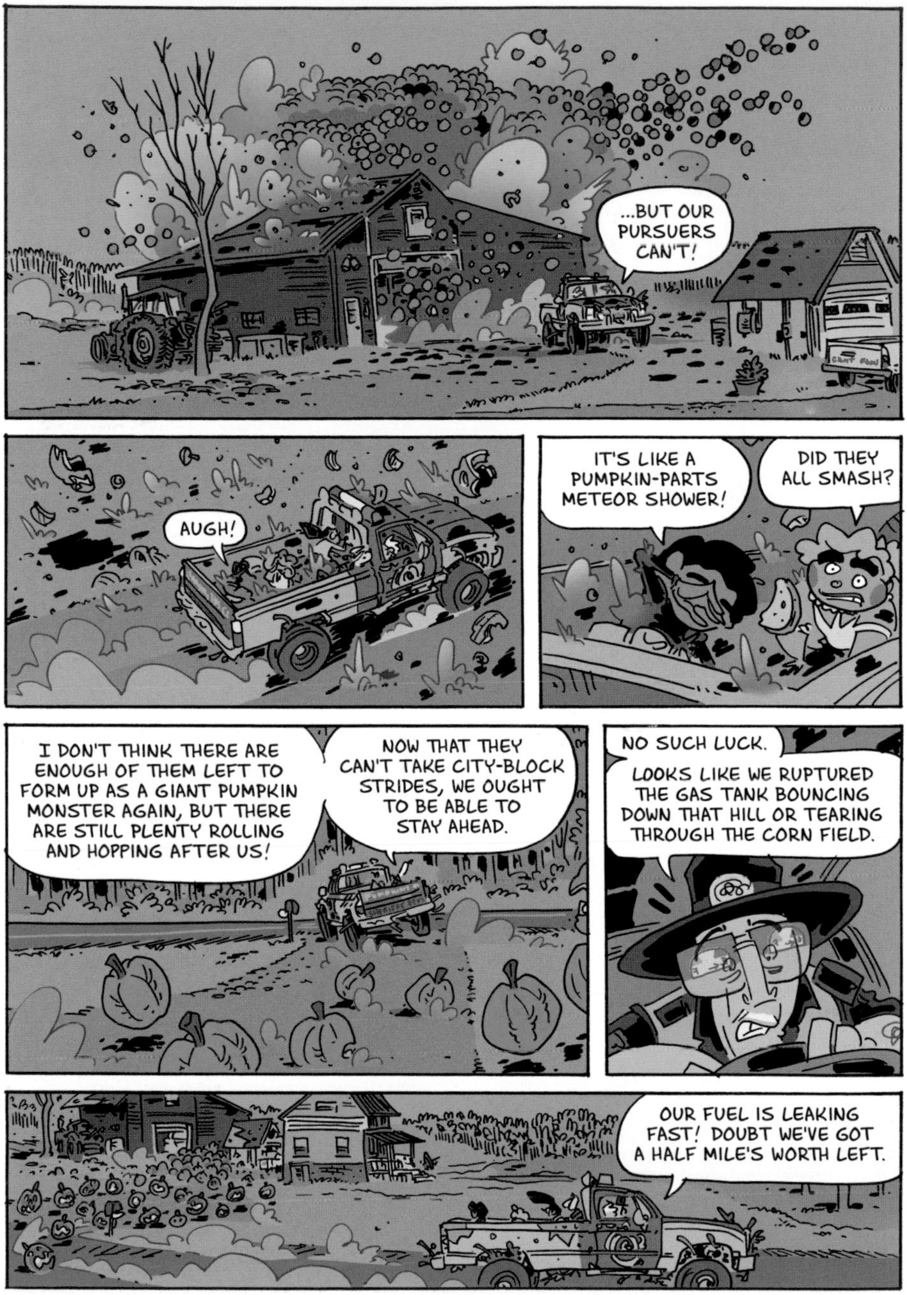
...BUT OUR PURSUERS CAN'T!
AUGH!
IT'S LIKE A PUMPKIN-PARTS METEOR SHOWER!
DID THEY ALL SMASH?
I DON'T THINK THERE ARE ENOUGH OF THEM LEFT TO FORM UP AS A GIANT PUMPKIN MONSTER AGAIN, BUT THERE ARE STILL PLENTY ROLLING AND HOPPING AFTER US!
NOW THAT THEY CAN'T TAKE CITY-BLOCK STRIDES, WE OUGHT TO BE ABLE TO STAY AHEAD.
NO SUCH LUCK.
LOOKS LIKE WE RUPTURED THE GAS TANK BOUNCING DOWN THAT HILL OR TEARING THROUGH THE CORN FIELD.
OUR FUEL IS LEAKING FAST! DOUBT WE'VE GOT A HALF MILE'S WORTH LEFT.

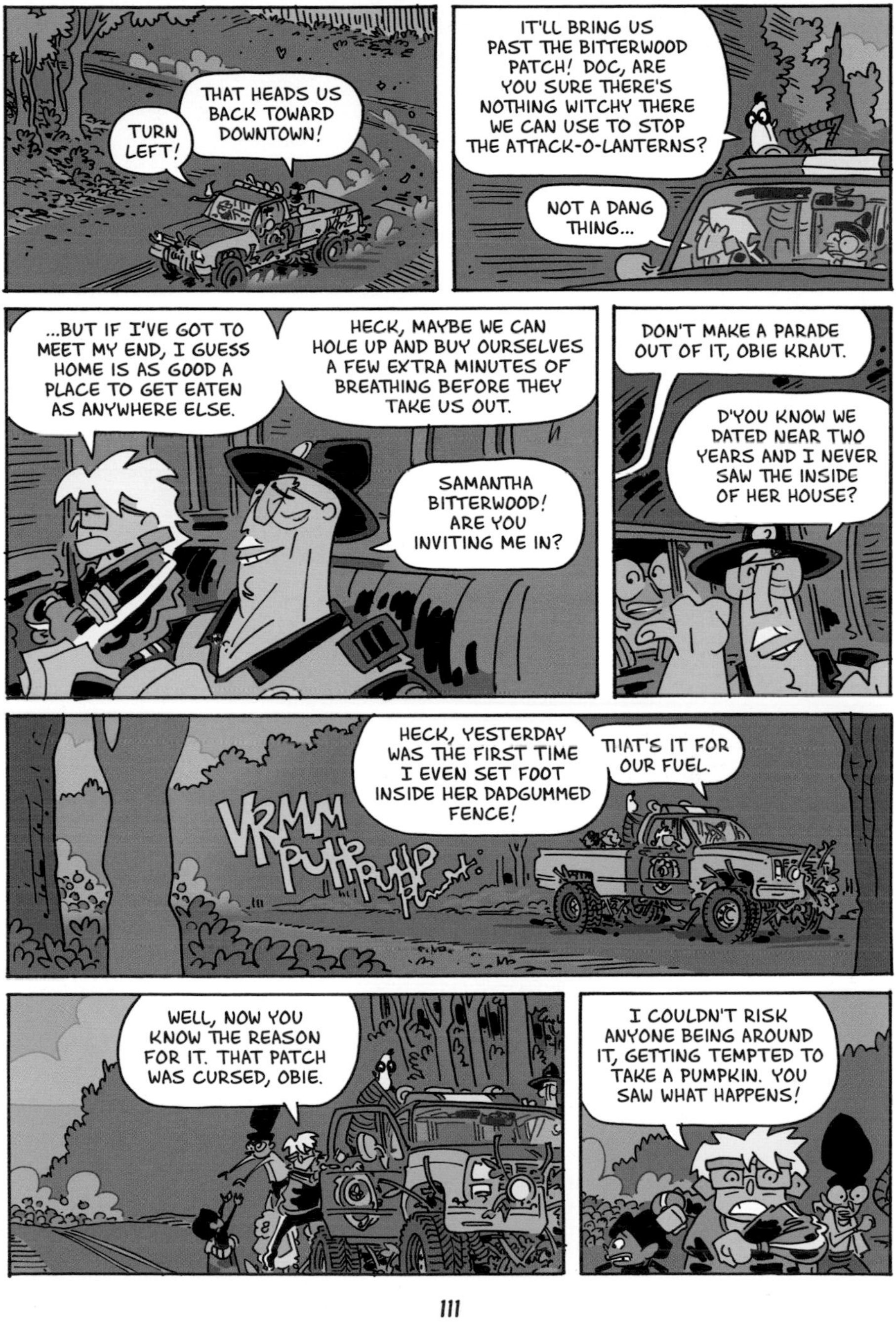
TURN LEFT!
THAT HEADS US BACK TOWARD DOWNTOWN!
IT'LL BRING US PAST THE BITTERWOOD PATCH! DOC, ARE YOU SURE THERE'S NOTHING WITCHY THERE WE CAN USE TO STOP THE ATTACK-O-LANTERNS?
NOT A DANG THING...
...BUT IF I'VE GOT TO MEET MY END, I GUESS HOME IS AS GOOD A PLACE TO GET EATEN AS ANYWHERE ELSE.
HECK, MAYBE WE CAN HOLE UP AND BUY OURSELVES A FEW EXTRA MINUTES OF BREATHING BEFORE THEY TAKE US OUT.
SAMANTHA BITTERWOOD! ARE YOU INVITING ME IN?
DON'T MAKE A PARADE OUT OF IT, OBIE KRAUT.
D'YOU KNOW WE DATED NEAR TWO YEARS AND I NEVER SAW THE INSIDE OF HER HOUSE?
HECK, YESTERDAY WAS THE FIRST TIME I EVEN SET FOOT INSIDE HER DADGUMMED FENCE!
THAT'S IT FOR OUR FUEL.
VRMM PUHHPUHP
WELL, NOW YOU KNOW THE REASON FOR IT. THAT PATCH WAS CURSED, OBIE.
I COULDN'T RISK ANYONE BEING AROUND IT, GETTING TEMPTED TO TAKE A PUMPKIN. YOU SAW WHAT HAPPENS!

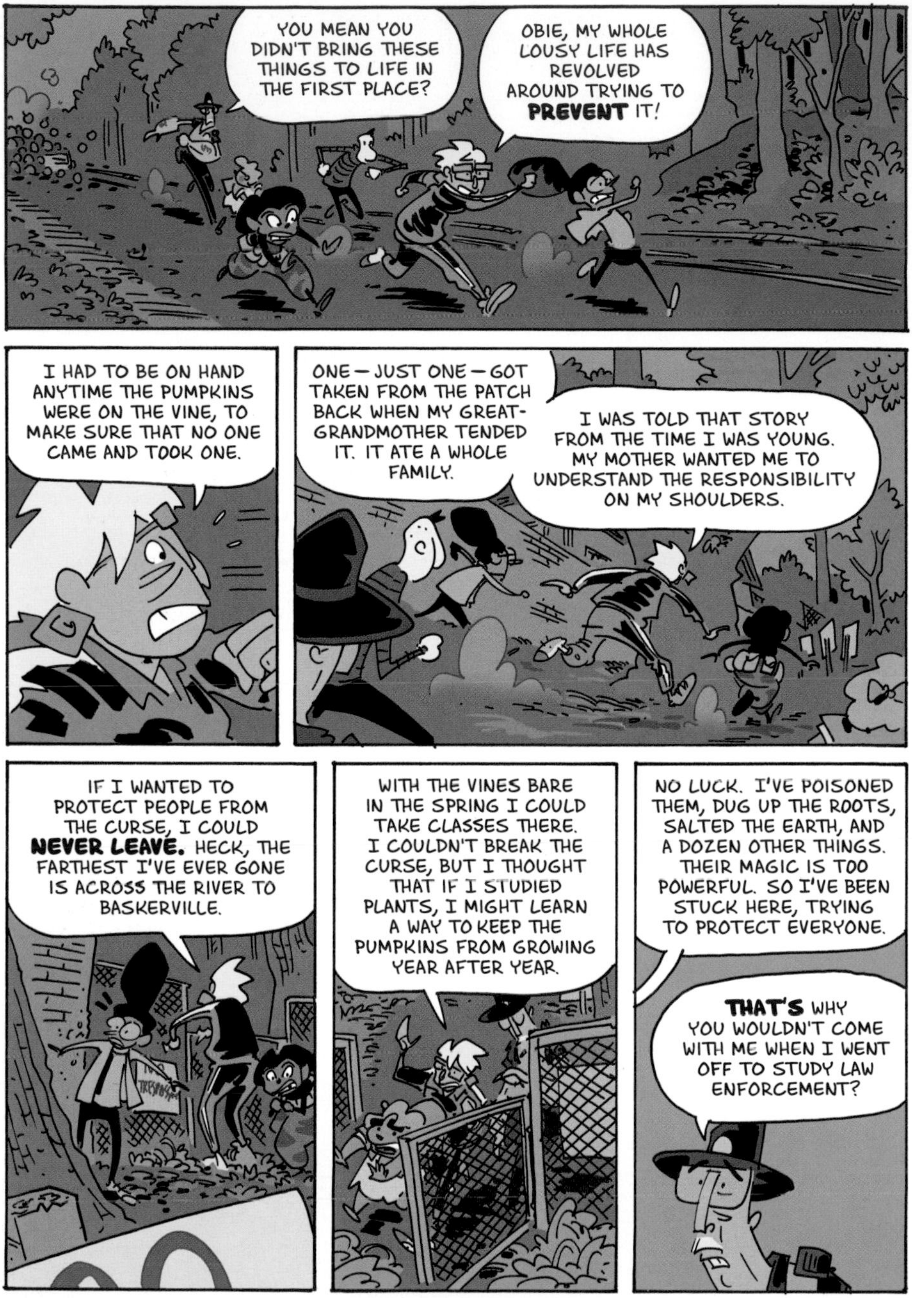
YOU MEAN YOU DIDN'T BRING THESE THINGS TO LIFE IN THE FIRST PLACE?
OBIE, MY WHOLE LOUSY LIFE HAS REVOLVED AROUND TRYING TO **PREVENT** IT!
I HAD TO BE ON HAND ANYTIME THE PUMPKINS WERE ON THE VINE, TO MAKE SURE THAT NO ONE CAME AND TOOK ONE.
ONE — JUST ONE — GOT TAKEN FROM THE PATCH BACK WHEN MY GREAT-GRANDMOTHER TENDED IT. IT ATE A WHOLE FAMILY.
I WAS TOLD THAT STORY FROM THE TIME I WAS YOUNG. MY MOTHER WANTED ME TO UNDERSTAND THE RESPONSIBILITY ON MY SHOULDERS.
IF I WANTED TO PROTECT PEOPLE FROM THE CURSE, I COULD **NEVER LEAVE.** HECK, THE FARTHEST I'VE EVER GONE IS ACROSS THE RIVER TO BASKERVILLE.
WITH THE VINES BARE IN THE SPRING I COULD TAKE CLASSES THERE. I COULDN'T BREAK THE CURSE, BUT I THOUGHT THAT IF I STUDIED PLANTS, I MIGHT LEARN A WAY TO KEEP THE PUMPKINS FROM GROWING YEAR AFTER YEAR.
NO LUCK. I'VE POISONED THEM, DUG UP THE ROOTS, SALTED THE EARTH, AND A DOZEN OTHER THINGS. THEIR MAGIC IS TOO POWERFUL. SO I'VE BEEN STUCK HERE, TRYING TO PROTECT EVERYONE.
THAT'S WHY YOU WOULDN'T COME WITH ME WHEN I WENT OFF TO STUDY LAW ENFORCEMENT?

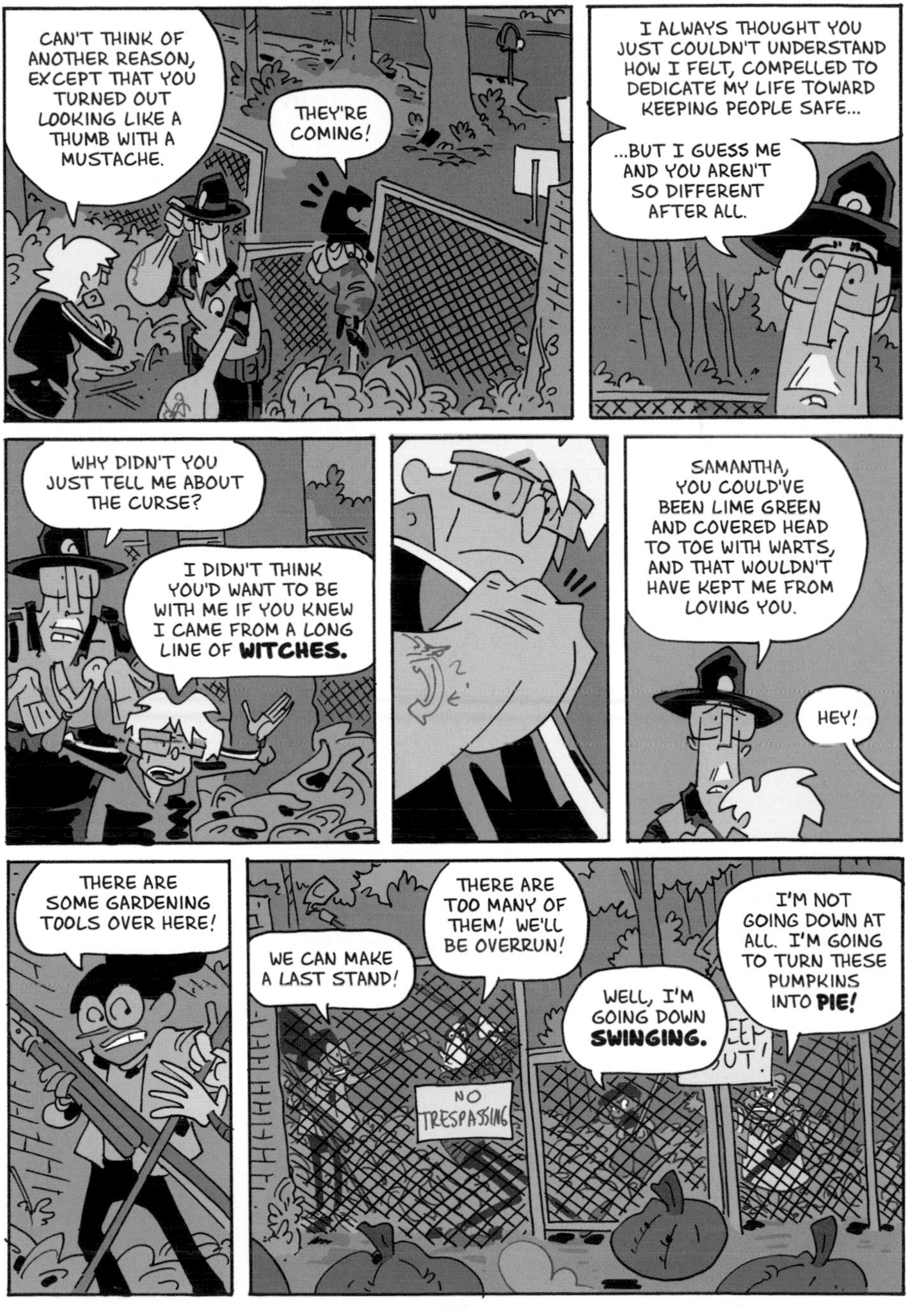

CAN'T THINK OF ANOTHER REASON, EXCEPT THAT YOU TURNED OUT LOOKING LIKE A THUMB WITH A MUSTACHE.
THEY'RE COMING!
I ALWAYS THOUGHT YOU JUST COULDN'T UNDERSTAND HOW I FELT, COMPELLED TO DEDICATE MY LIFE TOWARD KEEPING PEOPLE SAFE...
...BUT I GUESS ME AND YOU AREN'T SO DIFFERENT AFTER ALL.
WHY DIDN'T YOU JUST TELL ME ABOUT THE CURSE?
I DIDN'T THINK YOU'D WANT TO BE WITH ME IF YOU KNEW I CAME FROM A LONG LINE OF **WITCHES.**
SAMANTHA, YOU COULD'VE BEEN LIME GREEN AND COVERED HEAD TO TOE WITH WARTS, AND THAT WOULDN'T HAVE KEPT ME FROM LOVING YOU.
HEY!
THERE ARE SOME GARDENING TOOLS OVER HERE!
WE CAN MAKE A LAST STAND!
THERE ARE TOO MANY OF THEM! WE'LL BE OVERRUN!
WELL, I'M GOING DOWN **SWINGING.**
I'M NOT GOING DOWN AT ALL. I'M GOING TO TURN THESE PUMPKINS INTO **PIE!**
NO TRESPASSING

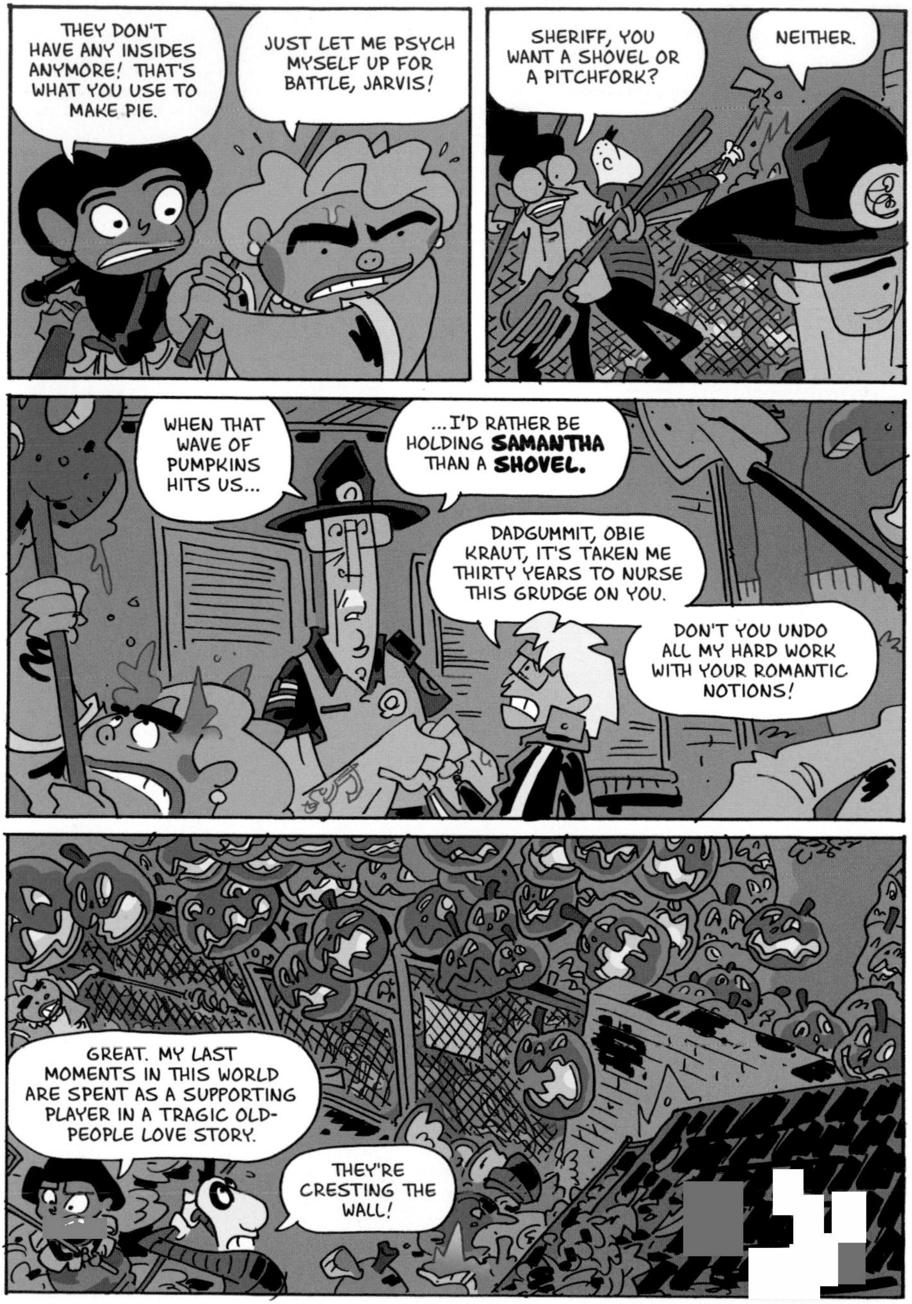
THEY DON'T HAVE ANY INSIDES ANYMORE! THAT'S WHAT YOU USE TO MAKE PIE.
JUST LET ME PSYCH MYSELF UP FOR BATTLE, JARVIS!
SHERIFF, YOU WANT A SHOVEL OR A PITCHFORK?
NEITHER.
WHEN THAT WAVE OF PUMPKINS HITS US...
...I'D RATHER BE HOLDING **SAMANTHA** THAN A **SHOVEL.**
DADGUMMIT, OBIE KRAUT, IT'S TAKEN ME THIRTY YEARS TO NURSE THIS GRUDGE ON YOU.
DON'T YOU UNDO ALL MY HARD WORK WITH YOUR ROMANTIC NOTIONS!
GREAT. MY LAST MOMENTS IN THIS WORLD ARE SPENT AS A SUPPORTING PLAYER IN A TRAGIC OLD-PEOPLE LOVE STORY.
THEY'RE CRESTING THE WALL!

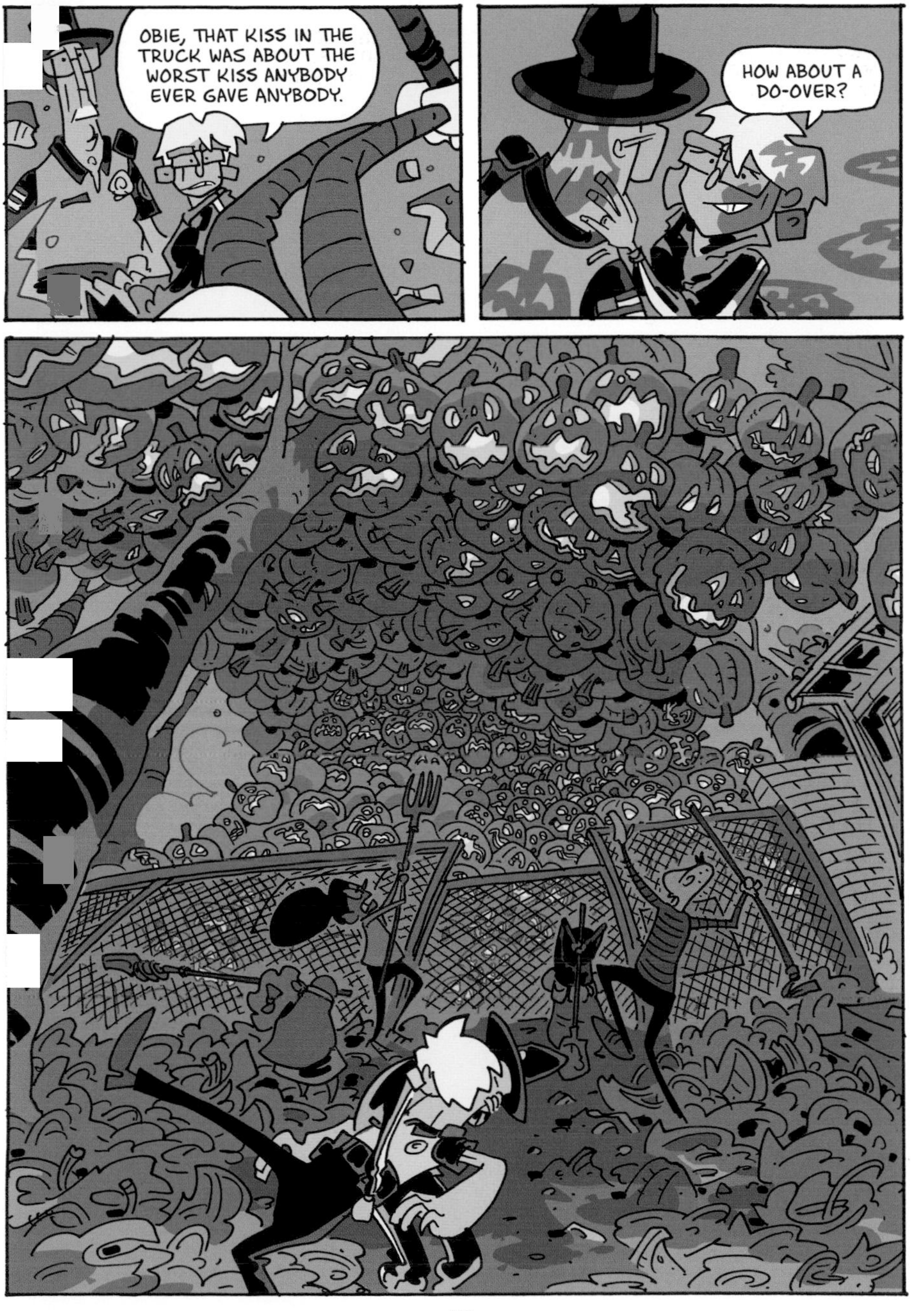
OBIE, THAT KISS IN THE TRUCK WAS ABOUT THE WORST KISS ANYBODY EVER GAVE ANYBODY.
HOW ABOUT A DO-OVER?

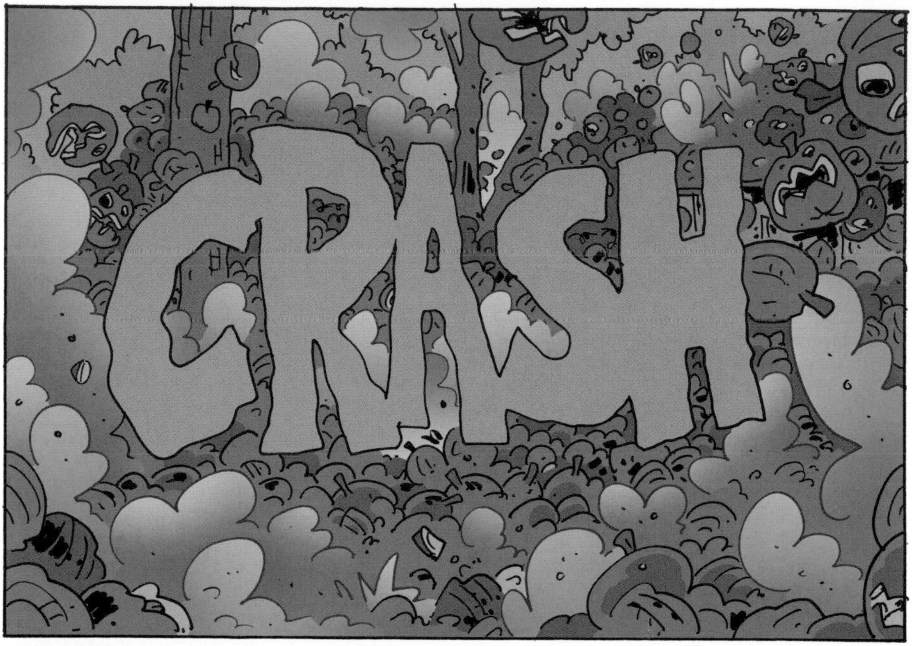
CRASH
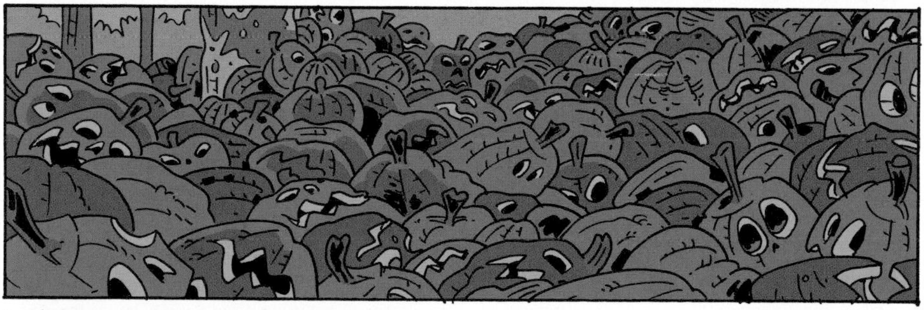
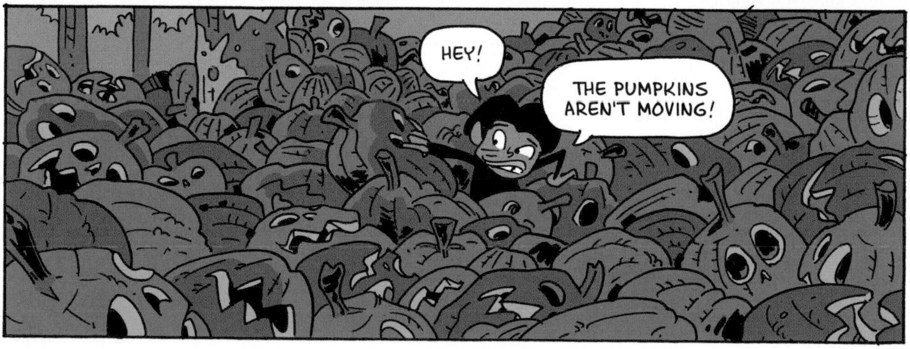
HEY!
THE PUMPKINS AREN'T MOVING!

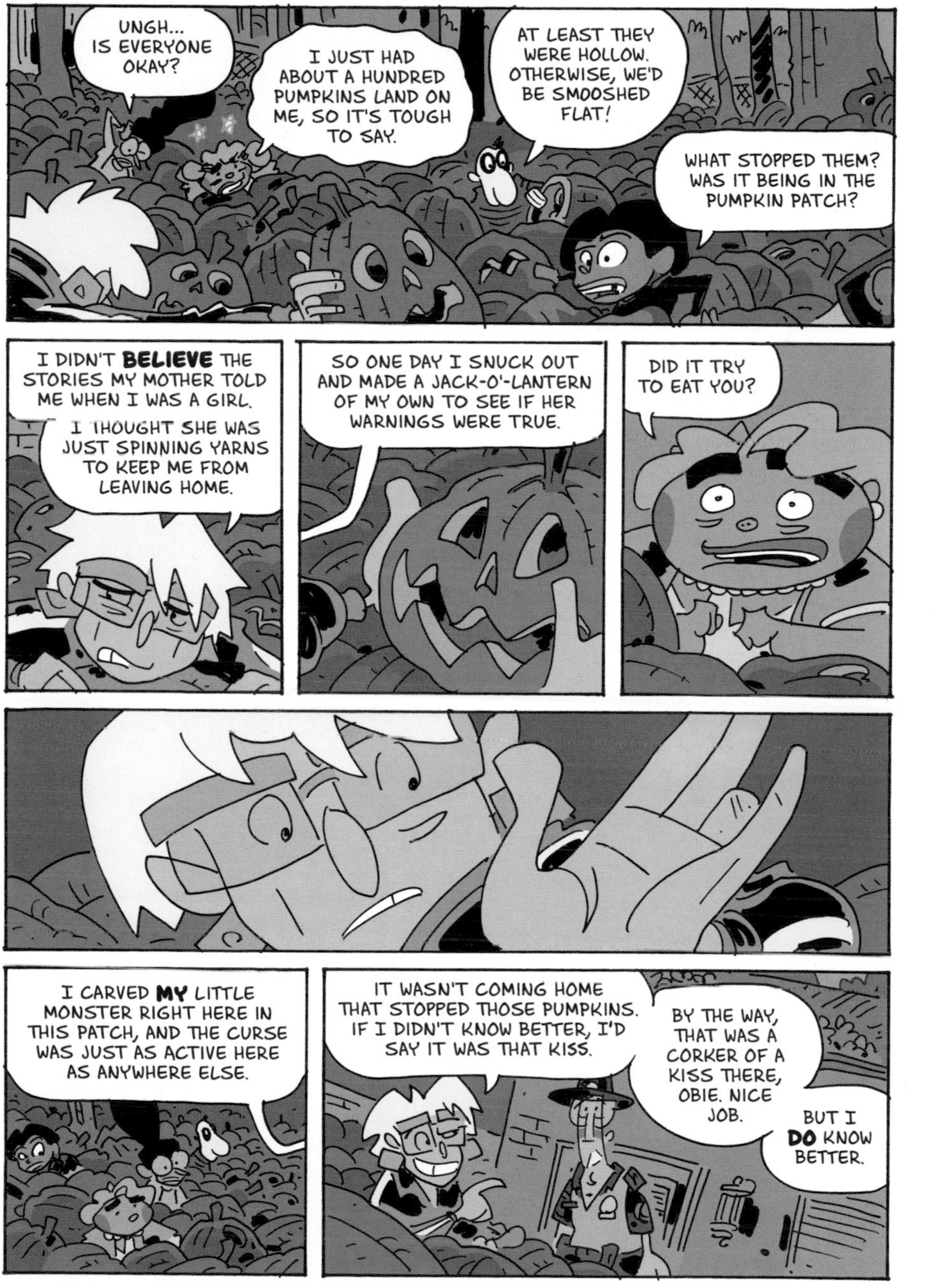
UNGH... IS EVERYONE OKAY?
I JUST HAD ABOUT A HUNDRED PUMPKINS LAND ON ME, SO IT'S TOUGH TO SAY.
AT LEAST THEY WERE HOLLOW. OTHERWISE, WE'D BE SMOOSHED FLAT!
WHAT STOPPED THEM? WAS IT BEING IN THE PUMPKIN PATCH?
I DIDN'T **BELIEVE** THE STORIES MY MOTHER TOLD ME WHEN I WAS A GIRL.
I THOUGHT SHE WAS JUST SPINNING YARNS TO KEEP ME FROM LEAVING HOME.
SO ONE DAY I SNUCK OUT AND MADE A JACK-O'-LANTERN OF MY OWN TO SEE IF HER WARNINGS WERE TRUE.
DID IT TRY TO EAT YOU?
I CARVED **MY** LITTLE MONSTER RIGHT HERE IN THIS PATCH, AND THE CURSE WAS JUST AS ACTIVE HERE AS ANYWHERE ELSE.
IT WASN'T COMING HOME THAT STOPPED THOSE PUMPKINS. IF I DIDN'T KNOW BETTER, I'D SAY IT WAS THAT KISS.
BY THE WAY, THAT WAS A CORKER OF A KISS THERE, OBIE. NICE JOB.
BUT I **DO** KNOW BETTER.

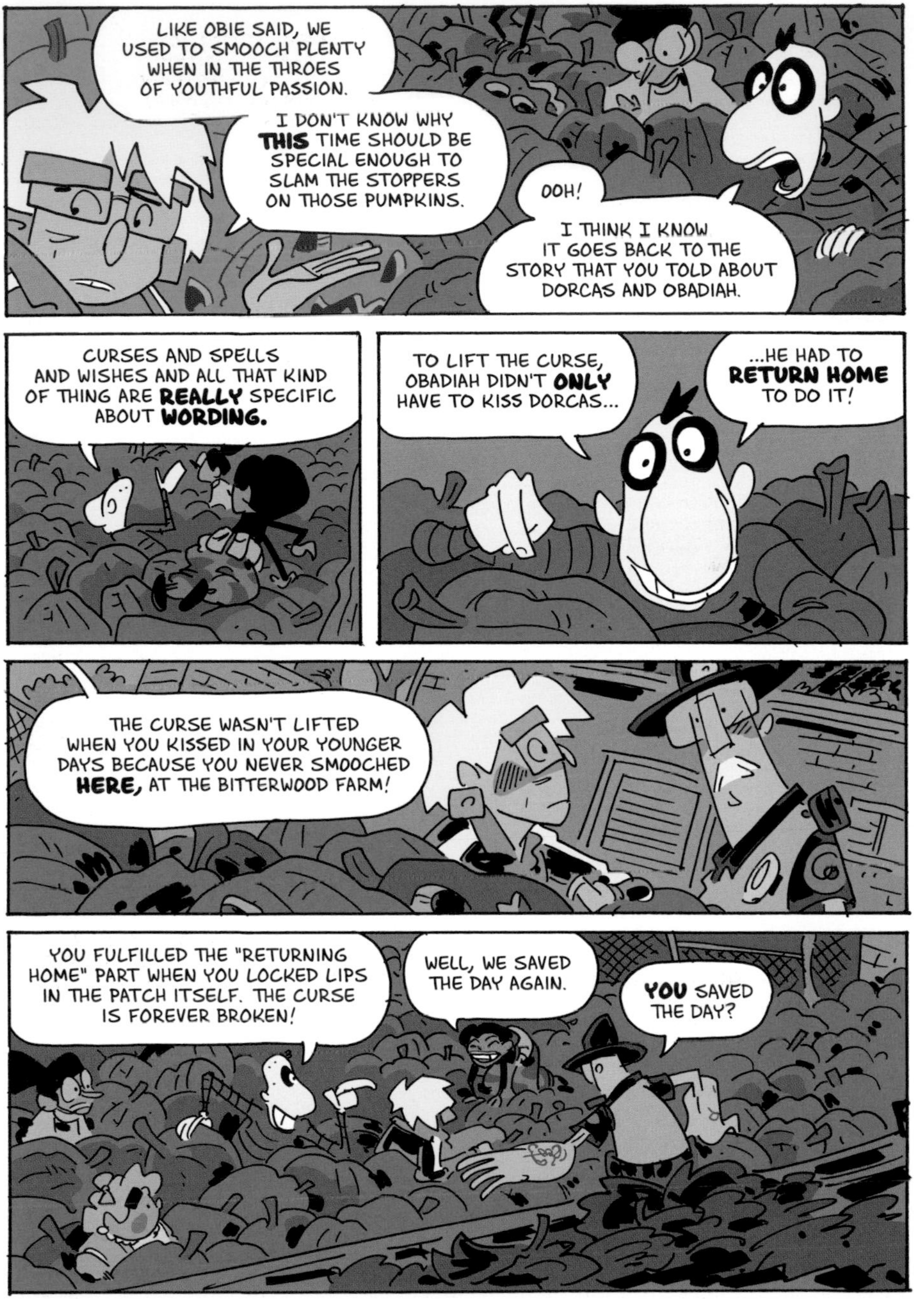

LIKE OBIE SAID, WE USED TO SMOOCH PLENTY WHEN IN THE THROES OF YOUTHFUL PASSION.
I DON'T KNOW WHY **THIS** TIME SHOULD BE SPECIAL ENOUGH TO SLAM THE STOPPERS ON THOSE PUMPKINS.
OOH!
I THINK I KNOW IT GOES BACK TO THE STORY THAT YOU TOLD ABOUT DORCAS AND OBADIAH.
CURSES AND SPELLS AND WISHES AND ALL THAT KIND OF THING ARE **REALLY** SPECIFIC ABOUT **WORDING.**
TO LIFT THE CURSE, OBADIAH DIDN'T **ONLY** HAVE TO KISS DORCAS...
...HE HAD TO **RETURN HOME** TO DO IT!
THE CURSE WASN'T LIFTED WHEN YOU KISSED IN YOUR YOUNGER DAYS BECAUSE YOU NEVER SMOOCHED **HERE,** AT THE BITTERWOOD FARM!
YOU FULFILLED THE "RETURNING HOME" PART WHEN YOU LOCKED LIPS IN THE PATCH ITSELF. THE CURSE IS FOREVER BROKEN!
WELL, WE SAVED THE DAY AGAIN.
YOU SAVED THE DAY?

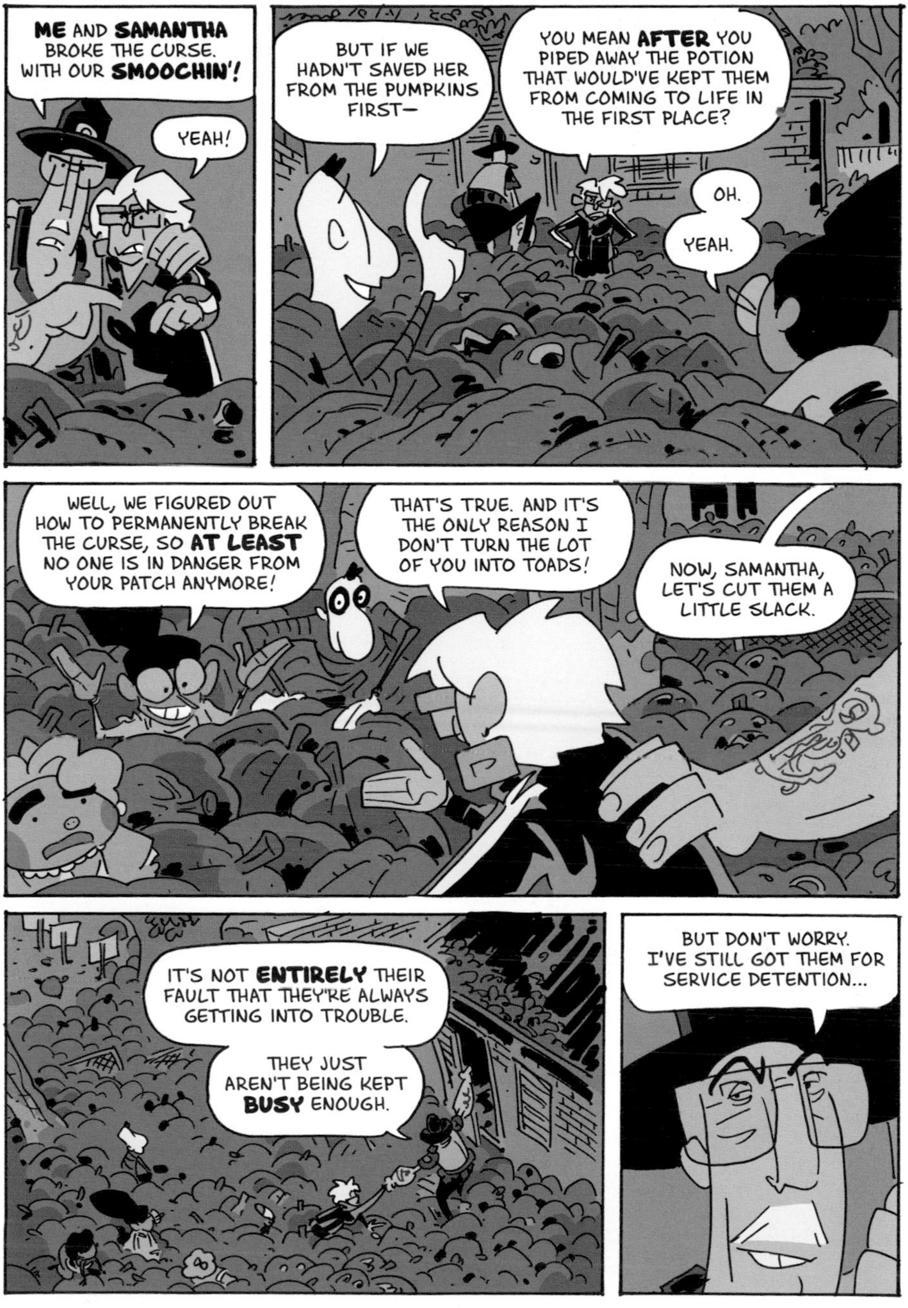
ME AND SAMANTHA BROKE THE CURSE. WITH OUR SMOOCHIN'!
YEAH!
BUT IF WE HADN'T SAVED HER FROM THE PUMPKINS FIRST—
YOU MEAN AFTER YOU PIPED AWAY THE POTION THAT WOULD'VE KEPT THEM FROM COMING TO LIFE IN THE FIRST PLACE?
OH.
YEAH.
WELL, WE FIGURED OUT HOW TO PERMANENTLY BREAK THE CURSE, SO AT LEAST NO ONE IS IN DANGER FROM YOUR PATCH ANYMORE!
THAT'S TRUE. AND IT'S THE ONLY REASON I DON'T TURN THE LOT OF YOU INTO TOADS!
NOW, SAMANTHA, LET'S CUT THEM A LITTLE SLACK.
IT'S NOT ENTIRELY THEIR FAULT THAT THEY'RE ALWAYS GETTING INTO TROUBLE.
THEY JUST AREN'T BEING KEPT BUSY ENOUGH.
BUT DON'T WORRY. I'VE STILL GOT THEM FOR SERVICE DETENTION...

...AND THERE ARE A LOT OF PUMPKINS TO CLEAN UP AROUND THE COUNTY. THEY'LL BE **BUSY** FOR A **VERY LONG TIME.**

WELL, WE'D BETTER LET THEM GET STARTED, HUH?

COME ON, OBIE. YOU LOOK LIKE YOU COULD USE A CUP OF COFFEE...

...AND I MAKE A MEAN **BREW.**

SLAM

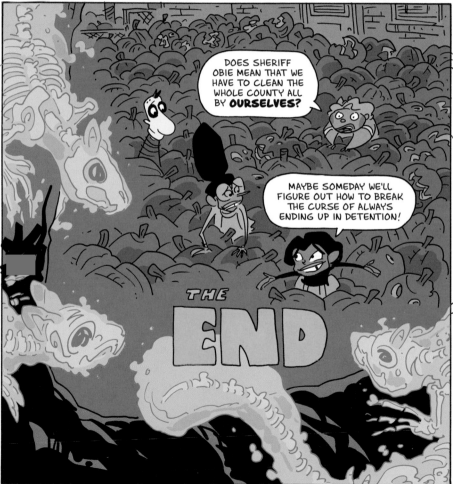

DOES SHERIFF OBIE MEAN THAT WE HAVE TO CLEAN THE WHOLE COUNTY ALL BY **OURSELVES?**

MAYBE SOMEDAY WE'LL FIGURE OUT HOW TO BREAK THE CURSE OF ALWAYS ENDING UP IN DETENTION!

THE END

ABOUT THE AUTHOR

Chris Schweizer has never seen a ghost, but he's worked in three places that were supposed to be haunted: an old restaurant, an old mental hospital, and an old hotel. When he was in college, he lived in a house that *The Week* magazine later called "The Most Haunted Place in England."

Chris has been a college professor, a hotel manager, a movie theater projectionist, a guard at a mental hospital, a martial arts instructor, a set builder, a church music leader, a process server, a life-drawing model, a bartender, a car wash attendant, a bagboy, a delivery boy, a choirboy, a lawn boy, a sixth-grade social studies teacher, a janitor, a speakeasy proprietor, a video store clerk, a field hand, a deckhand, a puppeteer for a children's television show, a muralist, a kickboxer, and a line worker at a pancake mix factory. He likes being a cartoonist best. He lives in Kentucky with his wife and daughter.

COLLECT THEM ALL!

THE CREEPS
1
NIGHT OF THE FRANKENFROGS
Chris Schweizer

THE CREEPS
2
THE TROLLS WILL FEAST!
Chris Schweizer

THE CREEPS
3
CURSE OF THE ATTACK-O-LANTERNS
Chris Schweizer

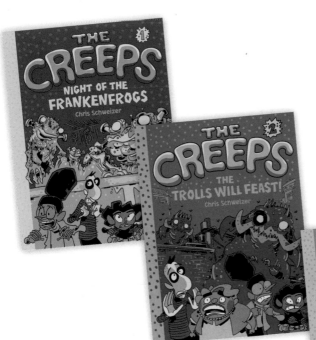

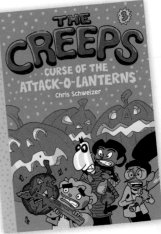